AND ONE RODE WEST

Other Dell Books by Heather Graham

AND ONE RODE WEST

HEATHER GRAHAM

A DELL BOOK

Published by
Dell Publishing
a division of
Bantam Doubleday Dell Publishing Group, Inc.
666 Fifth Avenue
New York, New York 10103

The trademark Dell® is registered in the U.S. Patent and Trademark Office.

ISBN: 0-440-21148-4

Printed in the United States of America

Dedication

This one is dedicated to some of the heroes in my own life.

In memory of my father, Ellsworth D. "Dan" Graham, who gave me wings with which to dream and fly. As long as I live, I will cherish his memory.

For my father-in-law, Alphonse Pozzessere, for being the kindest, sweetest man in the world, and having been there for us, so consistently, all these years.

For my stepfather, William Sherman, a gentleman beyond measure. Mom, you got lucky twice!

For my husband, Dennis, for keeping the love, the passion—and the conflict!—so fresh throughout all the boundaries of time. The years just make things better!

And for my three sons, Jason, Shayne, and Derek. I cannot imagine life without them.

Prologue

Late September, 1865

Slowly rousing from a restless doze, Christa became aware of the man.

Her heart seemed to fly to her throat, ceasing its beat, then pounding furiously.

He was tall, and he filled the entryway to the tent. His shoulders were broad, and cast against the darkness of the velvet, stormy night, he was touched only lightly by the blood-red blaze of the low-burning fire in the center of the tepee.

Terror filled her in those first few seconds. The red and gold light made him appear like some ancient pagan God of this wild, raw land, some indomitable being, created of muscle and sinew and vengeance.

Dear God! Who was it? Standing in the firelight and shadow, she knew he had come for her.

It must be Buffalo Run, she thought, coming to take his revenge. He would have what amusement he could find from her—and then he would have her scalp. She knew the Comanche sometimes tortured their captives, cutting their tongues out if they screamed in the night.

And when she died, her scalp, with a long black tress waving from it, would be stuck upon a pole high atop a plain's butte for some other traveler to discover.

Just as they had found that blond scalp themselves, not so very long ago. The blond scalp that must have belonged to a young woman, as Robert Black Paw and Dr. Weland had determined.

Dear God, no!

Jesu, sweet Jesu, let her open her eyes again and see that the man at the entry was gone! That she had imagined the towering figure of a man there in the darkness, touched only by that flickering light! Once it might not have mattered so fiercely. But it did now. She wanted to live. She wanted to live for her child. She wanted to live for the life that they might share together.

She opened her eyes. Her heart seemed to shudder. He was still there. He stared at her in the firelight, and she saw he had the advantage, for he was cast against the blackness of the night while she was bathed by the golden flames. She swallowed hard.

She didn't show fear, Jeremy had told her once, and that was, perhaps, the one thing he admired about her. Lying in their tent beneath the stars one night, he had admitted with a bitter tone to his voice that she was no simpering belle, no matter how she liked to play the part of the grand dame. Had she been in the midst of the fighting, Grant might never have taken Richmond.

She knew how to fight! But could she fight now? She had fought her way right into the middle of this disaster. Now the red and gold fire lit up the tepee from its center, casting some objects into amber light and some into crimson shadow. How menacing those dark shadows seemed.

How menacing the man who stood between that ominous play of light and dark!

Her heart slammed, seemed to cease its beat, then began to pound with a fury to rival the drumbeats.

The man cast in the light began to move. He took a step forward into the tepee.

Outside, it had been storming. Now, the rains had stopped. Only the chill wind remained. Anguished moans turned into tearing howls, cries that haunted the landscape. She could still hear the endless monotony of the drums as she watched that towering figure come toward her.

The night was savage. So seemed the man.

She placed a hand above her eyes, trying to see him. All around her, the pulse of the drumbeats continued as the seconds ticked by.

What did those drumbeats mean, she wondered desperately. Was she to become a sacrifice to a pagan god? Did each beat spell her doom?

Jeremy would know. He knew the Comanche ways well, just as he knew the Apache, Cheyenne, Pawnee, Ute, and the other tribes along the long trail west. To some of the soldiers, they were all just savages. But Jeremy knew them individually. He had taken the time to do so.

And he had warned her often enough about the Comanche. They could be savage, indeed. But there was more to it than that, he had warned her often enough. They were fiercely proud. They were independent.

She felt a scream rising in her throat. Instinctively, she cast the back of her hand against her mouth, praying that she might choke it back, then wondering why she even cared.

Maybe there was a chance. Comanche sold their captives too. Raped them and sold them to the Spaniards in Mexico, making sure that they only traded soiled goods.

It was warm within the tepee, she realized dimly, despite the pelting rain that had fallen, despite the howling cry of the wind. The Comanche knew how to keep their portable dwellings secure from the rain and the cold. They knew how to live off of this hostile land. They knew how best to torture captives.

She shivered fiercely. He was just feet away from her. In seconds, he would reach the center of the tepee. She would see him bathed in the red-gold glory of the fire, and she would see his eyes, and she would know why he had come.

"You!" she gasped.

He reached the fire. She blinked and her mouth went dry. She could scarcely move, could scarcely believe.

Indeed, the golden glory of the fire touched him. Touched his majestic height, played upon the fine breadth of his shoulders. Touched his eyes, and she saw the jeweled gleam of them. She saw the burning of emotion, but just what emotion, she could not determine.

He reached down his hands to her, catching her wrists when she continued to stare incredulously at him.

He wrenched her to her feet and brought her crashing hard against him.

"Tomorrow, madam, I may die for you," he said. His voice was rich and deep, his words harsh. The emotion that burned in his eyes brought fire to his fingertips, a touch of steel to the way that he held her. He brought her closer against him. His fingers stroked and cupped her chin, tilting her face, forcing her eyes to his. His fingers threaded into the wild tangle of her hair. His eyes traveled the length of her, assessing her for damage, so it seemed. His fingers, entangled at the nape of her neck, held her head steady as his lips lowered until they hovered just above hers. His grip was forceful. The length of him seemed to shake with electric energy, be it passion or fury.

He continued to whisper, the warmth of his breath bathing her lips and her face.

"Tomorrow I may die. Tonight . . ." He paused just briefly. She felt the fire in his eyes once again, and the tension of the blaze that burned within his body, as crimson and gold as the flames that lit the tepee.

"Tonight," he continued raggedly, "tonight, my love, you will make it worth my while!"

His lips descended upon hers, hard, questing, demanding.

And bringing all that fire within her.

"Jesu!" she whispered when the bruising force of his lips left her mouth at last. The fire coursed throughout her body. It felt like electricity, moving through her limbs and heart and womb. Her eyes searched his out. God, yes, she had wanted him before. Deeply, passionately. But never like she wanted him this night, with the wind crying beyond the buffalo-hide walls, with the pulse of the drumbeats never ending.

He had come.

She threw her arms around him, clung to him. His fingers moved over her hair, reveling in the length of it. He drew her away from him, the fury, the passion, still alive within him.

"Life—and death. Make them both worthwhile," he told her harshly.

She stared at him, and then he swept her up into his arms, and bore her down to the furs upon the ground.

"Love me!" he commanded her fiercely.

For a moment his handsome face hovered close over hers. She wanted to reach and touch him, yet she felt as if her limbs were frozen. He stood briefly, casting off his shirt, shedding his clothing, then coming down to her, sleek and naked upon the fur. The length of him was bathed in the fire-gold beauty of the flames. His hands were upon her, stripping her of the fine doeskin tunic the women had given her to wear.

And then she was against his burning, naked flesh.

The corner of his lips twisted into a self-mocking smile.

"Give in to me!" he commanded her. "Everything, Christa, everything."

Staring at him in the dancing light, she felt a pain like death steal over her heart.

She had given in to him—long ago. He knew that he had brought about her surrender.

But perhaps he didn't know just how completely he held her heart.

If she said it, he would never believe her. He would assume that she was deliriously grateful that he was here.

She had fought her battles all too well.

She had disobeyed him. In fact, she had betrayed him. Her reckless determination had brought them here, brought on this disaster.

And still, he had come for her.

He straddled over her, his naked thighs like oaks, the ripple of muscle in his arms and chest gleaming gold and bronze. From head to toe, he was tension, passion, and determination. She began to tremble, wanting him.

And knowing that she loved him.

She reached out her arms to him, her eyes wide and luminous. She moistened her lips to speak, and her words quavered.

"I will give you everything!" she vowed, and added in a vehement whisper, "And well, well worth your while will it be!"

He groaned softly, capturing her lips again with his hunger, a callused hand stroking and cradling the fullness of her breast.

Fire exploded.

And the words almost left her lips.

I love you.

What words to cry when there might be no future to prove them, she thought with anguish.

For fierce, fiery moments, it ceased to matter. His kiss claimed her and burst into her. The fire of need burst and spread rampantly. His touch encompassed her. The hardness of his body against hers aroused and awakened her to a fever pitch. She had sworn to make it real. She parted her lips to his kiss, and felt his tongue rake the insides of her mouth. His touch seemed to be all over her. Fingers touching her breasts, caressing her hips, stroking her thighs. His lips rising from hers, his mouth forming over the hardening peak of her breast, lapping sweet fire. His hands upon her inner thigh, his fingers touching, stroking, finding her cleft, diving within her. Soft cries escaped her. She shifted and undulated beneath him, and he stopped all but that touch, watching her in the golden red light. She heard his whisper.

"Death holds no threat, my love. Indeed, you have made it all worth my while!"

He would never see the flush that rose to her cheeks against the fire's glow. Perhaps he sensed it. Perhaps he would brook no hesitance or modesty on her part this night. He fell atop her again, kissing, stroking. She fought his touch, hungered then to give what he gave to her. Upon her knees, she kissed his shoulders, her fingers biting into flesh and muscle. She kissed his lips, his chest, dazed to be with him again. He caught her hand and guided it to the fullness of his sex, and she trembled, still awed by the size and vitality of his passion. Yet even as she stroked him, he cried out. He swept her up into his arms, then laid her flat against the hides and fur of the bedding. He caught her ankles, spreading her legs. He hovered over her, his lips ravaging hers again, his eyes seeking her own. He would take her now, she thought, for they were both well starved for one another. But he did not. He could not seem to have his fill of the touch and taste and scent of her. Again, his lips covered hers. He kissed her breasts, then bathed her belly, and even as she cried out, his lips and his tongue stroked and teased her in an incredibly bold and intimate fashion. The fire glistened, her body throbbed. She thought that she would black out from the force of her emotions. Within her a climax began to build unbearably. She whimpered and twisted, and then he rose above her again, his eyes on hers.

"Jesu!" It was his turn to whisper.

He scooped her into his arms and thrust into her hard. The force of his passion was breathtaking.

There was no subtlety now, just the hunger, let go at last to run rampant. Her arms entwined around him, she was near to sobbing as he thrust and stroked, as she strove to meet him, as the blazes burst high and climbed and soared around them. Senseless, she registered only the physical feelings. The buff color of the buffalo-hide walls. The never-ending gold and red of the fire. The feel of the furs and hides beneath her on her naked skin. The man above her. His muscles were slick with sweat now and glistening with every bit as much fire and gold as the blaze. Rippling, tense, constricted, easing.

His eyes, so demanding, hard upon her own. The planes of his face, both rugged and handsome. Fine lines, beautifully and harshly drawn. The feel of his flesh against her. The feel of his sex enclosed within her, slick, wet, hot.

She shrieked out, holding fiercely to him, limbs locked around him as her climax exploded fully upon her at last. She heard him whisper something, but she didn't know what. She drifted, aching, trembling, spent, delicious, still throbbing.

Seconds later, she was aware of the sudden, steel-hard constriction of his body. A long, harsh groan escaped him, and he shuddered, coming within her again and again. And more gently, just once again.

He held her, then sighed. He eased his weight from her and scooped her into his arms. He held her, stroking her hair.

I love you!

The words were there again.

But she couldn't say them. He had brought her to the plains of heaven. But that was only an illusion. The tepee was real. The fire was real. The threat of death was real.

She started to speak.

"Sh!" he said softly. "We have the night."

The night. They had the night.

Perhaps no future. Only a past.

Sometimes it seemed the past they shared had begun forever ago.

Sometimes it seemed as if it had been just moments ago when he had come to her, galloping up upon his horse.

An unwilling cavalier. One who wore the wrong color.

And one with whom she had made a devil's bargain.

It had been forever ago . . .

No, it had been just a few months ago, with a lifetime of living in those months.

The war had ended at the beginning of summer.

And their private battle had begun.

One
A Conquered Nation

June 1865
Cameron Hall
Tidewater, Virginia

The day was so hot that the sun seemed to shimmer above the ground, making the fields and the land weave in a distorted manner. The humidity was as high as the day was hot.

Christa Cameron suddenly stood straight, bone-tired from the heat. She arched her sore back and dropped the small spade she had been using to loosen the dirt by the tomato plants. She closed her eyes for a moment and then opened them.

If she looked to the river, it was as if the past years had never been. The river flowed on just the same as it always had. The sun shimmered above it, too, and the water seemed blue and black. At this distance, it seemed to be standing still. Pa had always said that summer in Virginia could be like summer in hell. Hotter than it was even down in Georgia or Florida, or way out west in California. The river might make it a spell cooler by night, but by day it didn't seem to help at all. Still, the heat was something she knew well enough. She'd lived with it all her life. The house had been built to catch every little breeze that might go by.

Turning around, Christa stared up at it. While the river gave away nothing of the tempest of the past four years, the house told it all. Peeling, cracking paint, loose boards, that one step from the back porch still missing. There were a few bullet holes in it from the day that the war had come right to them. Staring at the house, she felt ill. For a moment, she was dizzy. Then her anger and bitterness came sweeping down on her and her fingers trembled.

She should have been grateful that the house was still standing. So many other fine homes had been burned right to the ground. In so many places lone chimneys could be seen, rising up like haunting wraiths from the scorched earth around them. Her house still stood. Cameron Hall. The first bricks had been laid in the sixteen hundreds. The building was a grand lady if ever there had been one. Down its middle ran a huge central hall with broad double doors on the front and rear porch, all of which could be opened to welcome the breezes, to allow a host of beautifully dressed men and women to party and dance out to the moon-lit lawn if they so desired.

Even the lawn was ravaged now.

The house still stood! That mattered more than anything. The graceful columns that rose so majestically from the porches might need another coat of paint, but they stood. No fire had scorched them, no cannon had leveled them.

And though the paint was chipping and three-fourths of the fields were lying fallow, her home still stood and still functioned because of her.

The Yanks had been ordered to leave the place alone because of Jesse. Jesse was the oldest male heir, so the place legally came to him. And Jesse had fought for the Union. But the Rebs had left the place alone because her brother Daniel had fought for the South. Once, the Yanks had nearly burned it, but for a few bright shining moments her family had all managed to band together, neither Yanks nor Rebs, and fought to preserve it.

They had all fought for it, but she had saved it. She had stayed here while Jesse had gone north and Daniel had gone south. She had learned to keep the garden when so many of their slaves—freed by an agreement between her brothers—had begun to wonder what they could do with their lives in the North. She had watched them go—and she had watched some return. She had learned to garden, she had learned to plant. She had plowed, she had picked cotton. She had even repaired the roof when it had begun to leak in Jesse's study. She'd had help from her sisters-in-law, but they'd both been busy with their babies. Jesse, the Yank, had married Kiernan, the Reb, and Daniel, the Reb, had married Callie, the Yank, and so they'd all had each other.

Christa had had the house.

The softest whisper of a cooling breeze suddenly swept up. She lifted off her wide-brimmed straw hat and held it before her.

It might have been different. She might not have had to love a house—brick and wood and paint and shingles—if it hadn't been for the war. Once upon a time she'd been in love. And it hadn't been awful, like it had been for her brothers, loving women who were their enemies. She had been in love with a Confederate officer, Liam McCloskey. They'd spent what hours they could together, dreaming and planning and building a better world, one they could live in when the war was over, the brand-new and liberated Confederate States of America. They would have had a half-dozen children, and they would have raised them along with the cotton and tobacco that had built their world, that had made it rich.

But they wouldn't raise anything now. Her fair young officer was dead, fallen upon the field of battle. His uniform was his funeral shroud; the bare dark earth of his homeland, the Confederacy, was his coffin.

She and Kiernan and Callie had all worked endless hours, sewing beautiful beads and lace onto a white taffeta bridal gown. The war had raged around them, food had grown more and more scarce, and a pair of stockings had become a great luxury. But they had created a stunning gown for her to wear for her wedding.

But though she had dressed in the beautiful white gown, Liam McCloskey never arrived for his wedding. When Liam did not arrive by the time night fell, she had known with a sinking surety in her heart that he was dead.

They had taken the beautiful wedding gown and had dyed it black. Dressed in her mourning, she had gone to the train station to claim her lover's remains. All she'd received was word that his body had been buried with countless others in a mass grave.

At least he had died in Virginia.

Christa swallowed hard and lifted her face to the sun, her eyes tightly closed. She had ceased to cry. So many were dead. She had grown numb against the news of death. Both Jesse and Daniel had survived, and she was deeply grateful for that, but they had come home to wives with open arms. She had watched her brothers, one in blue and one in gray, coming home together. She had started to run to them herself, but then she had remembered. They had wives to run down the long road to meet them. She could not run, for the man she should have run to, ragged and worn in his gray, was no more than a memory now. He would never walk down any trail toward her, never smile his slow, warm smile, never open his arms to her again.

And so she had watched.

Now she was like the house. When the war had begun, they had both been beautiful, vibrant, full of life.

The house needed paint and repairs.

She needed her youth back. She had been so very young before it had all begun! The hostess of Cameron Hall, her father's daughter, her brothers' pride. Men from across the country had vied for her attention at parties and balls. She was known as the "Cameron Rose," for they joked that she was the beauty between two thorns, Jesse and Daniel. They'd all been blessed with the Cameron eyes, eyes that were near cobalt-blue, and the Cameron hair, a deep dark shade that was nearly as black as ebony. In those days her face had been ivory with just the right touch of rouge in her cheeks. She had been so quick to smile, so quick to laugh.

Maybe now she needed a paint job too.

Her big floppy hat hadn't kept the sun from her face. She had burnt, she had peeled. No matter what lotions Janey had given her for her hands, they had callused and grown rough. She'd acquired startling muscles. Very unladylike.

But Cameron Hall still stood. She had done it. Despite war, despite devastation. She had kept the hall standing, and she had seen to it that they all ate while they waited and prayed.

Now the war was over, and she was still out here working with the tomato plants.

It wouldn't be long now. She was alone with the house again because Jesse and Kiernan were in Washington on business and Daniel and Callie were in Richmond trying to help sort out some of the confusion of getting wounded Rebs back south from northern prison camps while returning wounded Yanks to their homes. The babies—her three little nephews and one little niece—were all gone with their parents. The Millers' twins, Kiernan's young sister and brother-in-law from her first marriage, were also in Washington. Janey had gone with them, just as Jigger had determined to go along with Daniel to help him and Callie with their little brood.

And so now it was just her again, her and Cameron Hall. She wasn't completely alone. Jesse and Daniel had agreed to free their slaves long before any emancipation proclamation had been written. Many of their slaves had left, but many had returned.

Many had stayed even at those times when she'd had nothing to pay them with but worthless Confederate scrip. Big Tyne, the huge, handsome black man Kiernan had brought home with her from Harpers Ferry, was with her, but his cottage was down by the stables.

She was alone in the house she had been born in.

She suddenly wondered if she was destined to grow old and die here.

She'd be Aunt Christa—a maiden relative. Living on the fringes. She could almost hear the children at some later time, telling a visitor about her. "Ah, yes, that's our aunt, poor dear! She is wrinkled and withered now, but once upon a time, she was one of the greatest beauties in all of the South. Men flocked around her like daisies in the summer. Her fiancé was killed in the war, but she's—well, she's been with us always, keeping up with us as children, making delicious little things to eat, knitting, sewing . . ."

Hanging on. Hanging on to other people's lives, Christa thought.

She should marry sometime.

There wasn't anyone left to marry. Far more than the devastation of buildings and land had been the devastation of human life. So many men, in the flower of youth, cut down to bleed, like her beloved Liam, that blood feeding the land they had fought for, died for.

It wouldn't matter if there had been a thousand men left to marry. Christa had been in love. She had buried her heart in that unknown mass grave along with the tattered remnants of her lover's body.

What was left? Cameron Hall. It had kept her going through the war. She had clung to one of the tall proud pillars while her sisters-in-law had rushed to greet her brothers. And there were those long empty years ahead when her nieces and nephews would say, "Yes, that's Aunt Christa, and there was a time when she was beautiful, when she was young."

She bent down again, pressing the soft dirt around her tomato plant. A faint trembling in the earth caused her to look up quickly.

Just around the corner of the house she could see the long elegant drive that led up to it. She frowned, seeing that an unknown rider was coming along the drive at a hard lope. She squinted to see better. The heat of the sun shimmered above the drive and the rider and horse seemed to weave and wave even as they moved.

The man on the horse was wearing a Yankee uniform. Her heart beat fast for just a moment, and she wondered if it was Jesse returning for some reason without Kiernan. But within seconds she knew that it wasn't her brother. There were no medical insignias on the uniform, nor was this man wearing a plumed hat the way that Jesse always wore his.

Nor did he ride anywhere nearly as well as either of her brothers, Christa decided matter-of-factly. This was a Yankee, and Yankees just didn't ride as well as their southern brethren.

The war was over. She wasn't going to be afraid of this Yankee. She dusted off the dirt from her fingers on the plain green apron she'd been wearing over the gingham skirts of her day dress and started to walk around the house to meet the man at the porch. A trickle of sweat ran down the back of her neck, then it seemed to turn cold, and a chill of unease swept along her spine. What did this man want?

He reined in, trotting up the drive. Christa began to hurry, catching up her skirts and running. As she neared the front porch, she could see that the Union soldier had dismounted. He had some kind of a flyer in his hand. He stared up at the house, then dug in his saddlebag and found a hammer and a nail, it seemed, shook his head, and started up the great sweeping steps to the porch. At the front door, he began to hammer in the notice he had carried.

"What do you think you're doing?" Christa demanded breathlessly, having arrived at the foot of the stairs.

The Yank turned to her, arching a slow, curious brow. He was a big, furry fellow with broad shoulders and a paunchy gut, sideburns and a full beard and mustache. His curious brow began to wiggle licentiously as he looked her up and down, and somewhere, in the midst of all that fur on his face, he began to smile.

"Well, how-de-do, ma'am! I heard tell there was a Rebel lived out here, but they didn't tell me it was a Rebel gal, pretty as a picture! It's right nice to meet you, girly. Right nice. And we're going to get along just fine!"

Christa ignored him. "What are you doing?"

"Uppity little miss, ain'tcha? Well, you'd better be nice to old Bobby-boy here. I'm slapping an eviction notice on this place."

"An eviction notice!" Christa exclaimed. She felt her temper flaring. Damn, if it wasn't one thing after another! She'd loved Jesse all through the war, even though he'd been a Yankee. He was her brother. She'd had to forgive him his confusion.

When the war had ended, she had tried to understand why it seemed to him that the sanctity of the Union had been so all-precious important. She hadn't really minded digging in the garden, and she hadn't even minded learning to fix the roof. But she did mind the scalawags, carpet-baggers, and downright trash that the Union had been sending down upon them now that the war was over!

"That's right, little Miss Uppity. An eviction notice. For crimes against the United States of America by one Colonel Daniel Cameron."

"Crimes!" Christa echoed incredulously. "He was a soldier, fighting in the war! You can't evict him for that!"

The soldier walked toward her, peering intently down upon her. He looked toward the house, then back toward her. "You Cameron's wife?"

"Who I am is none of your concern!"

"You a servant, then?"

"I'm Miss Cameron," she informed him, exasperated.

"His sister," old Bobby-boy said knowledgeably. "Well, where is he?"

"In Richmond—helping sick and injured people get back home where they belong! Rebs—and Yankees. The war is over, and you can't evict people anymore, and I don't think what you're threatening is legal to begin with! The house isn't really Daniel's—it's Jesse's. Who is your authority?" she demanded.

Bobby-boy was grinning. "My, my. Ain't you something. Whew! A wild one. I like that!" the soldier announced. He came down the steps toward her. Christa wasn't a tiny woman. She was slim—the war seemed to have made almost everybody more so, except for this furry soldier here—and nearly five feet six inches tall. Though this fellow was no giant, his girth was excessive, and despite the muscles she had acquired gardening, she suddenly felt another chill of unease sweep through her.

"I'll take this up with someone who actually has authority," she said. "For now, just state your business and get the hell off of my land!" she warned him, her hands on her hips as she took a single step back.

"Your land?"

"Yes!" she hissed. "It's Cameron land, and I'm a Cameron!"

He grinned again. "Yep. Even all kind of starved-up looking, Miss Uppity, you are a right fine portrait of southern womanhood! I hear tell that demure southern ladies get real fired up underneath all that magnolia blossom innocence. You could be nice to me. Real nice. Then, if you were nice enough, I could probably make things better."

He reached out and touched her, running his fingers over her cheek.

Christa didn't even think. She recoiled, furious. She lashed out in a flash, striking him in a slap that turned his cheek crimson with the imprint of her fingers. She hit him with such strength that he staggered back, his hand flying to his face with surprise.

"Why, Miss-Uppity-Southern-Bitch!" he murmured in a long twang, staring at her with eyes like little twin points of fire in the midst of all the fur on his face. "You just made yourself a mistake. A real mistake."

A mistake? Christa couldn't begin to see it that way. She stared him down, her own eyes sizzling. "You get your fat Yankee carcass off my land right now or—"

"Or what?" the soldier demanded in a voice that had grown very ugly. He took a step toward her, then another. He was smiling again. "All alone, eh, Miss Uppity? You got this nice great big old house, and you think you come from some goddamned kind of southern royalty here, huh? Well, you and your kind have been beaten, lady. You ain't no royalty no more and you're putting your nose up real high for a gal dressed in clothes just as tattered as this here paint job."

"Take one step nearer to me and I'll scream to blue blazes!" she warned.

He stopped for a moment, then his grin deepened. "Why, honey, even if you've got darkies lingering on here now that they've been freed, they ain't gonna raise their hands to help out the white woman who made them all slaves. Hell, honey, they'll just cheer me on!"

"Don't be a fool, Yankee. Our hands are all good people, and they know white trash when they see it."

"Well, you know what I think? I think there just ain't no one around at all. And you know what else I think? I think we're going to have a good time, and you're going to get your comeuppance."

"If you touch me—"

"I'd just say that you were willing, Miss Cameron. Willing to do anything at all to bargain for this old house of yours! You tried to seduce a Union soldier."

Despite his threats, Christa was amazed when his beefy hand reached out, his sausage-shaped fingers actually grabbing the folds of her bodice. He jerked her toward him. She smelled the scent of stale whiskey on his breath and realized that he was probably some lackey who sat around town all day drinking and whiling away time in the South. Reconstruction! This was it. Men like Bobby-boy.

They all said that it might have been different if Lincoln had lived. But Lincoln was dead.

And the powers in the North wanted to keep the South on her knees.

Bobby-boy was touching her now and the smell of whiskey on his breath was so bad that she was feeling queasy when it was important that she think and fight.

Fear suddenly coursed through her. Deep, gut-level fear. Tyne was here, but God alone knew exactly where. Tyne would kill the Yankee, but with emotions being what they were, someone would see that Tyne hanged for killing a white man. Old Peter was down in the smokehouse, but his hearing was all but gone and if he tried to help her, that fine old man would suffer the same fate as Tyne.

She stared into the soldier's leering eyes, feeling his hot, fetid breath upon her cheeks, feeling his pudgy fingers curved over her flesh.

The war was over. All those awful years were behind her.

Why was this happening to her now?

"Let me go, you repulsive gorilla!" she hissed, trying to strike out again.

He didn't let her go. He lifted her cleanly off the ground with one hand, then dropped her flat on the porch, crawling over her.

Christa's heart hammered at a furious beat. In disbelief, she began to fight the man in earnest, twisting, striking, kicking, scratching.

This couldn't be happening.

She grit her teeth, blinking back tears. Once, she had been so desperately in love. She had planned with Liam, waiting for the first possible moment for their wedding.

She remembered being in love, remembered his kisses. Remembered his touch, and remembered wanting more. But they had both been strictly disciplined. She would have been a bride in white, in love, waiting to be awakened.

They had waited to become man and wife. But bullets had severed the dream.

She had held back from the sweetness of desire, to come to this. Honor and innocence would be taken by this burly, bitter bear of a wretch in the dust on the porch of her very own house!

For a moment the fur-covered, pock-marked face rose above hers. She'd gotten in her digs, she realized. Bloody scratches tore his face. There was spittle on his lips and Christa inwardly recoiled again. "Hold still! You'll like it, I promise, girly!" he told her.

"I don't believe this!" Christa shouted. "They'll shoot you! They'll court-martial you. Rape is a crime—"

"A Yankee—against a Cameron? Why, honey, my commanding officer would give me a medal!"

He shoved her skirt up. Christa realized that she was really fighting a desperate battle. "You're insane!" she cried. "You and your commanding officer! My oldest brother, Jesse, is the legal master of this place. He's a colonel in the Yank army. He'll have your hide if you so much as breathe my way again—"

"Hold still, you wily she-devil!" he ordered, and punched her right in the stomach.

For a moment, her breath was swept away. Stars seemed to shoot in a black sky before her. Stunned, Christa lay still. Then every fighting breath in her body returned in a maelstrom. She cracked her knee up into his groin and sent her nails raking across his cheek. He howled and she twisted, managing to crawl from beneath him. On her hands and knees she escaped to the porch steps and then ran down them.

But he was behind her. He caught her arm and threw her down to the ground. Her hands clawing into dirt and grass, she tried to drag her way across the lawn, her heart beating in a fury, her breath coming in quick gasps. She kicked out with all her strength, blinded by the dust in her eyes.

She made it to her feet again, but fell upon the tangle and fullness of her skirt. She felt his hand around her ankle. "No!" She glanced back. He was about to pit the bulk of his weight against her again. She closed her eyes against the dust, crying out again. "No!"

Suddenly, she felt a violent rush of air. He was no longer touching her.

Bobby-boy seemed to fly up, as if he had been plucked away from her by some gigantic hand. He grunted, landing hard, several feet behind her.

She was free.

What in God's name . . . ?

She gasped in a great rush of air, trying to ascertain what had happened. Bobby-boy was reaching out a hand. Was he trying to reach her again, or was he protesting some new threat? She shrieked, still in a wild panic, backing away from him.

She crashed against something hard.

A body.

A man.

Someone else was with them. Someone who had the power to rip Bobby-boy off her and send him flying across the yard.

She twisted around to see that she had backed her way to a pair of shiny black boots. Cavalry boots.

"Touch her again and you're a dead man!" a deadly male voice warned Bobby-boy.

Gulping in more air, Christa allowed her gaze to rise. She was shaking.

This man, too, was in blue.

And it wasn't Jesse.

But like Jesse, he wore a regulation Yankee cavalry uniform. Blue pants hugged long muscular legs. A scabbard and sword clung to a taut waistline and hard narrow hips. As she lifted her head still further, the brilliance of the sun blinded her for a moment. All she saw was that the man was very tall, and that he wore a plumed hat. Leather-gloved hands were upon his hips as he surveyed the situation.

The sun shifted, and she saw the man's face.

Deep, rich russet hair framed handsome features tanned to a bronze color despite the rakish angle of his hat. Arched russet brows framed steel-gray eyes, eyes of a color so like quicksilver that it could change like lightning, being as stormy as a tempest one minute, and light as a mist the next. Gray like steel, silver like a glint beneath the sun. Eyes that touched her now, and flicked quickly past her.

Him.

Bitterness plunged through her heart. She didn't realize for a moment that she was safe, that she had been saved from rape. She thought only that he was here.

Him.

That Yank of all Yanks.

Jeremy McCauley.

Two

Hell, what a mess, Jeremy McCauley thought wearily, looking from the puffed-up soldier to Christa. Her brilliant blue eyes were on him. He couldn't read quite what emotion was in them, but he knew Christa, and he doubted, even under the circumstances, that she was glad to see him.

A shudder ripped through him, and despite Christa, a wave of anger washed over him. Jesu. The war was over! The damn thing wouldn't seem to end, though.

He'd seen too many instances now when the victors were acting like conquerors. We won the war! he wanted to shout at the soldier. We didn't win the right to rape and murder and plunder. And how the hell dare he touch Christa Cameron?

It startled him to realize that he felt like ripping the man's throat out for having touched Christa. They might be enemies, but Christa was Callie's sister-in-law, and so in a way, Jeremy determined, he was kin.

Christa was still down on the ground, staring up at him. Christa on her knees was a view to begin with. But even with her clothing disheveled and covered with dust, she was a stunning woman, proud and defiant.

Maybe she hadn't needed his help. Maybe she could have whipped Bobby-boy all on her own. It was possible. She hadn't his strength, but she had a raw willpower to match any soldier Jeremy had ever met.

She was still staring at him, and he suddenly found himself annoyed that she could be such a disaster—and still be so beautiful. Her hair was a tangle, falling down her back in blue-black waves. Her eyes were that uncanny color to rival a summer's sky. Her features were incredibly classical and beautiful.

And for just a moment he saw a flash of emotion in her eyes. She might still hate him. She might still blame him for the whole damned war, it was hard to tell with Christa, but she had been scared. For once in her life, she'd had the sense to be scared, and she was glad that he had come.

He remembered the first time he had seen her. He'd been standing on the porch just feet away from where he stood now. Callie had come out to throw her arms around him, and when he had looked over Callie's shoulder, he had seen Christa standing there. Tall, slim, regal, stunning, with an exquisite face and beautiful coloring. He had thought for an instant that she was the most beautiful woman he had ever seen, even more beautiful than Jenny.

He had felt like a traitor, and he had been furious with himself. She had muttered something about Yankees being everywhere and Daniel Cameron had accosted him. Jesse had appeared and it had been mayhem on the porch until Daniel had brought him into the office for the two of them to settle things between them.

Of course, he'd seen much more of Christa that trip. The very elegant Miss Cameron had begun to dine with them that evening, but she had chosen to take the children to the kitchen rather than sup with another Yankee.

Now here was Christa again, on the ground before him.

"Get up, Sergeant!" he commanded Bobby-boy sharply. He was just itching to touch the man again, to send him far across the yard.

"Now wait a minute, Colonel, sir!" he gasped out quickly. He looked still to be smarting from Jeremy's having plucked him off Christa and thrown him to the ground. "Colonel, I don't think you rightly see the situation—"

"You've got two seconds or there'll be pieces of you flying all over this grass, Sergeant!" Jeremy warned him, his voice low but deadly.

The man was quickly on his feet, keeping a safe distance from both Jeremy and Christa.

Jeremy reached a hand down to Christa. Her eyes were still on him. She was probably damned surprised to see him. He hadn't written, hadn't told anyone his intentions of coming down here. But he'd made some decisions in Washington just last week, and it had seemed important to come down and say good-bye to Callie. He wasn't quite ready to head out to his new post, but he didn't know if he'd get much time to come south again, and so it had seemed imperative to come here now.

Christa stared right past his hand, and he was certain she was trying to pretend she didn't see it.

She wouldn't want to take a Yankee hand. Though General Lee might have decided a surrender was in order, Christa had certainly never done so.

Christa, my dear Miss Cameron, he thought wryly, you are a witch! Maybe I should have rescued the soldier here from you.

Witch or no, she was a stunning young woman. And she was his kin. He'd just as soon see this soldier's face broken in a million pieces than see him dare to touch an inch of her again.

He arched his brow to Christa as she got up, then turned his attention to the errant soldier. He was tired. Tired of the North and tired of the South. He wanted no more of it, but if there were a problem here, he was honor-bound to solve it if he could.

"Who in blazes are you and what in the Lord's name is going on here?"

"Eviction!" the man said quickly. He was panting harder than Christa. "Any living folk are to clear out of this place. It's to be burned to the ground tonight."

"Burned!" Christa raged. "They're evicting us to burn it to the ground?" She wanted to scratch his eyes out at that moment. She took a step toward him furiously.

Jeremy McCauley caught her shoulders and jerked her back against him. His chest was rock hard, the grip his fingers formed was a forceful one. She grit her teeth, unable to fight him.

"This house is owned by Colonel Jesse Cameron, United States Medical Corp," Jeremy said over her shoulder.

"That's not what the records say. Seems the house was put in Daniel Cameron's name when these people wanted to keep it from being burned by the Confederates. Hell, it's real hard to tell just who is and who isn't the enemy, eh, sir? Or maybe these people just did whatever was convenient. Anyway, the house is down as having belonged to Daniel Cameron, Colonel, in that rebellious army that used to call itself Confederate."

"Convenient!" Christa choked out, wrenching away from Jeremy. How dare this stinking Bobby-boy say such a thing? Her family had been split and torn, and it had all been anguish. "Jesse is the oldest in the family and he never left the United States military, never!"

"It will burn for Daniel Cameron!" Bobby-boy said, a pleased grin on his face. He saw Jeremy's expression and the grin quickly faded.

Jeremy spoke softly. "You'd better explain this and explain it fast, Sergeant. You are going up on charges as it is—the war is over, and even if it weren't, soldiers do not resort to rape—"

"Ah, sir, she was asking for it, I swear!"

"Asking for it!" Christa exploded furiously. "Being mauled by corpses could not disgust me more!"

"Sergeant, I daresay that the lady was not 'asking for it,' " Jeremy stated flatly. He continued in the same dispassionate tone. "I know Miss Cameron. She might be guilty of many things—but never 'asking for it' from a man in a blue uniform."

"How gallantly you do rush to a woman's defense!" Christa murmured, irritated.

Jeremy didn't seem to notice. His attention was on Bobby-boy.

Bobby-boy seemed to have realized just how serious his situation was with Jeremy. His eyes remained glued upon the man. "I could see to it that you were court-martialed—"

"You'd take her side against a Yankee soldier—"

"Damned right!" Jeremy said softly. "Now tell me what's been going on here."

Bobby-boy was silent for a second, shuffling his feet. "All right," he muttered after a moment. "Well, it don't rightly seem as if it should be legal, and I don't really know just what is going on!" he said sourly. "Someone big, someone up top, wants this place razed. And the last taxes that were paid were paid in Confederate scrip, and the last persons to sign any bills were Daniel and Christa Cameron. So if Jesse Cameron is the real owner, he'd best get his Yankee body—and his Yankee dollars—down to the courthouse in Williamsburg by nightfall, else the place will be taken, lock, stock, and barrel, and burned. There's a new owner waiting to take over. And the new owner is waiting for the legal time limit to be up to take the place down."

"New owner?"

"Well, the party who intends to buy the place at sunset."

"And that's tonight," Jeremy said sharply. "Who's the new owner, and how come this notice just reached the house?"

Bobby-boy shrugged. "Maybe somebody didn't want it to reach the house until tonight. I'm just a soldier, just a messenger!"

"Who's the party intending to buy the place?" Jeremy demanded sharply.

"God as my witness, Colonel, I don't know. Lieutenant Tracy in Williamsburg gave me the order to nail the notice up this morning. He led me to believe that the house was a bed of rebellious vipers, just like the kind of folk what decided to kill Lincoln."

Christa hugged her arms tightly against her chest, staring from Jeremy to Bobby-boy. She shook her head, looking at Jeremy. "It can't be legal! What new game are you filthy, stinking, scalawagging, carpetbagging Yankees playing down here?"

"See there, Colonel? 'Filthy' Yankees. And you say that she isn't asking for it!"

Jeremy took a menacing step forward and Bobby-boy shrank back. "She may ask for a lot," Jeremy said, his eyes like a flash of steel, "but she most assuredly isn't going to get anything from you. Now you hightail it on out of here and fast. And if I ever hear tell that you've even been near this place I'll forget that I'm a Yankee officer and I'll hunt you down and rip you limb from limb. You got it, Sergeant?"

Pale as a sheet beneath the fur on his face, Bobby-boy nodded. On quaking legs he turned and hurried for his horse. He mounted and quickly rode away. In silence, Jeremy and Christa watched him go.

She felt a strange, cool breeze touch her. She was alone with Jeremy. Even though she had learned to love her sister-in-law, Callie, she'd never managed to accept Callie's brother in their home.

She'd never known quite what it was between them. Maybe it had been the war. Maybe she'd just been too bitter to accept any Yankee other than Jesse by the time that she had met Jeremy. But from that time when she had first seen him on her doorstep, she'd felt as if the air were charged with lightning anytime he was near her.

They'd been bitter enemies from the moment they had met.

Maybe she thought that he had never understood her. Perhaps he'd been expecting a very sweet and ladylike belle. Maybe she'd even been one once. But the war had forced her to take care of her house and her home.

And it had forced her to take up arms against the enemy.

She hadn't felt in the least obliged when Daniel and Jesse had determined to let Jeremy in because he was Callie's brother.

Admittedly, Jeremy had been caught up in a fight to save Cameron Hall once before. When unauthorized troops had come against him, Jeremy had fought alongside both of her brothers to save the place.

She hated being grateful to him. Hated to be obliged.

But there didn't seem to be a choice. If he could help her now, she was going to have to accept that help.

Sweet Jesu. She'd accept help from the devil himself to save Cameron Hall.

He was already caught up in this mess, so it seemed. He turned to Christa as soon as Bobby-boy was out of earshot. "Where's Jesse?" he demanded.

"Washington," Christa said quickly. "There's no way that he can be back here before nightfall. Even with the railroads all working, I'd have to reach him, and then he'd have to get back here. He'd never make it." She forgot for a moment that she needed his help. Feeling desperate and bitter, she lashed out, "McCauley, tell me that this can't be real! Not even you wretched Feds can come sweeping down here like a horde of conquerors—"

"We *are* the conquerors," he reminded her softly, but there was a silver fire in his eyes as he stared at her. She wondered at his thoughts as her temper flared.

"Ah, yes! Hail the conquering heroes! Bastards!" she spat out.

His jaw set. There was something different about him. She realized that the last time she had seen him, he'd had a mustache and beard. He was clean-shaven now. His jaw seemed even more square and determined.

"Christa, do you want to fight with me? Or do you want to solve this mess?"

She lowered her lashes, wishing that she didn't feel so compelled to battle Jeremy. She did need his help. "How can this be?" she cried out. "Aren't there supposed to be some laws?"

His silver gaze was assessingly upon her. What he saw in her, she couldn't quite fathom. The only thing she knew about Jeremy was that he seemed to have the ability to see right through her.

At the moment, he seemed nearly as disturbed about the house as she was. He sighed. "This shouldn't be possible, and who would do this except—"

"Except?"

Jeremy shrugged. "Someone acquired an enemy. An enemy with power. And then . . . well, then anything can be done."

"Because the North wants the South on her knees!"

"Christa! Some men are good, and some are bad. And some bad men do get into situations of power!"

She lowered her head again. She didn't want to fight with him. Not now.

He paused a moment, then turned his back on her, walking along the drive to where a big, handsome bay horse awaited him. He turned back to her as he mounted the bay. "I take it my sister isn't here? Daniel can't be."

"No, Callie is in Richmond with Daniel. How did you know that he wasn't here?"

"Because if Daniel had been here, that sergeant would have been a dead man," he said. "All right. I'll find out what's going on."

"I'll come with you—"

"No!"

"Dammit, it's my house, my home—"

"And you're very likely to get it burned before nightfall with your gracious way of addressing us conquerors!"

Christa braced herself, wanting to smack his handsome face.

He was all that she had at the moment. "Hurry. Get back here immediately."

He tipped his cavalry hat. "Yes'm, Miss Cameron. Let me see, save you from rape, and the home from demolition, and do it fast. I'll do my filthy Yankee best."

She felt her cheeks coloring. "Just go!" she hissed.

He inclined his head in a bow. Christa watched him race away on the bay, her teeth clenched bitterly. She hated to admit it, but he was one Yankee who could ride almost as well as her brothers.

An hour later she was pacing the steps before the house when she heard the sound of hoofbeats once again.

Her heart slammed against her chest as she rushed to one of the pillars, holding it for strength as she peered down the drive.

It was Jeremy, returning. Christa ran down the steps, ready to greet him when he dismounted from his horse.

"Did you do something? Did you stop it?" she asked anxiously. She saw from the storm-cloud gray of his eyes that nothing was resolved.

Tears welled in her eyes, but she wasn't about to shed them. She knotted her fingers into fists and slammed them against his blue-clad chest. "Damn you! You should have let me come! This isn't your home. You didn't fight hard enough. You don't care—"

"Shut up, Christa!" he commanded harshly, catching her wrists and jerking her close to him. Her head fell back, ink-dark hair cascading over the length of her spine as her eyes met his. "Don't you think I would have done something? Hell, I was on Jesse's side! My sister is married to Daniel. It's her home too."

"Then—"

"I found a friend in the courthouse, but not even Lieutenant Tracy knows who's after the place. A General Grayson is the one who gave the order that the house be confiscated, and he went about it all legally—at least, on paper it looks like it's legal. The notice was supposed to have been on the house thirty days ago."

"Supposed to have been!" Christa reiterated bitterly, trying to pull away from him. He wasn't letting her go. His jaw and his voice hardened as he continued.

"Well, Grayson must be playing dirty politics. Taking bribes. But the only thing I could do would be to call him out, call him a liar to his face. Then I'd have to shoot him, and then I'd be court-martialed and hanged."

He still wasn't letting her go. Christa swallowed hard, afraid that she was going to start crying in front of him. "Would that save the house?" she asked him.

He shook his head, his eyes narrowing. "No."

"Then don't bother!" she whispered miserably, pulling away from him and starting up the steps, her shoulders drooping.

"There's only one way to stop this. They need a signature before dark," he called after her.

She spun around. "I'll sign anything!" she whispered, still fighting tears.

"No, Christa, that won't do. A Yankee signature, that's what they want. If Jesse were just here!"

"If Jesse were just here, this would never be happening!" Christa said.

"You're most assuredly right," Jeremy said evenly. "But Jesse isn't here. And I've just walked into the middle of something that I don't understand. And though I know you'd like me to shoot every Yank in town, I just don't know who to shoot! Whatever is going on isn't my fight."

"Some dirty, lying vulture—"

"Yes, some dirty, lying vulture, sweeping down from the north," Jeremy finished for her evenly. "But I don't know who, Christa. And I'm not going to try to shoot every man in town, not even if you're still convinced it's your due!"

"It's our due!" she cried out. The tears were stinging her eyes again. She'd been to town. The blue uniforms were everywhere. She was damned sure that most of the men in town had never fought, they'd just seen the South like a wounded and dying creature, and they'd come just like a pack of jackals, sniffing opportunity. There were free blacks to exploit, starving women to proposition, near-slave labor in desperate straits, orphaned urchins—and there were houses to pick up for a song!

But whoever wanted Cameron Hall wanted to burn it!

She would never let it happen.

"There has to be something that can be done," she said vehemently.

"They'd even take Callie's signature," Jeremy told her. "Along with the money." He sighed. "Except that I'm not sure she ever swore any kind of an oath to the Union. Think, Christa, maybe there is someone. Some relation. You need a Cameron, or a Cameron spouse, who has sworn an oath to the Union."

"What?"

"You need a hundred and fifty dollars, but I can loan you a bank draft for that. What you have to come up with is a Yankee with a serious connection to this house." She was staring at him, too desolate to go to war with him at the moment. He stared at her, waiting for her to say something.

"I don't understand this. It can't be legal without warning—"

"Christa, don't you understand? They're saying at the courthouse that they've put up numerous flyers and warnings and that you've just ripped them all down."

"My God! It's a lie! It's a horrible, filthy Yankee lie—"

"Christa, dammit, whether it's a lie or not, it's what they're saying." He hesitated, staring at her. "And hell, Christa, like it or not, the South was beaten! Your word is just about worthless right now!"

She grit her teeth tightly together. She wanted to run down the steps and pummel her fists against his chest. She wanted to hurt him.

"I need a brandy," she announced tonelessly. She turned her back on him once again and started into the house.

No.

She paused a moment.

She could not lose it. Not after all this. Not after all these years. She could not lose the Hall. She had lost Liam. This was all that she really had left.

Jeremy followed behind her. She walked straight through the hallway to Jesse's desk and pulled out the brandy bottle. When she started to fill the entire glass, he jerked the bottle out of her hand. She swirled on him, staring at him hatefully. "How dare you! You're not my brother, my father, my husband—"

"That's right, Christa, I'm no one but a filthy Yank. And you're going to turn into a southern lush if you're not careful!"

She stared at Jeremy. He was too tall and too damned superior with his cockaded hat sitting low on his brow and his eyes flashing at her with silver scorn. She had never felt more bitter. Maybe that was why she longed to slap him all the more.

But she was careful with Jeremy McCauley. She had come to know a little about her sister-in-law's brother. He had a certain quality about him that might make someone else want to call him a gentleman.

He was extremely well built, with arms like iron and a hard, muscled chest. He was quick, and could be ruthless. He had no patience with her, and wouldn't even pretend to play any chivalrous games.

Not that she had really attempted to play any games with him. She'd tried to keep her distance from him.

He'd been fighting a war for a long time too.

And in an all-out battle with him, she wouldn't win. He was accustomed to snapping out orders, and he was always quick to give them to her. He must have known damned well by now that she would never obey him. He wasn't her brother! And most certainly wasn't her—

Husband.

A deep, searing chill came sweeping through her and her knees went weak. She took the chair before Jesse's desk just as Jeremy sat himself, watching her with narrowed, speculative eyes as he poured himself a brandy.

"What?" he demanded in something that sounded like a growl.

She moistened her lips. She couldn't do it. Not even for Cameron Hall. She'd do anything for Cameron Hall.

"You're trying to tell me that this has all been done legally? Or, at least, what you Yankees are calling legal these days?"

"Christa—"

"Someone hates either Jesse or Daniel. Probably Daniel—he was the loser here, right? Hates him enough to have gone through all kinds of machinations to burn this place to the ground."

"Christa—"

"Is that it?"

"Yes, dammit, that's it. So let's try—"

She leaned forward. "Wait. I need one hundred and fifty dollars and the signature of someone connected with the hall who has sworn an oath to the Union. And whoever is doing this must know that Jesse is in Washington. Jesse could stop it, but he can't get here in time. Someone knows that I'm alone here, and that I haven't any Yankee relations nearby."

"That's about the gist of it," Jeremy said. He tossed down the whole of his brandy, staring at her with his silver eyes. Then he sighed. "I'll stay here, Christa. I'll try to stop what's happening, but somewhere along the line, one of your brothers made an enemy. A big enemy. I don't know who. And I don't rightly know what I can do, but I'll try whatever I can."

"You can sign the paper," she said in a rush.

"Christa, I don't own Cameron Hall. I don't even have a real connection with it. Callie does, not me."

"But you would, if—"

"If?"

Why did he have to stare at her the way that he was staring at her now? He was a Yankee to the core with that hard-edged face of his and those flashing eyes. And that voice that could sound like a whip-crack.

How the hell did she do this?

She stood suddenly, trying not to appear as nervous as she felt. She had to sound offhanded. As if it were certainly no major task she was asking of him.

She folded her hands before her and sighed in what she hoped was a very mature and very matter-of-fact manner. "We'll have to be married," she said. "Very, very quickly, of course."

Maybe he would understand. It would just be something done on paper. It might be complicated to undo, but once they had saved the house, it could be done. Maybe, just maybe, he would understand, and make it easy for her.

"What?" he exploded, leaping to his feet and towering over her.

Then again, maybe he wouldn't understand.

And he sure as hell wouldn't make it easy for her.

It didn't matter. He was going to have to do it. And she was going to have to convince him.

"Jeremy, it's necessary."

He came closer. She had to lift her chin and lean her head back to attempt to stare him down.

She didn't like the disadvantage.

Her fingers curled around her glass and she tried to keep her gaze level with his. "Oh, you don't have to take it seriously. We can do something about it later, I'm sure. But we'll have to be married, and fast."

He sank down into the chair behind Jesse's desk again, a dark auburn brow arched high. "Oh, you think so, do you, Miss Cameron?" he demanded.

"Yes."

His brow arched still further as he stared at her incredulously. "Just like that?" he said softly.

"It's not such a big thing—"

His eyes narrowed sharply. She had come too close to him. He reached out, plucking the brandy glass from her hand, setting it on the desk. Then his fingers were suddenly wound around her wrist, and she was afraid of the strength in them, and afraid to fight him. Before she knew it she had been pulled down on her knees before him. "It's not such a big thing, eh, Miss Cameron? Ah, no, not for you perhaps. Liam McCloskey is lying dead in a battlefield and you don't give two figs for any other man living or dead."

She tried to free herself. "That's not true!" she cried out. "I care! I care about many people. I love my brothers—"

"And you love a hunk of bricks! Brick and mortar and glass and wood!"

She managed to jerk her hand free, lowering her head. "You don't understand! It's not a pile of brick! It's my family, it's history, it's—it's been here for centuries! It's not just a house!"

For a moment he didn't say anything. Then he ordered her, "Look at me, Christa!"

She did so. She wanted to be defiant. Maybe that would be the wrong ploy. In a way, Jeremy knew her well. He knew the gracious games that she could play, but he also always seemed to know what was in her heart.

"Christa, no."

"Damn you!"

She wanted to hurt him. To scratch and strike out and hurt him. He was the conqueror. She had already lost, and she was about to lose more.

Don't fight him! she warned herself. Play it softly, softly!

"Please!" she whispered, and she tried to give him a beseeching look.

"Don't bat your lashes at me, Christa. I know you hate the very sight of me," he said flatly.

Anger flashed through her eyes, making them brilliantly blue. "Then do it for your sister! Do it for your niece and your nephew. Do it because you goddamned filthy Yankees owe us something for this war!"

"Ah, with such a declaration of undying love and devotion, how could I possibly refuse you!" he retorted, a hard curve to his lip.

"Then you'll do it?"

"I already said no!"

"Oh!" she cried out. She freed her hand. She swung it at him with all her strength.

But he caught her wrist. "Christa! You have to stop fighting. You have to worry about—"

"I don't care! I don't care about anything. There won't be anything left to care about."

"Christa—"

His voice had changed. Just a little bit. She looked up into his eyes. They were pure silver now. Burning harshly within the handsome planes of his face.

"Christa, you hate me! And I must admit, you are not on the top of the list of my favorite Rebel women! You can't marry me."

"I'd marry that disgusting fur-face fleabag old Bobby-boy to save this place."

"You can't mean that!" he told her incredulously.

"I don't know what I mean! All I know is that I can't let it go!"

He pushed her away from him, furious. "It's a pile of bricks!" he roared.

Tears touched her eyes again, glazing them. "I'd do anything."

Before she knew it he was suddenly up again, his hands on hers as he wrenched her forcefully up before him. His eyes touched her like fire. "Anything, Christa?" he said. "Anything? What you're asking me to do is a mockery. So *you* had best mean it. You would do anything to save this place. You'd marry that white trash. You'd marry *me.*"

She opened her eyes wide, gasping. "You mean—you'll do it?" She couldn't believe it. He seemed angrier than ever with her.

And furious with himself.

"Miss Cameron, you are quite something, you know. Marriage doesn't mean a damn thing to you. You don't, in the least, mind selling your own soul for Cameron Hall. But what of mine? What if I were in love with someone?"

She grit her teeth, meeting his eyes. She felt a trembling inside of her. It was quite possible. He was a very handsome man. She wasn't blind and she wasn't stupid. He was tall, trim-hipped, broad-shouldered, lean, and muscular. His face was both ruggedly masculine and classically cast, with high cheekbones, startling eyes, and striking, deep russet, high-arched brows. He was a war hero. There might well be a woman waiting for him in the North.

"Are you in love with someone else?" she said.

"Would you really give a damn, Christa?"

She was afraid of his answer. "No!" she cried. "I care that your kind are threatening to tear this place down when I've worked my fingers to the bone for it, when it's all that I have left . . ." Her voice trailed away. "Damn you, Jeremy! Will you do it, or not?"

He stared at her long and hard. She felt the sizzling heat of his eyes rip into her, and then he turned away from her as if he were more furious still. He was going to refuse her! His back was as stiff as steel.

"You have sold both our souls, Miss Cameron. But yes, I'll do it. And we'd best hurry. We've just hours left before sundown and Richmond is a long hard ride from here."

"I would ride to hell!" she said.

He mocked her with a sweeping bow. "Perhaps, Miss Cameron, it is exactly where you are going!"

"Don't threaten me, Jeremy," she told him, lifting her chin, alarmed at the trembling that had begun within her.

"Don't worry, Christa, I would not dream of bothering with a threat," he responded quickly, silver eyes flashing, his fingers tightening upon her arms until she was afraid she would cry out. "To say that you have cast us into hell, my love," he murmured, his voice low and harsh, "is most assuredly not a threat."

"Then—"

"It's a promise. And I vow that I will keep it!"

Three

To Christa, it seemed the strangest wedding imaginable. The Episcopal priest agreed to marry them when the case was truthfully put before him. They were both obliged to swear that they meant to uphold the sanctity of their union before God. The words were spoken, and two choirboys witnessed them.

She had imagined once that when she did marry she'd be dressed in white, not in the cotton day dress she'd been wearing to dig in the garden. She'd have curled her hair. She'd have been surrounded by her family and friends.

She would have been marrying a man who loved her, and a man she loved deeply in return.

But the white gown had been dyed black and it was now a mourning dress. Her family was nowhere near, thus the forced wedding. Her friends, or very many of them, lay dead in battlefields and graveyards across the country.

The man she had loved lay buried along with the rest of the South.

She shivered, then mentally braced herself. She glanced at Jeremy, standing beside her. Once committed to her cause, he had done very well. He had explained the expediency of their need to the priest. Christa wondered what thoughts were passing through his mind. He looked so harsh beside her. What memories came to him as he agreed to this arrangement?

But he didn't mean it, she was certain. It was just to save the house. Once that was done, they could go their separate ways.

She looked around. They were being married in an empty church on the outskirts of Williamsburg. Cannonball fragments were lodged in the outer brick of the church. Some of the stained-glass windows were still cracked and broken from shots.

Christa barely heard the priest's words as he droned on and on. She heard just bits and pieces of the ceremony. Love, honor, and obey. She was supposed to vow to do so.

She would have agreed to anything.

She looked up during the ceremony and saw the large crucifix hanging from the altar.

Forgive me, God! she cried inwardly. She had to look away. God had to understand. He had let this happen.

He had let the Yankees win the war.

She heard Jeremy's vows. Surprisingly, his voice was strong and level. Perhaps it was not so surprising. His voice was laced with his anger. He had agreed to help her. But he was furious with her and himself for having done so. He was going to make her pay somehow for this, she knew. She tossed her hair back. She didn't care. She'd fight him from now until eternity, just as soon as her home was safe.

The priest cleared his throat. The ceremony was over.

"You may now kiss the bride, Colonel McCauley."

Jeremy's lips barely touched her forehead. Yet where his lips touched her, her flesh seemed to burn. And where his hands held her, she felt a riddling tension and a frightening pulse.

The wedding certificate was produced. Her fingers trembled so, she could barely write. McCauley. For the moment, her name was McCauley. She had given up the Cameron name to save her Cameron birthright.

The priest's wife managed to produce a little glass of sherry for them each. She chatted. She wanted to believe that it was a love match.

Jeremy tossed down the sherry, tipped his hat, paid the priest, and grabbed Christa's hand. They mounted their horses and raced like the wind into the town and down the street to the courthouse.

There, Jeremy produced their wedding certificate with the ink scarcely dry. He paid the hundred and fifty dollars and signed his name. A harried clerk assured them that the property could not be touched. Jeremy had gained a certain reputation as a cavalry commander. No one could deny that he was a stalwart Yankee.

Christa stood by his side tensely waiting as he filled out several documents.

Then he straightened.

It was over. Christa turned and hurried out of the courthouse into the yard, Jeremy following.

They stood in the yard and he stared at Christa, his silver eyes hard and enigmatic.

"Are you happy now?"

"Of course."

"You've lied under oath." Why were those eyes of his so damned condemning?

She tossed back her hair. "I would have wed the devil for the Hall," she told him coolly. "And I am going to hell when I die. You've already told me so."

He shook his head, his lip curling into a small, mocking smile. "Oh, no, Christa. I didn't say a thing about death. You're going to live in hell right now. But let's see, you would have married the devil—or old fur-faced Bobby-boy," he reminded her. "But I think fur-face might have been preferable to me. In your eyes, madam, you have married the devil, haven't you?"

"A Yankee devil," she agreed. It was already done. Why was he torturing her now?

"A Yankee devil," he repeated smoothly.

She lowered her lashes quickly, reminding herself that she was supposed to be grateful.

"I—I'm sorry," she managed to mutter. "I truly appreciate your help."

Her gaze was lowered, but she felt his, silver and steel, burning over her.

"My, my!" he murmured. "You're sorry that you called me a devil—or you're sorry that you married one?"

Her gaze rose quickly to his. He laughed with true amusement. "Never mind, don't answer that. Well then, let's see, the wedding is over and done with. Cameron Hall is free and clear from all liens, and cannot be sold to anyone for any reason. No one can torch it. So, where does that leave us? Dinner, I think."

"I'm not—really hungry," she murmured. She wanted to get home. To Cameron Hall—and away from him.

"I am. I'm starved."

She looked down at the ground. All right. They were here, he was hungry. She'd have to have dinner with him.

"Fine. Let's find somewhere to eat," she said, attempting to be gracious.

Her impatience was still clear in her voice. Jeremy seemed amused. He didn't give a damn if she was impatient or not.

There was a small inn down the street. Jeremy was determined to annoy her, telling their waiter that they were newlyweds, ordering champagne and the chef's special roast beef.

Christa forced herself to keep a dry smile on her lips. She wasn't going to let Jeremy's mockery disturb her.

"Let's see. To you—Mrs. McCauley." He hadn't addressed her so as yet. He rolled the words on his tongue bitterly. Still, he raised his glass to hers.

She lifted her glass in return. "To Cameron Hall," she retorted sweetly.

He tossed back his champagne. "And to all that we have done in its sacred honor!"

"Be that way, then!" she whispered fiercely across the table. "I don't care!"

"Just so long as I came in the nick of time, right?" he asked her, pouring more champagne.

She arched a brow to him. For the first time in the long day, she was suddenly curious as to how he had happened to be there at just the right time.

"What are you doing in Virginia?" she asked him, trying to sound polite and interested.

He set his glass down, watching her. "I came to say good-bye to Callie."

"Good-bye?" she said. "Where are you going?"

He waved a hand in the air. "West," he said simply.

She frowned. "But the war is over—"

"Yes, the war is over," he said, leaning back. "And my neighbors are all maimed, my fields are filled with decaying corpses in blue and gray. Your brothers fought on different sides. You should understand. Maryland's loyalties were split in two. Maybe some people can go home. I can't. Not yet, anyway."

She was startled to feel a certain empathy. Just how well did she know the man? It had been a long war. Like Jesse and Daniel, he had been in the first fighting, and in the last. He sounded bone weary. For a moment, she understood.

She picked up her champagne glass again. She suddenly determined that they could, at the very least, manage to get through one dinner together.

"You'll stay in the military?" she asked him.

"I was always regular army, so I'm retaining my rank. Some promotions were only valid while the war was going on, but I'll remain a colonel. So for the time being, I have determined I'll stay, yes. I'm bringing a regiment to one of the forts in the western territories. There's a lot of land to be had in the West."

"Indian territory?"

He nodded.

"You'll be going to war again."

"I hope not."

"But the Indians are all savages."

"Not all of them. Some of them are quite civilized. Especially when compared with . . ."

His voice trailed away.

"With Rebels?" she inquired icily.

His gaze settled on her. "No, Christa, that's not what I was about to say."

"What were you about to say, then?"

"That they are quite civilized when compared with some white men—and I wasn't thinking white northern men or white southern men—just white men."

She looked down at her plate. She had hardly eaten. Actually, she was hungry. She had been hungry a long time.

"You need to eat more," he commented, his gaze steadily on her as he poured more champagne.

For some reason, the comment hurt. Was she that gaunt? Was he implying that she was a skinny shell of an old maid? She smiled. "Maybe I do. But we southerners are accustomed to starving. Just as you Feds are accustomed to wolfing down our food," she said politely.

He set down the champagne bottle. Something that had begun to glow warm in his eyes turned chill once again. "Truly, Lord, I have been blessed!" he stated, and continued, "Starve then, Christa, if that's your pleasure."

She lowered her lashes again. She didn't mean to strike out with so much venom so quickly. She had been fighting too long. She had spent too many years fearing all blue uniforms other than Jesse's.

"I—"

"What?" he demanded.

"I'm sorry."

He was silent for a moment. Again, she felt him watching her. Currents of lightning seemed to riddle the air between them again. She had to quit being so antagonistic. Maybe he hadn't wanted to help her, but he had done so.

She was startled when his fingers curled over hers. "It was a damned long war, wasn't it?"

There was gentleness in his tone. She didn't want to hear it. She snatched back her hand.

"I would really love to get back to the house," she murmured uneasily. "I'm exhausted."

"It's a long ride back. We should stay here."

"No! Well, you can stay, Jeremy. I can't. I've got to go home. To make sure—to make sure it's still standing."

She felt Jeremy looking at her. He made no comment. He called for their bill and paid it. Christa watched in silence as he doled out the Yankee bills.

Dear God, but the world had changed quickly! Not so very long ago they had all mocked the Yankees.

Now even the southerners were scrambling for Yankee money, using their Confederate bills for the fodder and tinder they were worth!

She rose when he pulled back her chair, straightening her shoulders. "If you'd rather stay in Williamsburg for the night, I'll understand."

"No."

"I'm perfectably capable of riding home—"

"No."

"Really—"

"Christa, dammit, if you were a bare acquaintance, I'd see you home. And you're not a bare acquaintance. I'd hardly let my wife travel the night road alone."

She thought that she might be safer alone than with him. She wasn't quite sure what she had done to start his temper seething, but his mood seemed to be growing darker.

"Suit yourself," she told him.

He led the way back home. It was a long, hard ride. They rode it in near silence.

Halfway along the trail Jeremy glanced back, wondering with some concern if she had fallen asleep, if she was in danger of falling from her mount.

But Christa was in no danger. They raised horses at Cameron Hall. She'd probably ridden before she had walked and she was an excellent horsewoman. She sat easily in her saddle, but her lashes were low.

It had been one hell of a long day, he thought. And now, to finish it. He had a day or two before reporting back in Washington. He'd wait until he could get word to Callie to say good-bye, then he'd be on his way. He was sure that Christa could manage to get a divorce or an annulment. It might take some time, but then he didn't really care. He'd be in the West, and though Christa couldn't possibly know it, he'd buried his own heart in the ashes of the war. She was more than welcome to take her time ending their mockery of a marriage.

Suddenly he remembered the wedding ceremony. Remembered her vows, remembered his. Why had he agreed to this? She was his wife. Legally. It was an entanglement that would take years to end. And all of his life, he had imagined that marriage would mean love and commitment for a lifetime.

He locked his jaw. She'd done it for a house. And whether she really realized it or not, the house was Jesse's.

It would serve her right if I held her to her vows! he thought. She was always so damned determined to have things her way.

They came upon Cameron Hall in the moonlight. He reined in absently. It was a beautiful place. The red brick and the white columns rose majestically in the glowing light. It sat atop its knoll before the James like a castle.

Maybe that's what it had been, Jeremy speculated, before the war. Christa had ruled here like a goddess. People had attended to her every whim. Her older brothers adored her. And most certainly, young men had swarmed around her. She was probably accustomed to having her every wish obeyed. She had certainly expected *him* to do as she wished with no objection.

Marriage!

The word chilled him for a moment and he felt his temper rising. Ah, yes, Christa liked to pull strings. She'd pulled his, all right.

He didn't know why it suddenly sat with him so poorly. She hadn't said a word along the ride, but he had felt his temper start to grow at the restaurant.

"It's standing!" she said with relief. Behind him, she suddenly nudged her horse, and went galloping down the drive. She rode like the wind, one with the horse. He grit his teeth, then followed her.

She had already dismounted from her horse when he reached the front of the house. Yes, the house was still standing. She twirled before him, as smooth as silk, as pleased as a cat with a bird. "Thank God!"

"Indeed."

She didn't seem to notice his tone. She dropped her horse's reins. "Jeremy, why don't you see to the horses!" she commanded rather than asked and went tearing toward the house.

"Yes, ma'am!" he murmured. His voice was low. There was an edge to it, and she heard it.

Catching up her skirts, she suddenly turned toward him.

"The guest room is always kept ready for company," she said hurriedly. "You know where it is, right? Third room down the hall to the left."

"I know where it is. I stayed there several times," he told her, dismounting from his own horse. By then, one of the stable hands had appeared, and Jeremy quickly turned the horses over to the lad.

"Rub them down good, will you? They've had a hard ride," he told the boy. Christa was starting up the stairs. He realized that she intended to leave him out here in the moonlight.

Cameron Hall was standing. She seemed to have forgotten all that he had done to keep it that way.

His teeth grated. What was he going to do?

He was tired of being called a Yank and tired of being used. She could have things her way, but she was going to pay the price. He'd never forced a woman into anything, and he knew that Christa would fight him like a wildcat.

Maybe he wanted the fight tonight.

He didn't want to take anything from her. He just wanted her to know that she couldn't enter into any bargains—especially not with him, dirty Yank that he was—without paying some price.

"Christa!" he called after her. "I think you'd best wait a minute," he told her. He wasn't tired in the least. He was angry. Maybe if she had managed to be grateful he wouldn't feel quite so irritated. He just felt as if he wanted to shake her, and the longer she looked at him as if he were the hired help, the more irritated he became.

"Jeremy, I'm very tired," she said. It was definitely a "mistress-of-the-house" type voice she leveled at him. He had done his duty. He was dismissed.

Not so easy, Miss Cameron.

His fingers knotted into fists. Yes. Let it be that easy. Say good night. He didn't want to hurt her.

But neither did he want to let her walk away. Jesu! She had forced him into a marriage.

She stood regally beneath the moonlight, aware that he was watching her again, his hands on his hips.

Christa stared at him in turn, wondering at the twist of his jaw. "Oh!" she murmured. "Thank you, Jeremy. Really. And good night," Christa said and started for the house.

But when she started walking, Jeremy caught hold of her arm, spinning her back in such a way that she plowed right into his arm, her fingers splayed upon his chest while his hold then encompassed her. Her eyes widened with protest, but before she could speak, Jeremy did so, tauntingly. "No, no!" he warned softly. "Where do you think you're going?"

"I—I'm tired. I'm going to bed."

"Just like that?"

She stared at him and shook her head blankly. "It's over now."

"Over? It's just beginning! You're not going anywhere."

"I don't know what you're talking about. I'm going to bed."

He smiled slowly, shaking his head. "I don't think so."

Christa pursed her lips, feeling her temper flaring. "Who the hell do you think you are? You're not my brother, or my father—"

"But I am your husband now!" he snapped. "Dammit, don't you even remember what you did? You married me!"

So this was the way that he wanted to play it. She'd cajoled him into it, and he just wasn't going to be a gentleman about the whole thing. He wanted to make her suffer. Somehow. It was payback time.

Her temper flared. She was ready for battle again. "If I choose to go to bed, sir, I will do so!"

"Always the princess!"

"I'll do what I damned well please!"

"Have it your way, then," Jeremy said softly, and his eyes seemed very silver, cutting into hers like sword blades. "You will go to bed, Christa. But not alone."

"What?" she whispered in return, stunned. "What?" she repeated, both her amazement and her fury clearly discernible in her tone.

"Lady, you forced me into this. You were willing to sell everything, both of our souls, for Jesse's house. Well, we saved it. Jesse will come back to claim it. But you forced me to be a husband. Now, Mrs. Mc-Cauley, I'm afraid that I'm going to have to force you to be a wife!"

Her eyes widened still further. She wanted to strike him. Slap that taunting, mocking curl from his lip, the hard silver glitter from his eyes.

She pressed with a greater fervor against his chest. "Don't be absurd!" she hissed. "You can't mean—"

"Oh, but Christa," he interrupted her. His voice was low and husky and filled with a ring of steel. "That's exactly what I mean!"

Suddenly his fingers were threaded through her hair, pulling her head back, forcing her eyes to his. She saw the hard, handsome cast of his face, the rock-firm set of his jaw, and a sudden chill seized her.

"You married me, Christa. Marriage! It was a serious step. I warned you. As the saying goes, madam, you've made your bed. You're going to lie in it. You understand what I mean, Christa. I know you do."

She shook her head violently, freeing her hair from his fingers. Yes, she knew. She just couldn't believe what he was saying. Leave it to a Yankee! He couldn't just be pleased that they had saved the house. Oh, no. He wanted a real marriage. It was impossible. For many reasons—not excepting the fact that they could scarcely stand being in the same room with one another!

She swallowed hard and grated her teeth. "Leave it to a no-good Yankee varmint of a man to try to take the term 'husband' literally!" she whispered furiously. "This has to be a marriage in name only. I accept Jesse because he's my brother, but on the whole, Jeremy McCauley, I can't abide Yankees, and even if you weren't a Yankee, I'm not so sure I could abide you! All that aside, you're still in the cavalry. You'll be riding west."

"Then, Christa, my dear wife—and, yes! I do take that term literally!—then you will lie with me in the West." His face lowered toward hers, the silver gray of his eyes alive in a taunting sizzle. "I have a bad time abiding certain Rebels, Christa, and I'd have to say that you're right there among them. But this isn't going to be a marriage in name only."

She stared into his eyes and something hot raced through her. Something that seemed to touch her inside and out. Something that made her knees feel weak and her lips go dry. He meant to touch her. To have her. To do all the things that husbands and wives did together. Tonight. She was quite certain that she hated him, but suddenly she was imagining his bronze hands against her bare flesh. That hard, taut-muscled body against her own. Those curving, sensual lips pressed to her throat.

She couldn't breathe. Her heart beat painfully, and fire seemed to rage throughout her. She caught his gaze upon her, and suddenly she knew that he felt it too. It was hatred, it was anger, she thought.

It didn't matter what it was, it was explosive and it was frightening.

She shook her head again, desperate to find words. "No!" It should have been a cry of defiance and of rage.

But she hadn't the breath for it. It was a whisper. Barely a protest.

Because those silver eyes were on her. He spoke again in a voice that was shiver soft, and with an underlying current of rock. "Let me remind you. You did this. You begged, pleaded, and cajoled me into marrying you. I have done so. You said that you would pay any price. Well, my love, it's time to pay that price!"

She found her strength at last. Found strength and courage.

"You must be insane!" she hissed. "I am not bedding down with any Yankee vermin!"

"Even the vermin who saved your precious house?"

"The war is over!" she said desperately.

"No." He shook his head. There was challenge in his eyes, a wry grin that bitterly mocked them both curling into his lips once again. "No, Christa, you insisted on drawing fire. This war has just begun!"

Before she knew it, he had swept her into his arms. He carried her up the steps of the porch and burst through the front door. He reached the grand staircase leading to the second-floor bedrooms before she realized that he really intended to carry her up.

"Put me down!" she gasped, trying hard to struggle within his arms. "Dammit, I don't know what is the matter with you Yankees. You're done, you're finished, don't you understand!"

Done and finished? Jeremy wasn't really sure what he had been intending himself. Just a delivery to her bedroom door, perhaps. But suddenly all the anger that had been simmering inside all day came swiftly flying to the surface with her curt dismissal. All he knew at the moment was that Christa wasn't walking away from what she had done by throwing a blanket at him.

He was dimly aware that they passed the portrait gallery at the top of the stairs. Generations of Camerons looked down upon him. If he could have thrown a blanket somewhere, he would have liked to toss it over those faces.

He didn't need to hesitate in the hallway. He'd been a guest here three times now. Jesse and Kiernan's room was at the top of the stairs. Daniel and Callie's was farther to the right. The nursery was down at that end.

Christa's door was to the left.

Her fingers were burning into his arms as he kicked the door open with a boot. She was struggling so fiercely that he felt as if he was carrying a squirming greased pig.

She was going on and on, with every single word she uttered feeding fuel to the flames of his temper. She called him a small-time farmer, no-account white trash, and of course the very worst of them to her—a Yankee. "Who on earth would even think—oh! Leave it to a Yankee! Leave it to a Yankee!"

He didn't need light in the bedroom. The gas light poured in from the hallway, and a full moon was still up, casting a golden glow upon everything in the room. It was the first time he had actually entered the regal sanctity of Christa's room—the first time he had ever thought to do so.

It was beautiful. The bed was canopied with a white curtain and spread. There were huge wingback chairs by the sheer drapes that fluttered by the windows. A beautifully polished cherrywood writing table gleamed in the moonlight.

He walked her across the room suddenly aware that she had been pummeling and clawing him all the way. He tossed her down on the bed, leaning over her and pinioning her there.

Her eyes with their glittering blue fire and ice met his with a wild fury.

Her mouth was opening. She was going to say something about Yankees again.

"What?" he thundered before she could speak. "Rebels don't sleep with their wives, is that it, Christa?"

Her eyes widened. For once she seemed tongue-tied.

But only momentarily.

"You're no better than that fur-faced blue-belly who came here—"

"The one you said you'd be willing to marry?" he demanded quickly. Even in the moonlight, he saw the flush steal over her face.

"If you don't let me up—"

"Oh, you're going to get up," he assured her. His hands were on her waist and she was on her feet. He spun her around, his hands on the tiny hooks at the base of her spine. "I just sold my soul. I want to see what great and outstanding Rebel beauty I've achieved for my efforts."

He wasn't sure exactly what he wanted, and he wasn't sure himself exactly how far he meant to go with her. Maybe he had just intended to remind her that she was living now on his bounty, and that if she was lucky, he would be magnanimous.

But he never had a chance to be magnanimous.

She jerked violently away from him. It was her mistake. The worn fabric of her day dress ripped with a loud tearing sound and came away in his hands. She hadn't been wearing any of her multitude of petticoats that day, nor a corset. Her torn day dress slipped down the length of her one undergarment, a soft chemise left over from the days of glory. The fabric was cotton, elegant, sheer cotton. The straps were wispy and it was ribbed with lace. It molded her breasts, a garment that was soft, elusive, sensual, clinging to her waist, then flaring free—and sheer—to the floor. It did little to shield the rouge-colored crests of her nipples, nor did it do anything other than add mystery to the ebony-dark triangle at the juncture of her thighs. It emphasized her slender beauty in the glow of the moon. For a moment he stood still, looking at her.

It was impossible not to want her. She might have indeed been a goddess, created to be desired.

He started, drawn instantly from such retrospect as her hand cracked hard across his jaw. The sound echoed and echoed in the night.

Even Christa seemed surprised by it. She backed away from him, stumbling over the dress that had fallen to the floor.

"I—I—" she gasped, then she cried out, "You are a detestable Yank! Even married couples use dressing screens. Men turn their backs for their wives to change. They maintain decorum—"

"Decorum!" Jeremy interrupted. Despite the nagging pain that still stung his cheek, wry amusement tinged his anger. "You think that your brother makes love to my sister with decorum? For her sake, I hope the hell not!" With those words, he traveled the two steps between them. He didn't know what he was after.

He caught her shoulders, drawing her to him. He lifted a hand to her chin, cupping it.

His lips touched hers.

You may now kiss the bride.

The words echoed mockingly in his mind, then faded away. Christa protested. A strangled sound escaped her. She struggled against the rock-hard hold of his body.

In all his years of warfare, he had never felt more merciless. She'd married him. She could damn well kiss him.

But that wasn't why he had touched her. And it wasn't why he kept touching her.

Her lips were full and beautiful, the taste of them was sweet. More than that, the passion that filled her trembled there, within her lips, her mouth. Maybe it was the passion of hatred. That didn't seem to matter. Maybe it was the passion of his own anger. That didn't matter either. He wanted to kiss her, wanted to taste that sweetness. He didn't give a damn if she was protesting. His fingers curled into her hair, holding her to his will. His tongue broke through the restraint of her lips, forced her teeth, discovered the fullness of her mouth. Still the taste was so sweet. It seemed the smothered protests were being swallowed away as he held her.

Maybe it was more than her lips that spurred him on. The first time that he had seen her, he had been startled by her beauty, perhaps even a bit captivated by it. He could remember just staring at her and forgetting where he was and what he had come for.

Once again, he discovered himself startled, captivated.

Beneath the sheer fabric of her ribbed and laced chemise, he could feel the sensual curve and shape of her body. Full breasts crushed against his chest. Despite them, he could feel the wild pounding of her heart. Her legs were long and shapely, nearly entwined with his. He could feel the flatness of her stomach, and even the rise of her femininity, for he had crushed her very hard against him. The taste, the scent, the feel of her, all were suddenly blinding.

And suddenly so arousing that he could think no more. Her hair was silk to his touch. Her body was fire. He could forget pain touching her. He could forget the war. Forget love, and the dreams that had been cast to ashes. No matter that it was a passion born of anger, Christa seethed with it. She was raw and exciting to touch. More than her beauty made her arousing. The electricity that shimmered from her and around her evoked a shattering burst of desire within him. It made him long to drink and drink of her lips. To savor the sweet taste of her mouth. To delve further and further within it. As the seconds passed it seemed that she ceased to protest. Perhaps her body yielded to his. Perhaps her lips surrendered, parted of their own accord.

Let her go! he warned himself.

His mistake. He should have never come so far. Kissed her so. Taken her so into his arms.

She broke away from him suddenly. The back of her hand flew to her swollen lips. Her blue eyes were liquid as she gazed at him.

"You've no right!" she choked out.

He shook his head. "No, Christa. You had no right to slap me. I have every right to be here. You married me, remember? You insisted on it."

She bit her lower lip. Blue flames seemed to leap from her eyes. He crossed his arms over his chest. He might have been amused if he didn't feel as if he were suffering all the torments of hell.

"But you can't mean—"

"I don't know what I mean. I just want to see this incredible piece of southern fluff I've acquired."

"How dare you—"

"Take care, Christa. Get to know the enemy you've harnessed. I dare quite a bit. Let's go. I'll have the chemise—*Mrs. McCauley.*"

If she'd had a gun at that moment he was quite sure she would have shot him.

"Why, you—" she began.

He shook his head, his lip curling with dry humor. "Watch it, Mrs. McCauley."

"Why should I bother?"

"If you act the dutiful wife, I might decide to go away."

"And if I don't?"

"Well, the dress is in tatters. The chemise can follow the same route."

Her eyes narrowed. "You wouldn't."

"Want to try me? I am a Yank, after all. You need to keep that in mind."

She lifted her chin. "You can talk that way tonight, but if Jesse or Daniel were here—"

There was nothing she could have said to quite test his temper so far. His hand shot out, his fingers winding around her wrist. In a second she was in front of him again. "Don't threaten me with your brothers, Christa. Ever. Not unless you like the thought of more bloodshed. You married me. I warned you that you were selling both our souls to the devil. Jesse and Daniel are your brothers. Your name is McCauley now. I'm your husband. And so help me, Christa, you caused it, you'll remember it!"

He didn't mean to hurt her. He didn't mean to be destructive. His fingers gripped the bodice of her chemise at the cleft between her breasts. Alarmed, she tried to wrench free again. The fabric began to tear and she stopped, furious, shaking. She wrenched the garment over her head, throwing it at him.

"Bastard!" she cried. "Take the damned thing!" He was blinded by a cloud of white fabric as she started by him.

He threw it savagely aside, long strides bringing him to her. He caught hold of her elbow, swirled her around, and swept her into his arms. He cast her, naked, defiant, and trembling, onto her bed. Before she could think to spring to her feet he had straddled her, his weight bearing her down.

She was pure rebellion, staring up at him. A flush of color had risen to her cheeks, but her eyes were wild and furious and challenging.

Pure rebellion—and beauty. Her hair spilled about her like a black cloud, her lips were still red and moist from his kiss. Her coloring, even in moonlight, was glorious. Her naked breasts and flesh were radiant and beautiful. Heat cascaded from her in great waves. It seemed to touch him. To sweep into his body, constrict his muscles, quicken his pulse. The heat entered into his hips and his loins, and he was stunned by the savage and volatile way in which he wanted her.

He clenched his teeth hard together. He could walk away from her. Damn her, he could walk away from her!

She started to struggle. "Stop!" he warned her with a roar. He pushed back while she seethed, trying to remain still, her lower lip caught between her teeth, her breasts rising and falling with her exertion, her eyes alive with fire and vengeance.

He allowed his gaze to flicker over her. Not too slowly. A quick assessment.

"Well?" she flared. He could hear the grating of her teeth beneath the word.

He leaned close to her. "I think, Christa, that you are well aware of your own attributes. But are you payment enough for the price of a soul?" he murmured.

He felt her begin to tremble more fiercely. He pushed away from her, furious with her and with himself. He rose. He saw her eyes widen with amazement. She inched up quickly, grabbing for the coverings on her bed. He bowed to her. "My dear."

"You're leaving?" she said quickly.

"For the moment."

"But what—" She paused, moistening her lips. He could see her pride battling with her absolute relief that he seemed about to let her be.

"You'll do, Christa. But hell, I think I need a drink!" He turned and started for the door.

To his amazement, he was hit by a pillow. "Oh, you bastard!" she cried as he spun around. "This whole thing was just to torture me, to humiliate me, to strip me of my modesty—"

He walked back to her quickly, catching hold of her even as she shrieked, pulling her back up into his arms. "Christa, I can't strip you of what you've already given up. You said you would have married the blue-belly who would have raped you, so don't ask me to think too highly of your modesty. Maybe I did want to torment you." And God alive! I tormented myself! he added silently. "But there's more to it than that. You married me. You didn't care to first find out what it would mean. Well, it's done now. And you're going to find out that it does mean something! But for the moment, good night!"

He set her down. She sank back to the bed, her eyes spitting fire.

But when he left her this time, she was silent. Hatefully silent. Even as he walked away, he could feel the fire in her eyes.

Just who had taken whom tonight, he wondered.

For Christa might well lie awake worried.

But he was suffering the tortures of the damned.

Four

Jeremy came down the stairway with tense, heavy footfalls, trying once again to ignore the numerous Camerons who seemed to be still staring at him from their frames with silent reproach. He didn't want to see any more Camerons. The memory of Christa, naked and furious, seemed to be branded within his mind, and she was enough Cameron for him at the moment. He could still feel the sparks that had seemed to leap from her, like streaks of electricity. Christa in all her glory. All that magnificent black Cameron hair streaming down her back, every curve and nuance of her perfect young body.

Her eyes. Those blue fire-and-ice eyes. Revenge? Indeed, he'd had a taste of it. And it was sweet.

Then why was he the one so aflame now, the one suffering the pain of the damned? What a fool. How the hell could he want her so badly now? When there was nothing but hostility between them, after this travesty of a marriage, how could he have come to this position?

He reached the Camerons' study and burst irritably into it, lighting the gas light above the desk and sinking into the chair behind that desk. He poured himself a brandy from the decanter on a side table, then leaned back in the chair, swallowing it down, wincing at the fire that seared his throat. He didn't dare close his eyes, and he didn't dare open them. He saw her either way.

Christa. Naked. Maybe emotions didn't mean anything after so long a war, and so long a time since emotions had meant something. Maybe the wanting was just enough. Christa was perfect. Tall, slim, a little bit too thin, but not even the war could have taken too much a toll upon the natural dips and curves of her body. Her naked flesh was a beautiful ivory shade and it had the sweetest scent and the most inviting appeal.

He exhaled on a long groan.

He should have left her the hell alone.

He didn't know what force or demon was driving him tonight, he knew only that she had goaded him to a point where she was going to pay a price for what she had forced upon them.

If Christa Cameron thought it was an easy thing to twist and bend people to her will at her convenience, he was damned sorry, but she was going to have to see that her actions had serious repercussions.

Marriage. It had come so easily to her. Just a slip off her tongue. No more than a trip into town, an afternoon's escapade, easily done, easily forgotten.

In truth, she hadn't cared. Hadn't given a damn about his situation, just so long as she had gotten what she wanted, to protect the sacred halls of Cameron Hall.

Not that he resented having done something to salvage the place. Perhaps Christa had been right about one thing. The Hall was history. It was beautiful, gracious, a monument to centuries of a family that had found roots and flourished in a new world. Now Cameron Hall had weathered revolution and civil war, and all the trauma in between. It deserved to stand. He could understand her desire to save it, even if he was infuriated by the way she was willing to use him to do so.

Although he had fought all the long years of the war, although there had been times when he had watched his men fall and die and in his heart he had hated all things Rebel, he was disgusted with the way things were being handled in the South. Power was being put into careless hands. Lincoln had wanted peace. But Lincoln was dead, and Johnson's administration was determined not on peace but on punishment. Elections were being rigged, and half the men who had been in politics before the war—those who were still living—were being barred from office for having served with the Confederacy. Daniel Cameron had yet to receive a pardon from the United States government because of his high rank in the military service, and as things stood now, some men wondered if Jeff Davis might yet meet a hangman. But beyond the blatant abuses of power, there were smaller struggles going on. Officials—many of them opportunists who had come down upon the South like locusts—were taking all manner of bribes, selling out to the highest bidders. Such had been the case with Cameron Hall.

Jeremy liked his brother-in-law, Daniel Cameron, just fine. Daniel had been a Virginian born and raised, and there hadn't been a lot of help for the fact that he'd been a Reb. He'd just followed his own conscience. The war hadn't given them a lot of time to deepen their acquaintance, but from what they'd come to know of one another, they shared a common way of looking at the world, at responsibility, at life. And Jeremy's sister, Callie, loved Daniel. That said a lot for him, right there.

Jeremy was glad to have done anything that might have helped Daniel.

He lifted his brandy glass. "To you, Daniel!" The first time he had come here, looking for Callie, he had wound up in this room, drinking brandy with Daniel Cameron. It had been a strange day. He had come here ready to do battle for his sister's sake. He had come here an enemy. He had left here his brother-in-law's friend, even if neither of them had changed his colors.

Then there was Jesse Cameron. He'd had several occasions to get to know Jesse—they'd fought on the same side. Jesse was the finest physician and surgeon he'd ever come across. The war had taken a hell of a toll on him as he'd patched up his friends and old acquaintances—from both sides of the fighting field. In the regular cavalry, Jeremy had ridden in by the hospital tents often enough to see his sister-in-law's elbow deep in the wounded, that anguished look on her face that Jeremy could read too clearly.

Jesse Cameron was always afraid that someone would be bringing his brother in to him.

But the war had ended. Jesse and Daniel had both managed to stay alive.

Jeremy liked them both. It didn't matter which side they had fought on, he had no problem with the Cameron men.

It was the Cameron woman he longed to throttle.

Christa!

Damn her. Men knew how to fight, and they knew how to surrender. For Christa, the war would never be over.

Nor, he thought soberly, would she ever realize that she wasn't the only one to feel that she had lost a love, lost everything, in the carnage. For a moment the pain returned to him, though he thought that he had learned to suppress it a long, long time ago. It returned, harsh, brutal, tearing into his heart.

It had been one thing to see soldiers die. That had been anguish enough. But sometimes fire went awry. Sometimes cannonballs tore up far more than fortress walls or other cannons or fighting men . . .

Sometimes fire killed the innocent. Old men, children.

Women, trying to shelter little ones.

He grit his teeth. Jennifer Morgan had been killed during the long, awful shelling of Vicksburg, Mississippi. It had been over two years ago now. He could still remember how he had found her when the ragged, bone-thin little blockade-running urchin had brought him to her when the city had fallen into Yankee hands. She'd been in the caves beneath the hills. They'd folded her hands over her breast, and she might have been sleeping except for the clot of blood he found at the base of her skull when he'd tried to move her.

Jenny. He hadn't known her a year. He had first met her when his troops had encamped on her farmland and he'd gone to make what restitution he could for the destruction that his men were causing with their tents and multitude of horses. He had expected a haggard farm wife, but that wasn't what he had discovered at all. Jenny had been beautiful. Blond, green-eyed, delicate, and lovely. So very proud, but so sweet and soft-spoken. Three little children had clung to her skirts, and all were threadbare and thin-looking.

Jeremy hadn't just paid for the damage to her crops. He managed to pay her a small fortune for a broach she had. He was going home, and he had needed a gift for Callie.

Callie would take good care of the gift. And with his Yankee dollars, the widowed Mrs. Jenny Morgan—whose husband had been killed at Shiloh—would be able to buy food and clothing for her growing young brood.

Christmas had come and gone.

Jeremy had come back to Mississippi. He'd remained on her land while Grant determined to dig in until Vicksburg fell, no matter what the cost. Grant was the one damned smart general the Union had. He didn't retreat every time a southern force came near him. He knew that he had more of one important thing than any southern general out there—manpower. The Rebs couldn't afford to keep dying. The Union could keep replenishing her fallen forces.

But the war hadn't really mattered between them. They had never been at war with one another.

He didn't know when he had fallen in love with her. Maybe it had been one of those nights when he had stared at her windows so long he hadn't been able to take it anymore. He had mounted up and ridden over, and he had discovered that Jenny Morgan waited up nights for him. The hours of darkness became magic.

Jenny didn't have much interest in politics. But she had been born a Mississippian and she cared deeply about what was happening to the people around her. Jeremy never knew that she intended to go into Vicksburg along with her children *despite* his words of warning while the Union continued its siege of the city. She could help with the soldiers in the hospital.

Jeremy explained the futility of her wishes, and she listened to him.

While war pounded on around them, they formed a curious domesticity. The children loved him, and loved to pick his pockets when he came. Jeremy and she were on different sides of the upheaval, but Jenny, though she wouldn't say the words, didn't believe that the Confederacy could win the war.

Jeremy was ordered to take his company on a reconnaissance ride around the perimeters of Vicksburg. As it happened, the maneuver took them days. When he returned, Jenny was gone, leaving behind a note that she loved him and that she'd marry him as soon as the siege at Vicksburg was over. She was expecting their child in autumn.

When she was gone, he realized just how much he loved her. He tried to get word into the city to make sure she was all right. There were Union spies moving in and out, so it wasn't very difficult to discover her whereabouts. She was with many other citizens of the city, living in caves below the hills because so many of the houses had been hit with cannon and shell fire. The caves were the only place to avoid fire.

It was a terrible ordeal for the citizens of Vicksburg. The Union spies who returned shook their heads wearily at his questions. There was no food to be had in the city. Those who remained were cooking the rats that scurried among the refuse.

His heart sickened and he wrote her a long letter, begging her to come out. Yes, he wanted her. Yes, he loved her. He wanted their child, and he wanted to be a father to her other children. He didn't want her in Vicksburg. She needed to take the children, marry him, and find somewhere to live safely.

Somewhere where neither army came.

Days passed. A spy brought a letter back to him. He was grateful. He knew the man had put his life at risk. The letter was filled with Jenny's words, with her enthusiasm and empathy for all men, with all the beautiful things that had made him fall so completely in love with her.

She was unique. He hadn't lived so very long—he'd just turned twenty-four at the start of the war—but he'd put some mileage into those years. He came from a family of hardworking farmers. They were not rich but his father had earned a wealth of friendship and respect in his dealings, and he'd seen to it that all his sons had gone to West Point.

Once he'd graduated, he'd served some time in the West, riding hard on the Santa Fe Trail. He'd seen some action, enough to test his mettle under fire. He'd been initiated into battle fighting Indians, and he'd come to know a fair amount about a number of the tribes, from the civilized and fascinatingly cultured to the very savage and warlike.

He'd seen some other action in the West with the camp ladies who managed to trail behind any army. He'd even been growing serious about the daughter of an army major, but something had been lacking and so he'd backed away.

Once he realized just how deeply he cared for Jenny, he learned what had been missing. Love. She was, indeed, unique. Sweet and dignified. And strong, too, he realized. She pretended to bow to him in all things, then she went her own way.

She would not come out of Vicksburg. She had learned how to meet one of the blockade runners on the river, and she was determined to be of help to the citizens in the city. She could bring in food and morphine for the children.

She had been dead a long time now.

He had come in the very day the city had fallen. He had watched the women weeping in the streets as the blue-clad forces had marched through. He had felt the southerners' hatred.

He had ignored them all, demanding directions to the caves.

He had found her. She had been struck by a stray bullet just two nights before the surrender of the city.

She had died within twenty-four hours.

No one in the cave had said anything about his blue uniform. Maybe his grief had been that naked. Jenny's beautiful blond children had offered him more comfort than he had offered them. He had taken her into his arms, held her dead body. He had laid his palm over her belly, where their child had died with her. He had not wanted to give her up.

A woman like Jenny had stood in the entry to the makeshift home in the cliffs. He had looked up, his eyes glittering with his pain. "I can take the children. I'll adopt them if they'll have me, I'll find some place—"

"Sir, Vicksburg will be safe enough now," the woman said. "We've surrendered. The children will be safe with me. I'm Jenny's sister, and I've lost my husband and my only boy."

He could remember nodding. He could remember stumbling to his feet, still holding Jenny's body.

"She did love you," the woman told him. "And she knew that you loved her. She was happy about the new one, and it didn't give her any mind whatsoever that it was a Yank fathered her babe, she loved you that much. You put her down now. We've got to bury her."

Jenny was buried; Vicksburg was secured. Jeremy was transferred back to the East, whether he wanted to fight there or not. Grant was determined to trap the wily Lee, and it didn't matter what it took. He would lose battles, and he would lose men. He'd fight again, and he'd draft more men.

There was one benefit to being assigned back to the East. He'd have a chance to see Callie. He had been so angry with Callie when he'd first discovered she was about to have a Reb's child, and she was not married to that Reb. He might well have fathered a southern child himself. It opened a wealth of understanding. He had been so anxious to see her.

But he discovered that Callie had been spirited down south by that Reb and so he had come to Cameron Hall for the first time. He had come to know Daniel and Christa. The beautiful blue-eyed witch upstairs. The one who had married him, condemning him, hating him.

"To you, Christa!" he murmured, swallowing down another two-finger swig of brandy. He was certain she had sat at this very desk often enough, sipping brandy—or swigging it down—just as he was now. It was a fine old office with the massive desk and rows of books. The ledgers and all the books were kept here. And once, Jeremy was certain, gentlemen would have retired here in the midst of a party for brandy or whiskey and cigars and talk. Politics. Animal husbandry. Things in which the women wouldn't be interested.

Until the war had taken away the men and left the women.

For a moment, a heartbeat of pity slipped its way into his heart. She had managed well enough. She had a right to love the place. Working like a field hand, she had kept it standing. And she had fought for it. When Eric Dabney's Yankee raiders—out to bring Daniel in dead or alive —had come sneaking around the place, Christa had been armed and ready. She had shot a man in defense of herself and Kiernan and Callie. She hadn't killed him, but she hadn't hesitated to pull the trigger when she had been threatened. She was a fighter.

Pity. Because she was going to lose the place. The house belonged to Jesse.

He smiled suddenly. He *should* make her come west with him. She was a fighter; she had magnificent courage.

And she was beautiful. And desirable.

He set his glass down, sobering. The western plains were really no place for a woman, any woman. Some of the men did bring their wives, but those wives loved their husbands.

The West was wild, primitive, dangerous, savage. Then again, Christa was all those things too! Heaven help the Indians she got her hands on.

Somewhere in the house, a clock struck. He counted the chimes. Midnight.

It was his wedding night. He had imagined it so differently. He'd imagined laughter and caring, and making love deep into the night. He'd imagined sleeping with golden blond streams of hair tangled all over his naked flesh. He'd imagined her smile and her welcome, touching her stomach to feel their child grow.

"Anything! Anything but sitting alone in the Camerons' plantation office, sipping brandy."

It probably wasn't what Christa had imagined either, he reminded himself. Maybe it was worse for her. She'd been engaged, she'd waited.

Callie had written Jeremy when they'd all heard the news that Liam McCloskey was dead. She had told him how they had all dyed their wedding finery black. Christa hadn't mentioned her fiancé's name today, not once.

He stood up suddenly.

She wasn't going to sleep alone. One didn't marry an ebony-haired enchantress and sleep in the guest room—even if she was a shrew!

He took one more swig of brandy. He sighed out loud, lifting his glass again to the air. "To all of us poor wretches!" he said. He smashed the glass against the fireplace, left the room behind him, and started up the stairs.

The damned Camerons looked at him again from the portrait gallery along the upper stairway. This time he paused and looked back.

"Not a damned word out of a one of you! She's my wife."

The word sounded so damned strange in connection with Christa.

He walked purposefully past the portraits and to her room. The door was closed. He entered the room and closed the door behind him.

Moonlight streamed in on the canopied bed. He walked to it and looked down at her.

She had fallen asleep. Another woman might have cried herself to sleep, but he doubted that Christa had done so. She lay on her stomach, and the covers were pulled just to the small of her back. The beautiful curve of it was plainly visible in the moon glow. Black hair spilled all around her, and her fingers were curled just below her chin. Her lashes swept her cheeks. He reached out and touched her face, wondering if he didn't feel just a bit of dampness there, just a hint of tears.

"But this is it!" he said to her softly in the moonlight. "This is what you wanted!"

He sat at the foot of the bed and pulled off his boots. She must have been really exhausted—she didn't even stir. He watched her face all the while that he stripped off his uniform, folding it neatly, piece by piece, and setting it upon her dressing table. He crawled in beside her, not touching her. He stared up at the ceiling, then swore silently at himself once again.

He knew damned well he'd never intended to rape her in her sleep, so

what the hell did he think he was accomplishing by being here? He was
on fire again, from head to toe. He had tried to pull the covers over his
body, and now the damned sheet was rising, just as if there were a ghost
down in the center of the bed. It was impossible to lie beside her and not
want her.

Remember Jenny! he told himself fiercely. Remember what it should
have been. Remember Christa's words. The way that she says "Yankee"
as if it were the filthiest word in the English language.

It didn't work. He was as hard as a poker, and with the sheet flying up
he felt like a flagstaff.

Well, he wasn't getting up. They were married, and whether there was
anything between them or not, he was suddenly determined that they
were going to sleep like a married couple tonight.

She was his enemy, as no man had ever been.

But she was also soft and supple. Her flesh was silk, and he could just
feel the whisper of it against his own. He turned slightly and her hair
teased his nose, smelling like roses, feeling like a swatch of velvet.

He turned his back on her, making sure that their flesh didn't touch.
He slammed his fist against his pillow.

He started to count sheep.

It was damned funny.

No, it was torture.

But thank God for brandy, for long endless days, for total exhaustion.
Toward morning, he slept at last.

He usually awoke easily, at the slightest sound. All those years of sleeping on the field in tents, alert to the slightest danger, had done something
to his ability to sleep deeply.

But that night he slept as if he were dead.

And oddly enough, he had beautiful dreams. He was in some
meadow, somewhere. Maryland, probably. He had always loved his
home, where in the distance around him the land began to roll majestically and the mountains rose blue and green. The trees were rich and
beautiful, draping over the trails in natural arbors. He was coming home.
He was running because he could see her. Jenny. Delicate, feminine, her
hair a cloud of sunshine around her, she ran down the trail toward him,
her arms outstretched. He began to run. He could feel his heartbeat. He
could feel the muscles constricting in his legs. The war was over. It was
time to come home. She was reaching out to him.

Then the vision of her began to fade. In the dream he knew that she
was dead.

Vaguely, from the deep, deep recesses of that dream, he began to hear a noise, and he realized that the noise was coming from the real world of consciousness.

"Christa!" It was a soft, feminine voice. Then there was a rapping on the door. "Christa . . . ?"

He opened his eyes, fighting the last vestiges of sleep, pushing himself up.

He glanced to the right. Christa was just struggling to awaken. He was startled at just how quickly he found himself aroused at the sight of her. Her back was beautiful and sleek against the bedding that was falling from it, her hair was pure ebony against the snow-white coloring of the sheets. It fell in wave after wild wave down her back, and despite himself, he found himself making comparisons. Jenny had been so delicate, so ethereal. Blond, pale, soft. Christa was as slender, perhaps more so, but even slender she was richly curved, and she was not in the least ethereal. She was passion and fire and sensuality.

He wanted her.

"Christa . . . ?"

Someone was directly beyond their door. With his present feelings, he couldn't help but feel a malicious pleasure in the fact that Christa seemed so truly alarmed at the prospect of being discovered with him in her bed. She glanced at him with absolute horror in her beautiful blue eyes.

"What in God's name are you doing there?" she hissed. "You've got to get up, you've got to get out of here."

He leaned back against the bedstead, studying her, shaking his head slowly. He crossed his arms stubbornly over his chest. "I don't think so, Christa."

"That's Kiernan! She and Jesse have come back. If my brother finds you here, he'll kill you."

"Christa, I'm married to you. Remember? And what a pity! Jesse's back? Just think, for a matter of less than twenty-four hours, you've had to con me into marriage!"

She flashed him a furious look. "You're a horrible person, Jeremy Mc-Cauley. No less than I'd expect—"

"From a Yank. Yes, I know."

She flashed him another of her regally condemning glares, then started to push up from the bed determined to find clothing even if he wasn't going to do so.

He reached out quickly, sweeping an arm around her, and drawing her back down.

"Jeremy, let me go—"

"Cover up, my love. Someone's about to burst through that door."

And he was right. He'd barely brought the covers up over the two of them when the door did burst open.

A loud gasp sounded.

Kiernan stood there. And Jesse was with her.

But they weren't alone.

Daniel and Callie were beside them.

The foursome stared into the room, jaws gaping. "Oh, my God!" Kiernan breathed.

Five

Beyond a doubt, they had quite an audience. Jesse, still in the military, was in his blue uniform, a signature plume in his cockaded hat. Kiernan, at his side, was elegant in a yellow-and-mustard day dress that emphasized her blond beauty. Daniel had retired his butternut-and-gray uniform. He was dressed in fawn breeches, a black frock coat, white shirt, and red cravat. Callie wore a blue dress with modified petticoats and a velvet bustle. Her gray eyes were very wide with surprise, and he might have smiled at her expression—if the room were not so filled with combustible tension.

Beside him, Christa groaned. He kept his arm around her, wondering how—with this audience—he could still be so aware of her, of the feel of her hair tumbling over his shoulders and chest, of the silken feel of her naked flesh beneath his fingers. She was trembling.

He was certain that not one of the Camerons facing them intended to be so rude, filling the bedroom with their presence, gaping at them, slack-jawed and stunned.

"My God, how can you possibly be here?" Christa demanded, staring at the group. "I—" she began again, but she was cut off.

"Jesu—it's McCauley!" Daniel said. There was a raw edge of anger in his voice. Well, that could be expected, Jeremy thought. Daniel was more hotheaded than Jesse and fiercely protective of his sister.

How the hell do you think I felt about mine? Jeremy wondered in silence.

There was a long stretch of silence.

Then Daniel spoke again. "McCauley, if you've—"

Callie jumped to Jeremy's defense. "Daniel! That's my brother!"

"And my sister!" Daniel grated out.

"All right, all right!" Jesse lifted a hand, stepping into the breach. "Let's try to sort this out—"

"Dammit!" Daniel shook off Callie's restraining arm. "She's your sister, too, Jess—"

"Yes, and I'm sure we're not making her feel very wonderful, standing in here and staring at her like this. Jeremy, there is an explanation, right?"

Christa opened her mouth, about to speak. Jeremy tightened the pinioning arm he had around her. "You know, Daniel," he said smoothly, "you do, sir, have a hell of a nerve questioning me with such a damned note of accusation when I came home in the middle of the war to find my sister expecting a baby. And then to find that she'd clean disappeared, kidnapped south by some Reb the next time around!"

"I married your sister—" Daniel began heatedly.

"Whoa!" Jesse warned, coming to stand between them. Not only did they have an audience, Jeremy thought wryly, that audience was coming closer and closer. "Daniel, Jeremy, you made your peace about Callie a long time ago! Daniel, Jeremy fought with us to save this place. Let's have some reason here." He paused, then stared hard at Jeremy. "All right, McCauley. Just what the hell *are* you doing in bed with my sister? I need an explanation, and a good one!"

"There's a damned good one," he said lightly, addressing Jesse but his eyes narrowing on Daniel. "She's my wife."

"Wife!" Kiernan gasped.

"Christa, is that the truth?" Daniel shot quickly to his sister.

"Yes, I—"

"You married him?" Daniel said incredulously.

Callie cleared her throat. "Daniel, it's not so amazing that someone would marry my brother!" There was an angry emphasis on the last two words. She stared at Jeremy. "You married Christa?"

"Callie!" Daniel snapped.

Once again, Jesse stepped into the fray. "Let's not create offense where none is intended," he said flatly. "If we state surprise, Callie, it is merely because we never imagined Christa and Jeremy carrying on a civil conversation together, much less marrying one another. But it is the truth, right?"

"It's the truth," Jeremy said. "And I'm more than willing to explain it all, if you'd be so good as to excuse us long enough so that we can dress?"

"Oh! Yes, of course," Kiernan said. She started for the door. No one else was moving. She cleared her throat. "You all! They're naked and in bed and we're just staring at them!" she said in exasperation. "Jesse, come on. Daniel, Callie?"

"Oh," Jesse said quickly. Callie lowered her head and followed behind him. Daniel was the last to leave. "I'll see you in the study—" he began. But Jesse had his arm.

"Come on, Daniel. They'll be down in a minute!"

And Daniel, too, disappeared through the door. It shut with a small bang.

"Oh, my God!" Christa breathed. She leaned forward, burying her face in her hands. "How on earth did they all get here so quickly? Not just Jesse, not just Daniel. It will be so hard to get out of this now!" She leapt up, too distracted at first to realize that she was swirling around the room in all her naked glory as she searched for her clothing. The tangled fall of her hair was wild and sensual. The contrast between the rich color of her hair and the ivory of her flesh was exotic and tempting. He realized that she had two small dimples at the base of her spine, one over either buttock.

She wrenched open one of her drawers. "We'll have to try to explain it to them," she murmured, not even glancing his way.

Jeremy rose more slowly. He walked over to stand just behind her back. She found the pantalets she had been searching for. "I know that there's something we can say—" she started.

But he took hold of both of her shoulders and stared into her eyes. "No."

She shook her head. "What do you mean, no? I forced you into this, remember?"

"You forced me—and I did it. Well, now it's done. We're not getting out of it."

Her breath quickened. He was gazing into her eyes, but he could see the rise and fall of her breasts with his peripheral vision. Jesu. A part of his anatomy started to rise right along in response.

Christa's gaze slipped from his. A gasping sound escaped her and she tried to elude his hold, her chin rising, her eyes narrowing. "My brothers are home now, Jeremy. If you even think to touch me, I'll scream!"

He could hear the grating of his own teeth, the comment made him so furious. He jerked her hard against him. "Christa, this isn't a garden party any longer. Can't you understand the seriousness of what you've done? You'll scream?" he hissed. "Then you'll just have to go ahead and do so because I'll touch you when and how I like. They're your brothers. You married me. And unless you're really fond of bloodshed, you had best bear that in mind. Now, I'm sure you wouldn't mind in the least becoming a widow, seeing my Yankee carcass slipped into a shroud. Your brothers are good, damned good, but don't underestimate my abilities. I managed to stay alive through four years of fighting at the front too. So if you ever think about doing anything so stupid as causing a further friction between us, just remember that."

She had grown very pale. She no longer resisted his hold upon her. Her lashes, so long and rich a black, fell over her eyes. "Will you let me go, please? We do need to give them some kind of an explanation."

Instantly, he released her. She turned her back on him and stepped into the pantalets. He strode across the room and picked up his own neatly folded clothing, dressing quickly. He could hear the splash of wash water from the pitcher to the bowl as he buckled his scabbard in place. With his back to her, he waited for her.

"You can go down without me," she told him. Damn, how she wanted him gone! More time to plan a story for her brothers? Why a story, when the truth explained it all so clearly?

"You want to send me down to face the lions alone?" he drawled, turning to watch her. She was in the process of slipping into a dress. Christa certainly had enough gowns. This was another day dress, a handsome blue-and-gray plaid taffeta with black lace trim. It was elegant and very demure.

She dressed with care for every occasion. She stared at him, trying to do the hooks. He walked around behind her, impatiently grabbing her about the waist and pulling her back to him when she would have avoided his touch.

"My brothers are not lions," she said. "And I thought that you didn't give a damn about them."

"I'm not afraid of them," he told her. "I never said I didn't give a damn about them. There's a big difference." He rubbed his chin. He needed a shave. It would have to wait. The Camerons downstairs—including his sister—did deserve some kind of an explanation.

He was going to let Christa give it.

"Shall we go, Mrs. McCauley?" He offered her his arm. Christa ignored it, spun around, and started for the door. He followed on her footsteps.

Christa walked down the hallway through the gallery, painfully aware of him behind her. This could have been so easy. If Jeremy had behaved like a gentleman and kept his distance.

She suddenly felt a rush of blood rising to her cheeks. She could remember waking beside him. It had been almost like a dream. Being curled against him had been nice. She had felt the warmth of his body and the muscled length of him. She had also felt the hardness of him, warm and pulsing against her bare flesh. It hadn't been horrible at all, it had been fascinating, sensual, nice. She had wanted to turn around and curl against the strong male body. She had wanted to be held.

It's what it would have been like to wake up married.

She was married.

According to Jeremy, they were really married. She stopped short suddenly in the portrait gallery.

Camerons stared down upon them.

"What are we going to say?" she asked him.

"Let's see. I know. I rode by, you were swept off your feet, we couldn't wait a minute, you married me."

"How amusing," Christa murmured.

"How pathetic," he responded softly. He had dressed in his full uniform, down to his hat. It was a cockaded cavalry hat, just like Jesse's. Jeremy wore two plumes in his.

With the hat pulled low over his forehead, his eyes were barely discernible in the shadows of the hallway. He seemed exceptionally curt this morning, even for Jeremy. As if he were totally impatient with her now, and as if he truly regretted all that he had gotten himself into.

Except that he didn't seem willing to help get them out of it! He was a tall man and she felt again the disadvantage of looking up to him. His hair was still slightly askew beneath the brim of his hat, falling rakishly over his forehead. Her heart took a hard thud. He was a handsome man, but a very hard and unapproachable one at the moment. He leaned against the banister and casually studied her. "They're your brothers, Christa," he reminded her. "What's the matter with the truth?"

"I just don't want them to . . ." she began, but her voice trailed away.

"What?" he demanded sharply. She didn't have an answer for him—at least not one that she wanted to give. It didn't matter, Jeremy had the answer.

"Let me see, maybe I can answer this myself. You don't want them to know that you did something so desperate as to marry a man you despised to save a house. That you sold yourself for a pile of bricks."

She was itching to slap him, but he must have known it because he caught her wrist before she had barely made a move. "No, Christa," he warned her huskily.

She didn't want him as close to her as he was. She didn't want to feel the husky tenor of his voice, nor the heat of his body. She was very disturbed to realize that there were things about him that fascinated her. The size of him, the feel of him, the strength of him, the look of his bronzed hands with his long fingers and blunt cut nails against the pale ivory of her flesh. Something inside of her responded to him, whether she liked it or not.

She looked up into his eyes. They were steel gray with warning. His jaw was set at a hard-edged angle.

"Then quit being so horrible!" she charged him.

"All right." To her great unease, she was closer to him once again. He drew her very close, and whispered to her with his mouth just inches above her own. "We tell them that, yes, it was a matter of expediency. But the more we thought about it, the more wonderful it was. We're not really enemies at all, not now that the war is over. And of course, they're both home now. You don't need to guard the place anymore. You have your own life to lead. You're coming west with me."

She gasped. "I can't come west!"

"Whether you do or don't doesn't really matter at the moment, it's just something to say."

She stared at him. She wanted to wrench away from him, and she wanted to tell him that she'd never, never come west with him. But he was right—it didn't matter at the moment. She just had to get through today.

"Are you ready?" he said impatiently.

She moistened her lips. No, she wasn't ready. But he took her hand and started down the stairway, dragging her along with him.

The others were in the parlor to the right side of the entryway. Christa could hear their hushed voices as they came down the stairs. She bit her lower lip. She could hear Callie's voice. Though she couldn't hear her sister-in-law's words, she knew that Callie would be defending Jeremy. Then she heard Daniel, and she knew that he was concerned.

Then she heard Jesse. And though she couldn't make out a single word he was saying, she sensed that he was damning himself a thousand times over, certain that it was his fault that she had felt so forced to do something desperate.

"Well?" Jeremy arched a russet brow to her at the double doors to the parlor.

"Go on," she said.

"Oh, no, my love! After you."

She cast him a scathing glare and pushed open the double doors.

Four pairs of eyes turned to them instantly—and very guiltily.

Jeremy paused at the doors, closing them behind him, then leaning against them and watching Christa.

She was a wonderful performer, he determined.

She walked into the room with a beautiful smile—a Madonna's smile—

on her lips. "It's so wonderful! I can't believe that you're all home—together. Where are the children?" She kissed both her sisters-in-law on the cheek, then gave Jesse a big hug and turned to Daniel.

Daniel accepted the hug stiffly. The silence in the room was deafening.

Christa didn't let it bother her. She spun around, the perfect hostess in her own home. "How on earth are you here?" she asked.

Jesse, an arm on the mantel, arched a brow. "A little matter of the house, Christa," he said sternly. "A friend of mine in Washington heard that there was some dirty politicking going on here and that someone had made sure this house would go for back taxes. We picked up Daniel and Callie on our way through Richmond, and here we are." He paused, walking across the parlor to reach her. "I thought that we were going to be too late. I had this awful fear in my heart that we were going to get here to find the house burned to the ground." He took both Christa's hands. "What happened, Christa?"

Maybe it was time to jump in, Jeremy thought. No, not yet.

"Umm . . ."

All right. She could fume later. It seemed time to jump in and save her for the moment.

"Something was going on, Jesse," he said, eyeing the eldest Cameron squarely. "I came down to see Callie before being reassigned, and I happened on a slovenly misfit tacking a notice on this place. We had until sundown to do something about it." He walked across the room, setting his arms around Christa's waist and pulling her against him. Her hair just teased his chin. "The best solution in the world came to us," he said huskily. "Marriage."

"But you loathe one another!" Callie gasped out.

Jeremy smiled, amazed to discover that he was as good a performer as Christa. "Well, now, maybe that's what it seemed. But I swear to you, Christa wanted to marry me. More than she's ever wanted anything in the world, right Christa?" His arms tightened around her.

"Right!" she gasped out.

The Camerons still weren't convinced. "Dammit," Jesse swore suddenly. "This is my fault. I shouldn't have let them order me back to Washington. I should—"

"Hell, Jesse, it wasn't your fault," Daniel said bitterly. "I was the Reb, remember? The enemy to cause all this."

"Daniel, I'm the eldest. It was my responsibility—"

"Wait!" Christa cried out softly. "Will you two stop, please?" She leaned back against Jeremy, running her fingers tenderly over the arms that held her against him. "There's no fault here! My Lord, Jeremy and I are so happy! What's the matter with you all? We should be having a toast, you should be wishing me well!"

There was silence again. Jesse cleared his throat. "Jeremy, could I see you alone in the study?"

He released Christa, bowing his head in acquiescence. Jeremy opened the door to lead them out. Callie was on her feet in a split second. "Alone," Jesse said.

Callie sat. But Daniel was following him out.

"She's my sister too," he reminded Jesse.

Jeremy preceded the two to the study where he had overimbibed on Cameron brandy the night before. This morning he stood by the door, arms crossed over his chest, as he faced the two of them.

Jesse wasn't pouring brandy. He had the whiskey bottle out, even though it was still morning. "Jeremy, hell, I owe you," Jesse said, passing him a tumbler full of whiskey. He was quiet for a minute, and Daniel was silent behind him too. "I owe you for fighting here long before the war was over when the place was threatened by that misfit, Eric Dabney."

"Dabney was threatening my sister too," Jeremy reminded him. "You're not in my debt, Jesse. Neither is Daniel. Not now, not ever."

"Then what the hell happened yesterday?" Daniel demanded.

Jesse looked at his brother-in-law. The accusing tone was gone. There was anguish in his voice. Daniel adored Christa. He knew the feeling. Knew what it had been like to come home and find Callie gone.

He could have reminded Daniel of that now. He decided not to.

"It happened like I told you," he said. He set his glass down, leaning across the desk to talk to them both. "Look, I swear, I'm legally married to your sister. I've the certificate in my saddlebags. She would have liked you all to have been there, but it didn't seem to be worth the house being burned down to wait on the right kind of ceremony!"

Quick glances flickered between Jesse and Daniel. "We are in your debt," Daniel said. Jeremy knew that it must have been damned hard for him to say it. The Confederacy had lost the war, and Daniel accepted it, ready to go on. But some things were hard for him, like being in the debt of a Yank other than his brother, even though that Yank was now his brother-in-law. He inhaled and exhaled. Despite their differences—despite even the fact that they were both cavalry, that they might have met anytime in battle—they had formed something of a friendship. But this—this was hard for them all.

"Hell, Jeremy, it's just that Christa is our only sister!" Daniel said. "If you intend to divorce her—"

"I don't intend to divorce her," he interrupted quickly.

It was the truth. He hadn't really realized it until now. He hadn't known what to look for in the future. Now he knew. They might have no love lost on one another, but he didn't intend on a divorce. He had no heart left. Neither did she. Maybe they were made for one another.

He had discovered that he wanted her. Desperately. Maybe that was enough. Maybe it was much more than some had.

"You don't?" Jesse said.

He shook his head. "I admit, it was all rather sudden. I have to report back to Washington, and I have orders to head west. Maybe she'll come with me, maybe she'll stay here. There's a lot to decide about the future. But I don't intend on a divorce." He was silent for a moment, feeling them both watch him, feeling the relief that seemed to grow within them like something tangible. What else could he say with conviction? A wry smile touched his lips. "She's probably the most beautiful woman I've ever met. Why on earth would I want a divorce?"

Looks were quickly exchanged between the brothers once again. A slow grin broke out across Daniel Cameron's face. "Well hell, then, welcome to the family!" he said. He reached out a hand.

"Hell, nothing!" Jeremy murmured. "You already joined the McCauley family," taking the hand that was offered to him.

Jesse clapped him on the back. "That's between the two of you. For my part, congratulations."

"Don't worry," he heard himself saying. "I swear to you both, I would die for her."

Well, that much was true. He'd put his life on the line many a time for a man, woman, or child put under his care.

Yes. He'd die for her.

"The ladies must be chewing their nails to the bone in the parlor," Jesse commented. "Think we ought to rejoin them?"

They did so. When they came back to the parlor, three sets of feminine eyes stared at them nervously. "I don't even know anymore," Jesse said. "Have we got any champagne in the house, Christa?"

She had been sitting on the love seat, next to Kiernan. She leapt up nervously. "In the cellar, I think. I'll—"

"No, Jigger is here. He'll run down. He won't mind."

Jesse called to Jigger. Jigger was delighted to run down for the champagne. Everyone drank a toast.

Janey came back with the children. Christa delighted in playing with the whole brood of her three nephews and one niece while Jeremy looked more curiously to the two who belonged to his sister.

Her son, Jared, was the spitting image of his father. Blue eyes, black hair. The little girl, Annie, had McCauley coloring, almost as if it had been evenly divided. She had a riot of russet curls and huge silver eyes.

This is what our children would look like, he thought. Christa's and mine.

They couldn't have children, he mocked himself. They had never made love.

Yes, but they were going to. Maybe that would be his part of this bargain. Christa would have her house—Cameron Hall. May it stand forever.

He could have a son. Or a daughter. Maybe a girl as beautiful as Christa. But gentle, with eyes that grew wide with wonder at the world, with lips that turned easily to laughter.

His nephew toddled over to him and pulled at his pant leg. He reached down and picked up the little boy and held him close.

Soon after, Janey came in with a tea tray for a light supper. She promised a big supper for everyone by nightfall.

The afternoon passed quickly. Jeremy was glad to be with Callie, Christa was delighted to have everyone home. He was even drawn into conversation with both Daniel and Jesse about his new orders to ride west. They'd all been assigned to Kansas once, before the war.

Over lunch and dinner they discussed the Santa Fe Trail, the Indian lands, the civilized tribes, and the not-so-civilized ones.

But then dinner ended, and the entire family headed back to the parlor for coffee and brandy.

Christa quickly caught hold of Jeremy in the breezeway, before he could enter the room again.

"What?" he asked her impatiently.

She swallowed slowly. "I—I wanted to thank you."

He relaxed somewhat, watching her. It was nice to watch her squirm a little. "I don't know what you said to Jesse and Daniel but—thank you."

He nodded. "My pleasure."

"What did you tell them?"

"That I'm not filing for a divorce."

She inhaled quickly, watching him.

"And I'm not a liar, Christa. I'm a man of some honor, even if it's 'Yankee' honor. So be prepared. It's a real marriage. You do know what I mean."

She looked as if she wanted to slit his throat. He smiled. "You do know what I mean?"

"I know damned well what you mean!" she retorted angrily.

"And?"

Her eyes narrowed. "Camerons always pay their debts!" she whispered fiercely. And miserably.

She walked into the parlor. He held back, breathing deeply. It was going to be a real marriage.

He wanted children.

And he wanted Christa.

He went into the parlor. The children had been put to bed, the grown-ups were left alone. Jesse drew out some of the maps he had from his days in the West. He, Daniel, and Jeremy began to study them.

Kiernan excused herself first, saying that she was exhausted. Christa went next—right after she had fiercely hugged her brother and given Jeremy a very dutiful and wifely kiss. After a while Jesse excused himself. Jeremy and Daniel talked on a while longer, then Daniel suggested to Callie that they should retire too.

"I'll be right up," Callie promised her husband. When Daniel had gone, she turned to Jeremy. "You may have fooled them all," she said softly, "but I don't believe a word of it."

Callie stared at him with her wide silver eyes, and he found himself lifting his hands. "Callie, what do you want out of me?" he asked, rising, running his fingers through his hair, then leaning against the mantel. "They were going to burn the house down."

She stood and came over to him and began to speak softly in a rush. "It's just that you don't know Christa like I do, Jeremy. She's proud, yes. And she can be very stubborn, and she can fight harder than a catfish. But you don't know what it was like being here for the whole war, not knowing if and when the house would be taken—" She broke off, because he was looking at her, smiling.

"Callie, you're my sister, remember. I don't intend to do anything evil to Christa. She wanted to become my wife. That's all that I intend to ask of her."

Callie came up on her toes and kissed his cheek. "I'll pray for you both!" she promised. "Jeremy, you are my brother, and I do love you, and I want you to be happy."

"I'm going to be very happy," he promised her softly. "You'll see."

She smiled wanly, then walked to the door. "Good night, then. Don't stay up too late. Christa will be waiting."

He nodded. "I won't be long."

Callie left him. Yes, Christa would be waiting. Yes. Camerons always paid their debts.

Fine. He was going to collect.

He started to pour himself another brandy, then decided against it.

He left the parlor behind and started up the stairway. The floor in the upper hallway creaked beneath his footfalls.

She was in the bed when he entered the room. She was in some kind of an all-encompassing nightgown, and her back was to him. He was certain that she was feigning sleep.

He didn't care. He closed the door behind him with a definite click. He paused for a moment. Let her wait, let her wonder. Let the blood begin to flow too quickly through her veins. He knew damned well that she was awake.

He strode across the room to the bed. Once there, he methodically took off his clothes. When he was naked, he drew back the covers and crawled in beside her.

He wasn't going to make her wait any longer.

He put an arm around her, rolling her around to her back. Her eyes were tightly closed.

"Christa, I know damned well you're awake," he said.

Her eyes flew open. Burning blue in the night.

He ran his fingers around the beautiful embroidery and lace at the high collar of her nightgown. "Off with it," he told her flatly.

"You are a son of a bitch!" she told him heatedly.

He nodded. "A Yankee son of a bitch. One you're going to remember when I'm gone."

"You're leaving?" she said quickly.

He nodded. He had decided it just this minute, but it was probably the best thing for everyone involved. "First thing in the morning. I'm going back to Washington until the final order to head west is given."

He could almost feel her relief. It was not particularly complimentary.

She wasn't getting out of the night ahead of them. "Christa, get the damned thing off."

"But—"

"You can take it off, or I can rip it off. Either way, it goes."

Next thing he knew she was hissing that he was a Yankee bastard and scalawag, but she sat up and nearly ripped the gown herself, wrenching it over her head.

She didn't scream. She even cursed him just as quietly as she could manage.

She threw the gown furiously on the floor, then she sat there, naked beside him, seething and trembling, her eyes downcast. They rose to meet his, liquid and blue and shimmering. She threw herself back on the pillow. "Go ahead, then! Do whatever you've got to do!"

He was hard put not to laugh out loud. He leaned down on an elbow at her side, tossing all the covers back as far as they could go, then running his hand down the length of her body. How had she been created so damned perfectly? Moonlight fell over the rise of her breasts, and added mystery and shadow to the clefts at her hips and the dip between her breasts. At first he just touched her, running his fingertips lightly over her flesh. He felt her inhale sharply as he paused, running his palm over her nipple. Her breasts were perfect, firm and rounded, the peaks large and deeply rouge in color. Tempted, he leaned over her, running his tongue slowly around the aureole, then encompassing the whole of her nipple. She shifted beneath him. He felt the slam of her heart, the quickening of her body. He cupped her other breast with his hand, then rose, meeting her eyes before lowering his head to take her lips.

She didn't intend to respond to him. She didn't exactly fight him, but neither did she simply allow her lips to part to his. He intended to persist. He threaded his fingers into her hair, and with a growing passion he forcefully invaded her mouth, bathing her teeth with his tongue, then plunging deeply into her mouth. He could still feel her heartbeat. And he could feel the trembling that still riddled through her.

There was so much passion within her. If he could only reach it, touch it.

Her mouth was sweet. The taste and feel of it seeped into his system, adding to the hunger that had begun for her, creating a harsher throb of desire within him. She no longer protested the kiss. Perhaps she did not aid him, but she did not resist him either.

He lifted his lips from hers. Her eyes were open and on his. Her breathing came quickly and shallowly. Was she afraid? Christa Cameron, afraid?

She'd kissed a man before, he was damned certain. She'd been so in love with Liam McCloskey. Just how much else had she done? How much was innocence?

And how much was hatred?

"You've never done this before?" he queried.

"Oh, you oaf!" she cried out, struggling then to free herself from him.

He laughed softly, pleased, and not at all sure why. He caught hold of her cheeks and kissed her again, deeply, hungrily, giving her no chance to protest. The heat surged swiftly to his loins now. He tasted her lips and tasted them again. He rose above her.

"I will try to be very gentle," he told her.

She didn't answer him. Her eyes were closed. She lay, her beautiful face pale against the ink-dark cloud of her hair. He kept his eyes on her as he lowered himself against her. He caressed her breasts once again, feeling the pulse within her, feeling the heat. He lowered himself still, burying his face against the dip of her belly. Then lower. He brushed his fingers over the triangle between her thighs. Stroked her lower and lower. Forced her thighs apart.

He stared up at her. Her eyes were still closed. There was so much inside of her! he thought. He had felt the quickening in her when he touched her breast. He felt the rampant trembling within her now.

But she wasn't going to give to him. No matter what, she was determined to deny him.

Still, he didn't want to hurt her. He slid his thumb through the silk ebony of her pubic hair, and then into the damp softness of her sex. He felt again the trembling. Slowly, sensually he stroked her. He lowered his mouth to the tender, intimate regions of her flesh and began to tease her thus, moistening her at the least, if he could not arouse her.

But he did arouse her, he was certain! For scarce had he touched her before she jerked and surged. Her fingers tore into his hair. Whispered protests flew from her lips, but he ignored them all, delving deeper and deeper within her, bathing her, savoring her. She began to shake. Hunger gnawed raw and painfully within him, a surge of heat came like a rush of anguish.

He rose over her at last. And at last, those magnificent blue eyes were on his. He said nothing more but seized her mouth once again, taking her lips just as he took her body. He tried to take care, tried to go very slowly. She hadn't lied in her earlier protest—she had never made love with young McCloskey. Her body protested the invasion of his; she cried out briefly at the pain, catching her lower lip between her teeth to keep from letting out any other sound. He forced himself to stop completely, gritting his teeth against the will of his body as he awaited the acceptance of hers. Then he began to move with her slowly. Filling her with the length of his shaft, feeling the hug of her body around him. Dear God, it was good to be within her, sheathed by her. Even if she bit her lip. Even if she damned him for all eternity.

She had been made for this! he thought. For despite her protests, she gave to him, her body beautifully encompassing his. He thrust slowly at first, very slowly, bracing his arms at his sides, watching her face. But her eyes remained closed, her head to the side—her teeth upon her lower lip. Yet as he moved, she began to move with him, instinctively, naturally. The subtle undulation of her hips quickened the drive within him. He closed his own eyes, clenching down hard on his jaw, fighting for control. He maintained it as long as he could. Then his rhythm came faster, his drive stronger. He slipped his hands beneath her buttocks, molding her to him, and he gave free rein to the voracity of his hunger, taking her then with a volatile and fierce passion. Again and again he drove into her. Perspiration broke out in a fine sheen on his skin. He stiffened and thrust once, and once again, hard and deep within her, and his climax burst fiercely upon him, spilling his seed within her.

His weight was upon her, and his sex remained within her. She struggled beneath him, and, somewhat ashamed, he quickly lifted his weight from her, rolling to her side. Instantly she turned her back on him, like some creature deeply wounded. A rush of anger and impatience came to him. Dammit, she was his wife. And if he only saw her every five years or so, he intended to see her in bed.

He set an arm on the shoulder she had set so defensively against him.

"Christa, I'm sorry if I hurt you. It's fairly natural, I understand, for a woman to cry the first time—"

"I am not crying!" she whispered.

But he thought that she was. He wanted to comfort her. He ran his hand down her beautiful, sleek back. "Christa—"

Her back stiffened like a poker. "You've had what you wanted. Now, please, leave me the hell alone!"

He withdrew his touch as if he had been burned. He laced his fingers behind his head and stared up at the ceiling. Liar! he wanted to charge her. She could have responded if she wanted. He had felt the response of her body. She was beautiful, passionate, sensual, and he could feel it all. Feel it in her hunger for life, in her will, in her spirit.

Even in her hatred.

Hate me then, he thought. But you will respond to me, Christa, you will.

He let her lie there, fuming, stiff, and keeping her distance.

Then he reached for her again.

He saw her eyes. Blue ice and blue fire. Rebellious, furious, she stared at him.

"It's over—" she cried.

"It's just begun," he corrected. This time he swept her into his arms. From the very first touch of his lips to hers, he was filled with a force and passion that brooked no resistance. He kissed her until her lips were wet and swollen, then tasted her earlobes and her throat. He suckled her breasts, one then the other, taunting them with a slow rubbing motion with his thumbs, then suckling them again until she cried out. His hands, his lips, were everywhere. Hers flew about in protest, but he merely moved on. He rolled her onto her stomach, teasing the line of her spine with the caress of his fingers and tongue, nipping her buttocks, then

rolling her over once again, parting her thighs, and having his way between them. When he took her again, he was so fiercely hungry himself
that he could scarcely believe it. He should be sated with her. He wanted
more. He knew her from head to toe. He had touched her, tasted her,
from head to toe. But she moved, whether she wanted him or not. She
writhed, and trembled, and created an ever greater fire. And it burned.
Burned so that he stroked and drove until he was nearly mindless himself, and then amazed at the force of the climax that seized him again.
She shuddered as he filled her. But no sound escaped her, no surrender
even came in a whisper from her lips.

He fell to his side. Once again, she turned her back to him. Frustrated,
he stared at her in the moonlight.

"Christa—why?" he demanded.

"I don't know what you're talking about," she replied.

He touched her again, stroking her back whether she wanted his touch
or not this time.

He grit his teeth. "Christa, you're my wife. Why won't you give in to
me?"

"I don't know what you're talking about."

He rose up on an elbow. "Yes, you do. You're flesh and blood, and
you're very much a woman. And you're doing your damned best to deny
me."

"I didn't deny you anything," she said.

"You did, and you know it."

She was silent for a second, then burst out. "I don't owe you anything.
You take what you want. There's nothing else that should be yours.
You're not—"

She broke off suddenly.

He caught hold of her shoulder and rolled her around once again. He
met her eyes, those blue eyes that were brilliant with tears that she would
die before she shed.

"I'm not what, Christa?" he demanded harshly.

She shook her head.

"Answer me. No? All right, I'll answer for you. I'm not Liam McCloskey.
Well, my dear Miss Cameron, you're not the woman of my dreams either.
But you are my wife. Liam is dead, lady, and you're going to let him rest.
Do you understand me?"

She bit her tongue, staring at him. But then her lashes fell over her
eyes. "Hail the conquering heroes!" she whispered vehemently.

"Damn you, Christa," he said quietly. "Fine. Have it your way. It's a
conquered nation, Christa. Consider yourself beaten."

Her eyes rose to his again. "The South lost the war. I have never been beaten."

"Oh, I don't know. You'll surrender. I'll see to it. I promise it," he told her.

She wrenched herself from his touch once again, presenting him with the long line of her back. He lay back, staring at the ceiling.

He should have been feeling pretty wretched.

Oddly enough, he smiled.

It was there, somewhere inside of her. Something tangible to hang on to, to make a life with. Something made up of passion and spirit and glory, and all manner of hot and wonderful things. She might spend a lifetime hating him, but at the very least, they would have an interesting time of it.

He just had to discover the key to reach inside of her, to forge past the power of her will.

It would be something to think about in all the long nights to come.

Six

Christa arrived at Sterling Hall well ahead of the others. She observed the house as she patted her mare's neck, thinking that it was a very beautiful place and it was a pity it had been neglected so long. The majority of the construction was brick, and much of that had been plastered over so that the edifice seemed to be a large white building with symmetrical columns. It was very much like Cameron Hall, and like the age-old family estate it was still equipped with all its outbuildings, smokehouse, laundry, kitchen, and slave quarters. There were no longer any slaves but a lot of the household servants intended to come along with Daniel and Callie. Numerous Negroes—and poor lost white souls too—needed work and a place to live. Things would never be quite the same, and they'd probably have to sell off a lot of the land. Still, her brothers would manage both places well enough. Jesse wanted to resign his military commission soon and come home and practice medicine. Daniel was the natural-born planter and horseman. He could manage both estates.

And where would she live, she asked herself. As close as Jesse and Daniel were, they had both wanted their own homes. Sterling Hall had been in their family since the Revolutionary War when their great-great-grandmother had brought it into the list of family holdings. They hadn't worried about it much during the war years, but luckily neither had either of the fighting armies. Maybe that was because it had been cloaked by the overgrowth of shrubs and trees. The house was still standing, and except for the overgrowth and what some carpentry, paint, and a lot of cleaning would do to improve it, it was in very good condition. Callie would certainly make a very beautiful home of the place.

She slipped down easily from her horse and walked up the steps to the porch. With her hands on her hips she surveyed the place, trying to imagine it brought back to grandeur.

It had always been the family plan that Daniel would come here. The house had been willed to him. Cameron Hall for Jesse, Sterling Hall for Daniel. No home for Christa, since she would, of course, marry properly. A fine southern boy from a fine southern home she would take over as chatelaine when the time came. It was the way it had always been. The natural order of things. The Camerons had always prospered—more of the natural order of things. The very first Cameron had been a titled aristocrat, seeking more adventure than riches in the new world. Their great-great-grandfather had given up the title to cast his lot with the rebels in the Revolution. Through that rebellion they had prospered.

Now those who had rebelled had been beaten.

She had brought saddlebags full of things to start to build a household for Callie. Instead of bringing them in, she wandered along the porch and took a seat on the broad railing. She leaned back against one of the structural pillars and closed her eyes.

It had been so bitter for them to see Jesse ride away in his blue. Kiernan, in love with him then but not yet his wife. Daniel, the brother he had been as close to as his own conscience his whole life. And Christa, the baby sister he had halfway raised and lovingly protected. She hadn't understood Jesse's reasoning when he had sided with the Union. But not even the war had divided them. She had watched him go, loving him fiercely no matter what the dictates of his heart.

Still, not one of them had imagined that, eventually, they would all be grateful that Jesse had chosen to fight for the North. They had property left because of that decision. And they had Yankee dollars.

Actually, she reminded herself, they had property left because of her. And Jeremy McCauley.

She grit her teeth, suddenly feeling the breach between them and the worlds they knew to be incredibly great. Angry feelings were very high at the moment. With military occupation and harsh Congressional Reconstruction taking place, men and women were hostile enough. The lost cause of the Confederacy, and her failure to split from what she thought had been a voluntary union, was becoming something sacred. It lived with tremendous pride in the hearts of the vanquished southerners. Perhaps they could be physically beaten, but in the depths of their souls they would never give up.

Yet newspapers—North and South—had been filled lately with accounts of the execution of the "Lincoln Conspirators." Callie had read of the assassination of Lincoln and everything that had followed. John Wilkes Booth, the actor who had killed the president at Ford's Theater, had been shot and had died himself. But on July seventh, Mary Surratt—

the first woman ever executed by the Federal Government—was hanged along with others involved in plotting first the president's kidnapping, and then his assassination. Some said that Mrs. Surratt was guilty only of association with the killers, others that she had been as set on assassination as anyone else and that she had deserved to die. Mrs. Surratt's son had been involved to some extent, but he had escaped. The conspirators had been tried by a military tribunal that some considered to be a mock court. It was difficult to find the truth, Christa thought. Lincoln had been horribly murdered, and although many southerners had considered him an awful tyrant throughout the war, they now felt that he had been the one chance for a decent reconciliation. Booth had thought himself a hero but he had died despised by many of his own people.

The executions, just like the assassination, made public sentiment run high and volatile. Tempers flared, fights ensued. And chasms seemed to grow ever deeper, old wounds to bleed afresh.

Christa stood up, stretching her hands against her back. The lower part by her spine had been giving her trouble lately. It was because of this move, she thought. She and Callie and Kiernan had already been inside Sterling Hall, all scrubbing away with Janey, the ex-slave who knew her business like nobody else.

When it was done, what was she going to do?

For all his threats and promises, Christa had yet to see Jeremy again.

He wrote volumes to his sister.

He kept up appearances for Christa.

He was still in Washington—not so very far away. There were great upheavals in the army. Men staying in, men mustering out. New companies to be formed and assigned. Jeremy's command was being delayed. Since he really had nothing to say to her, he sent her newspaper clippings on the West, books by explorers, botanical articles, and the like. Occasionally he actually wrote a few words to her. Wonderfully tender, husbandly-type words like "Thought this might interest you" or "Pass on to Daniel."

She pressed her hand to her forehead, frowning, then shaking her head against a moment's dizziness that seized her. It was the sun. Or the fact that she hadn't been sleeping very well.

She sat again.

It was Jeremy's fault, she was certain.

He'd been gone a little over five weeks now, and she wished fervently that she didn't think of him. At first she'd been so delighted to wake up and discover that he was gone. On that morning she had been exhausted and sore from head to toe, and she had wanted nothing more than time in which to convince herself she had healed her wounds.

But days had passed. And when she thought about him, and that night between them, she had alternated between moments of deepest humiliation . . . and fascination.

Thinking of it now, she nearly groaned aloud, raising her knees to the rail and hugging her arms around them. Liam should have remained in her dreams. She should at least have fantasies of what might have been.

But thoughts of Jeremy preoccupied her too much now, when she was awake and when she was asleep. There was no denying the war-sharpened strength of the man, the size of him, the sleekness of his power. She tried to close her eyes and her mind from such thoughts, but they came to her again and again, unbidden. She could see his steel-gray eyes, warning her that his will was law. The rakishly tousled auburn hair, the naked length of him, stalking her, touching her.

Then all manner of heat began to rise in her, and her cheeks bloomed crimson and she swallowed down the thoughts. Thank God he was gone. She didn't have to submit to any wifely duty.

Or feel that shameful tug to surrender, the desire to reach out, to touch something sweet and magical and elusive.

She leaned her head back against the pillar, opening her eyes to watch the sky around her. It was so very blue today. The dead heat of summer was leaving, and fall was beginning to come upon them. It was such a beautiful time in Virginia. The air would be wonderfully cool, the sky still so beautiful, and then the leaves and trees would begin to change and the green landscape would be carpeted in color. She did love her home. Passionately.

She sighed, watching a spider build a web. Eventually, Jeremy would make the trip west. What then?

She bit her lower lip. She had caught Jesse watching her so frequently lately. And she had seen a heartsick expression in his eyes.

He wasn't going to play along much longer with the story that they had entered willingly into marriage. And then he was going to feel guilty the rest of his life, certain that he had caused her hardship by not being there when he should.

He had already torn apart half of the government offices in town trying to discover what had happened. But not even Jesse had been able to find out the truth. Everything had been in order on paper. There should have been plenty of time for Christa to reach Jesse, for him to have come home and straightened things out. Reconstruction staff had come and gone, men knew what they had been ordered to do, and the truth had eluded them all. The buyer who had been so frantic to buy the place and burn it down had disappeared without a clue.

So Cameron Hall still stood. And it was still her home. But Daniel and Callie were moving out with their children, anxious to set up housekeeping on their own. She would be welcome either place.

She rose, having forgotten the feeling of dizziness, and walked back to the brick pathway before the house where her mare was standing. She reached up to take down the saddlebags with their precious cargo of silver dinnerware and napkin rings. When she lifted the saddlebags down, the dizziness seized her once again. She swore softly—having learned some very colorful language during the war—and hurriedly set the bags down on the steps. She was startled by a sudden surge within her stomach. She leaned a hand against a pillar and paused for a moment. She'd felt queasy a few mornings ago, but she had swallowed hard and the feeling had passed. It would do so again.

She waited. The feeling didn't pass. To her astonishment, it worsened.

There was a well around the side of the house and Daniel had just tested it the day before. Cool water might help. She walked around quickly to the well and pulled up a bucket of water, drinking deeply from the ladle.

It didn't help. She clutched her stomach, and found herself being sick into the midst of a honeysuckle vine. She straightened, dismayed, wondering what sort of strange disease she might have caught. She ladled out more water, bathing her face in it, washing out her mouth, trying to swallow more down. It stayed. Maybe she was going to be all right.

The petticoat she wore was a very old one. It had already been ripped up once, the day Eric Dabney had tried to burn Cameron Hall down with his renegade forces. She had made bandages from it for Jesse to treat the wounded. It didn't seem much of a loss now to rip another panel of cotton from it to dip in the water and continue to cool her forehead. She soaked it, then leaned against the well, her eyes closed as she set the cloth against her face.

As she did so, she felt a curious feeling of unease slip over her, as if she were being watched.

She pulled the cloth from her face and stared across the weeded and overgrown yard.

A horseman had come upon her. A Yankee horseman. Jeremy.

As usual, he seemed to be in excellent condition. From his shiny black cavalry boots to his Union blue jacket and plumed hat, he was handsomely attired. When he dismounted from his horse and walked toward her, she noted that he hadn't lost a whit of his sleek muscled tone or suppleness. His hat was pulled low over still-relentless silver-gray eyes and neatly clipped russet hair. He was clean-shaven, and his features seemed exceptionally striking against the precision of his uniform.

Damn him. He had a habit of coming upon her when she was less than at her best. Last time she had been in the dirt, fighting off Bobby-boy. Now she was in old, worn clothing, her hair was damp and her cheeks were flushed, and she had just been wretchedly sick.

The closer he came, the more fiercely her heart began to pound.

"Want a hand?" he offered. "Are you going to faint or fall?"

She stiffened instantly. "Of course I'm not going to faint or fall. I—"

"You're a Cameron, right? And Camerons never falter." He paused, his hands on his hips, his head cocked at an angle as he watched her. Why did he make it sound like such a bad thing that she was determined to stand alone?

She stared at his face, and despite herself, she felt a slow flush coming to her cheeks. He was back. And despite herself, emotions seemed to be racing through her.

She turned quickly back to the well, using it to brace herself. "How long have you been there?" she whispered.

"Long enough."

"How did you—find me?"

"I've been by Cameron Hall."

She nodded. Needing something to do, and feeling so ridiculously flushed, she dipped her ripped piece of petticoat into the water again, pressing it against her forehead. "I'm sorry, I must be catching something. Perhaps you should stay away."

She was amazed at the crooked smile that slid easily onto his lips.

"You think that you're ill?" he queried her, an amused glint of silver in his eyes.

She threw up her hands. "Well, McCauley, I'm ever so glad my misfortune amuses you."

"I'm sorry to disappoint you, but no misfortune of yours would amuse me. I just don't think that you're ill."

"Then—"

"Christa, my sweet innocent!" he said with exasperation, making her sound anything but sweet or innocent. "Hasn't it even occurred to you that you might be expecting a child?"

Perhaps she had flushed red before. Now she felt every drop of blood seem to drain from her face. No! It never had occurred to her! She'd been busy, she'd been torn, she'd been wretched.

And she'd been queasy. Morning after morning now. If she'd given the least attention to the time that had elapsed she might have noticed that . . .

"Have you missed your monthly?" he demanded frankly.

The blood came surging back to her face. "How—how dare you speak to me about such things! A gentleman should never, never—"

"Jesu, Christa, spare me this!"

"You shouldn't even know about such things!" she charged him.

His smile was back. He was keenly amused once again. "Do forgive me. Christa, we both grew up on farms—be it true that mine was ever so humble while yours was ever so grand! And it's rather difficult for a man to have reached my age with a total lack of knowledge."

"I don't think you're lacking anything," she charged him miserably. She was going to be sick again. She couldn't be so. Not with him here right on top of her, asking such personal questions. "Could you please just go away?"

"Christa, I want to know—"

"Don't, please!" she whispered miserably. "Maybe you know such things, but you shouldn't talk about them!" She placed the rag against her forehead, suddenly wishing him away.

He didn't go away. "Christa, turn around. Look at me."

She shook her head. Damn Jeremy. He never just let her be. His hands were on her shoulders and he was turning her around. The glint of silver amusement was gone from his eyes. Before she knew it he was at her side, sweeping her up into his arms.

"I'm not going to fall!" she protested irritably. If she was lucky, she wouldn't be sick again.

He walked her around to the porch, sitting upon the steps where he could brace his back against a pillar. With his left arm supporting her, he used his right hand to gently press the cooling rag over her forehead and cheeks. She closed her eyes, most certainly unaccustomed to such a show of care.

It felt curiously soothing. Maybe because she was just worn out. He seemed a very strong protector at the moment, and it seemed especially nice not to feel the need to fight. His arm was very strong, his chest secure. His touch was gentle if not tender. He smelled nicely of clean soap and sweet tobacco, leather and brandy, all scents that she had known and loved all her life.

But they came with Jeremy McCauley, she realized suddenly. And if he was right, she was going to have his child. From that one wretched night when he had determined that it was going to be a real marriage, that he wasn't going to politely go away.

Well, maybe he couldn't have done so. Maybe he had salvaged something for her with Jesse and Daniel. Maybe she had owed him.

But not this much!

Her eyes suddenly flew open. His were on hers, deep gray, intense. "It can't be!" she whispered. "There was only the one night!"

Something seemed to shield his eyes. "Christa, it certainly can be—from only one night."

Something about his voice was very irritating, and she was suddenly frightened. She wasn't ready for this kind of responsibility. There was too much else to worry about!

No, not anymore. She didn't have to worry anymore.

He was watching her. "Oh, you'd like that, wouldn't you!" she snapped. "You'd get to feel wonderfully puffed up and arrogant and proud of your male prowess!"

He sighed, his teeth grating. "Christa, I wouldn't feel a thing. Jesse could explain it to you better than me, if you haven't raised your horses long enough to know about breeding! If it was the right night for you to conceive, it was the right night, and it would have damned little to do with any magnificent prowess on my part."

Her lashes fell quickly, covering her eyes. She was sorry she had snapped at him. Really, he managed to behave much better than she did upon occasion.

But he wasn't going to have a baby!

She opened her eyes again and met his. She didn't know if he was pleased or displeased or still amused. She swallowed, suddenly trembling from his touch and feeling as if she needed to escape it. "I'm sorry," she murmured quickly. "I'm all right now."

She was pushing away and so he helped her up, standing along with her, one booted foot on a step as he did so. He looked up at her on the porch. "Really," she said. "It may just be nothing, you know. The heat—"

"It's not very hot today," he said politely.

She couldn't be having his child! He was still a stranger, still the enemy, even if they'd fought alongside each other upon occasion.

Even if he had touched her. Made her feel . . .

She lifted her chin. "You act as if you know something about women expecting . . . babies. As if—" She broke off, some startling intuition coming to her. "You've had a child. I mean—you've fathered a child!"

It was an accusation. She certainly didn't expect the dark fury that constricted his features. After all, she was legally his wife. He was the one who should be apologizing, coming up with a quick explanation.

"I've no living children," he stated coldly.

"But—"

"I've no living children. Drop it, Christa, now."

The sudden cold from him seemed to wrap around her. Fine. She lifted her chin. "So what are you doing here? What has brought you back? What do you want?"

"What do I want?" he echoed, and he smiled again, but with no humor. "Why, I want my wife. My final orders have come at last. It's time for me to head out west."

The world seemed to drop from beneath her. Her knees felt weak, as if she couldn't possibly stand. She wouldn't reach to him for support right now.

Her horse. She started down the steps past Jeremy, anxious to reach her mount. He watched her running toward her mare until she spooked her, and the animal raced off toward Cameron Hall.

Home! Christa thought, her eyes stinging with sudden tears. Blindly, she reached out in the horse's wake.

He came up behind her, swinging her around, his arm about her in support. "Come on, we'll take my horse."

"I can't go west," she said tonelessly.

"We'll see."

She stumbled. He lifted her again, walking her around the side of the house to where his very well-trained cavalry horse awaited him. Her arms slipped around his neck, but she protested still. "I can't leave. I did everything. I kept it standing. I planted crops myself. I fixed the roof. I shot at a man once! I—I—"

"You performed the ultimate sacrifice!" he said, peering down at her. "Alas! You married me!" He set her up on his mount. She looked down at him, moistening her lips. She shook her head. "You don't understand."

"Christa, *you* still don't understand. It's Jesse's now."

She looked up, hearing the rumble of a wagon arriving at last. Around the corner of the building she could just see Daniel and Callie arriving.

Her sister-in-law jumped down from the front of the flatbed they were using to haul large belongings. "Christa!"

She started to reply, but Jeremy looked up at her, putting a finger to his lips. She didn't know why, but she obeyed his silent command.

Christa could see Callie on the steps, spinning around to meet Daniel as he walked up to meet her. "Daniel, the saddlebags are here on the porch, but Christa is nowhere to be seen."

"Jeremy must have found her."

"Yes, yes, of course."

There was just a moment's silence. Callie spoke again, softly, huskily. "Daniel, Kiernan and Jesse have the children. And we're alone—"

"And Mrs. Callie Cameron," Daniel finished. "Think of it! This is our threshold. Our very own threshold. It would be nicely fitting if I were to sweep you up into my arms and carry you over it and—"

"Oh, I like the 'and' part! Very much!" Callie whispered.

Christa could see them both—her brother, so tall, dark, and handsome, and Callie, beautiful with her rich red hair, slim figure, and beaming face. They'd waited so long for the war to end. They'd weathered everything that had happened since.

Christa closed her eyes. Suddenly, she heard Callie shrieking. Her eyes flew open. Jeremy was still just staring up at her. "He's hurting her!" she blurted out.

"Oh, Jesu, Christa! She's my sister. If he were hurting her, I'd have been in there with the speed of lightning. Don't be a fool. She loves him! And some women do enjoy being intimate with their husbands."

Crimson flooded her face now. Yes, she knew that Callie loved Daniel and Daniel loved Callie, and what a fool she had been! She knew, too, that her brother would never hurt Callie.

That fact was plainly evident in just seconds. They could hear Callie's voice again. Very soft, very low, and very intimate, whispering her husband's name.

"Daniel . . ."

The name was followed by a combination of sigh and laughter that gave no doubt as to the pleasure of her mood.

Jeremy was still staring at Christa. "Clearly," he murmured dryly, "she is in no pain!"

"Quit!" she whispered down to him furiously. Her cheeks were still flushed and she was painfully embarrassed. They had no business being here, listening.

Jeremy leapt up on his horse behind her. His arms encircled her. "I wonder. Can you say my name like that?"

"Must you always make a joke of everything?"

"Sadly, my love, I was not joking."

He nudged the horse quickly to take them away from the house—and from Callie and Daniel's chance to be alone.

They had ridden for several minutes before he spoke to her again.

"So, Christa, let's see, you can't go west. So which of your brothers are you going to grace with your presence in his home?"

"Stop it!" she whispered.

"Poor Christa! You worked for it all, you bled for it. And you married me for it. But it isn't yours anymore."

"Stop mocking me."

"I'm not mocking you. I'm pointing out the truth."

"I don't know why you're so concerned. I don't know why you're doing this. You don't like me. You don't like a single thing about me, and you can't possibly want me with you."

"There's where you're wrong, Christa. I admire your courage very much. And your strength. I think you'll make an exceptional cavalry wife."

Her head was pounding. Ah, there was something! He thought she was capable, at the very least! Just like an experienced field hand!

Within a matter of minutes, they had ridden the distance back to Cameron Hall.

Christa slipped down from his horse without his assistance. Her skirt caught on the saddle and he had to release it for her.

"Accept it, Christa. You're coming with me."

She tugged at her skirt, then looked up at him desperately. "Why? Because I might be useful? Just how much help can I be if—"

She broke off, lashes lowering, biting her lower lip.

"If you are expecting my child?" he asked softly. He leaned low, slipping her hem from his stirrup where it had snagged. "Well, there's one reason right there. Every man wants a son, Christa."

"Yes, and then I have callused hands and I know how to shoot and—"

"And at heart, Christa, you always were and always will be a pampered little belle!"

She gasped, jerking away. "Then—"

"Then there's the reason that, although I very much hate to admit it, to add any more flattery to that defiant Rebel head of yours, I do find you very beautiful. Exceptionally so. And . . ."

"And?" she whispered, startled by his last words.

"And you're my wife, and I've determined that you'll accompany me."

"I—I can't!"

"But you will. So prepare yourself, Christa. Willing or no, my love, you're riding west."

Seven

Jeremy stood by one of the wide windows in Christa's room overlooking the maze and the garden. From this vantage point, he could see the graceful slope of lawn that rolled all the way down to the river and the dock. It was beautiful country, rich country. And the Camerons were the royalty of it, he knew. The place was Christa's heritage.

His gaze fell from the distant dock to his wife's head. She was to the right of the house. She had walked out back a while ago with Jesse.

She hadn't asked him for time to be alone. He'd made it a point of telling her he'd had something to do. Maybe he needed time himself. It wasn't that Christa would have to find herself instantly swept away—on the contrary, she had some time. He'd had a long discussion with Jesse to work out the arrangements. He had to return to Richmond right away, and from there on to Washington where he'd be taking the railroad as far as Illinois. Once there, he'd be taking steamers down to Little Rock. Some of his troops would be accompanying him from Washington, and some would be assigned to him at Little Rock. He was glad to be going ahead, and he would be glad to arrive early enough in Little Rock to ride out into the countryside alone before leading his men and some of their wives across it. It was always good to know the lay of the land. He had been assigned to the West before, and there were dangers there.

Christa would join him in Little Rock. Jesse had assured Jeremy that he could extend his leave of absence even further, and escort his sister as far as Little Rock. Christa was upset, convinced that Jesse shouldn't leave his wife and children again, but Kiernan and Jesse had looked over her head to Jeremy. They all knew that Christa should not be traveling through the Reconstruction-era South alone, nor through some of the northern cities now either. The war was over, Kiernan insisted. She didn't mind seeing Jesse ride away one more time. And Christa had to have time to pack her household belongings as well as her clothing, and make all the arrangements to bring one of her favorite horses too.

Jeremy would return to Little Rock two weeks after his own arrival in the area, for Christa. Then they could begin their westward journey from fort to fort, camp to camp, together.

She wasn't saying good-bye to Cameron Hall for good today, but it felt as if she were doing so.

There was certainly no turning back for her now.

For a while he had heard the low murmur of voices on the back part of the hall's wraparound porch. But then the two, arm in arm, had walked down to the family cemetery that lay halfway between the house and the river. He couldn't hear what they were saying anymore, but he could see them. They were handsome people, these Camerons. Jesse, tall, with that ebony-blue of his hair, just now beginning to show a hint of silver at the temples. The war had brought on that silver early, Jeremy was certain. Jeremy had felt the division of the country very clearly—few states had been quite so wretchedly torn as Maryland. But until Callie had met and married Daniel Cameron, he'd never had kin fighting on the other side. It was a wonder Jesse wasn't solidly gray by now. Jeremy wondered how he had ever managed to walk away from all this never knowing if he could come home or not.

A soft tinkle of laughter rose up from below. It was faint, for Christa was at a distance, but it evoked all kinds of nostalgia and wonder within him. How had they been back before it had all begun? They would have been quite remarkable here, he was certain. Jesse, Daniel, Kiernan—in love with Jesse but not yet his wife—and Christa. Christa, so very young back then, the pampered pet of both brothers, uncontested mistress here since her mother's death. She must have been sheer elegance and beauty in those lighter days, allowing that spill of laughter to fill the halls, to brighten the days and nights of all their guests. She laughed so seldom now.

He closed his eyes. For a moment he could almost hear the clang of harness, the churn of carriage wheels. People would have gathered here from all corners of Virginia. Dignitaries had surely traveled down from as far away as Washington upon occasion. Ladies in their silks and satins. Men in their finest dress uniforms and most elegant civilian attire. Musicians would have played well into the night, and Christa would have tapped her feet and danced the night away.

What were they saying, those two Camerons below him? His eyes were sharp, and he could see her face, even as she turned to her brother at the gate before the ancient cemetery. She was smiling at him. Her head was tilted back, her hair, free and lustrous as the blue-black wing of a bird, flowed in rich waves and curls down her back, catching the sunlight. She laughed at something he said, threw her arms around him, and hugged him fiercely. Someone called from across the yard.

Daniel was back. He walked out to join his brother and sister. He slipped an arm around Christa. For a moment, the three of them were posed there, arm in arm, in a continuing triangle. Tall and handsome and beautiful and entwined by love—and that sometimes irritating Cameron honor!

He sighed, catching hold of the rise of his temper. He didn't begrudge her her brothers, or the love or loyalty between the three of them. It was something precious to her, something that he hoped they had forever. Things weren't so terribly different in his family. At least, not with his remaining family. The war had taken his father early. Their oldest brother, Josiah, had been reported missing in sixty-four. They'd discovered later that he'd died in some little skirmish in Tennessee. The second eldest in his family, Joshua, was back home now tending to the farm. He'd married his childhood sweetheart—who had waited out the war for him—and at least, for the two of them, there had been a happy ending. Josiah might be gone, he thought, but he and Joshua still loved Callie fiercely, and if they had been as close to the events in her life as Daniel and Jesse were to those in Christa's, she might have had a very wretched time, indeed, trying to explain Daniel Cameron. The war had kept Jeremy from her until she'd had her baby and come south and been duly wed— he never had found out just exactly in what order it had all happened!

His eyes narrowed as he watched Christa. She was so alive, so exuberant, so vivacious! Her spirit was as deep and bewitching as her vibrant coloring. Her passions ran so very deep.

But not for him.

How would it feel if she were ever to set her eyes upon him like that? So sparkling, so brilliantly blue, so tender? And that smile . . .

Ah, never in a thousand years!

Heaven help him, he decided dryly, if she did. He needed a strong guard against Christa Cameron. Her will was as strong as steel. If she ever felt that she really had any power over him, she would do her best to break him. She'd be free from him, taking what she wanted on her way!

He leaned back against the wall, closing his eyes for a moment. Maybe he judged her too harshly. Maybe he spent too many hours mourning a gentle blond woman who had never even thought to disagree with him. No, Jenny had been blessed with her own kind of strength. She hadn't needed to spend endless hours fighting him tooth and nail. But he was married to Christa, and unless he missed his guess, he was expecting another child.

They were going to make it work.

Every time he saw Christa, he found himself doing things he had never intended to do. He had never intended to marry her. He had never meant to order her to come west with him. He had actually come back to say good-bye and perhaps discuss the possibility of her joining him. But once he had seen her, the order had just come out. Once he had issued it, he realized that he had meant it.

He was a married man. He didn't intend to live without his wife, cold in the night. She might not be much of a willing partner, but she was beautiful. And in all the long nights he had been away from her, he had dreamed about her, and he had wanted her.

A slight sound from outside attracted his attention, and he took up his vigil at the window again. Jesse and Daniel were leaving her by the cemetery. She watched them go, smiling. But when they had come up the knoll leading to the house, when she felt herself sheltered by the foliage between them, she turned back to the graveyard. He saw her shoulders hunching over.

He knew that she cried.

She leaned against the cemetery fence, then slipped slowly against it to her knees. Her shoulders shook. She did not cry, she sobbed, in great, gulping waves. He clenched his teeth, torn by a wave of sympathy.

"Actually, I don't think it's all just because of you!" he heard.

He turned. Callie stood in the doorway. His sister was really beautiful too. There was an added luster about her. Callie was blessed. She was a woman deeply in love and, perhaps, more deeply loved in return.

"Thanks for such a vote of confidence. And from my own sister!" he reproached her mildly.

The others might have been well fooled, but Callie? Never.

He crossed his arms over his chest, leaning against the wall. "What brought on such a comment? What does she say about me?"

"Never a word. Even when I ask her outright. She stares me straight in the eye and reminds me that you're my brother, and that truly, I should understand what she has come to see in you. Then she very innocently and very sweetly, I assure you, reminds me that sometimes oil and water do mix, and that passion, hatred, and love are separated by very narrow lines, and surely I, of all people, should understand that!"

"Does she now?" he murmured. He shouldn't have been surprised. Christa would never give herself away. Not to Callie. Not to anyone.

"You forget, I know her well, Daniel. I came here uncertain, and she—

and Kiernan—were wonderful to me. She gave me the clothing off her back—"

"Hardly off her back," he commented wryly. "Christa has enough clothing to open a fashion shop."

Callie waved a hand in the air. "She shared everything she had with me."

"I grant you, in some things, she has a generous nature."

"But not in others?"

"Callie, there are certain things that are simply none of your business."

She flashed him a quick smile and came into the bedroom, slipping her arm around his waist and staring out the window with him. "I know what she's thinking."

"You do?"

He felt Callie nod slowly. "She's thinking of everyone that they've lost. Not just her parents. She's thinking about Anthony Miller, Kiernan's first husband. And about Liam. About little Joe Davis, Jeb Stuart, so many old family friends and acquaintances. Young, dashing, proud! A breed of cavaliers. The death toll was terrible, Jem."

"Callie, my God!" he said hoarsely. "We lost our father and our brother!"

"I know, but we won the war. They lost. You have to try to remember that!"

"It's tough," he told her, adding dryly, "Camerons don't surrender!"

"Don't I know it!" Callie laughed.

Christa had risen. As he watched, she came around the corner of the little cemetery and disappeared into a cover of trees.

"Where in bloody hell is she heading now?" he demanded, then realized his language, and remembered that once upon a time he would have never thought to have been so crude in front of any lady, much less his own little sister. He closed his eyes. "Sorry, Callie—"

"It's quite all right, I've most certainly heard it," Callie said, then asked, "Why are you so angry with her?"

"I'm not angry!" he denied. But Callie was right. Fine, Christa had her wonderful Cameron pride. She wouldn't cry in front of him.

But she was sobbing blue blazes behind his back and he wanted to shake her. He wasn't forcing her into a life as a scullery maid.

No, just into a life with him.

"Where has she gone?" he repeated.

Callie sighed. "The summer cottage. You can just see a corner of it through the trees right there. See, it's all whitewashed. I understand it used to be furnished quite elegantly during the summer months before the war. It overlooks the water, and if you open all the shutters the river breezes pour right in. There used to be a time when the ladies sipped mint juleps and lemonade while the male guests were offered stronger refreshment. There's not much there now. I think Christa had an old chaise brought down there last June. She told me that they all used to go there when they were children and in trouble. It's a habit that stayed with them all. Everyone knows it's off limits once another member of the family is in it. She'll come out of it soon enough, Jeremy."

"That's right, she will," he murmured. He started from the window, long legs carrying him quickly from the room. He was down the long stairway before Callie seemed to have found the energy to come after him. "Jeremy!" she called his name, but he pretended not to hear her. By the time he had left the porch behind him and passed by the extensive maze of rosebushes, he heard his sister reach the porch herself. But she was stopped there.

Daniel came beside her.

"Let them be," he warned her.

"He's angry, Daniel."

"They'll solve it. Callie, you keep reminding me—he's your brother. I can call him out and one of us can kill the other, and the one left alive can be arrested for illegal dueling."

"Daniel, don't be ridiculous—"

"Then leave them be."

The voices faded behind him. He came to where Christa had stood, to the low whitewashed fence that surrounded the graveyard. He'd come here before. Admittedly, the Cameron heritage had fascinated him, and on his first trip here he had come to the graveyard while awaiting a little time to say good-bye to his sister alone. That time he had been heading back to his troops in the field. He'd been transferred east along with General Grant, and he had left here with the very real possibility that he and Daniel might meet in combat. But they never had. In a cruel war God had, upon occasion, shown his small mercies.

He stared at the graveyard. There, in the far corner, were the first of the Camerons. Jamie and his Jassy. The tombstones were dated sometime in the late sixteen hundreds. The slate stones were very old, but the family had kept them all up and the writing remained clear. It was an oddly beautiful place, haunting, ghostly, but beautiful too. Magnificent angels hovered over some Camerons, while virgins cast their serene gazes down upon others. The funereal art was exquisite, history in itself, were there no beautiful house to grace the grounds. But of course, this meant so much more to Christa. Her parents lay within the gate. Her grandparents.

Aunts, uncles, and cousins and "greats" who had lived through two centuries of Virginia's history.

He walked around the cemetery at last. Through the foliage he could see the summer cottage. Like the main house, it seriously needed paint.

He came around the front. The door was closed but not locked and he came through it. There was a main room with a large fireplace.

With a smile he wondered if the cottage hadn't been used frequently in winter. He could just imagine how it would feel being here, a blaze snapping warmly from the hearth, cold winds blowing beyond, and a landscape carpeted in snow.

He walked through the room, not intentionally coming in quietly.

But Christa hadn't heard him. She was curled on a green brocade-covered lounge that looked out over large windows with a river view. The river rolled by, dark today, but enchanting. Its color, its slight turbulence, warned that fall was nearly upon them and winter was coming.

Some sound or instinct alerted her to his presence, for she turned, somewhat alarmed.

Women, he thought, didn't look good when they cried. Their eyes usually got all puffy and their faces became a blotchy red.

But not so with Christa!

Her cheeks were damp and flushed and her eyes remained crystal with the wetness of her tears. But as she stared at him she brushed her hands over her cheeks, and the wet glimmer of tears became that of defiance. He'd never seen eyes more vividly, beautifully blue. He'd been so sorry, so touched by the pain that she had been feeling.

But seeing the mercury-quick change in her, he felt his resolve concerning her stiffen.

Her pride was greater than any emotion within her heart.

"What are you doing here?" she whispered.

He lifted his hands. "Have I entered some sacred domain?" he asked.

She turned back around, staring at the river. "Of course not," she said. "It's a cottage on the grounds, nothing more."

He remained behind her in silence. His presence must have disturbed her though, for she was quickly up, swinging around to meet him as if she feared to have him at her back. She stared at him, and he must have betrayed some surprise at her movement, for she flushed slightly and strode toward the mantel. Her feet moved silently over the flooring. There was a handsome oilcloth on the floor, painted to look like marble. It was old and fraying now, but it had once been grand. Over that, before the hearth itself, was a rich stretch of fur rug, warm and very inviting.

Christa was glancing at the fur, too, he saw. She caught his gaze, then turned away very quickly.

"I think I know why you're doing this," she said. She was suddenly very prim, her hands folded before her, her eyes steady on his.

He took up a military "at ease" stance, legs slightly apart, his hands together at his back. "Oh?" he said politely. "And what am I doing?"

"Making me come with you."

"Why?"

She waved a hand in the air, unable to continue meeting his eyes. "It has something to do with Daniel and Callie. I believe you're trying to get even with him in some way." He was dead silent, and she continued in a sudden rush, "For taking Callie from Maryland. Well, for what happened between them in Maryland, and for taking her away. Perhaps you're not even aware of it. But if you stop to think—"

"If I stopped too long to think," he interrupted her at last, struggling to keep a cap on his rising temper, "I'd be tempted to wring your neck. Then your brothers would be obliged to come out and shoot me, but that's all right, my love, we'd expire in marital bliss!"

She didn't flinch. Her eyes narrowed and she stared him down in her very regal manner. "I didn't think that you'd begin to understand. I—"

She broke off because he was striding across the room to her. He caught hold of her elbows, lifting her, swirling her around.

"Let's get this straight right now, Christa. I said everything I had to say to your brother about Callie back then, but if you want to know something, my love, I'll tell you. Once I met him, I never felt much bitterness or anger toward your brother. It was too painfully clear that he was very much in love with Callie, and so damned obvious that Callie was in love with him. That makes up for a hell of a lot of sins, Christa. And just for the record, I'm not a Cameron. I have faltered and fallen upon occasion. But whether you believe it or not, we heathen Yanks raised in the Maryland farm country were brought up with a certain code of ethics too. I'd never use any animosity I had against Daniel against you in any way."

"Then—"

"No, no, no, hear me out. My turn, my way. This is between us, Christa."

"I see," she said coolly, staring at her arms where he touched her with a scornful command that he release her in her eyes. "All your animosity is strictly toward me."

He released her. He'd break a bone if he didn't.

"This isn't hallowed ground!" he told her.

Her lashes fluttered. She started to turn away. He grasped her back with a force that sent her spinning hard against him. "This is why you're coming with me!" he said sharply. He did what he'd been itching to do since he'd first seen her. He raked his fingers through the soft wealth of her hair, and kissed her. Touched those lips that were so quick to curl against him with his own. Hunger and dreams bubbled to the surface. He kissed her hard, ruthlessly, determinedly. Tasted the sweetness of her mouth, the mold of her lips, the very indefinable femininity about her that was so very elusive and so very beautiful and seductive.

Perhaps he took her by surprise. Perhaps he had been so forceful so that he left her no room to protest. A single sound escaped her; her arms rose between them, falling against his chest once, and then no more. His arms encircled her while his lips molded to hers. He sank down to the ground with her.

They were upon the fur.

He'd never meant to do this. To disappear such a length of time, then return and take his unwilling bride on a cottage floor.

But he continually discovered himself doing things he didn't intend in the least with her.

Her lips were parted to his. Perhaps she was not so willing a participant in the kiss, but she did not deny it. She made no effort to twist from him. He kissed her and kissed her, and her breath came too quickly and her heart hammered. When he brought her down, her arms laced around his neck. To keep her from falling, of course. But still, there was no protest.

She was laid down upon the floor, her hair spread across it, ebony blue. He leaned over her, aware of her eyes again and the sweeping richness of her black lashes. He stretched out beside her, cupping her breast beneath the fabric of her gown. Her lashes fell, her cheeks found color. He covered her mouth with his own once again, his hand tugging upon her skirt and petticoat. Damn women. They wore so much clothing. He was impeded further by the lacy pantalets she wore, but he impatiently found the tie to the garment and freed it. His palms moved over the naked flesh of her belly. He massaged it and slipped his fingers between her legs.

He heard the first rumble of sound from deep within her throat and ignored it. Touching her, feeling the silky hair of her triangle, the tender, damp flesh of her sex, added fuel to a fire that had tormented him all the time that he had spent away from her. He had sworn it would be hell. It was indeed his own hell, for he burned in it, wanting her. Now the flames were flaming to a peak. He wedged his weight between her thighs, fumbling quickly with his cavalry trousers. Some sense of sanity within him cautioned him that she was still new at this game, and not exactly an avid player—no matter the torment of his own desire. He touched her again, seeking erotic zones to tease, to arouse. To his surprise he was at the least rewarded with a startled gasp. He rotated his touch, moving more deeply inside her. She tried to clench her thighs against him but his body cleanly divided them and she was certainly at his mercy. Another sound escaped her as she felt the first thrust of his sex, just at the very vulnerable portals of her own. He could feel the charge and friction, the heat of his own desire. Her fingers bit into his blue-clad shoulders, she buried her face against his neck. He lifted his hips and thrust deeply and cleanly within her, feeling her arms tighten about him as he did so. He expected a cry, of pain or of protest. No sound escaped her. Slow! he warned himself. And he tried. But the dreams blended with reality. The sweetness of her scent pervaded his blood. The hunger he had lived with since he had left her gnawed with a burning ache for fulfillment. The flesh of her buttocks and thighs was like satin beneath his touch, and being within her, clothed and sheathed by the hot liquid heat of her body, touched off depths of desire he had scarcely known existed. As unwilling a bride as Christa might be, she was still, as she so often said herself, a Cameron. And her passions were all Cameron, wild and exciting. Whether she meant to give to him or not, she did. Perhaps she merely rode the storm. As the intensity of his need rose in a sweet and merciless spiral, he locked her into his embrace and rhythm. He forced her hips into a liquid smooth undulation. He swept her into his tempest, until it burst upon him, wonderful and volatile. He drifted downward, amazed at the sensations she created, at just how damned good it was to have her. Nothing had ever seemed quite so fierce or quite so sweet before.

Imagine! he mocked himself, if she were just willing!

She was quiet, breathing hard, her eyes downcast. She tried, which was futile with him still half atop her, to straighten her knees and bring down her skirts.

He bit his lip, rolling from her. He'd done well, he taunted himself. Let's see, he'd invaded her place of peace, then taken her nearly fully clothed on the very floor of her sanctuary. Now she was trying to cover a slim, shapely leg and to his annoyance, he was discovering that he could be aroused again himself by just such a sight.

Jenny would have taken a look at herself and giggled. And she would have whispered in his ear. "Well, that was fun, but really, Jeremy, shouldn't we shed our clothing this time?"

But, no! This was Christa, with her flaming blue eyes and midnight hair. And the sweet passion that simmered beneath everything, driving him to distraction. Making him want her more than he had ever wanted Jenny.

No.

Yes.

But denying him still.

She was uncomfortable, he realized. And she'd been in love once, yes. But she'd never married her Reb, never taken a chance on learning what it was to be in love and make love.

He rose, adjusting his trousers. He walked to the back window and looked out over the river before gazing back to her.

"I'm sorry," he told her quietly. It took some effort.

She didn't answer him. She was sitting up, her black hair a fall over her face, hiding her eyes. She was still trying to straighten out her attire. Her shoulders were squared. "It's really to be expected—" she began.

In that voice of hers. In that regal southern belle voice that set his nerves on edge.

He was back beside her in a number of seconds. He didn't touch her, but he hunkered down before her furiously. "All right, Christa, I'm not sorry. I'm not in the least damned sorry. You're my wife. This is what married people do!"

"Actually, most married people are completely polite and respectful of one another," she said smoothly, tossing back that mountain of hair. "They don't just couple like—"

"Jesu! Christa, you cannot be so blind! What do you think Daniel and Callie were so excited about this morning, sharing a cup of tea? Come, my love. Where do you think that damned fur came from in the first place?" He inclined his head toward the fireplace and the fur rug before it.

She was gracefully on her feet in seconds. "So why bother to apologize?"

He stood, hands on his hips, facing her. "I won't do so ever again, Christa, I promise." He smiled icily, remembering her secret torrent of tears over the fact that she was to come with him. He hadn't the least control over the malicious twinge that came to him when he reached for her, pulling her close once again. "Never. And so much—truly decadent, by your standards—lies before us. There is the dirt on the floor of a soldier's tent, and there's the dirt of the wide open fields! There are streams galore out there, abandoned Indian dwellings, wonderful, savage places to couple just like a pair of wild animals! And with my willing, imaginative bride, I just can't wait!"

She jerked her hand free. Her chin was high, her eyes blazing. "If you're trying to shock or frighten me, Jeremy, you can go to hell. I survived the war. And I'll survive you. I—"

"Yes, you are a survivor! No one fights so damned well, Christa. Had you just been in the damned field, Grant would have never stood a chance of taking the Rebs. I'm sure the goddamned Indians would be quaking in their buckskins if they knew you were coming."

She threw back her full mane of ebony hair, her eyes sizzling, her hands on her hips, the whole of her trembling. Actually, he'd never seen her quite so vital, so passionate, so wild.

So beautiful, sensual, and appealing.

"You sorry excuse for humanity!" she lashed out. "You can just stop it, or I'll—"

"You'll what?" he taunted. "Call in big brother? Tear me limb from limb?"

A cry of fury brought her flying across the room against him. He had goaded her on, and still, he hadn't quite been ready for her. She nearly knocked him flat. He caught his balance just in time. He caught her fingers just seconds before she could bring her nails raking across his face.

Husky laughter spilled from him then, even though he gave himself an inward warning. She was someone to reckon with.

"Christa—"

"Let go of me!" She kicked him hard, right in the shin. It hurt like hell.

"Christa!" He jerked her around so that her back was flat against his chest and her arms were tightly locked against his hold over her breast. She tried to bite him. He wrenched harder on his hold and she went dead still, rigid as steel.

"Don't raise a hand against me. And no more kicking. Or biting."

She remained still. And trembling. She tossed back her head. "Or what?" she whispered vehemently in turn.

He lowered his mouth against her ear. "Or I'll make you sorry, I promise."

He knew, from the feel of her, that she longed to tell him he didn't begin to know what sorry was—not yet. She'd see to it that he did.

But she was quiet for a long while. Then words seemed to explode from her.

"I'll best you yet, you Yank!"

"Ah, yes!" He pushed her from him. When she spun around quickly to face him again, he swept her a low bow. "You're a Cameron! God has nothing on you, my love!"

"How dare you—"

"How dare I? I've no choice, do I? I've wed into the Holy Family."

"That's blasphemous as well as despicable. Leave it to a—"

"Yankee bastard. Yes. Well, I do apologize for disturbing your peace. Jesse intends to accompany you into Richmond to see me off, but we don't need to start until sometime tomorrow. I'm interested in some of the books in your brothers' library, so, should you find yourself pining for me, you'll know where I'll be. You can have hours and hours to yourself to go cry over your tombstones. Enjoy yourself!"

With another exaggerated and courtly bow—certainly as well executed as any given her by a prewar beau—he left her.

But as he walked toward the house, his shoulders squared, a tempest of anguish seethed within him.

Jesu! He was sorry. Sometimes it seemed that the war was all that he had ever lived. He had despised the fighting of it, he had hated seeing his family, friends, and neighbors die, no matter which side they had fought for! It had been agonizing to watch the fall of Vicksburg.

A Marylander, he understood Christa, understood her pain and all that she had lost. But understanding hurt too. He didn't want to be crude with her. Or cruel. He kept finding himself wanting to put his arms around her. Soothe her.

And she would just as soon be soothed by a rattlesnake, he was certain.

He stood still, suddenly wincing. Damn her! Her pride, and her courage, and her beauty, and all the fire that spilled from her soul! Even before the strange day of their wedding, he had been touched by that fire. But he'd been able to keep his distance then, avoiding the fact that most of his hostility stemmed from desire.

Even now, he wanted to go back. Take her into his arms. Tell her that things would work out.

But no, because then she'd want her own way again!

He had to take care. He couldn't let her know just how much he understood all that she felt. Couldn't let her know how he dreamed of her, wanted her.

Damn! He stiffened and gave himself a mental shake. Yankee fool! he accused himself.

He would not weaken. And he wouldn't fall in love with her.

Unless it was too late already.

Eight

"They're vast lands out there," Christa heard Jesse saying when she came to the house at last. She didn't know where her sisters-in-law were, but she had heard the murmur of male voices coming from the parlor, and she moved toward the doorway, hesitating as she listened to the men speak. "It can be dangerous territory," he said.

"Especially approaching the Comanche and the Apache tribes," Daniel added.

Christa looked silently through the doorway. The three of them stood in the center of the room with a map spread out on the table before them.

"Up around Little Rock, the Indians are all fairly civilized," Jeremy was pointing out.

"Some more so than some of the white folk I know," Daniel agreed, grinning.

"If you're referring to Yankees, remember that you're outnumbered," Jesse teased.

"Only some Yankees," Daniel responded easily enough. Christa leaned back against the wall, biting her lower lip. Daniel was coming to grips with the fact that they had lost. Maybe it was easier for him. He'd told her once that by the time it had come to the end, he just hadn't given a damn. All that he'd wanted was for the dying to stop.

Jeremy was speaking. Because of his words Christa imagined that he was pointing at the map again.

"Once you enter the Great Plains, you're in the hunting grounds, and you can come across just about anyone there. Southern Cheyenne, their allies, the Shoshone, or the Snakes. Here we've got Kiowa, Kiowa Apache—"

"And Comanche," Jesse said softly.

"Is Christa going to be safe? Daniel demanded. Jesu, Jeremy, I'm not at all sure you've any right to be taking her out there." Christa smiled. Daniel was so blunt. Jesse would be far more diplomatic.

"Military wives often follow their husbands," Jesse said. "But Jeremy, it is a frightening thought. And if Christa is expecting a baby, it's more dangerous still."

"All right, Jesse, you tell me. Just from that standpoint. Do you think it would be dangerous to take her?"

Jesse hesitated. "No," he said at last. "I have always found that women who are more active during pregnancy do much better in labor."

"Will there be a company surgeon?" Daniel asked.

A match was struck. Someone was lighting a cheroot. Christa held her breath.

"Major John Weland," Jeremy said.

"John?" Jesse's pleasure at the name was obvious.

"You've served with him?"

"He was with me until the last year of the war. He is an excellent physician and surgeon."

Well, Jesse was not going to be worried about her medical welfare, Christa decided bitterly.

"It's still dangerous territory!" Daniel insisted. "You know that, Jeremy —you were just reading to us from Colonel Cralton's letter to you." She heard a rustle of paper, and then Daniel's deep voice as he began to read. " 'The twelve men were apparently attacked by hundreds of Sioux. Each had been pierced by at least fifty arrows. Their ears and genitals had been lopped off; the genitals were found stuffed into the men's mouths.' " The paper floated down. "Jesu!" Daniel exploded.

Christa swallowed hard, leaning against the wall. She felt as if she were going to pass out. No, she never passed out. She never even pretended to do such things. But the pictures Daniel's reading had evoked in her mind . . . She clamped her hand to her mouth. A wild panic seized her.

"And those men were on a search mission," Jeremy said. Christa heard the clink of glass. Obviously, everyone had seen mental images of the twelve unfortunate soldiers. "Sent out by a fool to look for a fool," Jeremy commented. "I intend to keep my regiment together."

"And you have a certain rapport with the Comanche, so I've heard," Jesse commented.

"No one really knows the Comanche," Jeremy said. "There are dozens of bands. But yes, I know Buffalo Run, and he does exert some influence."

"Enough to save Christa?"

"I don't intend to lose her." Jeremy sighed. "Listen, it isn't a perfect life. But I'll be in command of Fort Jacobson, we'll be just north of Texas, and I'll also be receiving a thousand acres of land. Yes, I chose to go west. Just like I chose to fight on the western front when I was given the option at the beginning of the war. I didn't want to fight my Reb friends from Maryland and Virginia. And now—well, hell, now we've won. And I've seen Johnson's idea of his great Reconstruction! Crooked politics, carpet-baggers, swindlers, and chaos. That's what's here for Christa if she stays. I chose the West before, and I'm choosing to go farther west now. Hell, yes! I prefer the Indians!"

Christa closed her eyes, bracing herself against the wall. There was silence for a moment. Then she heard her brother speaking softly. "Well, maybe you've got a point," he murmured. "Still, I wonder what Christa will think. Will she be afraid of the Indians?"

Yes! Terrified! She wanted to cry out. But she didn't.

Maybe Jeremy sensed that she was at the doorway listening. Maybe he even realized that she might be enjoying a moment of feeling just a little bit smug. "If I know Christa, she'll do well enough," he said. "It's the Comanche we'll have to worry about, I think."

"What—" Jesse began, but by then Christa was swirling into the room, her skirts rustling around her as she entered, her chin high. She smiled, although it felt like her smile was chiseled of plaster. Jeremy had seen her skirt, she realized, from his vantage point behind the map. He had known that she was there.

No matter.

She headed straight to the whiskey decanter, determined to ignore Jeremy if he should give her a look that insinuated she was being in the least improper.

So much for manners and mores. She poured out two fingers of whiskey, then stared at Jeremy. He didn't appear shocked. He seemed amused.

So that was to be her fate in life. To amuse him at every turn! She pushed the whiskey aside. Her stomach was churning. She didn't want it anymore.

"Well, what do you think, Christa?" Daniel asked her.

"You should think about this, seriously," Jesse said.

It was her opportunity. Her golden opportunity to tell Jeremy to play cowboys and Indians all on his own. She'd stay home. Her brothers would protect her.

But her brothers were, at long last, getting a chance to lead normal lives with their families. And, yes, she could stay. They loved her. She would have a place . . .

A place on the fringe of life.

Jeremy moved around the table, away from the map, fingering his whiskey glass. He strode over to Christa and added a new shot to his glass, his eyes probing hers, silver and steel.

"They're really fascinating, you know. We whites, especially here on the eastern seaboard, have a habit of grouping Indians together. Their societies are so unique. Take the Choctaw and the Cherokee. Christa, you'll meet several. They have excellent systems of justice, and their tribal laws are impressive. The Arikara, along the Missouri, tolerate such curious practices that their neighbors on the Missouri have moved away. They choose to live in earth lodges, keeping all their garbage between them. They practice incest, and spend the winter chasing one another's wives. The Cheyenne are famous for their chastity. The wives often belong to guilds, and brag about their domestic abilities with greater pride than the bucks brag about their hunting prowess."

"Then there are the Sioux, the Apache, and the Comanche," Jesse reminded him.

Jeremy was intending to shock her, she realized. Did he suspect what she had already heard? She wouldn't show him that she was afraid. Ever.

She smiled, determined that she would not crack.

"Tell me about the Comanche," she said pleasantly.

"Christa, maybe you shouldn't—" Daniel began.

"Oh, no! I'm just dying to hear anything that Jeremy can tell me!"

"They tend to be small and bandy-legged. They are the horsemen of the plains—no man rides better than a Comanche. They are inordinately proud of their stealth." He walked around her, his voice coming husky. "They say that a fellow named Walking Bear stole a Texan's wife away while he was sleeping right beside her. They are fond of taking captives, and sometimes they are fond of torturing them. At night, if their cries are too loud, they are fond of cutting their tongues out."

"Good Lord, Jeremy—" Jesse started to protest.

"Jesse, it's quite all right," Christa said quickly. "This is going to be my life. I should know about these things."

"You'll start a new life frightened and miserable!" Daniel warned her. "Perhaps you should stay home. Until the baby is born, until Jeremy is established, at the very least."

Here it was again—her golden opportunity.

"But Christa is never frightened, are you, my love?" Jeremy queried.

She spun around. His eyes were sizzling out a challenge. Or maybe he was goading her into doing his will. One or the other, it didn't matter. He was going to win.

She spun around to smile broadly at her brothers again. "My, my! I've married a Yank. How on earth could I ever be frightened of a short, little Comanche?"

"They tend to be short," Jeremy said suddenly. She spun around. His fingers were now tense around his glass, and his eyes seemed to blaze into hers. "Some are tall. And smart. And great forces to be reckoned with. They can be passionate, and very fierce. Perhaps you should stay home."

Even Jeremy was saying it now. All she had to do was speak.

But she didn't speak, and the moment was swiftly gone. He lifted his glass to her. "But Christa Cameron, the great Rebel, is coming west. I say that the Comanche, Apache, Kiowa—all—had best take care. Right, my love?"

"Certainly," she replied, and lifted her glass in kind. "After all, I shall have the great Colonel McCauley at my side. No brave would dare to steal his wife, I'm sure."

"Let's hope not," Jesse murmured. His eyes were darkening with concern. She could sense that Daniel was about to jump in and there was only so much that Jeremy could do to keep peace in the family.

"I know that I will be just fine!" she said enthusiastically, her eyes rising to Jeremy's. Damn him! He seemed to want her to back out now, to cause some problem. What was the matter with him? He had, at the least, helped her with her brothers before.

He sighed suddenly, reaching out for her. She remembered the last time that he had touched her, and a sizzle of burning heat came sweeping through her. But he merely slipped an arm through hers and led her back to the map. "Let me show you the way you'll be coming to join me. The train will take you from Richmond to Washington, and from Washington you'll pass through to Illinois, and then come south again down the Mississippi by steamer—"

"Washington?" she said, dismayed.

"It's the best way," Jesse explained to her.

"I'm going to travel north to arrive southwest?"

"Christa, half the railways in the South still need repairing," Daniel told her. She sensed just the slightest note of bitterness in his tone. "And even if they didn't, that's your best route. Honestly."

She nodded, staring at the map. It was going to be a long, long journey.

She looked up. Jeremy was staring at her again. She looked quickly back to the table. It was one of Jesse's old maps, one he'd acquired in Kansas before the war. There were no marks on it that drew lines between the North and the South.

There was no North, and no South. It was all one big country once again.

And here was a map with broad stretches in the West with names like "No-man's-land."

It would be wild and untamed. And it might even be free from the heavy hand of Reconstruction.

"It should be a fascinating journey," she said. Her head was pounding. There were more words on the map. Words that broke the big territory down into smaller, more frightening areas.

The words were Indian names: Shoshone, Cheyenne, Choctaw, Sioux, Blackfeet, Crow, Apache, Comanche, and more.

They were all looking at her now. She could feel their eyes on her. Jesse was worried. Daniel was growing hostile.

What was Jeremy thinking? Had he decided that he had been roped into this misery, but that she really wasn't worth the effort anymore? He might have decided that she simply wasn't enjoyable enough material, as far as a wife went.

To her astonishment, she felt a prickling of moisture at the back of her eyes. It was the baby, she thought. It was the exhaustion she so often felt.

There were so many things she felt for her husband. She could not forgive him—not so much for winning the war, but for being so damned certain that he had always been right. She hated him sometimes. Most men went out of their way to be charming to her, while Jeremy wouldn't give her the courtesy of believing in the smallest feminine lie. She hated him, yes, and she wanted to best him. She wanted to prove to him that southern "belles" had always been made of sterner stuff. She wanted to prove to him that she wasn't afraid, that she could do anything a northern girl could do, and better.

And she was intrigued. By his eyes, gun-metal gray one minute, silver the next. And she was fascinated by the hard-muscled grace of his body. She was determined to deny him, and equally determined that he would never lose his desire to have her.

She had married him, and she was going to have his baby. Her fingers trembled.

Twelve men had been found with fifty arrows apiece protruding from them. Their ears and their genitals had been cut off. Stuffed into their mouths. Comanches liked to cut out the tongues of their victims.

"My love?" Jeremy murmured, watching her.

She was going to travel west.

She ran her finger over the map. "I've never really traveled very much," she murmured. "Well, let's see, I came to West Point to visit you and Daniel that winter, Jesse. And I've been to Washington and down south as far as Savannah, but this . . ." She looked up, her chin high. "This will be quite different. How long will it be before I meet up with you in Little Rock, Jeremy?"

He smiled. Another of his taunting, amused smiles. Yet she thought that there was a glitter of admiration in his silver eyes. "Not that long, my love. Assuming you're ready to leave in another two weeks, the journey will take you about two weeks. We won't be parted more than a month. That shouldn't be too distressing, should it?"

"Oh, I shall just pine every day!" she murmured. She spun around suddenly, feeling as if she were choking. She wasn't about to let him know that she was feeling ill again—he might mistake it for cowardice.

"Gentlemen, do return to your whiskey and conversation. If you'll excuse me . . ."

She didn't give a damn if they excused her or not. She needed to escape.

In her wake, she was certain that she sensed Jeremy's silent laughter.

As they rode into Richmond late the following afternoon, Jeremy watched Christa's face and became heartily sorry that he had ever suggested that she ride in with Jesse and say good-bye to him.

Maybe they had all become hardened—he, Jesse, Daniel, and others. Maybe they'd just all seen so much battle that the aftermath couldn't seem too terrible.

But it was.

The streets of Richmond were filled with maimed and broken men. Amputations had saved thousands upon thousands of lives, but watching the results now was painful.

On every street they passed, there were men. Some were walking, some were just sitting. Half of them were missing some part of their bodies. Many were still clad in their uniforms, or pieces of uniforms. Tattered gray shirts covered scrawny chests. Many were unshaven, dirty.

But the worst of it was the look in their eyes. They looked as if they had lost everything.

They had. And the hopelessness was more difficult to see than death in battle. Death was sometimes merciful.

This endless anguish was merciless.

And there were more than just the tragically maimed, wounded, and lost to fill the streets of the city. Whores strode freely and boldly where the most chaste and modest of women had once strolled. Brazen, red-lipped and red-gowned, they shouted to any able-bodied man they saw. Soldiers in Union blue walked here and there, some on business and in a hurry, some off duty and strolling about, some saddened by the loss of humanity, and some pleased that the blasted Rebels had been broken.

Then there were the moneylenders and the businessmen. Garish folk, dressed in bright shirts and striped trousers, standing up on soap boxes. Mostly they promised the lost and wandering slaves wonderful riches for working for them. Paid labor from the first streaks of sunup to the last whisper of light in the sky. But they would work as free men for a pittance—not enough to feed the families now looking to them for food and sustenance.

He hadn't lied to Daniel or Jesse yesterday. He was heartily sick of Reconstruction.

Christa, attired in a maroon riding habit and actually riding sidesaddle and looking very composed today, reined in suddenly. He realized that they had come upon the large dwelling that had once been the White House of the Confederacy.

Through the long years of the war, the Jefferson Davises had resided here. Varina, gracious and beautiful, had entertained, always seeking to keep up morale, her husband's staunchest supporter no matter what his difficulties with the North—or with his own generals. In northern camps, the men may have poked fun at Jeff Davis before their campfires but Varina had earned a reputation that had made her the envy of many. Poor Mary Todd Lincoln was said to be part crazy, and now, with Lincoln murdered, the poor lady was in sad shape, indeed. She had never been popular with the northern troops.

Now, men in blue uniforms hurried in and out of the White House of the Confederacy. Christa stared.

"Christa!" Jesse said her name softly. She didn't seem to hear him.

"Christa!" Jeremy said more harshly. "Ride on by! It will be easier!"

She rode. She spurred her horse and rode on ahead of them. Jeremy glanced at Jesse. She didn't have any idea of where she was riding.

They both spurred their horses, hurrying to catch up with her. Christa was well dressed; her mare, Tilly, was an exceptional Arabian. Alone, she could be inviting trouble.

They rounded a corner where merchants were in the street selling goods for exorbitant prices. Yankee prices. Southern pride might remain, but no one wanted southern money. There was a stand where tomatoes were going for two bits a piece. Milk was sky high, meat almost untouchable.

As they rode by the booths, a high, venomous female voice called out. "Yankee-loving whore!"

A missile came hurtling toward them. Realizing that it was aimed toward Christa, Jeremy instinctively moved his horse forward. He stretched out a hand to catch the flying object. It seemed to explode in his hand, spewing red, like blood, around them. Someone had thrown a tomato at Christa.

He pulled off his glove, shaking the tomato from it. Christa stared at him in horror.

"By God!" she breathed. "So very dear, so expensive, and she was willing to throw it at me!"

"Stop!" cried another woman, apparently calling out to Christa's tormentor. "You'd have a Yankee, too, you old crone, if a Yankee would have you."

"Let's go on," Jesse suggested wearily.

But Jeremy started to dismount, determined to find the guilty party.

"No!" Christa cried. Jeremy looked at her. "Please!" she whispered. "Let's just go!" She flapped the reins over her mare's neck.

Once again, he was hard put just to follow her alongside Jesse. "I think maybe you'd best take her to the hotel, Jesse, right away, if you don't mind," he said to his brother-in-law. "She's not going to like seeing the people around the government buildings."

"I'll catch her," Jesse promised, riding ahead hard. Jeremy reined in. He watched them ride on, wishing with all his heart that he'd said goodbye to her at Cameron Hall. It was a bitter world. Maybe it was best she learned that now.

He reported in to a General Babcock, and was delighted to learn that he had a company of men waiting to travel with him, including a number of friends from his old regiment. He had barely left the general's office behind when he felt a tap on the shoulder. He turned around to see a very old friend standing there, a tall, lean black man. His name was Nathaniel Hayes, and he had never been a slave. He'd been born a free man in New York City, and from Jeremy's Indian days long before the war, Nathaniel had been with him. He'd carried firearms in the West, and he'd been dismayed to discover how many northern white men were against his carrying a gun against the Rebel forces; captured black men— free or not—did not fare well as southern captives. Especially if they'd carried firearms. So Nathaniel had just served Jeremy. He'd never carried a firearm, but he'd written many messages for Jeremy and he'd managed to attend to his every need.

"Nathaniel! You came all the way down here just to travel with me?"

Nathaniel grinned broadly. "Colonel, sir, I was delighted to come down. There's a number of the old regiment from the days we spent in Mississippi before you were sent east with Grant!"

"Tenting just outside the city?"

"That's right, Colonel. Waiting to travel with you. Are you joining us tonight?"

He shook his head. "My wife is with me."

"Traveling with us now, sir?"

He shook his head. "She needs to pack household belongings if we're to make a go of it out in the wilderness. She'll join me in Little Rock. You'll like her, Nathaniel," he heard himself saying.

He nodded. "Certainly, sir, that I will. She's a southern girl, I hear."

He nodded. Yes, she was that. A southern girl, very bitter at this moment that someone would hate her enough to throw a tomato at her—when tomatoes were so costly.

"Will you bring her tonight, sir? There's to be something of a barn dance. We've some young ones, new recruits, and they've managed to attract some of the young ladies hereabouts. With your permission, sir!"

"Permission granted," Jeremy assured him. "And yes, I'll come to see to my personal equipment, and to introduce my wife to the men."

As it turned out, Christa was not particularly interested in meeting his men. When he reached the hotel at last, he found her alone in their room. He unbuckled his scabbard, watching her as she sat staring silently out the window.

"Where's Jesse?"

"Bathing," she murmured absently, still staring out. She was so still and straight and miserable he wanted to offer her some comfort. She wouldn't want his comfort, though. It was because of him that someone had thrown a tomato at her and called her a Yankee-loving whore.

"There's to be a party, a barn dance of sorts, out where the men are tenting tonight. We're going to attend."

She shook her head. "You attend. I haven't the heart for it."

"We'll attend, because you're my wife."

"I don't feel well—"

"You're lying."

"I'm expecting a child!" she flared up.

"And you're feeling just fine."

She stood up, fingers clenched into fists at her sides, and accosted him. "If you were any kind of a gentleman at all—"

"If I were a southern gentleman, you mean, I would allow you to lie whenever it suited your convenience. Well, I'm not, and I won't. My men are eager to get a look at you. They've all heard that I married southern royalty. We're going to give them a good look. Make sure you wear something really lavish. They'll enjoy it."

He stalked out of the room, slamming the door behind him. How had he wound up fighting with her, when all that he had wanted to do was put an arm around her?

Easy. She'd insisted that he marry her but he'd insisted they make it real, that she accompany him. Why? Because he wanted her. He wouldn't have married her, not even for Cameron Hall, not for Jesse, Callie, or anyone, if there hadn't been something there.

He swallowed, grit his teeth, and went down to the taproom. It was a southern establishment, one Jesse had known well before the war. Its proprietor had a way about him—he was a man willing to roll with the times.

Jeremy was the only one in the public room. The innkeeper served him whiskey, then left him alone. Jeremy sipped it slowly, determined to give Christa more time alone.

What would he do if she flatly disobeyed him? Could he drag her along anyway? And what about Jesse? Right or wrong, he would have leapt to Callie's defense against Daniel if he hadn't been engaged in battle when the two had met.

When he'd sat with the whiskey long enough, he rose and returned to his room. To his surprise Christa was dressed, and beautifully so. She was in emerald-green taffeta and velvet, an off-the-shoulder dress that displayed the delicate beauty of her shoulders and the rise of her breasts. Her black hair was pulled into a riot of curls at her nape.

She sat by the window again, looking down, even though the night grew dark.

He held still in the doorway, watching her. Then he entered the room, closing the door behind him. To his surprise she turned to him at last. "Isn't this flamboyant enough?"

He discovered himself swallowing like a schoolboy. "It will do nicely," he said, then cleared his throat. "You're extremely beautiful."

She lowered her head. "For a Yankee's whore," she whispered.

"For his wife!" he reminded her harshly.

There was a knock at the door. He turned around. Jesse stood there. "Are we going to dinner? If you two would prefer to dine in—"

"No, no, Jess, thanks. We're going to something like a barn dance, and I think you'll enjoy it. You may know some of the men in attendance."

Jesse was agreeable. If he noted that his sister was pale and wan he must have thought it had something to do with her missing her husband once again.

Pray God we leave it that way! Jeremy thought. He didn't know what Christa would do once they reached the camp.

To his surprise, she did very well. She met Nathaniel first, and the two seemed to like one another immediately. He saw her eyes widen with surprise when Nathaniel first spoke, and he realized that she'd probably never met a black man without a southern slur to his voice. Jesse struck up a quick conversation with Major Weland, and Christa somehow wound up on Jeremy's arm. They joined the two physicians, and Weland assured Christa that he would see to it that she was safely delivered of a beautiful baby, no matter where they might be.

"I'll be—darned," Jesse said, looking across the large canvas mess tent where they had gathered for the dance. "Excuse me," he told the others. "That's Jules Larson. He's just turned twenty, I believe, but I thought he was fighting for the Confederacy at the end of the war. His family's from the peninsula."

Major Weland looked around Jesse. "The boy was a Confederate. He's joined on with the U.S. Cavalry again. Lots of southern boys will be doing so, you mark my words. A horse soldier is a horse soldier. The war is over. We've new worlds to conquer. The West is the future!"

There were a number of ex-Confederates who were going to be in his regiment, Jeremy learned. When the dance wound down to the final moments, the cavalry band decided to pay a tribute to them.

The last song played was "Dixie."

Jeremy watched Christa. She stood very tall and straight, and listened. She lowered her head, and he thought that tears must have sprung to her eyes.

But they had not. She lifted her chin. He thought that she had decided that she would cry no more for her homeland.

Pride was not such a terrible thing, he told himself. It had sustained many a man, many a time. If it would bring her west, so be it.

But she was so silent on the ride back to the hotel that he began to wonder again. He had determined that he would not press her that night, that he would leave her be.

But he could not bear to keep with that conviction. She had trouble with the hooks on her gown and he had to help her. When she stood in her corset and petticoats, he felt the familiar thudding of her heart, the ache in his groin. It would be their last night together for quite some time. He pressed his lips against her shoulder and inhaled the sweet scent of her. He didn't know if she issued a protest or not, but he swept her up, petticoats and all, doused the lights with a snuffer, and made love to her.

There was nothing different. She did not protest, she did not respond. Frustrated, he lay in the darkness and wondered if he hadn't made a horrible mistake. Then he leaned on an elbow and gazed at her. Her eyes were closed, her lips were damp, slightly parted. Her breasts rose and fell and her body carried a beautiful sheen, highlighting its perfection.

No, it could not be a mistake. She was his. They had cast their fates together.

But he thought of her in the wilderness. A fear gripped his heart. Did he have the right to drag her through savage country?

Her eyes opened suddenly. She flushed, reaching for the sheets as she caught him staring at her.

He closed his hand over hers. "Leave it. We'll be parted a long time now."

She didn't reply. Her lashes lowered. He sat up, then sighed. "Christa, don't come. Stay in Virginia. You don't have to join me."

Her eyes opened again. She looked at him. "I—I don't want to stay here!" she said softly.

He frowned, puzzled. "But—"

"I don't want to stay. I don't want—I don't want to see those maimed, hopeless men! I don't want to see the bastard scalawags tormenting the freed blacks and the whites who have been left with nothing. I—" She broke off. "I can't stay here!" she whispered.

He leaned low, watching her once again. "So you would escape—even if escaping means facing the Indians with me. Aren't you afraid?"

If she was, she wasn't going to tell him.

"I'm tired," she said.

He watched her for a moment. Then he slipped an arm around her and pulled her close. She stiffened instantly, but he merely smoothed her hair back.

"You're tired," he said irritably. "Sleep."

In a moment, she relaxed. And he held her, thinking that she was incredible. So taut and wounded, proud and fierce—and so infinitely beautiful and precious. His enemy, his love.

He didn't sleep that night.

They breakfasted at the crack of dawn, for he was to ride to the train station at the head of his troops. They moved so swiftly that there was no more time to talk, even though he could suddenly think of a dozen things to say.

They rode to the camp together, then he kissed her briefly, shook Jesse's hand, and prepared to take his leave. He was at the head of his troops, the bugler was calling them all in and they were ready to ride.

He turned upon his mount to look down at Christa one last time.

She returned his stare. She hesitated a moment, beautiful, elegant in her white gown with the lilac flowers. She began to move, hurrying toward his horse.

They were about to move forward. He reined in instead. She continued to come. Then she hesitated.

He leaned down, sweeping her up into his arms. She seemed startled for only a moment, her arms instinctively curling around his neck.

He lowered his head and kissed her.

And for the first time she kissed him back.

He tasted the marvelous sweetness of her tongue, felt the gentleness of her lips. Felt the subtle movement of her body, the brush of her fingers against his nape. Heat rushed into him, suffusing his loins, his thighs, his chest, his arms. He could have held her forever, kissing her, tasting her, holding her.

She was kissing him.

Because she would miss him?

Or because he was actually leaving, and she had gained another month of freedom?

It didn't really matter. A burst of applause rang out. His troops were certainly entertained. No matter what she was doing to his system, he had to ride.

Regretfully, he lifted his lips from hers. He searched out her eyes. They were fathomless. He set her down gently upon the ground and tipped his hat to her.

"Take care, my love!" he said. She stepped back, her fingers against her lips. She raised a hand as he lifted his own, moving his troops out.

Within minutes, she was a beautiful blur in the background with Jesse at her side.

Yes, that was it. It was a show for her brother.

But she had kissed him back.

Damn her.

The heat would haunt him all the long days until he saw her again.

Nine

Autumn, 1865

I have now been on the road (a steamer isn't exactly on the road, and I have traveled forever by steamer, so it seems) for ten days, and as Celia Preston has suggested, I am going to keep a journal. All good cavalry wives do so, for future waves of women and men who come this way and enter into the wilderness. Keeping a journal, so Celia tells me, is a quite popular thing to do, and as it is also a way to keep abreast of events when writing home, I have decided to set my hand to it. And so thinking, I will go back ten days, to the day I said good-bye.

I had help in preparing to leave. Although I couldn't take everything that had been acquired for my "marriage chest" throughout the years, Jesse warned me that I would need my good dishes and silver and table linens—Jeremy would be expected to entertain along the way, and no one can know who might come to visit. So when the day came to depart, I was literally surrounded with trunks. It was Daniel's time to then assure me that Jeremy wouldn't be in the least alarmed, that there would be plenty of ambulances to convey all these things. Yes, ambulances. That's the way frontier military wives travel, they both assured me. The vehicles are fitted out to carry the sick and wounded—and officers' wives. I have to admit the idea of seeing the countryside is beginning to intrigue me. And I have to admit, privately to my journal, that the idea of certain Indians terrifies me. But the die is cast—there is no looking back now.

As I stood in the entryway at Cameron Hall I thought of what lay before me. Although the weather was beginning to turn cool, both sets of breezeway doors had been thrown open for all the coming and going that took place as my things were being packed. I felt that touch of Virginia air, and I stood where my ancestors had stood for over two centuries. I looked up at the portrait gallery, at Jassy and Jamie who began the construction of Cameron Hall, and at Ma and Pa, and at the picture taken just before the war of the three of us, Jesse, Daniel, and me. I thought that not even Jesse's determination to be a Yankee had split us up, but now with the war over at last, we were surely being torn apart.

I looked away quickly. I love Cameron Hall with all my heart. It is Jesse's, it is Kiernan's. I must leave it to them.

Yet it wasn't the Hall that so broke my heart. I kissed the children and set them down. John Daniel was quite old enough to understand what was going on, and there were huge tears in his little eyes. Callie was crying and Kiernan was crying, and I kissed and hugged my sisters-in-law fiercely. No one, not Jesse or Daniel or Jeremy, will ever understand how close we became. The men fought battles together. We survived together.

And, of course, it was saying good-bye to Daniel that broke my heart the most fiercely. Jesse is still with me; I dread our parting. I had sworn I would not cry, but when I embraced Daniel knowing not when I would see him again, if ever (life being so precarious a gift as it is!), I felt the tears burning at the back of my eyelids. "Little sister," he told me. "You kept the home fires burning for us for years. Before God, Christa, we will always keep them burning for you!" He hugged me so fiercely that I thought I would break, and still, I could have clung to him forever. But Jesse plucked me away before I burst into a torrent of tears, and so we drove away, waving merrily. Yet, if my heart did not shatter in those moments, I know that I can brave what the future will bring. If I can only brave Jeremy!

Christa frowned, then scratched out the last sentence. She would be seeing him soon enough. Her stomach was knotting, and she was increasingly nervous.

If the Indians did get hold of her, she didn't want him reading in her journal that she had been afraid of him! And she wasn't afraid of him. Sometimes she didn't understand what she felt at all. Oddly, she would wake up nights and reach out, and feel empty to realize that she was alone. She would remind herself fiercely that she would be sleeping with him soon enough, in the rain, in the snow, in the elements. And being Jeremy, he would reach for her whenever the notion swept him.

And she would fight the onslaught of sensations that always seized her.

Why?

She bit her lip, determined that she wouldn't think about it, or Jeremy. But she paused again. There were times when she missed him, and she didn't understand why. She came slowly to admit that she liked the deep sound of his voice, and she liked the way that he wore a uniform—even if it was a blue uniform. She liked the strong feel of his arms, and she even liked the way, at times, that he could look through her. There was no pretense with Jeremy. She admired his raw determination, and she could never fail to be touched by the silver and steel in his eyes. Thinking of him holding her again made her breathless. She hated him for taking her away, and yet she was glad of him for that very reason. He made her furious, he made her weak. He always touched some deep emotion, some passion, within her.

What of Jeremy? He'd had weeks now to ponder all that they had done. Did he regret the marriage? Of course he regretted it. He had never wanted it. But he had insisted that she come with him. Was he sorry now? He could seem so bitterly disappointed in her. Or perhaps she would be better than nothing at all along the trail.

She wasn't going to think about it.

She looked back to her journal.

Coming through Richmond again was horrible, seeing all the wounded and maimed and lost souls upon the streets. No one hurtled anything at me, even though Jesse has accompanied me in uniform as he is carrying dispatches for several of the forts out west. He'll hand them—as well as me—over to Jeremy. Jesse has tendered his resignation. He is ready to set his hand to being a gentleman farmer and country doctor and live a peaceful life with Kiernan at Cameron Hall. It will take some time, however, for him to actually manage to leave the military.

Anyway, onward. A lot of rebuilding is being done. It is sad to see the burned and gutted houses, it tears at the heart. Yet rebirth is also going on. Fields are full, as there are no longer armies to tramp them down. One minute you can see a house that is nothing but a shell, smoke stains upon it and cannonballs within it. Then just along the road comes the scent of fresh lumber, the sounds of hammers against nails, and new structures can be seen going up. The South is repairing herself. Everyone says, "If only Lincoln had lived!" We all hated him for so long for his determination to keep the country together! But everyone knew of his gentle plans for the South to return to the Union, and everyone has seen that President Johnson is not nearly so mag-

nanimous! Perhaps the nation will heal. And perhaps the West is where the schism may come together at last, for I am traveling there with quite a mixture of people.

I met Celia Preston in Washington, where we switched trains for Illinois. She is very young, very pretty, and very frightened. She is a northern girl, traveling west to be with her James. Apparently James and Jeremy have served together before, and Celia is quite certain that the sun rises and sets in Jeremy. I have refrained from telling her that it is otherwise. I do intend to make an exceptional cavalry wife. I'm sure that Jeremy is expecting me to arrive all froth and lace, the very stereotypical southern "belle," and I intend him to know that few of us were ever so flighty as men seem to wish to believe. Running a plantation was hard work. From sunup to sundown. There were always candles and soap to be made, meat to be smoked, linens to wash and change, and even if a household did keep slaves it was up to the mistress of the house to see that it was all done, that hundreds of people were fed, that things ran so smoothly that the master of the place could come in at any moment, set his feet up, and call upon his beloved for a brandy, never realizing what she had accomplished.

Those days are over. I have come upon an easy lot in life. Jesse assures me that there will be a company cook, and that men often come up from the ranks to cook specifically for the officers' wives. Also, we will be followed by a host of laundresses.

All that I shall have to do is try to assure the other wives that we will not be eaten by cannibalistic Indians.

Actually, that is not fair. None of the tribes I have heard about is a cannibalistic one. They are just murderers, savages, and thieves.

She paused again, chewing upon the nib of her pen. She couldn't write all negative things about the Indians. She was traveling with an Indian. His name was Robert Black Paw, and like James he had served with Jeremy before. He was a Cherokee. A tall man who could move like air. His eyes were very dark and serious. He wore Union issue navy trousers with a deerskin shirt and hide boots that laced up to his knees. He was soft-spoken and his English was excellent. Whenever she needed something, he miraculously appeared. When she wished to be alone, he just as miraculously disappeared. He and Jesse had seemed to hit it off very well and they spent a great deal of time together.

Robert was a Cherokee. Cherokee were among the Five Civilized Tribes. Jesse had told her that actual companies of Cherokee had fought for the North—and for the South. She knew that Jesse considered the

Cherokee to be at least as civilized as the white man—Jeremy probably considered them to be more so.

Back to travel. It seemed difficult for me to go through Washington, but actually it was far easier than seeing Richmond. Nothing was bombed, nothing was burned. We had some time before the train was to leave and Jesse already had his dispatches, so we went for a ride. My mare, Tilly, and Jesse's horse will now be pent up in a railway car again for a long stretch, so it seemed only fair to exercise them. But then we came upon the very sad part of that journey, for Jesse rode toward Arlington House, General Lee's old home.

He and Daniel had been General Robert E. Lee's pupils at West Point. To this day they both adore Lee, as does a countryside now, it seems. (Other than that awful General Pickett who blames the entire disaster of Gettysburg upon Lee.) Even Daniel admits that Stuart did not have the cavalry where it should have been and so failed Lee. And with Stonewall so recently deceased, Lee was so alone! Do I defend him too rashly? Yes, perhaps. Stuart is gone now along with Jackson and so many others; Lee has aged ten years for every one in which he fought the war.

"He can't come home," Jesse told me. And I saw in his eyes that he was remembering all the times that he had come there in happier days. The moment Lee agreed to serve the Confederacy, the Union seized his home. They could not afford him his little mount that overlooked the city of Washington. The house still stood. The house where Lee's wife, Martha Washington's great-granddaughter, had grown up and raised her own family. It had been a home to the Lees as precious as Cameron Hall is to all of us.

Lee cannot come home, for the government still has the place. The grounds are filled with the bodies of innumerable Union soldiers. Someone once thought that it would be a fine retaliation against Lee to bury Yankees on his grounds. Jesse told me that there was talk that the place might be made into a national cemetery, like the grounds in Gettysburg, but at the moment it is all in the air. Perhaps Lee's family will try to get the property back or demand some recompense. Bitterness remains, although Lee himself has said that the war is over and that he is determined on healing—a healing as quick as can be accomplished.

We rode back from Arlington House and saw that the horses were boarded and then found our own accommodations. I have a beautiful sleeper to myself. The upholstery is velvet, the furnishings are mahog-

any. Jesse is traveling on my one side, and Celia on the other. There is a handsome dining car just beyond us, and beyond that a smoking car for the men. Jesse has refrained from spending much time there, as he is so tenderly determined to share what little time we have left together.

Celia is lovely, Robert Black Paw is fascinating. There is one more army wife with us, and she is not quite so lovely. She is Mrs. Brooks, wife of Lieutenant Brooks, and I do not know her first name because she has not offered it. She raised a huge stink that we must all stop and observe the Sabbath properly. She was furious with some of the men— enlisted men—in the far cars because they dared to use profanity in her proximity. Of course, I'm certain the poor fellows had no idea they were anywhere near her. She has assured me that she will insist my husband do something about it since I refuse to be concerned. Where is my proper respect and belief in the Lord?

I was so stunned by her that I'm afraid I took several moments to reply. I assured her that my God was still busy collecting souls from the battlefields, which brought a gasp from her. She huffed herself around and left and I haven't seen her since, so I'm quite sure she will complain to Jeremy. I don't care. Jesse was behind me, and he was amused and assured me that Jeremy would probably be too. Of course, Jesse doesn't know how Jeremy really feels about me, but I do hope that he'll support his men over that harpy. I walked to the rear of the train, stood out by the rail, and watched the countryside. We were traveling through the mountains and their beauty, captured in so many colors, was awesome. I wondered what had happened to so many of our own convictions. When we were young, we never failed to make Sunday church services. But then the war came and all men, Yanks and Rebels, prayed to the same God. I don't think that I have lost Him entirely. Perhaps I shall find Him again in the West, alive in the savage wilderness.

We left the mountains to travel through Cincinnati, Ohio, and I saw just a bit of the bustle of that city. It is so untouched by the war. The next day brought us to Odin, Illinois, where I was startled when Jesse insisted I not leave the station. "They call it the hellhole of Illinois," he informed me, and really played the big brother. I chafed at the bit, of course, and saw all that I could through the windows. In the dining car I managed to pick up quite a bit of gossip and was heartily sorry that I could not see the place, for it is truly reputed to be a den of iniquity. I could see some of the women in the streets, and certainly some of them were engaged in "the" profession, for their clothing was loud and garish and their faces were very painted. One young lady was wearing black stockings that could be seen beneath a rise in her skirt—which was crimson! She seemed a happy-go-lucky thing, and I imagined that she was probably much more down on her luck than evil in any way. Of course, there was more to be seen. Drunkards careening down the street, gamblers in very fancy black. Oh! There was a gunfight! Not that I could be a Cameron and be unaccustomed to guns, but this was quite different from anything in my experience. The two men were wearing slovenly long railway frocks, teetering about, and calling one another out. Fortunately—or unfortunately— they were both so drunk that they missed one another several times.

Jesse pulled me in from the window and warned that I had best watch out—they were such poor shots they might well catch my nose since it was protruding so from the train. I cuffed him soundly on the arm, then started to laugh, and he laughed, and then I was nearly crying and in his arms, but I sobered quickly. I will not cry again.

From Odin, Illinois, we came to Cairo and caught a steamer that would take us down the Mississippi. I was delighted with my beautiful stateroom, though that delight was somewhat dampened when the captain, a kindly old bewhiskered fellow, assured me that there would be nothing less than the finest for "Colonel Jem's" wife. I tried not to think about the future too much, for the steamer is a fine southern vessel and there is a certain feeling about heading down into Dixie again. There are several ex-Confederates aboard. None of them seems to bear a grudge. Jesse has come across some old friends, and Rebel and Yank alike, they are all interested in a game of poker. Being Jesse's friends, they were more than willing to allow his sister to play, and Jesse thought it was all right since I would be in his company and the stakes would be very low. Mrs. Brooks is, of course, quite horrified, and I'm certain she is going to find a way to inform Jeremy fully about his wife's outrageous behavior. Well, she will just have to do so. I am enjoying myself tremendously, and I am very afraid that far too soon a noose will slip around my neck.

I had been sick mornings. Jesse had been afraid that the steamer would make me doubly so, but oddly enough, I feel very well now.

In Memphis we left the steamer and caught a new one headed down the White River. The ride became fascinating, for the scenery was haunting and mysterious. Swamps and deep, submerged forests sur-rounded the river. Darkness descended quickly, it seemed, yet sunsets and sunrises were glorious. There was the constant hum of insects at night, and though it seemed somewhat dismal, it was also very beautiful.

Four days out of Cairo and we reached DeVall's Bluff, which is a teeming, busy port. Not even the war seems to have changed that here. Ships were coming and going, goods were piled high on the docks, and people bustled about with purpose, busy with their lives. It was wonderful to see.

I am, however, growing very nervous. We leave here on the noon train, and will reach Little Rock by five. My heart is racing, I cannot breathe very well. Women, especially women in my "condition," are supposed to have such difficulties, but I don't think that this has anything to do with my health. I think that it has everything to do with my husband, and I cannot, for the life of me, begin to understand it. We are enemies. It is more than the color of his uniform, for from the day we first met we were natural enemies. A fire would grow hotter if he entered a room, a clear soft day would seem charged with the force of a storm. Now, things are assuredly worse for he seems to think that this marriage business has made him lord and master. Perhaps there is some sense to that, for I am here, the old life falling behind like clothing that has been shed, the new life stretching before me, frightening and wild.

We are approaching Little Rock. My fingers are trembling and it is difficult to hold the pen. I look at what I have written and am amazed —these words be but for my eyes only! Any minute, I will be with him again. I am so very nervous! I will end here.

Five forty-five. I will not, after all, end here. We've just received a message that Jeremy moved out into Indian territory with a small company of men on a search mission. He has left word asking Jesse to bring me down to his regiment's encampment outside of Fort Smith. We will leave by boat again in the morning.

I have just read over my last entry. I wish that I might have enjoyed Little Rock more. Jesse was wonderful, taking me out for a delicious steak dinner at a very nice restaurant, joking and warning me that I must now be prepared for life in the field and that I should embark upon that life well fed. It was an interesting evening, for I met the matronly wife of a colonel just coming in from the Indian territory, and she has been wonderful. She warned me that, yes, I must have crinolines and petticoats for special occasions, but that if I were to be a truly respectable cavalry wife, I must dress the part. Simple cottons and, with the colder weather coming on, warm underclothing, nothing frilly. There will be occasions when one must dress up, but on a day-to-day basis the simpler the better. A bonnet is a must if a woman is to have any skin left whatsoever upon her nose. The dust will be horrid, the cold will be bone chilling, and the rain will come in torrents. But she assured me that she valued every minute of her experience. I hope that I can be like her. She is charming and bubbling. Her interest in the flowers and plants and the beauty of the scenery is contagious. Most of all, I am delighted because, thanks to this dear lady, Jeremy will not be able to find a bit of fault with me. He will meet the perfect cavalry wife. However else I may fail him, in this I will succeed.

We left Little Rock early the next morning. The steamer seemed excessively slow, and though the days should be turning cool, the ride seemed very hot. I could not seem to still the onslaught of nerves that had assailed me, and all because of Jeremy. I am afraid to see him, I am afraid of Indians, and I am afraid of the unknown. I cannot be afraid of any of these things—especially Jeremy. I am also anxious. The blood seems to race through my veins. Though Jesse assures me that blood moves through the body at a constant rate, this is different. I lay awake last night, almost all the night, and I thought that it might well be the last time that I lay alone. Then I am anxious again, because he does strange things to me, things that I can't combat, things that I must surely combat.

I haven't thought of Liam in days. I loved him, but Jeremy seems to have overpowered that loss, and if I let myself think about it I will be glad to have him beside me, glad to feel his arms, for he does give me that feeling of belonging. He is fascinating to me, and I am compelled by him nearly as much as I am infuriated.

We have reached the camp. I am in Jeremy's tent. I think that I am quite ready for a ride across the plains. I have folded up my crinolines, my dress is simple (I learned a great deal about simple clothing while picking cotton and tomatoes!), and I am trying to be very composed. Jeremy was still not available when we arrived, but his aide, Nathaniel, the curious black man I met in Richmond, has been very kind and efficient. My trunks are all arranged within Jeremy's tent. It's a large one. Even his bed, a folding apparatus, is large. The weather is fair, the flap is lifted, the insects are at a low, Nathaniel has assured me, and I have been supplied with a bottle of sherry, a small writing desk of my own—facing Jeremy's larger one—and I really think that I am doing quite well. Nathaniel has assured me that there is a hip tub that was ordered especially for my use, and that he will be delighted to fill it for me if Jeremy does not return by mealtime. He has been gone several days, but they expect his return very soon.

Camp is a very busy place. Jeremy is commanding a regiment of eight companies, with each company consisting of eighteen to twenty-four men. Each company has its own captain, with various sergeants and corporals, and there are usually four lieutenants beneath Jeremy, but sometimes officers come and go, and there are others among them not necessarily accountable to any particular group of men. Dr. Weland, or Major Weland, is here and has already come by to see to my comfort. Celia is settled—and I'm assuming that Mrs. Brooks is settled, too, eagerly awaiting her chance to leap on Jeremy with tales of my evil deeds. She may go right ahead and do so. When he returns he'll find me well composed—the sherry will see to that. I'll be tremendously prim and proper with my hair pinned and my clothing plain, and hopefully he'll have no complaint.

As it happened, her hair wasn't pinned up and she wasn't wearing clothing at all when he reached her.

But he certainly had no complaint.

While Christa was coming down to the encampment, Jeremy was busily engaged in a painful discovery.

He had come out to find an earlier company that had been headed for Fort Union had lost its regiment and bogged down somewhere in the vast country in between.

He knew the country and he had known where to look.

The Great Plains drew many tribes seeking the hunting grounds, the bountiful water, the rich grasses. Many of the tribes were peaceful, many were settled in reservations, and many were still at war.

He had come upon a place where they had dug into trenches. They had built up a wall of small rocks and mud to one side, and trenched in on the other. It had been a good maneuver to outsmart and outfight a band of horsemen. Some of the Indians had had rifles, but only a few. The others had been armed with bows and arrows.

But oh, how they had used them.

He could see the battle even as he walked around the trench of dead men.

The Indians had encircled the the cavalrymen. The cavalry had first used their horses as shields, forming a circle with their backs toward the middle, every man shooting as the Indians rode around them. It was the natural, textbook way to fight. It was perhaps the only way, under the circumstances. Perhaps night had then fallen. The men had dug in. The Indians had come again, but they had discovered that the white men were so well dug in that they were losing far too many braves with each encounter.

So the Indians had used different tactics, finding a distance from which to shoot their arrows. They had staked out the area with feathered shafts that remained to mark the grave the men had dug themselves. Someone had called out the order to fire—just like an artillery officer might have done in any battle of the war. Then adjustments had been made. A little to the left, a little to the right. Dead straight closer, perhaps a little farther. And so the arrows had flown. Perhaps twenty-five at a time. Once, twice, again. Until the men all lay dead.

"My God, Colonel! This is a sorry picture!" Captain Thayer Artimas of Company G told him. "Jesu, sir, but the poor fellows never had a chance."

Jeremy stepped forward, pulling the arrow from the heart of a very young private with wide open, staring blue eyes. He knelt down and closed the boy's eyes. He looked at the arrow. "Comanche," he said softly. "They've come in quite far east. They don't usually ride in this far."

"They've been hot to fight lately, sir," Captain Artimas said.

"I imagine they've been attacked a lot lately," Jeremy murmured dryly.

Artimas shrugged. He looked around himself uneasily. "Think we ought to be moving onward, sir?"

Jeremy nodded. Night was coming. Comanche seldom attacked at night, but he wanted to be out of the area. He had only twenty-five men with him and he didn't want another massacre.

"Let's get a burial detail going here!" he called to his men. But even as he said the words, he felt a peculiar sensation stirring at his nape. The wind seemed to have picked up. There was a trembling in the ground.

"Dismount and circle!" he ordered quickly. Jesu, it could be the same thing! Even as he gave the order, he heard the first war whoop of the Indians. They were coming around the scruff of trees that stood over the one hump of dirt near them that might be construed as a hill. He narrowed his eyes against the rising dust, trying to count. It was a small party —perhaps twenty or so braves.

He shoved his horse's rump, aiming his rifle, calling to his men. "Wait to shoot, then shoot straight. We have to take them the first time, we can't give them a chance to come back. Understand? We'll be trapped like these poor fellows here if we make a mistake."

There was no answer except for the rise of the war whoops on the air. The Indians were bearing down on them quickly. They were in buckskin breeches, only a few of them wearing shirts despite the fact that the nights were growing cooler and cooler. The paint on their faces, the feathers in the hair, all denoted them as a war party. They had come to kill.

Jeremy took careful aim at the warrior who seemed to be in the lead of the group. He squeezed the trigger and the man flew from his horse. He took aim again, steadying his nerves. He had learned long ago that no matter how difficult it was to stay still and take aim while Indians were bearing down on him, it had to be done. Steadily and quickly.

He fired again and caught a second warrior. At his side, Captain Artimas was also firing and firing fast. Private Darcy, an exceptional sharpshooter, was reaching for his carbine in his saddle. Indians were falling quickly. Darcy brought down another.

Jeremy noted Willy Smith, a new recruit, standing straight and staring at the coming promise of death with wide-eyed horror. He looked just like an animal caught in a sudden bright light.

He was a target as big as the side of a barn to the Comanche.

"Get down!" Jeremy shouted, leaping toward the boy. He brought them both flat on the ground, not daring to look at Willy again but keeping both eyes on the horses that pounded surely toward them.

He kept shooting, emptying the six chambers of his revolver. He released Willy as he hastily filled the chamber again as the Indians raced around them in a complete circle.

"I'm all right now, Colonel," Willy choked out. "I'm all right. I can shoot pert near as good as Darcy, and I won't lose my senses again, sir."

"I'm sure you won't," Jeremy told him.

Dust rose, choking them.

Willy Smith took aim. He fired. A shrieking brave came flying from his painted pony, landing dead just in front of Willy. The boy stared at the dead Indian a second, then took aim again.

They were doing well. They had downed at least ten of the warriors in the first go-round.

"Injured, dead?" he shouted.

Artimas called out for an assessment. No one dead yet. Two wounded.

"We have to take them all this time around!" he called. "Else we'll be sitting ducks for target practice!"

"Right, Colonel!" Darcy called and grinned. "I'm going to get me the first one this time, Colonel."

"You do that."

As he had expected, the remaining warriors began to circle again. They were lucky. If the Indians had thought to pin Jeremy's troops down in the same trenches, they might have done better. Except that Jeremy wouldn't have stayed in the death trap—he would have charged the Indians.

The circle began again with the braves crying out their horrible war cries.

Darcy caught the first of them, just as he had promised. Jeremy began to fire. Aiming, squeezing, aiming, squeezing, faster, faster. He caught one, lost one, caught two. His men were good. By the time the second circle was completed, only five of the braves were left to ride away.

"Mount up! We've got to stop them before they bring more warriors against us!"

He leapt upon his horse, spurred the creature into motion, and started after the retreating Indians. Darcy and Artimas were right with him; the rest followed at a gallop behind. Darcy aimed his carbine and brought down one Indian. Jeremy caught two more in rapid succession. Artimas caught the fourth, and a man from the ranks brought down the last of them.

"Let's leave them where they fell!" Artimas said bitterly, after dismounting by the first of the fallen Indians. The brave was half naked, his chest and face painted, his lance, still curled in his fingers, decorated with several scalps, some white, some Indian from other tribes.

"No. We'll bury them all. Maybe that will delay their discovery for a while, and buy us some time."

Darcy had already started digging with his gun butt. He looked at Jeremy. "Colonel, sir, what's going to happen when we ride this way with the whole regiment?"

"They won't attack the regiment, Darcy."

"Why?"

"Because they haven't the numbers to do so."

"Why, Colonel, sir, there's hundreds of them stupid savages out here—"

"First lesson, Private! They're not stupid. See how they planned the artillery arrow attack that did in these men from Fort Smith? Second, don't go causing a big war by assuming they're all savages—we're very friendly with a number of tribes."

Near his side, Sergeant Rodriguez, a Mexican-born soldier who had served most of his life in the West, spit out a big wad of tobacco. "*Madre mío, niño!* Some of them are much more clean and smart than lots of the gringo riffraff we get in the West, eh Colonel, sir?"

Jeremy smiled. "Right," he said. But his smile faded quickly. It was growing darker, they were miles and miles from camp, and they still had lots of burying to do.

"Let's get to it, shall we?" he ordered.

This was a new company for him. Darcy had served with him just briefly before the end of the war and he knew that the man was a tremendous sharpshooter. He was grateful to have him.

He wondered if Darcy didn't hear Rebel yells in the Indian whoops when he shut his eyes, just as Jeremy had.

He suddenly broke out in a sweat. God help him, but this was easier. Easier than shooting at men in gray uniforms and wondering if he might be aiming at his brother-in-law.

They finished with the burial detail, dusting over the Indians, packing down the trench dirt over their own dead. In the midst of it, a groan had been heard, and they had discovered one man just barely alive. They had gone back to thoroughly look over every dead man to be sure that he was dead before finishing with the burying. The survivor had an arrow in his upper back, but they had managed to extract it without further injury, get some water into him, douse the wound with whiskey, and bandage it well. Jeremy was certain that the young man would make it.

He had survived this far—he could go all the way.

He forced his own men to ride until the moon was high in the sky. They rode for over seven hours and they rode hard, but they covered nearly fifty miles. He knew they would not be attacked if they camped on the plains.

He lay beneath the stars, watching the sky, exhausted but anxious for morning.

Christa should have arrived. He stared at the sky, but he saw his wife's face. Beautiful, delicate, refined.

Passionate, alive, stormy, disobedient, and defiant, her blue eyes flashing.

He winced. What would it be?

Well, she would learn a few lessons in the West, he thought. She'd probably pass out from the weight of her petticoats on the first day!

Whoa, don't be malicious there, sir, he warned himself. But she did have a few lessons to learn.

He inhaled deeply. So did he.

Jesu, he couldn't wait. All the long nights without her he had lain haunted by her memory. What was it with Christa? What tore at his body and emotions so deeply? He had longed for her to arrive, then he had berated himself for ever suggesting that she come. This was no place for Christa.

But dear God! He wanted her. He didn't give a damn how he found her when he returned. He felt torn by the pain and waste of his discovery on the plains, and he wanted nothing but comfort.

Christa? he thought, bemused. Comfort? She was like a little tigress, a wounded animal, proud, fierce, and ever on the defensive.

Yes, maybe they were both like wounded animals. Maybe time would heal some of the lacerations.

He closed his eyes tightly. Maybe he was falling in love with his wife. Maybe he had always been just a little bit in love with her.

Aroused yes, but more. She infuriated him, but there was more. Christa would not be beaten. And he could not help but admire her for that. Exactly what were his feelings? He didn't know.

He did know that he wanted to see her, no matter what her mood. Whether she was pleasant or furious because she'd realized just what a life he had brought her to!

He smiled, and pulled his hat low over his eyes. Tomorrow he would cleanse away the sight of the men in the trench. He would do so in her arms.

He didn't know how he would find her—clinging to Jesse perhaps, or sitting in his tent with her toes tucked under an elegant gown.

But as it happened, he found her in a more delightful manner than he had thought to imagine. She was in his tent, in the hip bath, surrounded by a froth of bubbles. She didn't hear him when he first came and he paused, unable to resist the temptation to watch her for a while.

Where had Nathaniel gotten hold of those bubbles?

They were wonderful. They covered her body, they popped, and then they no longer covered her. She leaned back, surrounded by bubbles. She lifted them and smoothed them over her shoulders. She seemed as sleek and luxurious and sensual as a cat, deliciously enjoying the feel of the hot water and the bubbles. Her hair was drawn up in a loose tie. Tendrils escaped, damp and curling, framing the delicate, perfect beauty of her face. Her eyes were half closed. Ink-dark lashes fell against her cheeks.

Suddenly, she sensed that he was there. Her eyes flew open and she stared at him. God, they were blue. Bluer than any sky in deepest summer, richer than any sea.

She was definitely startled by his appearance. Obviously, she hadn't intended to be discovered so.

He smiled slowly, crossing his arms over his chest. "Hello, darlin'!" he murmured softly.

"You're—you're here!" she whispered, dismayed. A flush rose to her cheeks.

"It is my tent," he pointed out. "You did come here to join me, remember?"

"Yes, of course. I—it's just I intended to be in the perfect plains garb! I meant to be ready for you," she murmured, her lashes sweeping her cheeks again.

It seemed that all the wicked fires of hell came bursting to flame within him. "Christa!" he promised her hoarsely, "trust me! At this particular moment, there couldn't be a more perfect garb for you to wear—nor could you appear to be the more perfect wife!"

And with that, he took his first, swift steps toward her.

Perhaps she wasn't ready for him.

He was more than ready for her.

Ten

So much for being entirely dignified upon his return, Christa thought quickly. Her fingers curled around the rim of the tub as he swiftly approached her.

She hadn't realized how anxious she had been for the sight of him. She studied him avidly, noting every little thing about him. There was a slight stubble on his cheeks and he needed a hair trim. His eyes seemed very dark, gray as storm clouds. His hair was tousled when he tossed his plumed cavalry hat aside. He was usually so impeccable in his uniform; today he was covered in a light coating of dust. He seemed taller than ever, broader in the shoulders. His cheeks seemed just a bit gaunt, but they added to the hardness of his rugged good looks. Her heart seemed to slam and scamper. She hadn't realized just how anxious she had been for this moment, just how hungry she had actually been for the sight of him.

It frightened her.

And just what was his intent? Did he mean to dive, uniform and all, into the small tub with her? A stray lock of deep auburn hair fell over his forehead, giving him a rakish look. As he came nearer she searched frantically for something to say, but no words came to her lips.

She shrieked out softly, discovering his intent. He didn't crawl into the tub with her, he reached inside of it and plucked her out. She felt absurdly faint for a moment, clinging to him. His arms felt incredibly hot and incredibly strong. He held her and long strides brought them quickly to the bed. He laid her down upon it and paused, taking a long look at her. Then he was beside her, wrapping her into his arms, and his lips were upon her naked throat, touching, tasting, licking away the drops of water that lay there. She began to tremble, feeling an overwhelming urge to simply give in to it all. But words came tumbling from her lips because he was always so quick to take her, and always so distant when the fire was quenched!

"How was your journey, Christa?" she asked herself out loud, trying to ignore the masculine lips upon her nudity. "It was fine, thank you. And the babe? Fine, too, I believe. Were you ill at all? Just a bit. Amazingly, it ended aboard the steamer, and I did very well from then on. How have you found the camp? The men, for Yanks, have been as pleasant as can be expected. How—"

She broke off. She had caught his attention at last. He leaned upon an elbow, staring down at her. His eyes were silver with laughter and appreciation now, even if it was a dark silver, and none of the determination or intent had left them.

"I had intended to get to all that," he assured her.

"Well, you hadn't done so!" she whispered. "All this time since we've seen each other, and you just grabbed me up and brought me to the—"

"All this time! That's quite the point, Christa. All this time! My love, believe me! This is the first act to be expected of any loving husband!"

Any loving husband, she thought.

He did not love her, but if she closed her eyes at that moment, she might well believe that he did. His lips were against her earlobe and his words were hot and evocative. "You smell so sweet, taste so sweet . . . Jesu, all of you!" He moved like quicksilver. One minute his lips were upon hers, the next second his tongue stroked her breast, and a spiraling began deep in the pit of her belly. Words of protest bubbled in her throat, but she did not issue them. Her fingers fell upon his waving russet hair, but briefly, for he was moving again, touching all of her, whispering more feverishly against her flesh. Her fingers fell upon his shoulders and she felt the dust upon him.

"You're covered with dust!" she whispered.

"Sorry!" he apologized briefly. Moving back he stripped off his jacket and shirt. She closed her eyes quickly, alarmed at how pleased she was at the sight of his chest, how fascinated she would be to touch it. When she opened her eyes again, he had stripped naked and was coming for her, and it seemed the devil's dance had begun within her, all at the sight of his nudity and the protruding hardness of his arousal. When he crawled atop her again, she noticed a streak of red running down his neck and she cried out in earnest.

"You're injured!"

"I'm not."

"Let me tend to it!"

"If it's anything, it's a scratch, and I'd far rather you attend to other things at the moment!" he cried in frustration.

He had other things on his mind.

But she didn't mind. He was always, even in his most fervent moments, a considerate lover. And there was a curious sense of rightness when he was with her so, when she felt his body blanket her own. When she felt his body enter her own. Taking her, making them one. Moving. Even as she twisted her head, biting into her lower lip, feeling the rugged heat and rhythm of his motion, she discovered that deny it or not, she was pleased that he did want her so. Her fingers rested on his shoulders, and she felt the tremendous tension in the rise and fall of his muscles, felt the hunger building and building within him.

She had imagined something like this. But she had never felt this with Liam, never sensed that this could come.

Her breath caught with the sudden force of his movement, and she very nearly felt something exploding within her, something promised, something wonderful. Then she was washed in the rich expulsion from her husband and felt the shuddering that shook through him again and again.

She bit her lip hard, something inside telling her that it was wrong to deny him, that perhaps she could give them both a chance if she could quit denying him. But they had been apart too long. She didn't know his feelings, and she certainly didn't know his mood.

He fell to her side and was silent for a while. She curled to her side, not facing him, but not moving away from him. His fingers moved idly over her back.

"Liam McCloskey is dead," he told her. The words were soft—she still thought that there was a note of anger to his voice.

Her lashes fluttered over her cheeks. "I know that very well," she murmured. Darkness had fallen since he had come. Just dusky at first, then darker and darker. Outside the tent, the stars would be dotting the heavens. The moon would be rising. She had slept here last night alone, but she hadn't felt the wilderness so keenly.

Neither had she felt so truly alone then, for she had been waiting for him. But now she felt his withdrawal. He rolled to his back. She thought that there was now a note of grave disappointment in his tone, more jarring than the sarcasm of his words. "Liam is dead, the war is over, but you're still fighting. And you may look as sweet and southern and delicate as magnolia blossoms but we both know that you're no simpering belle! It's a pity, my love, a true pity, that you were not in the field. No matter how many had died, you'd not have allowed Lee to surrender!"

She stiffened, stunned that tears could suddenly burn so hotly behind her eyes. "All this time we've been separated," she charged, "and you're being exceptionally cruel!"

"All this time! And you're still as cold as ice. Well, my love," he said wearily. "You may not believe this, but I do not *try* to make you so wretchedly miserable."

She frowned, glad of the darkness. "I'm—I'm not wretchedly miserable," she said softly.

The tent had grown very dark. She felt him looming over her again. "No?" he queried. "You don't hate me, or"—she felt his slight hesitation —"this?"

Even in the dark—and even after the incredibly intimate things they had just shared—she felt herself blushing. "No," she murmured. "I—I don't hate this. I mean, I don't find you physically detestable. I mean—"

He laughed. She wasn't sure if he was amused or if the sound was entirely ironic. His lips touched hers again briefly. "Welcome to camp life, my love," he murmured. "My fair, sweet cavalry wife!"

He rose from the bed. "You need to dress quickly, Christa. I want a bath, but not one filled with rose-scented bubbles. The men might find it difficult to take me seriously if I smell too sweet."

He lit the lamp on his camp desk. Soft light flooded the room and Christa looked away from his nakedness, but he quickly drew his trousers back on and walked to the flap of the tent, lifting it to call to Nathaniel. Christa dived beneath the covers as he did so. She opened her mouth to warn him that she needed some time, but the words died in her throat.

There was something in the bed. Something very warm and furry. Something that moved.

She shrieked out, jumping from the bed. Jeremy stared at her, astounded.

"There's something hairy in there! That moves!"

"Thank God it isn't me!" Jeremy murmured, then ripped the bedding aside. Christa gasped again as two little creatures leaped up, flew from the bed to the ground, then raced wildly in opposite directions, finding the way out at last. She stared in astonishment and horror. Jeremy was doubled over in laughter.

Her eyes narrowed. "What—"

"They were just two little polecats, Christa!" he assured her.

Polecats. They wouldn't have hurt her.

"Sometimes the men keep them as pets. Lots of Indians do—they eat them when they're done being entertained by them. They say polecat can be very tasty."

He was still laughing, watching her in wry amusement.

Ah, yes. The girl from the plantation. The foolish little spoiled creature.

"I was startled," she said coolly. "It will not happen again."

He must have realized that he had offended her. He slipped his arms around her and she was reminded that she had jumped up naked. "I rather enjoyed your reaction," he told her.

She pushed his arms away. "Your man is going to be returning any minute." Freed from his touch but not from his gaze, she hastily found the very plain and sensible dress with the split skirt she had chosen for their first days of travel.

"How *are* you feeling?" he asked her.

"Fine," she said curtly.

"No more sickness?"

"No."

"You can still barely tell," he murmured. "Except that your breasts are larger."

Christa swung around. "You are outrageous!" she charged him.

He grinned, boyish and very appealing at that moment in his trousers and nothing more.

"Colonel?"

He was called from outside the tent. Nathaniel had come. Jeremy quickly asked for new water for the bath.

"It was a bad one, Colonel, eh?" Nathaniel asked.

"Yes," Jeremy said simply. Nathaniel tipped his hat to Christa, then went about his business.

"What was bad?" Christa asked.

"Nothing. I don't want to talk about it."

She grit her teeth. "I'm here. I have a right to know."

"All right, maybe you should know. Never, never wander away alone. One of the companies from another regiment did so. And they were wiped out by the Comanche. Are you afraid?"

She felt weak.

"No," she lied.

"Well, you had better learn to be very afraid. Never, never go off alone!" he warned her.

"What about—your men?" she asked.

"My Yankees? A few were wounded." He relented and added, "No one was killed. Is that what you meant?"

"Yes," she said softly. "I'm—I'm very sorry for those who were!"

"Are you?"

"Yes." She turned to him, eyes blazing. "Don't you believe me?"

"Yes, I believe you," he said tiredly. Maybe he was being wretched to her because he was still haunted by the sight of all those men dead in the trench they had dug.

He turned away from her. Nathaniel called out again, and entered with two other men to empty the tub and fill it again with water heated over a fire. When they were gone, all tipping their hats to Christa, Jeremy climbed into the tub. He winced suddenly, touching his neck. "I was nicked!" he muttered. "Want to come over here and take care of it now?"

"No!" she muttered. But she came toward him, fascinated. She picked up the washcloth and dabbed at his throat. "An arrow came that close?"

He caught her hand. "A bullet, I imagine. That close—you were nearly widowed. What a tragedy."

"You're a fool," she informed him coolly.

"Be tender. Take care of it."

She smiled. "I will. I'll get Jesse and he'll give you a stitch or two."

He shook his head. "Scrub my back—and tell me more about the trip out here."

"Ask me nicely."

His silver eyes touched hers. "All right. Please scrub my back and tell me about the trip."

She smiled, and tossed the washcloth his way. "No!"

"All right, you little southern vixen," he warned. "Scrub my back or—"

"Or what?"

"I'll climb out of this tub, drag you back into it, and scrub yours."

She bit her lip, picked up the cloth, and gingerly scrubbed his back. She liked the feel of it.

She even liked the intimacy of it. It seemed like a good time to warn him about a few things. She talked idly about Washington and the train. Then she told him, "You have a Major Brooks in your command."

"Yes?"

"He has a wife."

"Lots of men do."

"She, er, she traveled with us."

"Tell me about her."

"Oh, I think she's going to be much happier telling you about me."

"Oh?"

He turned around, staring at her. "What's she going to tell me?"

"Well, she was being rather self-righteous, I thought. I think I said something about my God still being on the battlefields picking up lost souls, and she went huffing off because we weren't observing the Sabbath properly. And then she didn't like the fact that I was playing poker—"

"With Jesse?" he said sharply.

She sighed. "Of course with Jesse! Oh come, Jeremy, had you sent me with the Virgin Mary, I couldn't have had a more proper escort!"

She thought that he smiled. His dark lashes fell and he leaned forward. "Down a little. Did you win?"

"Pardon?"

"Did you win at cards?"

"Yes, as a matter of fact, I did. I'm a—"

"Cameron, yes," he murmured. "And Camerons don't like losing."

"I wasn't doing anything wrong—"

"Then you don't have anything to worry about, do you?" He leaned back suddenly, and he looked very tired. "Go on and find your brother. I've hired a woman, Bertha Jacobs, to come along with the laundresses specifically to help with whatever we might need. She and Nathaniel will be serving us a private dinner here tonight." He hesitated a minute. "I saw your brother coming in. He's leaving in the morning at the same time we pull out from this camp."

Christa felt the blood drain from her face. Suddenly, she could care less about Mrs. Brooks. Jesse would be leaving her. Tomorrow. She stood up, and hurried from the tent, anxious to reach him, to hold tight to every minute they had left.

Jesse had to go home. He had a wife and children. She had borrowed him for as long as she could.

She wasn't going to be able to bear to watch him go.

They had a decent dinner, Jeremy thought. He and Jesse had become good enough friends, and Christa was always on her best behavior when she was with one of her beloved brothers. Weland stopped by for coffee which Christa had made herself over a fire after the meal. He smiled, thinking of her screaming over the polecats, then tilted his hat down, watching her. She was very sensibly dressed for the plains, no frills, just comfortable, durable cotton. Her face was flushed as she worked over the fire, and he felt a peculiar pounding in his heart. She would succeed. He could mock her all that he wanted, she would succeed. Even in the wilderness, as simply accoutred as nature deemed wise, she would still be beautiful.

If only he could reach her.

Jesse was watching her, too, Jeremy realized. And Weland was watching Jesse.

"I promise you, Jess," Weland said, "I will see to it that Christa has care almost as tender as that you'd give to her yourself!"

Christa, startled to be the sudden subject of conversation, looked up. "I wasn't worried," she said. Was she lying, Jeremy wondered. What woman wanted to have her baby in the wilderness?

But Christa stood, walked over to Jesse, and set her hands upon his shoulders. "Dr. Weland, I helped deliver my last little nephew and my niece too. Jesse and Daniel were still—" She broke off.

"At war," Jesse finished for her. He caught her eyes and patted her hand. She offered him a tender smile. One that dazzled. Were she to look at a lover that way, Jeremy mused, he would be smitten for life.

Were she ever to look at him that way . . .

"She won't mind labor," Jeremy heard himself saying. "She will mind the urge to scream, right, my love?"

The look she cast him was one of daggers. "My husband is so concerned!" she murmured.

"Your husband is very concerned," he said, rising. "And that's why I'm going to insist on you getting some sleep. We break camp tomorrow. It will be a hard ride."

Her eyes widened. "But—"

"We'll have time in the morning," Jesse said, rising too. "Christa, you do have to get some sleep."

"Jesse, Dr. Weland, may I offer you brandy and cigars beneath the stars?" Jeremy suggested. He caught hold of Christa, drawing her unwilling figure to his. He kissed her on the forehead. "My love, that way you may retire undisturbed and at your leisure!"

She cast him another look with eyes of shimmering blue fire, but Jesse kissed her good night and Weland thanked her for the delicious coffee. The three men then walked beneath the stars, seriously discussing the western question. Jeremy was sorry that Jesse was going to leave; he liked his brother-in-law more and more and felt he had very intelligent attitudes about the Indians and the western expansion movement.

When he returned to his tent, Christa was curled up in bed. He didn't know if she pretended sleep or not, but he quelled the urges the very sight of her created within him. It had been a long day for her. Tomorrow would be longer.

He kissed her gently upon the forehead and let her sleep.

The day began with rain.

The bugle sounded with the dawn and men were quickly up and preparing to ride, breaking down the tents, packing the equipment. All of his and Christa's personal and household items were packed into the ambulance he had outfitted for Christa to ride in when she chose. It was soon packed with their trunks, with his hunting guns, with his dress saber, with pots and pans and lanterns. There was a long bench where she could sit and where they could carry wounded men, if need be. The regiment was outfitted with several other ambulances, and the men who had been wounded in the Indian skirmish on the plain would ride in one of them.

He wasn't sure he trusted Christa with wounded Yankees just as yet!

He was busy that morning, but if he hadn't been, he would have found some way to stay away from her. She breakfasted alone with Jesse. They had several hours together. But still, the time came when they had to part. The regiment was ready to go west.

Jesse was ready to start the long journey back east.

Jeremy found them by an oak tree, and so he stood in the drizzling rain watching as she said good-bye to Jesse. She clung to him and he held her tenderly in return. There were no words between them. Maybe they had all been said already. Christa's eyes were closed. Her face lay against her brother's chest. At long last, Jesse pulled himself away from her. She wasn't crying. The effort not to do so was etched clearly into her face, and the sight of her trying so very hard not to give way to tears was far more heartbreaking than had she shed buckets of them.

Jesse's eyes met Jeremy's over Christa's head. "We have to go, Christa," he said quietly. She nodded. She still didn't release Jesse. Jeremy walked to her at last, taking her by the arm. She was wooden as he pulled her to him.

He offered his hand to Jesse Cameron, and Jesse took it. "Take care of my sister," Jesse said huskily.

"I certainly intend to look after my wife," Jeremy replied with a slow grin. "Give my best to *my* sister, and Kiernan and Daniel."

"I'll do that. You know, you will always have a home in Virginia," Jesse said.

"I know that, and I'm grateful," Jeremy told him. "I know we'll be back, for a visit at least, soon enough."

Jesse nodded. He reached out and lifted Christa's chin. "I'll see you, Christa. Take care now."

"You too, Jesse."

He nodded. He stroked her cheek one last time, then turned to walk away, a tall and striking man with his dark hair graying slightly at the temples, his posture straight and sure. Christa watched him for a moment.

"Jesse!" she cried out. She broke free from Jeremy and went running after him. He swung around, caught her, and hugged her one last time.

Then he set her firmly upon her feet. He said something to her and she nodded. Jesse walked on. She waved from where she stood.

She had never looked more forlorn. She stood very straight, her shoulders squared. Her chin was high and her eyes were damp. Her fingers were knotted tightly at her sides.

Jesu! He wanted to go to her, to put an arm around her in comfort. But she didn't want him now. He was the damned Yank who had brought her out here.

"We have to go, Christa," he said firmly. "Will you ride Tilly, or do you wish to start out in the ambulance?"

She didn't answer him. She was still staring after Jesse.

"Christa!"

She swung around. "What!"

He repeated his words. He had wanted so badly to be gentle, but there was a terse note to them now.

"I'll ride Tilly," she said. She started to walk past him. He caught hold of her arm. She stared at him furiously, and he saw that she was still fighting tears. "You take Tilly, you stay behind the front of the line, do you understand me?"

"I'll do—"

"You'll do as I tell you!"

She wrenched her arm free and saluted him sharply. "I'll do as you tell me. Now leave me be!" she hissed. He let her go.

She did not want his comfort. With a sigh, he strode down the line of horses and men until he reached his own mount. He yelled to the bugler to call the men to their horses. In a moment, he was swinging up on his horse. He had a hand lifted in the air. It fell, and the long column began to move.

He rode back, seeking Christa.

She sat upon Tilly, watching Jesse mount his horse to ride in the opposite direction.

"Christa!"

Jeremy called her name.

She looked at him, then spurred her horse and cantered by him.

He followed her to very near the front of the line. She fell in as he had commanded.

She didn't look at him.

But neither did she look back again.

Eleven

Christa did not have much time to brood over Jesse's departure during the next three days. The rain that had begun that morning continued to plague them, and she was quickly initiated into the cavalry life full thrust.

She rode the first day on Tilly until even she was exhausted, but the regiment was not stopping to camp for the night until they reached higher ground. So she traveled on in her ambulance for some time, watching the pots sway over her head, a lamp and kettle dance, and Jeremy's dress saber clash against the edge of the canopy. There was a litter of crying pointer pups in the wagon with her, along with their mother, Pepper, and she amused herself for a while trying to keep the pups quiet.

She became bored after a while, and the constant sway and jiggle of the ambulance felt even more miserable than riding, so she took to Tilly again. She saw Jeremy briefly, barely recognizable in his rain gear. He was telling James Preston that it was amazing to be able to cover over fifty miles in one day when he was riding with one company, but not quite manage to make ten when he was riding with the whole of the regiment. He seemed neither impatient nor frustrated, and she realized that he was very accustomed to this way of life.

She was not, but she would become so.

She scarcely saw him that first night. It was nearly dark when they stopped for a meal. They had reached high ground and the order was given not to pitch the tents, they would move out with the dawn. Men slept on their saddles.

Christa slept in the ambulance—tossing about as she listened to the whining puppies. She wondered if Jeremy's determination to drive the men so hard had been to avoid her. Since she had said good-bye to Jesse, he hadn't seemed to want any part of her. Thinking about it, she tossed and turned all the more. He must truly be regretting not just his marriage, but his determination to bring her out here.

The following morning was a wretched one. She had hardly slept; she felt as if she were twisted up like a pretzel. She didn't see Jeremy, but Nathaniel directed her with his slow beautiful speech to the creek nearby so she could wash, and he brought her coffee and some bread and porridge from the main mess pots. It was barely light before they started off again. She rode Tilly and kept abreast with Lieutenant James Preston, Celia's young husband. He told her stories about the territory they were traveling, about the Indians in general, and then cast her a quick glance, apologizing profusely.

"It's all right!" she assured him. "I'm here—I need to know things."

He shook his head. "I don't tell Celia anything. She is afraid of her own shadow. I'm very grateful that you've befriended her so. She's already having a horrible time of it, back in her ambulance."

"I'll see to her," Christa told him. She rode back down the long column, moving along slowly in the endless drizzle until she reached Celia's ambulance. She tethered Tilly to the vehicle and spent time in the wagon with her. She was heartily entertained. Celia knew many of the northern officers who were little more than names to Christa. She had Christa laughing with her stories about George Armstrong Custer, the brash young cavalry officer who had given Stuart such a nightmare of a time at Gettysburg.

"He is much, much more attached to his hounds than he is to poor Libby!" Celia laughed. "I've heard she can scarce fit in bed with all of his pups!" Then she sobered suddenly. "How unkind of me!" she said in horror.

"Oh, Celia! She's not about, and I don't intend to repeat a word. And we have to get through all of this somehow, don't we?" She grit her teeth as she finished, for they had hit another horrible rut in the road and the ambulance swayed so precariously that she was afraid they were about to go over. "Ugh!" she said, making a face for Celia. Celia smiled wanly, but Christa told her a story about burying the family silver while planting tomatoes and she had Celia smiling again in a few minutes. When the rain stopped, Christa left Celia's ambulance and rode along behind it with Nathaniel for a while.

By the end of the second day, they had traveled twenty-two miles. They set the tents up that night, but Jeremy never came to theirs. At midnight Christa still lay awake, oddly miserable that he did not come. She closed her eyes and told herself it was because no matter what, it hurt to feel unwanted.

They left Camp Creek at dawn, and managed to travel nearly fifteen miles. The rain had stopped. They encamped by another beautiful creek and there were wonderful wildflowers everywhere. Christa took a walk into one of the open fields beside the array of army tents. She was picking something with delicate little bulbs when she sensed someone behind her. She turned, and nearly screamed.

Two Indians stared at her. The man wore pants that looked like old army issue clothing, but the woman wore a loose buckskin dress with intricate embroidery. The man said something, and she shook her head, looking toward the camp. She had been warned not to wander away, but she had done so. Now she was facing these two Indians. The man spoke again, thrusting what he held in his hands toward her. Her heart started hammering.

"Two bits," the man repeated insistently.

"He wants you to buy his berries," she heard. She swung around. Jeremy had come up behind her. His hands were on his hips, the low slant of his hat covered his eyes. "Two bits?" he said to the Indian.

The Indian nodded, and said something in his own language. Jeremy replied, then produced the right coin from his pocket, and the Indian woman hurried forward with the basket the man had been carrying. The pair turned around and disappeared across the field.

"Did they frighten you?" Jeremy asked.

"I—no, I just—"

"They should have," he said curtly. He looked in the basket. "Dewberries. I told you not to wander off!"

She swallowed hard. "They were—Comanche?"

He shook his head. "Choctaw. They're a very civilized people."

"Then I had nothing to be afraid of."

"But you didn't know that. You wouldn't know a Comanche from a Seminole."

She stiffened. "But I will know the difference," she told him. "I learned to plant cotton, McCauley. I can learn to know one Indian from another too." She lifted her chin and walked back toward the tents, leaving him standing in the field. He didn't follow her.

That night she met Bertha, who was a plump, wonderfully pleasant Irish woman. She'd lost her husband back home years before to the potato famine, then she had lost two sons to the war. Now she was traveling to Santa Fe where her grandson was just starting a family of his own. She was a cheerful soul, a great believer in the will of God, and Christa was grateful to know her.

Later, Nathaniel brought her a freshly shot quail. "The colonel took her down, Mrs. McCauley. He says he's bone tired and hungry as a wolf. He'll be finished for the day in about an hour, and if you don't mind, he'll have dinner with you."

Christa was certain that Jeremy could care less whether she minded or not. She was being put to a test tonight.

She smiled sweetly. Did Jeremy have the audacity to think she'd never had to pluck a chicken before?

She smiled. "Thank you so much, Nathaniel."

"If I can help in any way—"

"Just get me a good fire started, if you'll be so kind. I'll manage from there."

She did manage. There were several cows among the animals trekking along with them, so she had fresh cream for the berries. She spitted the quail and seasoned it with their supply of salt and pepper. There were large bales of potatoes that the cooks had bought from the Cherokee encampments down the trail, and so she peeled and sliced and boiled them along with some salt and pepper and butter. By the time that Jeremy returned, she had finished cooking and eating, and had left his meal on his desk, covered by a silver tureen. She'd even seen to it that a glass of wine sat before his place where she'd folded the napkin elegantly. Determined to ignore him, she gave her attention to her journal, describing the prairie around them and the Choctaw who had sold her the berries.

She felt him staring at her when he came in, then he inquired, "Aren't you eating?"

"I've had quite enough, thank you."

"Who cooked for you?"

She looked up at him, her brow arching high. "I cooked myself. If things aren't to your liking, however, you shall certainly not offend me if you choose to take your meals elsewhere."

"I could eat horsemeat right now," he told her, and sat, throwing off his hat to land at the foot of their bed. She pretended to continue giving her attention to her journal, but she glanced at him now and then. He was hungry and he ate quickly. But all the while that he ate he was sketching on paper. He pushed his plate aside when he was done, not giving her the least attention.

She rose at last and cleared away his dish, washing it in a bucket of fresh creek water Nathaniel had brought. "Is there anything else you'd like?" she asked at last, annoyed. He could have said something.

She continued to stand there. Finally he looked up, frowning. "What is it?"

"Nothing."

A half smile curved his lip. "I'm sorry. I didn't realize that we had been gone so long you might crave even my Yankee company."

"I don't," she informed him coolly.

He watched her for a moment. "Then go to bed. It's going to be another hard day tomorrow."

"And you're making them harder and harder because of me, aren't you?" she demanded.

His brow hiked up in surprise. "Actually, no, I'm not. I just want to get settled in at Fort Jacobson before we start hitting really bad weather. And before some fool out there has a chance to cause us some really serious Indian problems." He looked back to his paper and began writing again. Christa clenched her teeth together and moved past him. Keeping her back to him, she changed into a warm flannel nightgown and curled into bed. She hated to admit it; she was exhausted.

She was also confused and hurt. He hadn't said a word about any of her efforts, and he'd made no effort to come near her. Not that she wanted him near her.

But she did. She wanted the comfort of being held.

She stayed awake awhile, but then her eyes closed and she slept. When she was very deeply asleep, she began to dream that she was being very gently kissed and caressed. Slow, sensual circles were being drawn over her back, lusciously brought to her buttocks, her hips, her belly, her breast. Sweet wet whispers touched her earlobe, her nape, her throat. She woke up, startled, and very aware that she wasn't dreaming because he had thrust within her from behind, and was not so gentle anymore but making love to her with a raw, wild fervor. Her fingers curled over his, holding tight, while the storm thundered. He went taut, then slackened. His arms remained around her, but she sensed that he lay awake. She wondered why she was so determined to keep something of herself from him. Maybe it was just all that she had left.

His temper was somewhat better in the morning. He rode with her for a while, pointing out some abandoned Indian huts as they passed them, reminding her again that the tribes could be very different. Here they often lived in these huts with land about them that they cultivated, growing potatoes and beans and corn and other vegetables.

"Soon, we'll be on the plains. You'll see some of the tepees of the nomads."

"Nomads?"

He glanced at her. "The Indians who follow the buffalo. In winter the buffalo go north. We'll still see them now along the trail we're following."

He hesitated, then continued, "And the Comanche usually only travel just so far north. Their territory tends to be Texas down to Mexico, west into Arizona and New Mexico."

"You all talk as if the Comanche are the only Indians you worry about."

Jeremy smiled, glancing up at the sky as if he weighed its color. "Oh, no! There are lots of Indians to worry about. Apache can be terrifying. The Sioux can be extremely fierce. But when we get to Fort Jacobson the Comanche will be our nemesis. They are noted for being some of the most savage warriors ever to ride the plains." He reined in his horse, pointing across the landscape. "There are more Choctaw homes over there. They're bringing in some of their harvest, see?"

She nodded, seeing the neat little row of huts, the Indians busy in their fields.

"Choctaw," she murmured. She felt him watching her, but when she turned to him again, he was already looking forward once more.

"I'm riding on ahead. I want to make up some mileage today."

They rode hard that day, and she fell into bed exhausted that night. Very, very late, he woke her again. She didn't mind because it meant that she slept held in his arms.

It was clear and beautiful, growing slightly cooler, the next day. She rode with Jeremy for a while and with James for a while, and spent time with Celia in her ambulance. She was coming to know a few other wives. In those first days she became very aware that they talked about her all the time, and she became very aware of certain attitudes. Some of them were fascinated by the very fact that Colonel McCauley had plucked her off a southern plantation. Some of them were glad that the war was over and anxious for peace. Some of them were bitter, and, Celia admitted, hated her for being a Confederate. "Just as you hate the Yankees," Celia told her.

"I don't hate the Yankees. I don't hate all Yankees," she amended. She sighed. "One of my brothers was a Yankee all through the war."

"And then, of course, there's the colonel!" Celia said, a touch of awe in her voice. "Any of them who have anything to say at all are just as jealous as can be. He's such a handsome man with that thick red hair and those piercing silver eyes of his! And you are beautiful, Christa, you must know that, and you're both so wonderfully brave and full of life!"

Christa blushed. She wondered what Celia would think if she knew the circumstances of their marriage. She bit her lip, tempted to confide the truth, then determined not to do so. She didn't want any of the wives within the regiment to know that they were anything but the absolutely perfect couple.

That night when they camped on the Sans Bois, she walked down to the water and looked across it. The land was beautiful here, very green. It was very broad, and the area was deeply forested, which made her wonder about the name given the creek. With twilight falling, she felt a sudden, fierce twinge of nostalgia. She fought the urge to cry, the desperate yearning for home.

Jeremy came upon her. His hands fell on her shoulders. "We're about forty miles from Fort Arbuckle," he told her. "We'll be into buffalo territory soon."

She nodded.

"What are you thinking?" he asked. His voice was soft, his whisper near her ear.

"I was thinking that this particular area right here reminds me of home."

He was silent, and for a moment she didn't realize that her words had sounded like a reproach. His hands fell from her shoulders.

"It won't for long. The prairie can be dry, the grass scruffy, and when the buffalo come stampeding over a ridge, you'll know you're west and far from home."

He left her there. She stared after him and felt a fierce pain suddenly stab into her heart. Despite herself, she remembered Celia's words about him. Yes, he was a striking man with his deep russet hair and unique, silver-and-steel eyes. Besides the appealing cut and angle of his face, there was the broadness of his shoulders, the strength and heat in his arms, the taut ripples in his belly, the tightly compacted muscles of his buttocks and . . .

She straightened her shoulders, trembling suddenly. She had to be so very careful! But suddenly she wanted to talk to him and tell him that she didn't mind so much being away from home. She missed Virginia, God help her, she missed Daniel and Callie and Kiernan and Jesse and her nephews and her little niece. But the West was wonderful. The flowers were beautiful. The Choctaw, the Cherokee, and the Creek were fascinating. She couldn't wait to see a buffalo or dozens of buffalo grazing on the plain. Things were new and exciting every day—even if they were frightening.

She hurried back toward the encampment, but when she reached their tent she found Nathaniel sorting papers on his desk. "The colonel went on to the headquarters tent, Mrs. McCauley."

"Oh." She hesitated. "I guess I shouldn't disturb him."

Nathaniel shook his head. "You'd be fine and welcome. He's just received some army dispatches from a messenger, a Captain Clark, whom he hasn't seen since the second year of the war. I'm sure they'd both welcome you."

She hesitated. Would he welcome her if he was visiting with an old friend?

She thanked Nathaniel, then walked idly through the tents to headquarters. Along the way she heard a group of young privates discussing the battle of Antietam, arguing over whether they'd won or lost. A little farther on, she could hear shrieks of female laughter, softly muffled.

A number of the laundresses were tending to needs other than that for clean clothing, she determined, hurrying on by. She wondered if Mrs. Brooks knew what went on when the men were at their leisure for the night. If she did, she'd demand that Jeremy get the whole regiment down on its knees to cleanse them of their sins.

A few minutes later she saw the grouping of the command tents, the medical tent next to the headquarters tent. With the weather fair, the large headquarters tent stood with its flaps lifted high, the night breeze moving through. Dr. Weland was there along with Jeremy and the visitor. Jeremy was deep in conversation with the man, but Weland saw Christa coming, said something softly, and the three men quickly stood.

"Christa, how nice of you to join us," Jeremy said. She didn't think that he was finding it nice at all, but she smiled and turned curiously to the visitor. He was tall and sandy-haired with a sweeping mustache and full beard. When he greeted her, she thought there was just the slightest hint of a southern slur to his voice.

"Captain Clark, it's a pleasure," she murmured.

"No, Mrs. McCauley, the pleasure is all mine," he assured her.

"Sherry, Christa?" Dr. Weland offered.

"Thank you." He poured her the sherry from a portable leather bar. She accepted it, taking the camp stool Captain Clark was quick to offer her.

"How are you finding the trail?" he asked her.

"Intriguing."

"She's quite a trooper," Weland said. "Mrs. McCauley is in, er, a family way, and still enduring all the rigors without a blink."

"Another baby, how wonderful!" Captain Clark said.

Christa frowned. "Another—?" she began, but Captain Clark was sitting back, tilting his head curiously "I hail from an area that's now West Virginia, and I would swear, Mrs. McCauley, that your accent is a Virginian one. But I remember distinctly your husband telling me years ago he was marrying a girl from Mississippi."

Christa's gaze shot quickly to Jeremy. She'd never seen him appear quite so tense or pale. His jaw was tense as if he were in great pain.

"I'm from Virginia, Captain Clark. Right from the heart of the Old Dominion." She sat back, still staring at Jeremy. "Darling, do you have another wife from Mississippi?" she asked lightly.

Captain Clark evidently—and far too late—realized the error of his ways. "Oh, I am so sorry. I beg you both, forgive me. It's just that—"

"It's all right, Emory!" Jeremy said, exasperated. He carefully controlled his annoyance, determined to make his visitor at ease once again. "I was to have married a girl from Mississippi. The fall of Vicksburg changed that. Christa is the queen of Virginia, Captain, beyond the shadow of a doubt. Perhaps you knew some of the same families?"

Jeremy was the one to start them comparing notes, Christa would remind him later.

At that moment though, he was hard put to curb his temper as the two of them leaned forward, talking a blue streak. Yes, they knew several of the same families. He had known the Millers, frequent guests at Cameron Hall. Kiernan had been married to Anthony Miller before he had died at Manassas, his younger sister and brother were still her charges. Emory talked about the dances, the estate, the sad shape of Harpers Ferry now that the war was over. Christa reminded him that at least the new state of West Virginia, established in 1862, didn't have a Yankee sent down by President Johnson to be governor of the state, and Emory laughed and told her that any governor would be a Yankee governor.

His Yankee jokes made her laugh.

They began talking earnestly about Reconstruction. "Of course, Lincoln meant to be far more magnanimous!" Emory declared. "Numerous members of Congress were furious when he so arbitrarily declared his will on the southern states. But dear Christa, you must remember! Many northern mothers lost their sons; wives lost their husbands. Some are very bitter, and yes, they do want the South to pay. What if the South had won, Christa?"

She sighed. "Don't you see? It was a cause! A bid for freedom—no different from the American Revolution! Had we won, we wouldn't have caused any hardship to the North. We'd have merely gone our separate way."

"It wasn't meant to be," he told her. "I don't even know why. There is something special, something grand, about this Union."

"You sound like my brother, Jesse," she said.

Weland was sitting back, watching the whole thing.

"Her brother fought for the Union," Jeremy explained, smiling over his grating teeth.

"One of them did, one of them didn't."

"They both came home?"

"Yes."

"You were very lucky."

"I know!" she said fervently.

Jeremy had had enough. He stood. "Well, we're riding hard tomorrow, and Emory will have a very long ride back to Fort Smith. We'd best call it a night."

Christa rose, wondering at the tone of his voice when he was the one who had so much explaining to do. Emory Clark leapt quickly to his feet, and Weland followed them all, rubbing his chin. Emory took her hand and kissed it, and told her what a pleasure it had been. He turned to Jeremy, saluting him and telling him he was glad to have him in the West, and very glad to be serving in a messenger capacity beneath him again.

Outside, Emory went on to his assigned quarters for the night. Weland tipped his hat, smiled curiously, and headed for his bed in the medical tent.

Jeremy took hold of Christa's arm and steered her toward their own quarters.

"It's amazing just how much you can like Yankees when you choose, Christa!" he told her. His escorting of her through the tent flap was much more like a thrust.

A lantern had been lit for them. Nathaniel, always seeing to their welfare, Christa thought.

She spun around, facing Jeremy. "Me? You have a problem stomaching Rebels, but apparently you were very fond of one in Mississippi. Why didn't you marry her? Did you change your mind? *Do* you have another child? What is it, Jeremy, a girl or a boy? Do you at least send the poor woman some sort of—"

She broke off with a gasp because he was striding toward her looking murderous. He paused just before he reached her, his eyes closed tight, his teeth nearly bared. She heard them grating. "Don't you ever question me about my past again!" he hissed, turning away from her, unbuckling his sword belt.

A trembling shot through her. She moistened her lips as he stared at her again. He had started this, not she. She just wanted the truth, even if she was going about it the wrong way.

"Then perhaps you should refrain from commenting on me!" she whispered fiercely.

He spun around to face her. "I wouldn't comment on your past. It's the present I couldn't quite help but notice! You might have been sitting on the lawn at Cameron Hall tonight, the queen-of-all-she-surveyed, the damned belle of the ball, flirting as if every swain in twelve counties was after her."

"How dare you!" Christa began, her voice low and throaty and dangerous. "When you've been running all over the South procreating!"

She cried out because he held her shoulders in an awful vice. "I have no children, madam. None. The lady is dead, the child with her. And I don't care to hear about it from you again, are we understood?"

"Yes!" she cried out. "Just let me go!"

He loosened his hold, and she wrenched herself away, turning her back to him. Angry, hurt, frightened, she found words flowing from her. Words that would hurt.

"I was trying to be pleasant to your friend!" she said. "And he was very much a gentleman. He might have been a Yankee, but he reminded me of—"

"Jesse?"

"No . . ."

"Who, dammit?"

"Liam!"

"Ah, yes! The wondrous Liam!" Jeremy said. He sat down on the foot of the bed and wrenched off his boots. "Well, that is one thing I can promise you. I will do my best never, never to remind you of Liam!"

He was usually so meticulous with his clothing, but tonight he nearly ripped every button from his cavalry shirt as he stripped it off. Christa moved away from him, unnerved by the depths of his temper.

She recalled the timbre in his voice when he told her that the Mississippi girl was dead. He loved her still, she thought.

"What the hell are you doing!" he snapped out suddenly. He was up, shedding his trousers, then standing naked in the lamplight, his hands on his hips.

Again, in the midst of all this anger, she thought of Celia's words about him. She swallowed, trying not to allow her eyes to roam down the hard-muscled length of his body.

"I'm keeping my distance," she murmured.

"Get in bed."

"I am not getting in bed with you when you're in this mood!"

Two long strides brought him across the tent before she could retreat further. "You're getting in bed with me no matter what my mood!" he informed her. He swung her around, undoing the buttons on her dress. She felt a trembling begin in her and she started to move away.

"I'll rip it into shreds," he warned, and she stood still.

"If you think—"

"I think I'm getting some sleep!" he announced.

He spun her around again, shimmying the dress from her body, then picking her up in chemise and pantalets and setting her down on the bed. He blew out the lamp on his desk and joined her.

She waited.

Waited for the touch of his fingers, for the heat of his desire.

They did not come.

An hour later when she knew that he slept while she was still lying there awake, she wondered if he dreamed of a dead girl.

And if he compared Christa with the sweet Mississippian of his past.

And if he didn't find Christa to be lacking in comparison.

He had been up some time before she rose the next morning. Nathaniel called her from outside the tent to warn her that they were nearly ready; the tent needed to be broken down, she needed to be ready to ride herself.

She started to rise, then stared down the bedding at her blanket.

There was a creature on it. A spider. Not just any spider. A huge, massive, hairy spider. Step by step it came crawling up her blanket.

She felt a scream rising in her throat. She fought it. The spider was moving slowly enough.

"Nat—Nathaniel!" she cried. It should have been loud. It came out like a whisper.

"Mrs. McCauley? What is it?" She could sense his confusion. He couldn't come bursting in on her. Then she heard him calling to someone, saying that something was wrong.

She was staring at the thing when the flap flew open. Jeremy burst back into the tent.

"Just stay still," he told her. He slipped a glove from his hand and slapped the thing from her blanket to the ground. He crushed it with his boot. She heard a strange crackling and popping sound and felt ill for the first time in ages.

She moistened her lips. "Was it—lethal?"

He shook his head. "It was a tarantula," he told her. "The bite can make you very sick, but it's seldom lethal. Are you all right?"

No! She wasn't all right! She hated spiders, especially big brown ugly spiders like that! She hated polecats in her bed, and most of all she hated feeling alone, the way that she had felt last night.

"Yes, I'm all right," she told him.

For a moment, she thought that he would come to her. Hold her. But he didn't. "Come on, then. Get up. We've got to move," he said softly.

Then he was gone.

She dressed quickly, fervently shaking out her clothes. Nathaniel brought her coffee. He tried to tell her that she might well have scared the spider more than the spider scared her. "They're really mighty curious creatures, Mrs. McCauley. They can build little trap doors for their nests that open when they leave and close tight when they come back. They spin webs finer than any silk cocoon you can imagine!"

"That's wonderful," she told him.

"I'll look things over real good tonight, I promise, Mrs. McCauley."

She smiled, then gave his arm a quick squeeze. "You're a godsend, Nathaniel. Thank you."

He managed to cheer her up, being so considerate and in a very good mood himself.

"We're out on the prairie today, Mrs. McCauley. Beautiful country with high plains and deep ridges. Wild things as far as the eye can see! We might even see a buffalo or two today."

"You think so?"

"I think so. If the critters haven't headed too far north by now!" he said.

Robert Black Paw came riding by. "Are you riding in the ambulance, Mrs. McCauley?"

"I think I'll take Tilly this morning," she told him, her hand over her eyes, shielding them from the rising sun.

He nodded. "I'll bring her up."

Robert was as good as his word. She had just finished packing the last of the overnight gear when he returned with Tilly, saddled and ready to ride. She didn't see Jeremy when they started out, but two hours into the day he rode back to her at last, tipping his hat to her.

"You've survived?"

"Yes, so it seems."

"If we don't come upon a buffalo we can take today, we'll take out a hunting party tonight. We'll stay close to camp, but we'll find fresh meat."

She nodded politely.

"If you're frightened because of the spider—"

"I'm not frightened," she said irritably, "and you needn't strain yourself to be nice because of a spider!"

She regretted the words as soon as they left her mouth. She bit her lower lip, but it was too late. He tipped his hat to her. "If you'll excuse me, then . . ."

He galloped on ahead, moving to the front of the ranks.

It wasn't much after that that Nathaniel rode back to her. "There's been a buffalo spotted up ahead!"

"Really?"

She started to ride forward with him, but then she suddenly felt a curious shifting in the ground.

It came again and again.

She saw Nathaniel's dark eyes widen. "God above us!" he whispered.

Then someone else shouted out. "It ain't a buffalo! It's hundreds of buffalo!"

"Jesu!" came a cry. "Jesu—stampede!"

Twelve

"Stampede!" someone yelled again in warning.

The earth didn't tremble—it shook.

Christa knew the feel of cannon fire and the feel of shot. She even knew the feel of the earth when hundreds or thousands of men were marching over it.

She had never felt anything like this. It was as if the whole world was giving away. The noise of it began to rise. It had started off sounding so low that she had barely heard it, and then it grew and grew. It was becoming a whirl, a cacophony of rhythmic pounding, a force that knew no bounds.

She was so absorbed with it that she was startled when Tilly suddenly reared high, letting out a snort of terror. She just barely brought the horse under control, her eyes meeting her husband's. "You!" His finger leveled at her. "I told you not to be riding in the front!"

"I—" she started to argue, but she could see them coming now, just over his shoulder.

They were horrible, they were magnificent. They came in a wave of brown and black, in a cloud of dirt and earth they kicked up in their frantic run. They looked like a swarm of locusts descended upon the plain, except that they were massive. Such strange creatures! Their heads so large, their shoulders huge, and their legs seeming so spindly to hold that bulky weight! But hold it they did. The creatures raced. Their great heads downward and butted forward, they ran with amazing speed and amazing dexterity. Beneath them and around them the earth continued to move. Great billowing clouds of dirt and dust rose and rushed before them, around them, and in their wake.

Indeed, they had changed the very landscape! It had been a simple plain, dry and dusty, with tufts of grass here and there, low, lonely foliage, and a blue sky overhead. The plain ran flat except for a ridge here and there, such as the one they stood on. Undulating only slightly, with that soft roll beneath the sun and blue sky, the place had seemed secure, serene.

Until the buffalo had begun to move.

More dangerous than any storm, more merciless in their mindless rush. The sky had turned gray; the sun was gone. The sound was becoming deafening.

Nothing could move them! Christa thought. Nothing could stop or move them. And anything caught in their path would be brutally, horribly crushed and broken beneath them. A man or woman would be left in torn and bloody pieces.

She moistened her dry lips, her eyes wide when she glanced at Jeremy again.

He wasn't in awe of the creatures—he was angry with her. Sitting atop Gemini—the well-trained cavalry horse who had carried him through the duration of the war—he rode with his customary easy grace, barely aware of the animal beneath him. This was his command.

The massive animals charging toward them were his concern.

"Get back!" he ordered her, his eyes blazing silver. "All the way back where you were told to ride!" He turned from her, a yellow-gauntleted hand raised to the whole of the company behind them.

"They'll be over the rise in a matter of minutes!" he called. His arm was moving in a circle, ordering the company back against its left flank. "Major Brooks! Hold the lead steady here, I'll bring in the rear. Not a horse, mule, or beast forward!"

He nudged Gemini and the experienced war horse moved forward. Christa hadn't had a chance to move; she had that chance now. Jeremy caught hold of Tilly's reins. He pulled her along behind him as he rode down the length of the ranks, shouting out his orders. Christa felt like a punished child, being dragged along.

But she also felt the keen edge of fear. All around her the noise of the stampede grew. Hundreds and thousands of buffalo were coming their way, climbing over rises, dipping into valleys. The air was already filled with dust and dirt, and the earth continued to tremble and shake as if it would disintegrate at any moment.

They galloped down the line of the men. Jeremy was making no attempt to move the whole of his column of men, horses, and wagons. Instead, he lined them in a narrow band just beneath the butt of the ridge, hard to the left flank. At the tail end of it, he released her reins, jumped down from his horse, and lifted her from Tilly. He thrust her toward Robert Black Paw, who, with Nathaniel, was helping calm a pair of mules.

Robert took her instinctively. "Get her below the ridge!" Jeremy commanded.

He leapt back up atop Gemini. Christa pulled from the Indian's hold, dismayed by the fear that surged through her. "Jeremy—"

But he had turned his horse and was riding hard down the line again at a full gallop.

"What's he doing?" she demanded miserably.

"He's going to see that the lead animals steer clear of our line," he told her.

"He's going to go out there? In front of them? That's insane! He'll be killed." She started to struggle.

Robert Black Paw held her back. "No! Come, Mrs. McCauley, down below the ridge."

She had no choice. Robert Black Paw dragged her stiff body down beneath the knoll of the rise and close against it. She was sheltered here from the swirl of dust and dirt. But the noise of the buffalo's pounding footfalls seemed all the more increased. Horses were screaming now in panic; the men were shouting, trying to hold them, to calm them.

Jeremy continued to ride straight toward the stampeding herd.

"My God, let me go! What is he doing! He's got to come back!" she cried, struggling against Robert.

He held her politely, but firmly. Robert Black Paw took his orders from her husband well, Christa thought bitterly. If he'd been shot dead, he'd die holding her tight!

But he was a good man, too, she knew. And if his hold was rigid, his words were gentle and reassuring. "He knows what he's doing. He's ridden these trails before."

"He's not a rock! A buffalo will crush him—"

"Watch!"

Robert pointed a finger past her nose. Over the ridge of earth at her side she could see the path that the buffalo were running. Their narrow line offered the buffalo a wide path. They were beginning to arrive, with just a few of the strays edging to the side. Then she saw Jeremy. At the least, he wasn't alone. Two of his officers were with him. They were waving brightly colored blankets and making almost enough noise to be heard above the stampede.

Christa's heart seemed to fly to her throat. One of the massive creatures had veered Jeremy's way. To her astonishment, Jeremy started to ride down on it, hard, headed for a collision.

A cry escaped her.

But at the last moment the creature turned and ran toward the clear path, and those behind it followed suit.

She sank back against Robert. She hadn't felt ill in a long time now, but she was suddenly afraid she was going to lose everything she had consumed for the last two weeks.

She heard a shot and jumped in panic, leaping away from Robert.

"What is it? What's happened now?" she cried out.

Smiling, Robert Black Paw set his hands on his hips. "There'll be fresh meat for supper tonight, Mrs. McCauley. Your husband brought down one of the last of them." He hopped up the short distance to stand atop the ridge again. He reached down a hand to her.

As she crawled atop it, the world around her seemed to be split by a cacophony of noise once again.

The buffalo were gone. The earth was still trembling slightly, as if the aftermath of some great cataclysm. The buffalo were still running, but far past them now. In their wake gray dirt and dust followed them like a windstorm.

Closer to her immediate vicinity, the noise was caused by the pick-up measures necessary after the stampede. One of the wagons had fallen over and a group of soldiers was righting it. Some of the horses had run off and Jeremy was now giving orders to men to go after them. The columns were re-forming. Sergeant Jaffe—Jeremy's favorite among the company cooks—was busy supervising men over the buffalo carcass.

Robert Black Paw, his duty to her ended, was leading a pair of mules and a wagon back onto the trail. Jeremy was still riding around giving orders. Christa saw that Tilly had held her head and remained nearby, and was now eating up little pieces of grass from the stampede. Christa caught hold of her reins and mounted her horse. She cantered over to the buffalo.

She felt sorry to see the great creature down. Close up, the head seemed even more ridiculously large in comparison to the body. Except that its eyes were tiny in that huge face, and part of the reason the head seemed so big was that it was covered with shaggy fur. Alone and downed it didn't seem such a menace. A streak of pity danced through her. It was an ugly beast, but in some curious way it was beautiful, too, by simple virtue of its magnificent size and power.

"Now, don't go feeling sorry for it, Mrs. McCauley!" Sergeant Jaffe told her. "Rations can get mighty lean out here, and the way I see it there ain't nothing like starving through winter! God put these creatures out here to feed us all. Don't you go turning up your pretty nose at buffalo meat!"

From her seat atop Tilly, Christa shook her head. She could have told him that she had watched a whole nation almost starve, but she kept her silence.

"I'm sure the meat will be wonderful," she murmured. "It's just—rather sad, for some reason!"

"Yes!" Jaffe said, cocking his head toward her. "It's always sad to see something so damned strong brought down. Don't know quite what it is myself, but I understand what you're feeling." He grinned. "Still, when it's either him or me, then I'm mighty glad it's him!"

She shivered suddenly, inching Tilly toward him. "Sergeant Jaffe, do stampedes happen often? We must be moving more deeply into buffalo territory and—"

"Don't you worry your pretty little head none, Mrs. McCauley. We keep our eyes open. It's strange though. You can ride up on a ridge and see a few buffalo grazing on the plain just as nice and peaceful as can be. Then you can see one or two of them running and you don't know if you've come across a couple of strays, or if you'll have a couple hundred thousand racing at you in a matter of minutes!"

"I'm sure my wife will rest well after that!"

Christa swung around. Jeremy had come up behind them. His hat was low over his head. She couldn't see his eyes. She was certain that he was still angry with her.

After last night, she felt as if a wall had risen between them, higher than ever before. Upon occasion, it had seemed as if they just might broach the barriers between them. Now those barriers seemed more insurmountable than ever.

On top of that, she thought wryly, she had disobeyed his orders to ride behind the front of the line.

She tore her gaze from his, determined to ignore him. He'd have his chance to chastise her as soon as they were alone.

Jaffe was apologizing profusely. "Didn't mean nothing by that, Mrs. McCauley, except that we keep our eyes open and our ears to the ground."

Jeremy led Gemini close to the fallen buffalo. "How are we going to make out with this one, Sergeant?"

"Right fine. We'll have buffalo stew and buffalo steak! Dried buffalo and smoked buffalo! We'll make out right fine. Good shot, Colonel."

"Thanks. See to it that my wife has some tender cuts. We've got a general riding in with an escort of officers, and I think we'll do a little private entertaining in my tent. And if you don't mind, Sergeant, she might need a little instruction. We'll be laying over for a few days, making camp, so you'll have some time tonight to deal with the kill. So will my wife."

Christa felt a soft wave of color touch her cheeks. He was making it sound as if she were the most worthless of fluttering belles. How could he! He knew damned well she'd managed with all manner of meat and meals before. The war had taught her an amazing array of crafts. She'd done just fine with his quail.

But then again, "the general" was arriving? This was the first she had heard of it. What general? Captain Clark must have brought the message that someone was coming.

What in God's name made Jeremy think she was about to entertain any Yankee general? She had done exceptionally well, she thought, living with Yankees up to this point! She'd been polite, she'd even been friendly with Celia and James, Robert Black Paw and Nathaniel—and Captain Clark.

Jeremy didn't intend to give her any explanations now. He wagged a finger at her. "You'll ride at the back, with Robert at your side. If you don't, I'll take Tilly and set you into an ambulance and that will be that. Do you understand?"

She saluted him sharply. "Yes, sir!"

Gemini pranced forward. Jeremy adjusted his sweeping cavalry hat. "You are quite all right, I take it?"

"Fine."

"Then perhaps you'll be so good as to see to some of the other wives. Celia is shaking like a leaf, they say, and her husband is at his post."

"Yes, sir, Colonel, sir!" she responded. Jeremy didn't give a damn about her sarcasm. He didn't care how she obeyed his orders, just so long as she did. But the sarcasm in her reply was not lost on Sergeant Jaffe. He looked at her rather sorrowfully when Jeremy rode away, convinced that his order would be obeyed this time.

"I'll make you a cloak out of this here hide!" Jaffe told her. "Why, you just wait and see! It'll be the most wonderful warm thing you've ever owned, Mrs. McCauley."

"That's very kind of you, Sergeant," she told him. She didn't know if he meant the words or if he was just trying to make her feel better.

She smiled, waved a hand to him, and rode from the scene of the buffalo kill. Jeremy had asked her to see to the other wives. She cantered along the line until she came to Celia's ambulance. The young girl was shaking away and her husband, at her side, was looking very helpless, loath to leave her.

Christa dismounted and came to the rear of the conveyance. She offered Lieutenant Preston a reassuring smile.

"Celia, look who's here. Mrs. McCauley."

Celia released her death grip on him at last. Lieutenant Preston leapt down from the ambulance, thanking Christa with his eyes.

"Celia, come on now!" she said. "It's all over!"

"It was terrible!" Celia moaned. "Why, the ambulance almost turned. I saw your husband—oh, how could you bear it!"

"It's all right now, Celia, I swear it!" her husband said.

Christa was startled by the tug of envy that touched her. Preston was so tender, so caring of his wife!

She gave herself a mental shake and reminded herself bitterly that it was all right for Celia Preston to be a fluttering little female. She was a Yankee.

"Celia, come now!" she said impatiently, as her husband strode for his horse. "It's over!"

"Oh, Christa!" Celia said miserably, "I'm such a failure. He shall hate me!"

Christa sighed. She assured Celia she was no failure. Then she told her what a marvelous meal they would have that night. "And we're making camp for a few days, Jeremy said so. We'll be stationary for a few days. It will be fun!"

Celia was slowly mollified. Christa rode down the rest of the line seeing to the other ladies, but by then, though many had been shaken, they were all fine. Mrs. Brooks informed her that the Lord worked in mysterious ways against those who did not properly respect him. Christa smiled sweetly, her face feeling like wood, and told the woman that the Lord had chosen to protect them all from the buffalo—and to supply them with buffalo stew, so perhaps they were all respecting Him properly after all.

They made eight miles that day. Christa rode in the back of the line with Robert as she had been ordered. She wanted to hate the journey, she was so angry with—and admittedly hurt by—Jeremy, but it was difficult to do so. The landscape was still so different from anything she had ever known. With the buffalo gone, the sky was incredibly blue once again with just a shadowing of puffy white clouds against it. The land seemed so barren, but little flowers grew here and there. The day remained pleasantly cool, their path unobstructed, and the ride was not a hard one.

When the spot Jeremy had chosen for their camp was reached, a young private took Tilly from Christa, promising to rub her down well.

The men, busy and competent, immediately started to raise the tents. Christa wandered over to where Sergeant Jaffe was making supper for the hundred and twenty-three men in the command. He talked to her about the value of good seasonings and gave her a sip of buffalo broth. It was sweet, she thought, but good. The taste was like beef, but different. It had more of a wild, gamy taste to it, but still the sweetness was inviting. Perhaps this buffalo was a little tougher than some of the steak she had had, but in the end she decided she liked the taste very much.

"It'll be stew in a matter of minutes, Mrs. McCauley. We'll have a big dish over for you and the colonel soon enough."

"That's very kind of you."

He shook his head. "I never did understand much how the officers' wives felt so obligated to cook for their husbands when there's so much food being prepared for the enlisted men."

"Well," Christa pointed, "because sometimes the men do cook at their own fires."

Someone cleared his throat behind her. It was Nathaniel. "Mrs. McCauley, your tent is up. Since we'll be here a spell, I've seen to the arrangement of your belongings to the best of my ability. I hope you'll be satisfied. And I've taken the liberty of bringing in the hip tub for you. Some of the boys are boiling water and filling it now. We figured that a lady like you—what with the buffalo dust and all—might be wanting a bath."

"How very, very kind of you!" Christa told him. She walked to him and took his hand, shaking it. She smiled at him as well. "How very thoughtful and gracious you all are to me! I should be learning about the tents and doing these things myself."

"We're always so proud of our cavalry wives, ma'am, braving buffalo and dirt and Injuns! We don't mind a bit what we can do," said Sergeant Jaffe.

"Well, I'm afraid I'm not much of a cavalry wife!" she admitted. "But I thank you both from the bottom of my heart. Nathaniel, a bath!"

His grin split his dark face handsomely. "Come, Mrs. McCauley, I'll show you to your tent."

"Mrs. McCauley!" Jaffe called after her. She turned around.

"You're wrong, you know. You make a right fine cavalry wife!"

She smiled. "Thank you."

Nathaniel led her to her tent. It was pitched some distance from the field of smaller tents, yet not far from some of the larger tents that had been pitched for Jeremy's officers. She was also quite near one of the large supply tents.

Maybe that had been done on purpose, she thought, if Jeremy was entertaining a general. Who? she wondered.

Then she ceased to care. Nathaniel had opened the flap to her tent. She cried out with a little sound of delight.

He'd fixed it beautifully. Jeremy's camp desk and her own smaller one had been set up on opposite sides of one of the structural poles. Their bed had been set up and made with the sheets and blankets arranged in a very inviting way. Their trunks had been set conveniently by the bed. Brandy and whiskey had been set out, and even the boxes with her china and silver had been thoughtfully supplied, ready if she should need them to entertain.

Best of all, a tub sat in the tent and the water that rose from it was definitely steaming.

"Bless you, Nathaniel!" she cried, clapping her hands together.

Again, he smiled broadly. "Someone will be near, Mrs. McCauley. You needn't worry about being disturbed." She flashed him a smile of gratitude. He disappeared outside the tent.

Christa thought of nothing but the heaven the water in the hip tub would offer her. She quickly stripped off her blouse and chemise, and then her boots, riding skirt, and pantalets. She shivered until she sank into the water. The heat wove its way into her tired muscles, feeling wonderful.

After a moment, she sank all the way in, soaking her hair, allowing the water to close over her head. She came up, eyes closed, reaching awkwardly for the trunk near the tub where her soap and cloth and the vial of her lavender-scented shampoo had been left.

Her hand came in contact with something that she hadn't expected. Flesh.

She sat back, her eyes flying open. Jeremy was standing beside her. It was his hand she had touched. She stared at him balefully.

It had been such a beautiful moment for him to interrupt.

"My, my! You do have a knack for finding luxury, my love. Even in the wilderness."

She ignored his tone. He was going to yell about the fact that she had disobeyed his orders. She didn't give a damn. She wasn't wasting her hot water.

"Would you hand me my shampoo, please?" she said icily. "And then if you don't mind . . . ."

He dropped down beside her, the vial in his hands. He poured out a portion into his palm. She pursed her lips, staring forward. A second later, his hands were moving in her hair. She closed her eyes. The movement was gentle, mesmerizing. She didn't want to enjoy it, but she did. She closed her fingers over the rim of the tub, clenching them. Then they eased their grip.

And just as soon as she was at ease, he spoke. "You pull a stunt like that again, and I'll take your horse away from you. You'll spend the rest of the trip in your ambulance. Do you understand?"

Her eyes flew open. "I'm not one of your men, Jeremy McCauley. I'm here under duress. And you're not acting like this because I was too close to the front of the line. You're still furious with me over last night. I—"

"All right, Christa. Yes, I'm still angry over last night. But you're truly a little fool if you think that has anything to do with my determination to keep you safe. You'll do what I say!" he told her sharply. "I'm not writing home to tell your brothers that you were mauled by buffalo or picked off by a Comanche scout, his arrow having found your heart since it was right there in perfect shooting range!"

She ignored him, sinking into the water once again to rinse her hair. It took her some time. When she came up again, she realized that he had stripped off his boots and cavalry jacket and that he was undoing the button at his shirt's cuff. Her eyes went wide with amazement. "You're not coming in here."

"I am."

"Then—"

"Nathaniel used to see to my needs. But now he and the others are always running themselves ragged to tend to the needs of my fragile little bride. I want some of that water while it's still hot."

She gripped the edge of the tub. "You're not doing this!" she whispered vehemently. "You always think that you can yell and scream and snap out your orders and then just—just do whatever you want with me! Well, it doesn't work that way. It—"

She broke off for a moment because he hadn't paid her the least heed. He had stripped naked and was striding the few feet toward the tub. For a moment she was taken aback by the sight of him, even though she had seen him hundreds of times.

He was startling to look at. His flesh was so bronzed. His movements were so supple. Quick, silent, powerful. His easy strides belied the knots of muscle that formed him, the breadth of his chest and shoulders, the tautness of his hips and belly, the bulge of his arms and rock hardness of his thighs and buttocks. She felt as if the water suffused with heat all over again just because he approached it.

"Jeremy, I'll get out—"

"The hell you will," he growled.

And he was behind her, his back against the tub. He pulled her back against him as some of the water sloshed over to the ground. She felt his chest and his hair-roughened legs. And between them, just teasing her back and buttocks, his sex.

"You'll get nothing from me—" she began.

"I never get anything from you, Christa," he said flatly. "Worrying about your mood doesn't result in a hell of a lot. But rest your sweet head. At the moment, I want the warmth of the water. You, my love, are like hugging ice, and I think I may be too weary for such an encounter tonight."

She stiffened. He ignored her, finding the soap and sudsing the washrag between his hands before her eyes. "Let's get back to where we were. I won't have you disobeying orders."

"Me!" Miserably torn between comfort and agony by his hold, she bit her tongue. "Of all fool things to do, you go racing right at a buffalo! Riding into the things, for God's sake! It was—"

She broke off.

Suddenly, he went tense behind her. "It was what?"

"It was foolish!" she charged. "You might have gotten yourself horribly trampled!"

He was quiet for a moment, then she felt the warm whisper of his breath as he spoke softly near her ear. "I'm the officer in command. It was my duty to see that the fool creatures turned away. And I do know what I'm doing. I've been out here before. But how nice. It sounds as if you might have been concerned."

"Of course I was concerned!"

"Why? If I had been trampled, you would have been free. You could have returned to your beloved Dixie and your precious Cameron Hall."

"What an awful thing to say!" she charged him, trembling. "How could you?" she whispered. "After all the years of death and destruction I witnessed, how could you even mock me so!"

She whirled to face him the best she could within the confines of the tub, his chest, and legs. There was nothing to be seen in his gray eyes other than speculation. One dark russet brow was slightly raised, and there was a curious, small curl to his lip. For a moment she remembered him riding out, reckless, fearless, precision perfect in his uniform, rugged and striking in his appeal. They were so intimately close. Warmth spread through her. She'd always admitted he was a handsome and appealing man. He had courage, and his own sense of honor. She'd never really realized until this moment that she admired him very much. He was many things, daring, bold, determined, sometimes reckless, but always aware of his responsibility for others.

No, he was not Liam. In many ways, he was very, very different.

She was coming to care about him. Deeply. She didn't mind him so much anymore. Not even his intimacies. Being with him grew more and more exciting. The men admired him very much. The women sighed when he passed by, and envied her.

Maybe, if he just hadn't been such a diehard Yank?

"Do I take that to mean that yes, you would have been distraught had anything happened to me?"

"Oh, stop it!" she murmured, twisting around, suddenly very anxious to be free of him. She tried to rise but his arms wound around her bare midriff, pulling her back down against him. She felt his fingers beneath the fullness of her breasts and she was startled by the streak of sensation that swept through her.

Her heart was beating hard as he pulled her closer against him.

"It was a terrible thing for me to have said, Christa. I'm sorry," he told her.

She didn't reply right away. He was idly running his fingers over her midriff in the warmth of the water. To her amazement, the feel of those fingers shot through her. It seemed to sizzle and burn its way right to the apex of her thighs.

She tried very hard to ignore the growing heat within herself. "It was horrible," she murmured softly. "And you might discover that I am capable of understanding things when you explain them instead of just bellowing out orders! If you could just be polite upon occasion—"

"Polite!" he murmured, his whisper very close to her ear, his tone amused. He seemed to think it over. "Well, I have considered it upon a number of occasions."

"And?" she persisted.

He moved his cheek gently against her temple. The warmth flamed more deeply within her. The gesture made her feel both very comfortable and stirred.

"Do you remember the very first time we met?" he asked her softly.

"Vaguely," she said. "You were ready to hang my brother. You were looking for Callie. What does this have to do with being polite?"

"I wasn't ready to hang your brother. I had to find out what had happened to my sister. Now—"

"You were a Yank deep in Rebel territory." She reflected on that for a minute. "Definitely an idiot," she told him frankly.

"Maybe. Callie is my only sister. We were always close. But that's beside the point. The very first time we met, you were ready to shoot me."

"Daniel wouldn't let me," she said regretfully.

She felt his smile.

"Let me see," he continued. "I think it was the same occasion when you left the dinner table simply because I was at it."

"There was a war on," she reminded him. "And we might have all been shot as traitors for entertaining you."

"Jesse was there."

"It was his house."

"Not during the war."

"What is your point?" she asked him, not really seeking an answer. For once, it seemed nice just to be with him. His touch upon her was easy, light. She felt secure in his arms, almost like a sleek cat being very nicely stroked. She closed her eyes. Maybe it was a time of truce.

"The point," he said, and again the hot whisper of his words touched her earlobe, sending little shivers down her spine, "is that there was always something between us."

She shifted slightly, smiling incredulously. She wanted to see his eyes. They were very silver. Amused. Tender. "The fact that I wanted to shoot you meant that there was something between us?"

His smile deepened. He nodded. She arched a perplexed brow, but eased back against him when his arm encircled her, pulling her back. "Anger, hostility—but sparks. Anyway, once in a while, I've wondered what it would have been like if I'd met you before the war."

Callie hesitated a moment. "Perhaps, if I hadn't met you as the enemy you would have been quite tolerable."

He laughed. "But then again, I might not have been all that tolerable. I can just imagine the type of occasion when I might have met you. Your brothers and I never met at West Point, but just say we could have. Jesse might have brought me home for one of your big barbecues. There would have been fellows all over the place, just tripping over themselves to get near you. Daft fellows with stars in their eyes. They would have been begging for dances, dying to bring you some punch, standing on their heads just for one little smile."

"Jeremy—"

"And there I would have been. Some poor farm boy from Maryland!"

"McCauley, we never judged any man by his money—"

He laughed, his knuckle running over her cheek. "No, I'm certain that you didn't," he assured her, and she bit her lip, pleased, because he seemed to mean it. "But you're not seeing the picture I'm painting! All those fine young strapping fellows! They would have all been as nice as was humanly possible! And you would have twirled every single one of them around your little finger. You would not have listened to a word any of them had to say. You would have thumbed your nose at any one of them who might have even thought of telling you what to do! And they would just have kept on being nice, begging and pleading and falling in love like a pack of fools—and never, never once managing to get you to do a thing by being polite!"

She shifted again, meeting his eyes. "Well, you are mistaken, Mc-Cauley!" she said with her nose just a bit in the air. "I always responded politely in return—"

"You were nice as can be—and went about doing just as you damn well pleased. I can't always afford to be nice, Christa. And heaven help me, I certainly can't afford to act like those poor boys so mesmerized by your beauty and your smile!"

"We didn't meet before the war—" she began.

He interrupted her with soft, husky laughter once again. "If we had, Christa, you wouldn't have given me the time of day!"

"If you had been nice—"

"I would have loved being nice," he whispered. "Very, very nice . . ."

His lips touched her damp shoulder. His teeth slightly grazed it, his tongue bathed the region. His kiss moved closer to her ear. Little rain-drops of sensation danced through her flesh. She gripped the rail of the tub tightly. His palm was fully against her breast now. Cradling it. Tenderly cupping its weight, the center of his hand going round and round her nipple.

Her breath caught.

"Jeremy, it's not even supper yet," she breathed. "Sergeant Jaffe is sending buffalo stew. It's even light out. It—"

"It will wait," he told her. "Believe me, no one will disturb me now. Robert Black Paw is aware that I have joined my wife at her bath. If the Comanches raided, he would fend them off."

Perhaps the last was an exaggeration, Christa wasn't really sure.

And she wasn't sure in the least if she cared. She was always fighting him. This afternoon she was weary of the fight.

And she was so very aware of the way that she was feeling. Sweetness and fire seemed to pervade her to the depths of her soul. She was amazed that the tip of his tongue could create such havoc all through her. She didn't mind just lying back, feeling his arms, feeling his caress.

She felt his arousal hardening against the base of her spine, hotter than the water, exciting. She closed her eyes, catching her breath. She wanted him. She'd felt the sweet promise before. Now something golden and wonderful seemed to stretch before her. He had made comments enough about her refusal to give in to him.

Maybe this time it would be different.

She closed her eyes. He was stroking her, his touch sliding through the water, down along the flesh of her inner thigh. Closer and closer to intimate places. Touching her there. She froze, afraid to breathe, then exhaled in a gasp. She heard a soft groan behind her. He buried his face against the wet hair at her nape. "This is wonderful, but I think my body is breaking." He balanced her weight and stood, crawling from the awkward tub before reaching down to sweep her up, dripping.

"Do that again," he murmured.

Her arms locked around his neck as he held her. "Do what?" she whispered.

"Sigh. Softly. As if you wanted me too."

Color touched her cheeks, and he laughed. There was something different in his expression. Something anxious and pleased as he watched her.

She lowered her lashes. A drop of water came trickling down the center of his chest. She wanted to lean against him. Taste it with her tongue. Panic seized her suddenly. She couldn't surrender to him, no matter how sweet the feelings. Her distance was all that she had left of her pride and heart. Daily, she forgot more and more the look and feel and texture of Liam's face.

And daily, she came to discover more about Jeremy and his feelings toward her. He must have resented her heartily when he had married her. He had been in love before. He had been expecting a child. She'd been a southern girl, so he must have loved her very much. And he must surely lie awake beside her at times, feeling that bitter disappointment with her that he did, and wonder why God had chosen to take the woman and the child he had wanted, and saddled him with Christa and her baby.

"I . . . there's so much we need to discuss," she said.

"There's suddenly so much to discuss?" he said, laughing. "I don't think so. I don't want to talk," he said, walking her over to the bed. He pulled back the blankets that Nathaniel had so meticulously prepared for them.

"Jeremy, Nathaniel spent a lot of time—"

"Nathaniel would certainly forgive me," he said, lying her down flatly. His kiss touched her upper breast. Then covered the fullness of it. Amazing sensations began to seize hold of her. His tongue licked over her

nipple. She clenched her teeth so as not to cry out. Her fingers fell into
his damp hair. "It's—daylight still. Jaffe is coming. Because of the general. Remember, a general is coming!"

"Umm."

Maybe he knew just how close to surrender she was at that moment.
Maybe he even sensed that she wanted him. Really wanted him at that
moment, for the first time. He didn't intend to be dissuaded.

His tongue skimmed down the valley of her breasts, rimmed her navel.
An ache was burning between her thighs. She was dying for him to touch
her.

In anguish, she pulled upon his hair. "Jeremy!"

He came up against her. His smile was sensual. The silver gleam in his
eye was wicked. Luxuriously lazy. "I can't believe it. My little ice maiden
so warm. Trembling."

She moistened her lips, shaking her head. His smile remained. He
stared at her mouth and then seized it in a sweetly savage kiss. She loved
the feel of his mouth and the taste of it. Loved the way that he raked hers
with his tongue, filling it, again and again. She was breathless when he
broke from her. Breathless and staring at him. Her hands were upon his
shoulders. She hadn't even realized it. She was stroking his arms. Her
heart was thudding at a frantic rate. Her nipples were taut and hard,
teased by the hair on his chest, delicate, taunting pinpoints against him.
She flushed, the length of her feeling the hard pulse of his arousal.

His knee urged her thighs apart. He held himself above her. She trembled with a surge of anticipation for the silver in his eyes, a fire unlike
any she had seen before. The feel of his hardened sex pressed against
her own was dizzying. "Jesu!" he whispered, both tender and urgent.
"Damn General Sherman! Were he due in ten minutes, my love, I could
not leave you now!"

He pressed his lips to her throat, thrusting smoothly into her body.

Sherman!

The name went off like a burst of cannon in her head.

"Sherman!" She gasped it aloud.

The feeling of desperate desire that had been so strongly aroused in
her slid from her like bathwater sluicing from her body. She braced
herself, trying to deny him. It was too late. She had so nearly been the
seeking force in this tempest. She clenched her teeth, twisting her head
to the side. Tears stung her eyes and she held herself rigidly against him,
not protesting, not even hating him, but becoming once again his ice
queen. She closed her eyes. In time she felt the hardness of his constriction, felt his body tense rigidly from top to bottom. The warmth from him

spread into her and she bit her lip, longing to run her fingers through his hair, to cradle his head.

But he had uttered the enemy's name.

"Sherman?" she repeated coldly.

He groaned, falling wearily to his side. Damn. What an absolute idiot he had been. So seduced and so enchanted that he hadn't even thought of what that name meant to her, he had spit it out just as if he were one of her prewar beaux, tripping over his own tongue in his desire for her.

He'd come so damned close!

"Jesu, you couldn't have waited to discuss this?" he demanded irritably.

"*You* brought up that name!" she cried, coming up on an elbow.

But he didn't look at her, and he didn't seem to care to have her staring at him either. He rose angrily and walked back to the tub and used the water to strenuously wash his face. When he was done he grabbed her towel and wiped his face and body and began to dress impatiently. Christa watched him, her anger growing.

"Sherman?" she said again, her teeth grinding.

He buckled his scabbard on, swinging around to meet her. Oh, God, no. This was going to turn into another battle. A serious one. He should have been more prepared.

Sherman hadn't gone into Virginia. But that didn't matter. He'd come through her precious Confederacy and had definitely done severe damage.

Dear Lord, he didn't *want* to hurt her and he did understand her feelings. But she was going to have to deal with them. She was going to have to accept the man. Sherman was his superior officer and they were both military men. He had no choice but to entertain the man when he came to the camp.

"Sherman," he said flatly. He didn't dare give her even an inch of leeway.

"As in William Tecumseh?" she demanded.

"The very same."

She leapt up, heedless of her nudity. She flew at him, slamming her fists furiously against his chest. He caught her wrists. She grit her teeth. "You expect me to entertain General Sherman?" she nearly screeched.

"Dammit, Christa, you should be used to Yankees by now!"

"Yankees, yes!" she spat out. "But not Yankees like Sherman! He ravaged the South! He raided it, raped it, destroyed it. He made women and children starve and freeze—"

"He fought an all-out war to win. He had a 'scorched earth' policy and

Thirteen

Jeremy didn't return to his tent until it had grown very late.

Sergeant Jaffe had seen to it that his buffalo stew made its way around the camp and so there was no reason for him to go hungry. He ate with Celia and Jimmy Preston, then made his escape because Celia couldn't say enough about his prowess against the buffalo and Jimmy just couldn't quit shaking his head with wonder at the magnificent way Christa could handle herself in any situation.

For a while he walked along the river, glad of the spot he had chosen for their camp. There were two things the army needed when they camped for a stay of any duration—water and grass. He'd found both here in abundance. The river ran strong and pure here, surrounded by endless plains where the grass was deep green, rich, and abundant.

It was beautiful out here. The air was dry and cool, the horizon seemed to stretch for miles while mountains rose in the distance. It was a rougher place than his home, perhaps. Maryland was so very green, shaded with blues and purples. Out here, the landscape was tinged with earth hues, golds and tans, deep burnt oranges and scorching reds.

This was Comanche land, he reminded himself. He was in Buffalo Run's territory. It could be as wild and savage as the Comanche themselves, and as strangely beautiful.

He paused, listening to the run of the river at his side and looking back at the low burning fires of his camp. A sentry saluted him and he saluted in return. Fourteen men were on guard watching the perimeters of their camp. In four hours they would switch with others. They were spaced fairly tightly together, and they were wary.

Jeremy had been warned by his superiors at Little Rock that Buffalo Run was on the warpath.

But he knew Buffalo Run. He had met the Indian when they had both it worked. And he did his damnedest to give Confederate General Joe Johnston the best surrender terms possible. He was called a traitor by Stanton for the terms he tried to offer—"

Christa could hear him. "How dare you!" she gasped. "How dare you even think that I will entertain that man."

"Because you're my wife, that's why!" he thundered. "I am the commanding officer here and you're my wife!"

"No! I won't do it."

"You will!"

"I won't!" she vowed, breaking his hold on her. "You can't expect this of me! I've done everything that you wanted. But I won't, I mean it, I won't have Sherman to dinner!"

"You will." He reached out for her, bringing her hard against him. His fingers were taut, he was shaking her and her hair tumbled down her back. Tears stung her eyes and she began to laugh.

"I will not do it!"

"Jesu! You will!"

"You can beat me black and blue—"

"I'm not beating you!"

"You're damned close!"

He stopped. He stared at her, his eyes silver and narrowing like daggers. He swept her up and deposited her back on the bed. "Damn you!" he cried. His eyes swept over her and he inhaled sharply. "And damn me for a fool!" he added. He turned on his heels and left the tent behind him.

been quite a few years younger. Buffalo had not yet risen to become the great war chief that he was today. He had just been one of Gray Eagle's many sons, a handsome Indian, sleek, lean, as cunning as a fox, as strong as a bear.

Jeremy would never forget the first occasion he had met the Comanche. Cavalry and Indians had met in a skirmish just north of the Texas borderline. The cavalry had been doing well enough, until their commander had realized that they were running out of ammunition.

They had made a break for it. Jeremy had been bringing up the rear. They'd raced long and hard, losing the majority of the Comanche following in their wake. But then Jeremy's horse had suddenly and silently dropped beneath him and Jeremy had gone plunging into the dry dirt. Before he had much managed to catch his breath, he'd been attacked by a man like a five-armed creature out of hell.

He'd managed to dislodge the knife that nearly slit his throat from the Indian's hand, but the fistfight that had followed between them had gone on endlessly. It had felt like hours.

They very nearly killed one another, but when the sun went down they were both still breathing. Jeremy looked over to see that the Indian had closed his eyes. He picked up a large jagged rock and came up on his knees, ready to strike the weapon against his enemy. For some reason he held still, unable to kill such an enemy in such a way.

He dropped the rock and began to walk away.

It was a good thing that mercy had tempered his decision. The Indian opened his eyes. The two of them stared at one another for a long while. Then Jeremy felt a creeping feeling at the nape of his neck. He turned.

Around them were grouped five Comanche braves who had come for Buffalo Run. Jeremy was certain that he had breathed his last. His scalp tingled.

But Buffalo Run called out to them and stood slowly and painfully. He spoke again and someone trotted up with a paint pony. The pony was offered to Jeremy. Hesitantly, Jeremy took the reins, still staring suspiciously at the Indian.

"You can go, white man," the Indian said in well-enunciated English.

Jeremy frowned, surprised by his excellent English, and more surprised by the mercy he seemed to be receiving.

"Just like that, I can ride away?"

"I am Buffalo Run. Remember my name."

"And if I mount this horse and turn my back to you, I will still live to remember your name?"

"You would be a dead man now if I chose it so. Maybe you will even choose to understand. We are raided, and so we raid. Our lands are ceded to us and then snatched away, so we seek to take them back. You fought a brave battle. You would not kill a man who could not see his death. You will not die by my hand, white man. Ever." He suddenly extended his buckskin-clad arm, then pushed up the sleeve. Jeremy stared in fascination as one of the other young bucks brought up a sharply bladed hunting knife. Buffalo Run slashed his arm deeply and offered it up to Jeremy.

Jeremy had heard of the custom. Blood brothers. It meant they would fight no more. He took the knife and ripped up his cavalry sleeve. Buffalo Run's slash had been deep. He made his equally so, looking at the Indian, taking great care not to flinch even as he felt the pain. He melded his arm to Buffalo Run's.

"Go back. Tell them to leave me in peace."

"They will not believe that a Comanche seeks peace."

"Tell them anyway."

"I will try."

"We will meet again."

Jeremy didn't think so. The rumble of war was already growing deeper back home—he knew that the government would start sending troops eastward very soon. He'd already determined that he'd do his best not to fight in Maryland or Virginia, but he knew he'd soon be sent back to a battle line.

He mounted bareback the paint pony he had been given. He didn't turn around. He knew that no arrow would pierce his back, no shot would be fired, no knife would fly.

As it happened, he did see Buffalo Run again. He was sent with a commission to visit Buffalo Run's father. Jeremy sat in the Comanche village, fascinated. He had come to know the people of many Indian tribes, especially the Cherokee, members of the "Five Civilized" Tribes! Their manners were gracious, their desire for learning was a deep thirst.

The Comanche were different. They were a warlike tribe, and the chief's tent was decorated with many war drums, across which stretched animal sinews that held any number of human scalps. Many were Indian scalps. The Comanche went to war against the Apache and other Indian tribes, as well as the white man.

Tonight, they were invited guests. No one commented on the scalps—few of them could. White men in the West were sometimes as quick to take them as Indian braves. There was also a rumor that the taking of scalps had spread west from the East—that the first white settlers had started the custom by scalping Pamunkey Indians. Jeremy found such a thought difficult to stomach, but in his heart he knew that he had met both white men and Indians capable of taking scalps, and so he could not discount the rumor completely.

Buffalo Run greeted him with a nod. He spent a day in the sweat lodge with Buffalo Run and his father and brothers and other cavalry, and he sat for hours around a fire listening to the singsong of the shaman's chants. The medicine man threw powders from his bag upon the fire, causing it to flare up. They drank some concoction the Indians had brewed, and Jeremy saw—as the Indians had suggested that he would— many things in the flames.

It was an interesting occasion for Jeremy. He knew that many white men felt the only good Indians were dead ones, but he had seen many commendable things even among the savage Comanche. They were a fiercely loyal people, protective of their own and fearless when they were threatened.

He inadvertently received a valuable lesson that night too. When the cool night breeze soothed his flesh after the hours of the sweat lodge, Buffalo Run told him that the Comanche had been watching. They had watched the tribes come west of the Mississippi. They had watched Andrew Jackson try to strip Florida of the Seminole, they had seen the Cree taken from Georgia. Then they had seen the white man lick his lips and try to shove the Indians ever farther west.

"None can be believed," Buffalo Run told him. When a white man sees an Indian village and destroys it, he tries hard to murder the children for they will grow to be braves. And he tries harder to murder the women, for they will carry the future generations."

"Not all white men!" Jeremy protested. He pointed out that Indians were known for equal cruelty. In fact, part of the reason they had come was for the return of a young Texan girl.

Buffalo Run told him that neither did all Comanche choose to kill young people. Young white boys could grow to be fine braves, and young women the mothers of fierce warriors.

His mother had been one. The white man had come to rescue her, and she had refused to leave Buffalo Run's father. "The choice was hers. She saw the two worlds, and she knew."

"I find your tribe admirable," Jeremy told him.

They parted that night, intrigued with one another. They met up one more time on the plain, right before Jeremy came home. Buffalo Run was amused. "They mock us that we are all alike, and that Indians make war upon Indians. Now you will go home and fight your brothers." He pointed to Steven Terry, a friend of Jeremy's from Alabama. "You will fight one another. Shoot one another. Take your swords and bleed one another."

"It doesn't give us any pleasure," Jeremy said. He felt forced to explain. "We are fighting for ideals. For the whole of our nation."

"You will band together, all you different tribes, on either side of a line. One day, white man, you should take care. The Indians might well band together too."

When he had headed back east, he had spent much of the journey thinking about Buffalo Run. He understood many of the things that the Indian had said to him. For one, the whites were always overestimating the number of Indians. Some chronicler had written down that there were twenty thousand Comanche in Buffalo Run's territory. There were, perhaps, four hundred.

But Buffalo Run had given him fair warning too. The Indians could band together. The Comanche could band with the Kiowa and the Apache and others, and then they would indeed be a powerful force. Perhaps the alliance could spread north and farther west. Navaho and Hopi could join in, and Cheyenne and Black Feet and Oglala Sioux.

Someday, if the Indians were pushed too far, it could happen.

But then Jeremy had come home. He'd had a long leave to be with his family. They'd all been home, he, Josh, Josiah, and Callie. There had been long sweet days when he had gone back to an earlier time, tilling fields with his brothers, listening to his father read into the night, even indulging in a food fight when they put together a picnic on the lawn, laughing when they'd all managed to miss one another completely and catch Callie right on the nose with a blancmange. She'd managed to pay back the lot of them with a meringue pie, and then they'd all been sorry that they lost out on dessert. Their father had indulged them, smoking his pipe, watching with knowing eyes.

They'd all been there to see Callie wed to Michaelson, beautiful in her white, and then they'd all been together one last time to say good-bye and then leave Callie all alone as they traveled off to join their companies in distant fields.

Their father had been the first to fall. Then Michaelson, then Josiah. Their losses had been great. Yet all that was behind them now. The war was over. Callie had found Daniel—or Daniel had found Callie. Men and women struggled to understand, to come to grips with the war.

Admittedly, some men struggled still to see the South pay for all that had happened. It was said that Sherman's men had gone into South Carolina with an especial vengeance.

Some Yanks, like Christa's carpetbaggers, would take advantage of the

South's defeat. Those in high political places would take their revenge against the men they held captive, like Jefferson Davis. Some Rebels would never surrender, like those he had heard were heading for South America to form a new Confederacy there. Like Christa herself.

He sighed, ready to kick himself again. He'd had her right where he wanted her. In so many things she was the dutiful wife, not because she gave a damn about being dutiful to him, but because she was determined to prove that a Cameron could do anything. She was an extraordinary cavalry wife. Hell, tarantulas hadn't sent her screaming, they had intrigued her. Buffalo hadn't brought about the first flicker of fear in her eyes.

She had faced Yankees. Nothing else compared to that ordeal.

She slept with him every night because she was his wife. She never protested his touch. But night after night he felt the passion simmering there, felt that she could be magnificent, that he had only to coax her surrender.

And that was it, of course, in a nutshell. Christa was not about to surrender.

Yet he had come so close. There had been a languorous look in her crystal-blue eyes. She had leaned against him so softly, she had sighed, moved so sweetly. The slightest smile had curved her lips, and even the promise that she might return the least of his desire had sent a near-maddened longing to his senses. He must have been insane. He had said the hated name. Sherman.

Dammit, he mentioned Grant's name all the time. He had served almost directly under Grant during most of the war, having been his aide-de-camp for a few months before he had been ordered directly to logistics. He talked about Sheridan. They talked about battles around the campfires sometimes, and Christa had never reacted so violently.

Maybe because his men were gentlemen for the most part, he thought, especially his officers. In all this time, there had never been a negative comment made about the Rebs. The North had won. His men were willing to speak the truth. The Rebs had been damned fine fighters and their leadership had been extraordinary. Jackson and Lee would go down in the history of military annals, just like Stuart with his magnificent, lightning cavalry raids. So many men were dead, blue and gray. It seemed the kindest thing was to offer them up a salute for their honor and let them rest. In her way, he thought, even Christa saw this.

Damn. He just couldn't wait until later to mention Sherman's name.

The fires were burning lower. The air was beautiful, but growing colder. He stared back at the camp. All was well. A horse whinnied from somewhere. The scene was peaceful.

Somewhere out there, he knew, Buffalo Run watched his movements.

And tomorrow he had Sherman and his party of officers arriving. It would be a very long day.

His set his jaw, his teeth grating. He was the ranking officer. He'd be expected to entertain Sherman. Christa would have to swallow hard and accept it.

But what if she didn't?

He determined that he'd best be prepared for the worst.

Jaffe, he thought, would be doing the cooking for the general's arrival.

He started back along the water, through the myriad tents of the enlisted men, and finally to his own.

Robert Black Paw, silent and nearly blending in with the shadows of the tent, saluted him and slipped past him. His vigil was over.

When Jeremy slipped inside, he found that she had doused the kerosene lamp on his desk, making it difficult for him to move about in the darkness. He would manage.

He crawled into their camp bed, wondering for a wild second if she would be there. Yes, of course, she would. Though she didn't know it, Robert always kept vigil, and if she had thought to go somewhere, Jeremy would have known it long ago.

No, she was there. As his eyes adjusted to the total darkness, he realized she was bundled from throat to toe in a flannel nightgown. She was as far to her side of the bed as she could manage and her back was to him. She was awake, he was certain. She was lying there too tensely to be asleep.

He leaned close to her. But before he could say a word, she whispered fiercely, "Touch me, and I'll scream until every man in this camp is awake!"

"My love, I am far too weary to touch you tonight. You should know that I don't give a damn if you scream until you're hoarse. In fact, princess, I have a word of warning for you. Be courteous tomorrow. Be courteous, or I will tan your hide. I will do so with an audience of dozens of men, and I will not care in the least what a single one of them has to say. Am I understood?"

"You wouldn't—"

"Dare. Yes, I would. But don't worry about your precious solitude this evening. My pillow offers far more comfort and warmth! But take care tomorrow!"

He turned on his own side. He didn't touch her. The inch between them lay like a great chasm.

General William Tecumseh Sherman arrived with a small party of officers and their wives, some who would now be joining Jeremy's ranks, and some who would be moving on with the general.

He arrived early and was greeted with a bugle salute. The men not on guard duty presented him with a show of their horsemanship.

Christa was not with Jeremy. He had slipped from bed while it was still dark to dress, and he had mounted his bay to ride out with James Preston to meet the approaching party as soon as the messenger had arrived to announce the imminent appearance of the great general.

He was an interesting man. A ruthless one in his way, Jeremy thought, but not an exceptionally cruel one, and certainly not cruel by choice. Like so many others, Sherman showed the wear of the war on his face. It was deeply lined, never a really handsome face, but now one with haggard cheeks beneath a full beard and mustache and with soul-weary eyes that looked upon the world with a weary wisdom.

He was accompanied by a Lieutenant Jennings and his wife, Clara, Captain and Mrs. Liana Sinclair, Captain and Mrs. Rose Claridge, and two bachelor officers, Captain Martin Staples and Captain Dexter Lawrence.

The younger women, Liana Sinclair and Rose Claridge, were both charming and sweet, if somewhat wide-eyed and ill-prepared for the rigors of the western roads. Liana giggled a bit excessively for Jeremy's taste, and Rose shivered every other minute. Yet both ladies seemed pleasant enough.

Clara Jennings, however, was a virago.

Jeremy had been in their company for not more than ten minutes before she had managed to complain about the ruts in the road, the dirty taste of the water from the streams, and the awful way they had been bumping along since coming into Comanche territory. Jeremy chanced a glance at Sherman and realized that the general was going to be overjoyed to leave the woman behind.

Through the presentations and ceremonies, Sherman was polite and cheerful due to the presence of the ladies. Despite a generally stern nature, Sherman could be a very polite and pleasant social companion when he chose to be.

But toward midafternoon, the ladies were escorted to their newly erected tents, and when he and the other officers sat around the field tent drinking coffee, he was much more blunt.

"Colonel McCauley, there is going to be trouble ahead for you. It's as clear as day, the handwriting is on the wall. Comanche."

"I've heard that Buffalo Run is on the warpath. They warned me about him in Little Rock. Has something else happened?"

Sherman waved a hand in the air. "A great deal has happened, sir. Some regrettable. Some, perhaps, unavoidable. Captain Miller, in charge of Company B of the Third, raided one of the Comanche villages. I understand that his men panicked and that it turned into a slaughter. It's been said that Buffalo Run promised retaliation. Now, you know my stand on the Indian issue pretty much, I think."

"Yes, I think I do, General." Sherman was a soldier, first and always. He didn't mind the Indians who behaved—those who bowed to the white decree and obediently went to live on their reservations. But he intended to be hell on those who were determined to go their independent way. Sherman knew that Jeremy felt far more sympathy for the Indians and the loss of their way of life than he did, although he didn't agree. From some of the things that Sherman had written and said, Jeremy was certain that he actually favored extinction of the tribes who continued to be warlike. Sherman was a man who tended to resent the point of view of another man, especially when it disagreed with his.

Lieutenant Jennings, the middle-aged man saddled with the harridan, Clara, made a sound and pointed his pipe at Jeremy. "Colonel, I believe I saw some of his work not an hour's ride from here. We couldn't detour much from our path with the ladies present, but I saw smoke rising and I rode out a bit. If I'm not mistaken, I saw smoke. I'm not sure where off the trail, but I'm sure that some mischief was afoot."

Jeremy was damned sure of it. He'd heard of Captain Miller. The man hated Indians, he'd had a brother killed in a prewar clash with them. Buffalo Run was sure to be on the warpath if one of his villages had been raided, if the innocent, women, children, and the aged, had been killed.

"I wish you had mentioned it earlier," Jeremy commented. It was too late to send his men out tonight. He'd send a party out with Robert Black Paw in the morning. If anyone could find the faint embers of a dying fire, it would be Robert.

"Gentlemen, perhaps we should retire for an hour. Sergeant Jaffe has taken it upon himself to create an excellent dinner, and I believe that Celia Preston is arranging entertainment. She determined to drag her spinet out to her husband's new post. We've also a fiddle player and some of our men are talented harmonica players. After everyone has freshened up, we can meet again at the officers' mess tent."

Jeremy rose and the others joined him, filing out. Sherman was watching him. "I look forward to this evening. It's my understanding that you have wed one of the most beautiful women to reside on either side of the Mason–Dixon line. I regret that I've yet to meet her."

Don't regret it! Jeremy thought. He smiled stiffly. "My wife is very beautiful. She is—she is with child. In the early stages, sir, but you know women and their moods."

Sherman laughed, rubbing his beard. "I know she's a Cameron, and a Rebel one at that. I imagine it will be a lively evening."

"Sir—"

"You mustn't expect too much of her, Colonel. It was a long, bitter war. Few people understand that I bear no rancor toward our southern brethren. A 'scorched earth' policy is the fastest way I know to win a war. It gave me no pleasure to hurt people."

"I know that, sir."

"I'll try to tell your wife," he said lightly, and winked. "But, yes, I think it will be a lively night!" He walked out.

You don't know how lively, Jeremy thought with an inward groan.

He hadn't gone near her himself all through the day, but he had asked James to see to her whereabouts now and then, and he knew that she had spent the day with Celia. She was in camp. Presumably, she would at least show up at the dinner table. He thought that he had made his threat strong enough for that.

When he returned to his tent to shave and change for the evening, she was nowhere in sight. She had been there recently, for the hip tub had been brought in for her use and the water in it was still tepid.

Whatever she intended to do to Sherman, she intended to do it clean, he thought wryly.

He hadn't intended to bathe, but the water was there, and so he made use of it, shivering when he rose—it wasn't quite as warm as he had thought and the night was growing chill. He dressed and shaved quickly, and came out in search of Christa.

Sergeant Jaffe stopped him, presenting him the full menu for the evening. They would begin with a buffalo broth soup. There would be a mixed vegetable platter composed of the yams and fresh greens they had purchased from the peaceful group of Choctaw the week before. He'd arranged for the best buffalo steaks. And one of the messengers had brought with them some strawberries from St. Louis last week, so they would be able to have a fine dessert with fresh cream.

"Very commendable, Sergeant."

"And we'll be eating on your wife's fine plates, sir," Jaffe said happily. "I think we'll do you proud, sir."

"I'm sure you will. She helped you today with her plates and silver?"

"Oh no, sir. She trusted us with the boxes. She's been busy with little Mrs. Preston all day. I'm sure they're planning a delightful entertainment for you."

"I'm sure," Jeremy agreed.

When he came past Jaffe, he nearly tripped over a dozen of the hunting hounds that accompanied the troop. He swore beneath his breath, then realized she was definitely getting the best of him.

He strode into the officers' mess tent. Nathaniel was in the corner, softly playing the fiddle. Officers in their finery were standing by their ladies, definitely decked out in theirs.

But there was no one there so striking or beautiful as his wife.

Christa was engaged in conversation with Jimmy and Celia. A delicate champagne flute was in her fingers, and he imagined that the glass had traveled with them from Cameron Hall.

Christa had eschewed her usual trail clothing for the most elegant wear. She was in a gown of rich blue taffeta with velvet and black lace trim. The gown had a slightly high collar at her nape, but the handsome edge work was cut low across the bosom. It hugged her upper body, and the skirt fell in elegant folds down to the ground, the rear caught up in a bustle at the back. Against the rich coloring of the gown her hair had never appeared more midnight black, nor her eyes so endlessly blue.

She had dressed for the occasion, he thought uneasily. She had drawn out her plates, her silver—and her own finery. Magnanimous. And frightening.

He strode across the tent, acknowledging the men and women as he did so. The company was not a large one. Tomorrow there would be an officers' picnic to which all the officers and their wives would be invited to meet the newcomers. Tonight was a smaller grouping, just the general, the newcomers, Lieutenant and Mrs. Preston, and a few others.

Christa's eyes rose to his. She studied him for a moment, her eyes grave, and he wondered what went on within her head. He tried to convey his own warning to her through his eyes.

Coolly, she looked away.

He came beside her, slipping an arm through his. "Evening, Jimmy, Celia."

"Colonel!" Celia always had a smile for him, even when she was frightened of something and her smile was wavering.

"Has he arrived yet?" he asked Jimmy.

"Just coming in now, sir."

Freshened, smiling, Sherman came through the entry, Lieutenant Jennings and Clara right behind him. His eyes fell instantly upon Christa. Naturally. He was intrigued with her.

Naturally. She was exquisite. Every man in the tent had looked her way.

"Ah, the elusive Mrs. McCauley at last!" Sherman said. He strode to them, ignoring the salutes of his officers. "McCauley, so here she is. No wonder you hide her. She is a treasure."

He reached for her hand and kissed it. Jeremy saw the blood drain from her face. She snatched her hand back quickly. "General Sherman," she murmured.

"I know of your brother, madam," Sherman said. "Men who should have died considered his skill a rare gift from God."

Her eyes narrowed. "Jesse is quite talented, sir. Have you heard of my other brother?"

"Daniel Cameron? Indeed." Jeremy waited. Every eye in the place was on the two of them. Tension rose. Sherman continued, "Time and again, Mrs. McCauley, we shook our heads at his exploits. Had he and his like but been on our side, the war might well have been won much earlier."

It was a gracious comment. Christa said nothing.

"I believe myself, General, that had Christa but been on our side, the war might have been won much earlier."

A burst of laughter rose. Christa still didn't reply, but the tension had been broken. Jeremy tightened his fingers around her arm. "Suggest we sit, madam!" he hissed to her.

She freed herself from his touch. Short of creating a disturbance, he could hardly pull her back.

"We need some dinner music," she said, walking over to Nathaniel and whispering something to him. Jeremy grit his teeth.

"Shall we sit?" he suggested himself.

As it happened, Christa was on his right—and Sherman was on her right. He was sure that Christa hadn't planned it that way—perhaps Sherman had. Sherman had been designated a seat beside Clara Jennings.

Maybe that was why his seat had been changed so that he was placed beside Christa.

Whatever the reason, Jeremy inwardly braced himself for the coming storm.

It arrived within minutes.

Sherman politely complimented the soup, and Christa assured him she'd had nothing to do with it. The subject of fine dining came up, and then the subject of dining on the trail.

Wine was served. A Bordeaux that they had carefully packed with them for special occasions. To Jeremy's surprise, Christa drained her glass immediately.

It was refilled. The men were serving them without a flaw.

"Mrs. McCauley," Sherman complimented Christa, "you have done remarkably well with practically nothing to work with here in the wild."

She was sipping her wine again. She smiled sweetly. "Well, I've years of training! I am a southerner, sir, very accustomed to doing the best one can with nothing! And even that nothing was so easily snatched away!"

"She should have been in the field," Jeremy said pleasantly, his fingers curling tightly over hers. Their eyes met. Christa flushed, snatching her fingers away.

Once again, silence fell over the table. Sergeant Jaffe and his crew served the main dish.

Christa's wineglass was refilled. She wanted to drain it once again. She was a Cameron. Southern belle or no, she had shared wine—and whiskey—with her brothers on plenty of occasions.

Since the baby, it made her ill. She needed it tonight. She couldn't do more than sip at it.

Jeremy asked the general to join him in a whiskey, and it was brought.

"Lord, but whiskey is in plenty out here in the wilderness! And to think it was not so long ago there were places we had none and soldiers screamed beneath the amputation saws!" Christa said.

It was shocking dinner conversation.

"She's so accustomed to her brother being a doctor!" Jeremy said, slipping an arm around her. His fingers threaded tightly into her hair. He smiled icily while turning her beautiful face toward his. "Beat you, eh?" he whispered softly. "I'm going to tan you to within an inch of your life!" he promised.

She smiled, gritting her teeth against the pain of his hold.

"Of course, it's true," she told Sherman sweetly. "We did survive much better in my part of Virginia than did those who lived off the land farther south. All of that deprivation, in comparison, makes the trail much, much easier to endure!"

Jeremy started to step into the breach, but inadvertently Clara Jennings did so.

"Well, I don't think that I shall ever be happy on the trail. The bugs! The rain. The terror of the Indians!"

"All trials the good Lord sends for us to endure, so that we see to the error of our ways!" Mrs. Brooks advised.

"Ah, well. The good Lord seemed fond of sending us southerners many trials!" Christa murmured, with a smile that seemed to make light of her comment. "We were ever afraid of Yankees invading, especially after having heard that our good General Sherman was on the march. Having lived with that fear so very long, I cannot worry too much about simple heathens like Comanche!"

"But as you said, you are a Virginian, Mrs. McCauley. I cut my path through Georgia and Carolina."

"We were ever in sympathy with our more southernly sisters!"

Her eyes were wide. Her tone was innocent. Christa knew how to cut to the bone. Sherman might long to strike her, Jeremy thought.

But apparently, the general had taken her on as a challenge. He leaned closer to her, speaking softly. "I swear to you, Mrs. McCauley, I fought a war the best, and oddly, the most merciful way I knew how. I offered generous terms of surrender. So generous that Secretary of War Stanton slandered me, calling me a traitor in numerous publications. I renegoti- ated with Joe Johnston as I was ordered, ma'am, but I was ever sorry that my original terms did not stand, for they were right, honest, and good."

Christa appeared just a little bit pale. Maybe Sherman had managed to touch something inside her.

"I'm a soldier, Mrs. McCauley, not a politician. It's to the politicians now to reconstruct state governments. It is to the sorrow of all good men when those chosen for such tasks do not prove themselves equal to them."

"Reconstruction is a bitter thing!" she said.

Jeremy stood, thinking that this company would be fool enough to stop him if he did set his fingers around her throat. He dragged her to her feet nevertheless.

"We've music. Shall we dance while the plates are cleared and dessert is served?"

The suggestion was well met. He pulled Christa along with him over to Nathaniel. "Nat, how about a jig on that fiddle for me, please. A lively dance tune."

Nathaniel nodded. A private who had been standing in the shadows behind the spinet piano stepped forward and took a seat.

The music was coming a little early. It didn't matter. Nat and the pri- vate broke into a lively rendition of "Turkey in the Straw."

Jeremy held Christa in his arms, whirling her through the song. Be- neath the cover of the music, he gave her fair warning once again.

"One more thing, Christa. Just one."

Her eyes were blazing. The wine was giving her courage. She tossed her hair back. "And what?" she challenged. She didn't let him answer but rushed on. "You had no right to do this! No right at all to expect me to meet that man—"

"He's been exceedingly gracious. He's made every attempt to be pleasant—"

"And that atones for what he did to my people?" she said incredulously.

"Christa, the war is over!"

He felt a tap on his shoulder.

Sherman.

There was nothing to do but relinquish his wife to the general.

He did so, then stepped back, watching the pair. They talked animatedly throughout the dance. What was being said?

The music ended. Sherman led Christa back to him. Just as she reached him, her back went very stiff.

The men were playing a new tune in honor of their guest.

It was called "Marching Through Georgia."

The company began to sit. Christa's eyes were on his. He led her back to her chair, but she didn't sit.

"I think that I shall help with the entertainment," she murmured, pulling away.

He watched her walk to the spinet and speak with the private. He rose, and she sat.

She started off gently. As strawberries and cream were served, Christa played and sang.

She sang "When This Cruel War Is Over," a song so heart-wrenching that many commanders had ordered that it not be played in camps, for desertions often followed its playing.

It went well enough. Both troops embraced the song. She went on to "Amazing Grace." She had a beautiful voice, crystal clear, sweet, and pure, and she played just as beautifully.

Of course she played beautifully. She'd been bred and trained to play beautifully, to sing like a lark, to flutter her eyelashes, to rule like a queen. She'd spent years learning all the subtle arts so as to marry a man like Liam McCloskey, to supervise his household, to entrance his guests.

Perhaps she had prepared more for a military life than she had ever intended. The whole tent seemed enraptured. They were seldom treated to such a lovely display in the wild. She was doing it all on purpose, he knew.

She had them all!

She slipped into a song called "Southern Girl," a song in defiance of the Union, and went on to "I'm a Good Old Rebel," a song for those

Rebels determined to die in rebellion. To make absolutely sure that no one could miss just where her loyalties lay, she broke into a soft, heart-rending edition of "Dixie."

A wondrous finale. He couldn't say a word about it. Lincoln had ordered it played in honor of the South before that fateful night at Ford's Theater. Jeremy's own troops had played it before they left Richmond.

While the last echoes of the music remained on the air, Christa rose from the spinet.

Celia Preston began the applause.

General Sherman seconded it mightily.

Christa bowed low in a mocking curtsy. She rose and her eyes met Jeremy's. He could have sworn that for a moment she was very still, and that a slight tremor swept through her.

"Gentlemen, ladies, you will excuse me?" she pleaded politely, offering one of her beautiful smiles to the whole group. "I tire so easily!"

They all tripped over themselves to excuse her!

Jeremy awaited her at the exit from the tent, arms crossed over his shoulders. A flush suffused her cheeks as she looked up at him. Her lashes quickly lowered. "Excuse me."

He caught hold of her arm. To anyone viewing them, he might have been whispering the sweetest endearments.

"They might have excused you, my love. But be forewarned. I most certainly do not! When I get my hands on you, Christa . . ."

He let the warning trail away. She pulled away from him, her eyes blazing. She was flushed. Was it the wine, was it her temper, or the heat?

"Good night, Colonel." Her words were definite. Mistress of Cameron Hall definite.

He smiled, his fingers itching to touch her. If she had been determined to single-handedly destroy his career, she was well on her way tonight. It was good that Sherman, remarkably, had a sense of humor.

He still blocked Christa.

"I said, good night, Colonel," she enunciated carefully. "The night is over!"

His smile deepened. "Oh no, Christa," he assured her. "The night has just begun for you."

She pulled away from him and exited the tent. He let her go.

He would find her in time.

She had nowhere to go.

Fourteen

Christa did find somewhere to go.

Jeremy remained with the company of officers and their wives while Nathaniel began the strains of "Beautiful Dreamer." A number of the ladies patted their fans and assured him that they understood Christa's exhaustion.

He refrained from telling them that Christa had spent perhaps three weeks with some discomfort, but since then had seemed to feel more healthy than most of his men. He listened gravely to Sherman's warnings about the Indians, and he danced with a number of the women including Clara Jennings, a feat that did not in the least ease his temper.

By the time he left, he'd heard half the company cluck over what a beautiful and brave figure his wife was, poor child, always doing her best to make do.

That didn't improve his temper much either.

He was not far from his own tent. When he had said good night to the last of the guests, he strode the few feet to it, angrily jerking open the flap.

She wasn't there.

Fear drove into his heart, and while it did so he tried to assure himself that nothing could have happened to her. They were too large a camp, too well armed for the Comanche to attack.

He spun around, nearly crashing into Robert Black Paw. "She is by the river, some distance from the tents. I left Private O'Malley to guard her. I didn't know whether to bring her back or not. She is beyond the circle of our night guard. I'm afraid she strays too far."

"I'll bring her back myself, Robert. Thank you."

The scout nodded and disappeared into the blackness of the night. Jeremy started the long walk down to the river. Near its edge, he found

Private O'Malley and sent the young man back to camp. He walked through the trees himself, amazed that Christa would have come here, so far from the camp. He saw her, standing with one foot upon a log, staring into the cold black water. The folds of her skirt fell elegantly about her, her hair cascaded down her back like a wing of the night. If any young Comanche brave had come upon her so, he would have thanked the gods for his incredible good fortune.

The thought spurred his anger, and he thrashed on through the trees, his eyes narrowed on her. She heard him coming and spun around, her eyes wide. The look on his face must have been as savage as his temper because she turned to run, when there was nowhere to run. She had barely taken a step before he was upon her, swinging her around and against a tree trunk.

"Get your hands off me!" she commanded him quickly.

"What the hell do you think you're doing?"

She interrupted instantly. "Jeremy, your swearing is excessive—"

"And you can swear with more ferocity than any mule driver I know. I repeat, what the hell are you doing?"

"Looking at the river. I needed some fresh air."

"So you just walked away from the camp?"

"All right, I needed to be away from you. And your Yankee company!"

"And you didn't give a damn that I'd come back, worried sick, wondering if the Comanche hadn't walked off with you?"

"I—" She faltered for just a second, then lifted her chin. "I thought that you'd be occupied, impressing the great general! The man who won a war by starving innocent women and children."

"He's not a monster, Christa! Jesu, madam, he did his best! Stanton tried to have him barred from riding at the head of his army when it passed the review stands in Washington because of his efforts! He risked his own career, and was as angry, I've heard, as a caged lion when Washington forced him to renegotiate his peace with Joe Johnston. Hell, Christa, if you want to crucify someone, let me try to get Phil Sheridan out here! He's a firm believer in a 'scorched earth' policy!"

"What difference does it make who you get out here?" she hissed. "We'll never agree. I just decided that I needed to take a walk."

"A walk! In the dead of night? In Indian territory?"

"I needed to be alone—"

"Like hell. You were hoping that I wouldn't find you. That I'd give up and go to sleep before you came tiptoeing back. That I wouldn't strangle you over what you did."

"I will never be afraid of you!" Her chin was high, her words scornful.

Maybe the wine she had drunk was giving her an added boost of bravado. She still seemed flushed. "Never!" she repeated.

His eyes narrowed on her. "You'd best be—tonight."

She was breathing hard, both defiant and uneasy. He wished that wanting her, aching for her, desiring her so desperately would not plague him so when he longed to shake her. He couldn't keep his hands off her, despite his most stalwart efforts. He shot out, gripping her wrists, wrenching her toward him. It might have been a mistake. He could feel the trembling in her now. Her eyes were luminous with her fury. Her hair tumbled about her shoulders and fell down her back in a wild disarray. Her scent was sweet against the rich, earthy smell of the river and the breeze and the embankment.

"You let go of me, Jeremy!" She jerked free from him and started to walk away. She stumbled and caught her balance. Was it a root in her path, or a reminder of the wine she had drunk.

"Get back here!" He jerked her back into his arms. Her eyes went wide. Maybe she wasn't frightened.

"Let go of me!" she insisted.

He smiled crookedly. Let her go? Never, not tonight. He wasn't quite sure what seized hold of him, but he knew he would never let her go. Not tonight. Maybe it was her defiance, her passion, maybe it was even the depths of the hatred she seemed to bear him. But it felt as if an inferno had suddenly found roots within him, streaks of the blaze tearing throughout his body. Tonight? He wouldn't let her out of his sight again.

"You're not afraid of me, remember?"

"Jeremy—"

He lifted her up, flinging her over his shoulder despite her outraged shriek of protest. He instantly started his way back to camp.

She pounded fiercely against his back. "Put me down! Your friends might still be awake. What would they say, what would they think?"

"One, I don't give a damn. Two, any friends of mine would probably want to thrash you as well after that marvelously stirring rendition of 'Dixie.' "

She thudded his back again. She started to bite his shoulder and he gave her a sound whack on the buttocks, certain that he hurt the bustle— and her pride—far more than he hurt her. They had reached the outer rim of the tents.

"Damn you! Put me down!" she whispered fiercely.

"Soon enough, my love."

She fell silent, braced against him as he strode his way to their tent. In seconds he had set her down hard on the bed. He tried to walk away from her. He spun around. She lay there in the blue gown, her face flushed, her eyes flashing, her hair a magnificent spill around her, her breasts heaving over the velvet bodice of the gown. She sat up, then stood quickly, her hands clenched into fists at her sides. "I won't stay here, Jeremy. I can't. I told you that I couldn't be expected to entertain Sherman—"

"You did nothing, in fact. I took no chances on your cooking for him, lady. He might well have left here poisoned. And I never asked you to entertain the man. You took that on all on your own!" He stripped off his dress military frock coat, then removed his cuff links. " 'I'm a Good Old Rebel'! My God, you do have bravado, ma'am, I'll grant you that!"

She started to walk past him. "I have really tried to be an excellent wife—"

He interrupted her with a loud snort.

She stood still, stiffening. Her eyes were blue fire. "Since it appears you are determined to sleep here tonight, I shall find other accommodations."

"Oh? And where will you go?"

"Elsewhere!"

"I see. Perhaps that dear charming Captain Clark—who reminds you so much of your poor deceased Liam—will be willing to take you in."

"Perhaps I'd even prefer the Comanche tonight!" she hissed back furiously.

He caught hold of her wrist, throwing her back toward the bed. "Sit down. You sure as hell aren't going anywhere tonight."

She lay flung atop the bed, watching him, catching her breath. She wasn't about to stay down. Not yet.

She sprang up easily again, determined on walking out of the tent. She was no fool. He could see her weighing her options. Since the opportunity to best him was probably not going to come her way, she was seeking her ever majestic lady-of-manor dignity to use against him. She inhaled, as if with a great deal of patience. "I will not stay here and listen—"

"Sit down," he repeated, stripping his shirt over his head.

She swallowed hard, gritting her teeth. He knew she was fighting to think of some way around him. He was far stronger.

She tossed back her hair, smoothing it down. Her words were polite enough, but he heard the grate of her teeth that preceded them. "Perhaps this thing can be discussed at some later date. If—"

"It will be discussed right now. I warned you to be courteous, Christa. I warned you."

She stood once again, her chin up, her hands folded before her. He hated the stance. It was her lady-of-Cameron-Hall stance, and it was so damned superior. "You've had a fair amount of whiskey with your Yank cronies—"

"Oh, that's rich!" he exclaimed. "From the delicate belle who was downing wine like water? No, Christa. That won't work. I've had some whiskey, but I'd need a hell of a lot more to forget your performance this evening!" He kicked off his boots and pulled off his cavalry pants.

She seemed to pale somewhat. She was accustomed to the sight of him naked. Tonight it seemed to disturb her.

She pressed a hand dramatically against her temples. "I have a tremendous headache and you're making it far worse. I'm leaving!" she said flatly. "You'll just have to pretend you're capable of being a gentleman for once. I mean it, Jeremy. It was a wretched night!"

"Christa! The war is over!" he growled. "You're married to a cavalryman, and my future is at stake here. Did you ever think about that?"

Maybe she hadn't. For a second, she was silent. "I'm not terribly worried about your future, Jeremy. From what I understand, you're an excellent swordsman, you know the Indians better than their own mothers do, and you're even a friend to the buffalo! You'll rise high—with or without me being decent to Sherman."

"How amazing! I never knew I had such a vote of confidence from you. Especially after following in the wake of such men as your sainted brothers!"

"Don't you dare speak about—"

"Madam, leave it be!"

"Yes, leave it be!" she whispered. "Let the great Indian hunter have the last word! And the war is over, is it? Daniel still hasn't received a pardon, carpetbaggers are passing themselves off as politicians in Richmond, and the entire South is being run by Yankee riffraff opportunists! Don't tell me the war is over!"

"Christa—"

He moved toward her, at that moment wanting to comfort her, no matter how angry he was himself about the evening. But she backed away quickly. She was still too upset to accept anything from him. She jerked back. "Touch me and I'll scream. I'll scream and scream—"

He reached out with such a vengeance that his hold upon her sleeve tore the gown. She glanced down where the sleeve and bodice gaped from her body. "How dare you . . ."

He'd never meant to hurt her, or to rip her gown. The damage was done.

She wasn't going anywhere, and she wasn't going to threaten him with

screaming ever again, he determined fiercely. Eyes on hers, he caught
the fabric once again and ripped harder. She gasped as the whole of the
garment began to fall from her, exposing her corset and petticoats. She
tried to slap him and he caught her wrist. "I gave you fair warning,
Jeremy, I'll scream—"

"Then start screaming!" he advised. She gasped out instead, her fists
slamming against his chest as he plucked her up and threw her down on
the bed, straddling over her. "Despicable Yank!" she hissed. "You'd rape
me—"

"Not on your life, lady."

"Then—"

"Buck naked, darling, you might decide to stay in the tent!"

He flung her over on her stomach, trying to loosen her corset ties. The
petticoat resisted him and he ripped it impatiently, only to be greeted
with another flurry of her venom. "You're wrecking my things! You're—"

"Christa, for a poor vanquished Reb, you've still got more clothing than
most birds have feathers! And you're damned lucky I'm ripping fabric,
and not your irresistible, delicate, wonderful southern flesh!"

She stiffened, going dead still for a second. He used the opportunity to
untie her pantalets. When she choked and began swearing again, fighting
to unseat him from his perch atop her, she afforded him the chance to
strip off the last of her garments. She lay facedown and bare, still fighting.
Her back was sleek, her hips and rump rose smooth and delectable—and
tempting.

"Despicable Yankee bas—" she began.

"One more word, my love, and—"

"And!" she cried in desperate challenge.

He tensed, swallowing hard. He didn't want the battles. What could he
do when it seemed that something from the past always arose to come
between them? Tonight, it was Sherman.

Damn Sherman. Couldn't he have traveled to some more northern
Indian district this year?

Christa was shaking. Never, ever ready to surrender, never ready to
call a truce. He bit into his lower lip and pressed a gentle kiss against the
small of her back.

He might just as well have burned her with a branding iron. She
shrieked out with rage, bucking against him and turning beneath him.
Tears of fury stung her eyes. Her fists landed against his chest. Very
suddenly, she went still. He became aware that he was straddled over her
now with his sex laid low against her stomach and it was aroused and
hard against her softness.

Her eyes narrowed on his. She moistened suddenly dry lips. "I hate you, Jeremy. I hate you for Sherman, and I hate you for the war. I—"

"Listen to yourself, Christa! You *hate me* for *Sherman!*"

Tears stung her eyes. "Can't you understand?"

"I can't change the past. And I'm not sorry that the North won, that slavery is dead and the Union preserved!"

"Get—"

"Christa! You don't hate me—"

"Trust me, I do!"

He shook his head again vehemently, his eyes dark and intense. "I don't really believe that. And I want you, Christa. I want to touch the spark of magic that is always there, just below the surface. So let's pretend that you don't hate me tonight. Lie still beside me. You claim that you are such an excellent wife. Be one for me."

"Jesu!" she rallied. "I ride the trail, I sleep in a tent. I have encountered tarantulas and buffalo. I lie with you night after night—"

"You are here, yes!" he continued for her. "And you refrain from protesting when I exercise my matrimonial rights. Dammit, Christa! The fire is there, I can feel it! I can nearly touch it. But you deny me and yourself, again and again!"

"I don't know what you're talking about!" she cried.

He pulled her up by the shoulders, searching out her eyes. "But you do, Christa, you do! You fight me, you fight yourself. You could taste the sweetness of fulfillment, but you deny yourself the chance. It's there within you, I know it. You possess a rare passion. Why fight me so?"

Her eyes were liquid. With emotion, with anger? "Perhaps I do not fight you!" she whispered vehemently.

"I know that something rich lies locked within you!"

"Perhaps, Yank, you haven't the key to unlock it!"

He eased his weight back, holding her still, shaking his head slowly. "No, Christa, it's not me. Maybe I'm not your Rebel lover. Maybe I am your Yankee husband. But in every way, I swear to you, I've sought to give what I would take. And I know that I've touched your senses. You hold back because you would continue to wage war in our bed. But I tell you, my love, no more. No more, after this night!"

"Don't—" she began.

"Jesu, Christa! Give me a chance, give us both a chance!"

"Jeremy—" she began anew. But he was done arguing.

His lips touched hers. For a moment, he felt her resistance, tasted the salt of her tears. Her fists banged against his shoulders and she tried to writhe out of his hold. No! He could not let her go!

"A chance, Christa!" he whispered, lifting his lips just a breath from hers. His voice was low, rich, deep. Demanding, pleading.

She inhaled on a ragged little sound.

He touched her lips once again. Tasted them, pressed past them, felt the desire in him flame wildly as he took in the sweetness and warmth of her. He wanted her so badly. She was in his arms, and he could have her. They'd waged this battle before. All he need do was take her. Ease the hunger.

He lifted his lips from hers. Thought himself insane. Her sky-blue Cameron eyes were on him, her lips were damp from his touch, still so tempting.

He smiled ruefully. "Your choice, Christa."

"What?" she whispered, amazed.

"I will not force the issue."

He rolled beside her. She quickly turned her back on him. He ran a finger seductively down the length of her back. Up again, down again. What was the matter with him? What if this didn't work?

It had to work!

The most seductive touch he could manage, down the bareness of her back, caressing the very base of her spine. Softly, gently, over the rise of her hip. The fullness of her buttocks. He drew circles with his fingertips.

Pressed his lips to her back. Followed the touch of his fingertip down her spine. Up again.

Jesu . . .

Please, God . . .

She swung back around on him.

"You said—" she began to accuse him, her eyes wild.

"I said your choice!"

"It's not my choice when Sherman—"

"Jesu! Christa! Could we please get Sherman out of this tent tonight!"

"Let's get him out of the camp!" she challenged.

"We'll start with getting him out of our bed!"

"But—"

His fingers threaded into her hair. His lips silenced her protest.

She still tried to keep up the fight, shaking her head slightly when his mouth rose above hers. "Christa, do you know what you're doing to me?" he groaned softly. "If the war were still on, I think I'd be willing to change sides at this point!"

Despite herself, she smiled. But she was ever determined. "You said—" she began again stubbornly.

"Your choice," he finished on a breath.

But he couldn't really leave it that way. Not as things stood. She still needed some persuasion.

He swept an arm around her, bringing her fully against him. The length of his body shuddered. He found her lips. Caught them, held them. Stroked the rim of them with his tongue, parried between them. She would fight him now.

To his astonishment, he heard a soft moan rumbling in her throat. Her hands pressed upon his shoulders, then went still. Her fingertips dug slightly into his flesh.

Holding him. Not pressing him away.

He took her tightly into his arms, afraid to let her go. He kissed her lips, stroking her back softly, feeling the sensual curves and planes. He broke from her lips to touch them again, his tongue tracing the shape of them before slipping deeply into her mouth again. He caressed the silky skin of her back, sweeping the length of it, creating sensual swirls once more at the base of her spine with his fingertips, stroking the curve of her hip, the rise of her buttocks.

There was a difference tonight. She hadn't returned his hunger as yet, but the pulse was there, as was the heat. The promise was in his arms.

Determined to discover it, he trailed his kiss to her earlobe, along her throat. He lifted the mass of her hair and kissed the nape of her neck, then shuddered, sighing deeply, burying his face within the ebony cloud of her, enjoying the scent and silken feel of it. He moved her about, shifting the fall of her hair once again and pressing a kiss against her upper spine. He bathed her shoulders with his caress, then moved lower against her spine, his fingers stroking fire while his lips delivered their liquid heat, down to the very small of her back, over the rise of her hip. He paused, sensations sweeping through him in a staggering manner from the taste and feel of her, as she suddenly sighed and shuddered.

He held her in his arms once again. Her eyes met his, very wide, soft, dazed.

Perhaps she hadn't really expected this. To feel the burning inside, the need like raw hunger. She shook her head wildly again. "No!" she mouthed.

"Yes," he insisted, both tender and determined. "Tonight, my love, we have twisted the key already."

"It's the wine!" she whispered. "You're taking advantage of my confusion."

"Damn right!" He laughed huskily. "I take every advantage that I can get. And it isn't the wine so much, because I've noted that you barely touch the stuff since you've been carrying our child."

"I tell you—"

He pressed his case, capturing her mouth, and feeling at long last the duel of her tongue with his own. Hunger seared through him. His hand moved fervently over her breast, discovering the peak pebble hard. He delivered his kiss there, teasing the peak, savoring the sweetness of it, suckling upon the fullness of it. She shifted beneath him gloriously. Even as she did so longing gripped his loins tightly, a savage heat swept through him and he moved against her, his hands never still. There was a greater demand to his touch now, an urgency that filled his body.

She could always arouse his desire. But tonight, she was a breath of magic. Perhaps hatred was close to love, perhaps the passion of anger danced narrowly close to that of desire. Maybe they had just been building to this.

But she was moving too. She was liquid and supple in his arms. He stroked her breast, and she rose against him, and he whispered soft words to her. "Feel the touch, my love. Here, and here . . . feel it become a heat that begins a swirl inside of you, deeper and deeper, here." He stroked her upper thigh, set his palm over the rise of her ebony triangle. "Here," he whispered, then slipped a finger deep and hard inside of her. "And here . . ."

She gasped and trembled massively against his touch, and shifted as if she would deny it. If the fires were not sizzling through her then, they were running rampant within his own body. Still, he took his time. She was stretched out on her back. Her flesh was damp with an exotic sheen, touched by the gold lamplight. Her hair was a tangle. Her limbs were long and beautiful and her breasts were rising and falling in a rush. Her eyes were soft glazed as if he had taken her quite by surprise. Perhaps he had. And perhaps it had been building as he had said, and tonight he had finally bridged the last of the walls of her defenses.

An anguish tore through him. He wanted her, then and there. But he wanted more tonight, too, than he had ever wanted before. He wanted those blue eyes to fill with the passion he knew lurked behind the midnight shadow of her lashes. He wanted to feel the bowstring quivering of her slender form, the ardent rhythm of her hips. It wasn't time to seize hold of her, not yet.

He rose above her and gently touched her lips with just the breath of his own. He drew a pattern between the valley of her breasts with his finger. He followed it with his tongue. He lowered himself slowly against her. Wherever he caressed her, he kissed her. Lower and lower until he lay between her legs. Touching her, parting her, caressing her, kissing her.

A soft, fervent cry escaped from her. Her fingers tugged upon his hair. He caught her hands and held them firmly within his own. She moaned softly. Her head began to toss, her body to writhe.

If it was the wine, then bless that wondrous fruit of the vine! Perhaps they lay in the wilderness, but magic surrounded them. Beyond the canvas of their tent, the night breeze stirred, making their flesh seem all the more searing. In the endless sky the stars rode the heavens. They seemed to also dance within the tent. They rained down upon him in bursts of radiant light. Jesu, she was beautiful, alive with her passion.

He smiled wickedly. All the torments of hell could take hold of him now and he would endure them gladly. He found the tiny bud of her greatest sensuality and played mercilessly upon it, laving, teasing, demanding with the caress of his lips and tongue. She began to shudder, and the golden gleam of light upon her began to shimmer with the growing undulation of her hips. "Please!" she whispered suddenly. "I can take no more!"

And she could not! What had happened tonight, she wondered. Why couldn't she fight this fire?

It mattered not, she could not, and that was simply that. She couldn't think, the sensations were so strong.

And it was wonderful, erotic, and sending her into such a sweet spiral of sensation that she couldn't fight. He was whispering things to her and in her mind's eye she was seeing things of startling beauty. A rosebud, so dark and rich a pink, flowering beneath a radiant heat, stretching, growing, parting to burst into an open beauty. Even as she saw the image of the rose she was aware of the very graphic reality around her, the camp bed, herself, the glow of light that touched them, the bed beneath them. Jeremy. The power of his hands, his fingers locked around hers. The taut muscled feel of his body. The weight of him between her legs. The way that he touched her. The things that he did. The tension grew inside of her, hot, warm, wonderful, painful, and sweet. It grew until it was anguish, until she was arching wildly against him. Until sounds filled the night, soft, desperate, breathless. Sounds that she was making herself.

Then something seemed to explode. Sweet, so achingly sweet! It burst with wonder over her, with light, and then with dark. With stars across a velvet sky. Like a million shots firing into the night. It was the sweetest thing she had ever imagined, like a taste of honey burning throughout her system. It was so, so good. She floated with it. Saw the light, saw the darkness.

Then he was atop her. His eyes silver and wicked in the gleam of light, his naked body slick and hard and muscled and fascinating still. She cried out softly, closing her eyes, trying to turn away from him. He wouldn't have it. His body slid into hers hard. "Oh, no," she whispered.

"Oh, yes," he corrected.

Her fingers fell upon his shoulders. She shifted, amazed that he could feel so wonderful within her so swiftly. Even denying it, she had liked the feel before.

Tonight, the spiral began again. The heat deep inside of her. Curling, deepening. It couldn't come again. The velvet black, the bursting of light, the liquid stars bursting warmly throughout her body, so sweet, so delicious, so wonderful. It couldn't come again.

But the spiraling, the hunger, that led to it were so easily coming alive again. She was achingly aware of him, as if all sensation of her flesh had become heightened. She felt his hair-roughened legs and chest, the hardness of his arm muscles, the rock of his hips, and him, inside of her. The fullness of the movement, the thrust . . .

She gasped. The spiraling was rising again. She arched to meet him. She dared open her eyes. His blazed into hers, and she bit her lip, her lashes falling. His face remained so taut, his length so vital yet rigidly hard. He moved, demandingly. His arms held his body above hers. He thrust into her. And into her again, his eyes locked with hers. He moved faster and faster, his face fraught with tension. She cried out, unable to deny the quickening within her. Her hands fell upon his shoulders. Her fingers raked across them. She was pulling up to him, meeting his thrust with a rhythmic arch of her own. Her lips fell upon his shoulders. She covered them with ardent kisses. Her fingers played upon his back, massaging, digging, clinging. She felt him thrust incredibly hard against her just as the sensations seemed to split and explode within her in a wild frenzy of fire and hunger. She gasped, clinging to him, as she felt the force of the climax that seized her. Darkness fell. Light burst. The liquid stars seemed to rain down upon her once again. For a moment she was so absorbed with the shimmering feel of ecstasy that she did not realize that he remained above her, that the heat spilling from his body was just filling her own.

He fell to her side, slick with sweat, breathing hard.

She shuddered, turning to her side as sudden tears warmed her eyes. Dear God, she'd never imagined such a piece of heaven.

But yes, she had. She had known that Jeremy could bring her to it, and she had been fighting it fiercely. Why? Because it was wrong that it should be Jeremy when she had once loved so innocently and so sweetly? When Liam lay cold and buried. When all her world lay in ashes.

She had married Jeremy.

She could say what she wanted, to him, to herself. He was not so detestable. He had seized hold of her life. He had shaken her in the midst of defeat.

He had given her something more.

She bit her lip.

She cared for him. Cared far more than she wanted to know. They were enemies who had clashed head-on, but they were enemies, too, because they were both strong, determined, willful.

And he was honorable. She had demanded that he marry her, and he had done so. He had read her heart and eased the way with her and her brothers. He had brought her with him, and he had forced her to live.

He was beautiful, whipcord strong and lean in his physique, rugged and handsome in his face. Indeed, he held the key. He had touched her and found all that he had demanded of her.

He stroked her shoulder gently. "Madam, I take it back!" he murmured. "You are an excellent wife."

Was he gloating? She had certainly given him all that he wanted, whether willingly or not. Every word that he had spoken had been true. She had teetered on that precipice night after night, tasting the wonder, refusing to let it come to her.

Yet tonight it had been undeniable. It had taken her in a flood.

"Excellent . . ."

He was gloating. Yankees. Once they won, they just didn't let up. That's why it seemed tragic to surrender.

"It was the wine!" she whispered.

"Was it?" he murmured.

She started to stiffen, not sure if he mocked her or not. But then something miraculous happened. She felt something. Not wild and magical and exciting . . .

Different. She inhaled sharply.

The baby. Deep, deep inside of her the baby was moving. It was just a flutter. So curious. So light. Then it came again.

She gasped.

"What is it?" He was over her instantly.

She shook her head. "The baby."

"My God!" His voice was harsh, rasping. "Is it all right? Did—"

"No, no! It's fine. He's moving! I can feel the baby. It's so strange!"

His palm moved over her abdomen. "I can't feel it!" he said.

She shook her head again. The darkness cast shadows over them both. "No, you can't feel him, not yet. It's just inside. I think it takes time to feel the movement from the outside. But—oh, there again! He's alive, he's moving, he's kicking, he's . . ."

"He's what?" Jeremy said. His palm still lay gently against her flesh.

"He's real!" she breathed. "He's real, he's going to be born, he's going to live."

His hand went rigid. He pulled her back against him. "Go to sleep. Tomorrow is going to be a long day."

His body enwrapped hers. The comfort was there.

But she wondered if he thought of another unborn child. And of that child's mother.

Fifteen

"Christa. Christa. You have to wake up. Now."

She came awake from a deep unconsciousness. There had been a strange cocoon of comfort in her sleep. Last night, she had given in to him. She had given in to far more than duty. She had felt so very weary, and even in her surrender she had discovered a certain peace.

But now, awaking, she felt a tinge of fear encroaching upon her comfort. She had given too much. Surrendered too much.

She had tried to tell him that it had been the wine. Now all that she wanted to do was crawl beneath the covers and not have to face him until she was ready. Until it was dark again. Until forever. She didn't know which.

She shook her head, trying to pull the sheets tightly around her. "Leave me be!" she pleaded.

"Christa!" His voice had been fairly gentle. Now that old snap of command was back in it. If that weren't irritating enough, she felt the palm of his hand fall sharply upon her derriere.

Indignantly, she opened her eyes, staring at him with all the evil reproach she could muster. She turned her back on him again, murmuring. "Please, just—"

"Up!" he repeated, catching her shoulder and rolling her over to face him. He had apparently risen some time ago. He was fully clad in his dress uniform. She heartily resented the fact that he could appear so striking in the cavalry dark blue, and that most women would find him a handsome figure indeed.

Yes, he was a striking figure. Yes, he had done things to her that she had never imagined. Yes, now when he touched her, she remembered and grew warm.

She hugged the sheets tightly, determined to stare him down—even after last night. "Jeremy—"

"You have to get up."

"You did tell me a wife belonged in bed!" she snapped.

A smile curved his lip and he leaned against her. "I do like you there, Christa. Very much so. And I would dearly love to join you again. Especially after last night. You were wonderful. Extraordinary." He started to stroke her cheek.

A flood of color rushed to her cheeks. "It was the wine!" she whispered.

"The wine! And I thought it was my devastating charm! Ah, Christa, are you sure that it wasn't? Perhaps I should cast duty to the winds and crawl back in to discover the truth!"

"Trust me!" she murmured, inching herself against the rear of the bed. "It was the wine—"

She didn't want to remember how completely she had surrendered, how desperately she had wanted him.

And there was still the Sherman matter between them!

"If you'd please just leave me be—" she began.

But she broke off. She swallowed hard, shrinking back as he suddenly pinned his arms on either side of her, bracing himself as he studied her eyes. "Christa, I won't go back," he said softly. "Everything I longed to find was there within you. I won't let you deny it again. I never meant to press my point with as much anger as I did last night, but hell, who knows? Maybe the only way to ever get anything from you, Christa, is to take it by force."

She felt a trembling deep within her. She didn't want to have the surge of emotion that flowed through her. She didn't mean to be so hostile to him. There were times now when it seemed that he was trying to find peace, break down the wall between them.

This morning, she needed the wall. She was suddenly very afraid. Afraid for her own heart.

"Don't talk to me like that!" she said heatedly, and she saw the silver in his eyes glitter and harden but she couldn't seem to stop. "I'm not one of your privates to be ordered about. And don't think yourself such a great commander! You're only a colonel because the Rebs managed to kill so damned many Yankee officers that they had to scrape the bottom of the barrel to fill their ranks!"

His brow arched. His lip curled. She wondered fleetingly whether he was amused or furious. She hadn't meant to say the words. She was sorry that hundreds of thousands of Yanks were dead as well as Rebs. She was sorry for the whole damned war.

And she was heartily sorry that she kept finding herself fighting it again and again when it should have truly been over.

"I'm a colonel because too many Yanks are dead," he said softly. "And you're my wife because too many Rebels fell. And it's all a travesty, but it's the way that it is, my love, and you had best get used to it. I found there does exist a match to strike the fire within you. By God, Christa, I swear I'll not let that flame go out."

"I told you, it was the wine—"

"Then perhaps we shall have to douse you in the stuff nightly."

A sense of panic was rising within her. He could hurt her all too easily. It seemed best to strike out first.

"Have it your way, then! Dead Yanks, dead Rebs. But a few too many glasses of wine and you're no longer a Yank. You're a Reb officer, a ghost come back to life—"

She broke off with a little cry of protest as his fingers wound around her upper arms, lifting her from the bed and hard against him. "We'll have to see to it that next time, Mrs. McCauley, you are well aware that you're not sleeping with a corpse!"

The tension within him was suddenly frightening her. She wanted to cry. Last night had begun with anger, yes. But they had come so close to something being right between them.

Daylight always seemed to bring back the war.

"Let me go!" she cried. "If you even think about touching me to-night—"

"I'll think and do whatever I please, Christa. But cheer up—perhaps you're not so all damned alluring as you seem to believe. Maybe I'm weary of sleeping with someone who seems to be one of the walking dead herself at times. For now, just get up. Or stay there. My staff sergeant is due here any minute. Maybe you'll give him the entertainment of his life, lying there naked. The picnic for the officers and their wives is at eleven. You'll be there and you'll behave politely. And you won't sing a single note under any circumstances!"

He was balanced upon their bed on one knee, his fingers tightly vised around her arms. She should just give in, she thought.

But she wouldn't lie and promise that she'd behave any differently if General Sherman made an appearance.

She narrowed her eyes at Jeremy. "Will he be there?"

She almost cried out. It seemed impossible, but his hold upon her tightened.

"What difference does it make?"

"All the difference in the world."

He released her so suddenly that she fell back, unprepared. Her hair spilled over her shoulders and breasts, and the covers fell away from her. He stepped back, his hands clenching into fists at his sides, then unclenching again. "The war *is* over!" he exclaimed. He stared at her and she was startled by the depths of the passion in his eyes. She wondered if the burning emotions within him then were hatred or desire, or perhaps a combination of the two. Despite his anger, despite his harshness, she wanted to cry out, to reach out to him. To tell him that she wanted it to be over! I just don't want to have dinner with George Tecumseh Sherman!

But she didn't cry out. He had turned and was walking away from her, ready to leave their tent. Before lifting up the flap he paused. His back to her, he spoke again. "Sherman will not be there. He is reviewing troops farther along the trail." He turned back to her. "I'm not asking you to like Sherman or anyone else. I'm not asking you to forgive the war. All I want is for you to extend whatever courtesy you can manage to our guests in this godforsaken land. Will you be so kind?"

She tried once again to assemble some dignity about herself, flipping back her wayward hair, tugging at the sheets once again to cover her breasts. "I tried to be courteous last—"

"Try harder. I'm warning you."

"Oh? And if I don't?"

He smiled, and doffed his hat politely. "My love, you will *please* try harder!"

When he turned to leave this time, he did so without another word. Christa threw herself back on the bed, fighting a new rise of tears behind her lids. He didn't understand. She didn't hate the cavalry wives. She felt sorry for so many of them! She, at least, had been forced to raise her own food. She'd smoked meat and made soap and baked bread. She might have been raised a lady, but life had already taught her hard lessons.

Little Celia Preston had been practically raised in a nunnery. From her home in Maine, she'd scarcely known that a war was on! An Irish maid had doted on her all her years, and she had come here totally unprepared for the hardships that faced them.

It was just Sherman.

How could any Reb be expected to tolerate the man?

She rolled over with a groan, her face against the sheets. As she lay there she became aware that there was a faint smell of her husband about the bedding. It was rich, pleasant, masculine. It reminded her of the night that had passed between them. She'd never imagined such a night. Not even when she'd been young and in love with Liam. Maybe a few previous occasions had hinted at such glory, but she'd been too naive to imagine what incredible physical sensations could be reached. Jeremy had known, of course. He had known long before he had known her.

And yet she had to give him credit where it was due. No matter what her protestations he had always been determined to sweep her into his fire. He had been a giving—if a forceful—lover. Because he had wanted her surrender.

He had wanted her to know the richness of sensation and emotion that could be reached. Any time that he had touched her with lovemaking in mind, he had been determined to teach her the sweetness and the beauty of the act.

She grit her teeth. She did not want to appreciate or admire the man. Or love him.

A sigh escaped her and she shivered suddenly. The bed had grown cold without him. Her head was aching. She was tired and she suddenly wanted very much to close her eyes and go back to sleep. She wanted to forget the world.

Her lashes fluttered closed. Then they flew back open. Jeremy's staff sergeant was due any minute.

She flew up, dragging the covers with her. Jeremy had already brought in wash water. She bit her lower lip. He had left her a clean pitcher and bowl and towel. He was, she thought, always courteous in such things.

She hurriedly washed and more hurriedly dressed. She wanted to be out of the tent before Jeremy or his staff sergeant arrived. She needed some time alone if she was going to appear calm and poised—the subjugated and polite Rebel—for Jeremy's officers' picnic.

He hated to admit it—even to himself—but there were moments when Jeremy wondered if Christa would defy him so far as to refuse to show up for the impromptu social event, much less assist with it.

But when he had finished the morning business with Staff Sergeant William Hallie and then spent an hour being briefed on recent Indian events along the westward trails by Jennings, he came around to the center of the clustered tents to discover with definite relief that Christa was already there busily preparing plates and offerings alongside Bertha and Nathaniel. She glanced up briefly at his arrival, then looked quickly back to the chore at hand. She was busy twirling fine white linen napkins into silver holders.

Indeed, the camp tables that had been stretched out on the grass were covered in the same white linen. They were using Christa's china and silver, and even here in the wilderness she had made an elegant scene of the buffet table.

There were benefits to marrying a southern belle, he told himself wryly.

Her eyes rose to his again. Beautiful, as blue as the summer's sky. She hadn't wound up the bountiful wealth of her ebony hair but rather left it loose upon her shoulders. She was probably the most fascinating woman he had ever seen and the most beautiful. He felt a flash of heat come searing through his body, and he knew that the one benefit to the marriage had been Christa herself. No matter what words passed between them, no matter what gulf separated them, he ached for the nights. Even when she lay stiff. He had felt sometimes that he lived through the day just to touch her by night.

He lowered his head, determined not to let her see his smile. It wasn't amusing. It was painful to want his wife the way that he did.

But there was something special deep within her. A passion sweetly strong, feverish, dynamic. He had sensed it, felt it, longed for it. And now he had touched it. Briefly. For one night. And as he had suspected, there was nothing in the world like making love with Christa when she made love in return. Nothing. It was dangerous to remember last night, because it made him forget everything else that he was doing.

Night would come again.

He had to keep a smile from curving his lip once again.

Poor thing. Sherman, it seemed, had caused another southerner to fall.

She would certainly not see the amusement in it. And if she spoke today anything like she had spoken yesterday, they could all be in for a fall. He sobered quickly, determined to make his gaze a warning one as he watched her finish with the table.

Even as she did so, a number of the officers began to arrive with their wives. James Preston came with his lovely young Celia on his arm. Then Major Tennison with his wife, Lilly. Several of the captains came, some with their wives, some alone. Nearly all the invited men had made their appearances when Major Paul Jennings arrived at last with his wife, Clara.

Jennings wasn't a bad sort, Jeremy had decided. Sherman seemed to think highly enough of him. But though he liked Jennings well enough, he wasn't particularly fond of the man's wife.

Though most of the men on the trail, the officers and the enlisted men alike, were eager to see to the welfare of any of the ladies along with them, Clara Jennings was proving to be something of a harridan. She was a good companion for Mrs. Brooks. Since her arrival she hadn't done much other than complain. She had imagined they would be given real officers' quarters, not a canvas tent.

There were no real quarters, Jeremy explained. Clara didn't understand. Real quarters should have been built.

But they would soon be moving on.

Clara didn't seem to care.

She kept the men moving throughout the night, bringing her blankets, warming bricks for her bed, brewing her a cup of tea.

Now, as the others laughed and chatted and enjoyed the picnic, Jeremy noted that Clara was having difficulties again. She was complaining to Bertha about something.

Jeremy excused himself from the young captain he had been speaking with and placed himself strategically beside an oak that looked onto the buffet table and the scattered camp chairs and tables that had been set out.

Christa had finished preparing and serving and was leaving the rest to Bertha, who remained contentedly behind the tables. Christa, he noticed, was actually smiling. She was standing with James and Celia and Emory Clark, and Emory was saying something that pleased her. She laughed out loud.

Jeremy wondered at the rush of resentment that filled him. Why was she so quick to smile for Emory? Hell, he was as much a Yank as any man here. Maybe it was Celia, he tried to tell himself. Christa liked Celia. But then, who could help but like the young woman? She was small, delicate, lovely, with an innocence and wide-eyed wonder as big as the West. She had instantly formed an attachment for Christa, and not even Christa could find fault with her.

Christa was blushing, laughing at something that *Emory* was saying.

Emory. Who reminded her of Liam.

Jeremy tightened his lips. His attention was momentarily drawn away from his wife when there was a commotion at the buffet table.

"Oh! I'm afraid that it's sickening, just sickening! I can't possibly eat this meat! I need something quickly!"

It was Clara Jennings. She was waving her handkerchief before her nose.

Bertha, alarmed, had hurried around the table to her. "Mrs. Jennings, what can I do?"

"Some bread, please! That will help, I think!"

"Nathaniel, Nathaniel, please! Get Mrs. Jennings some bread."

Nathaniel was circulating around the tables, picking up plates as the men and ladies finished with them. As Bertha called him, he hurried over to the table.

Clara Jennings saw him for the first time. She watched as he cut her several slices of bread from the loaf.

"Oh, dear, you don't mean for him to give it to me after he's touched it, do you?" Clara Jennings said, horrified.

A silence fell upon the gathering.

Nathaniel, in the act of cutting the bread, went dead still.

Clara felt the silence. She waved herself with her handkerchief profusely. "Well, the man is a Negro!" she said defensively. "And he's touched the bread!"

Jeremy saw Nathaniel's face. The face he had known and trusted so long. A face he had come to care about greatly.

And he saw the weariness and the hurt on it.

He had to say something. As politely as possible, the woman had to be put in her place.

But he didn't have a chance to speak.

"Excuse me!" came a feminine voice with a ring of steel.

Christa stood up and came beside Nathaniel, slipping her arm through his. "Nathaniel, please, would you be so good as to go back to my tent for my shawl?" she asked him quickly.

Proud, wounded dark eyes touched hers. "Please, Nathaniel?"

"Yes, Mrs. McCauley. Yes, right away."

Jeremy could have spoken then, but he was too curious to see what his wife intended to do next. He leaned back against the oak, watching her.

Her back was very straight. Her hands were folded in front of her. Her chin rose as she stared coolly at Clara Jennings. "It always seems to me to be such a curious thing that so many northerners fought such a passionate battle as abolitionists when they were so ignorant of the people they longed to free. Mrs. Jennings, Nathaniel was born a free man. He's received a finer education than most white men I know. I don't know if that matters to you or not. I come from a family that owned slaves at one time. Black people fed me and bathed me as a child, and they stood by me as an adult while the world around us crumbled. I'm lucky. I know that they have hearts and souls—and that the black of their skin can be very beautiful, and that it isn't something that comes off when touched! Perhaps I was one of the wretched southerners holding a people in bondage. At least we knew that they were people. Now, if you'll excuse me, Nathaniel is my friend. I think that I need to see to his welfare."

She had never appeared more the great lady, Jeremy thought, his gaze keenly upon her as she swirled around. For a moment, her eyes touched his. There was an instant of wariness within hers. She thought that he would chastise her for rudeness to his associates again. But she didn't care. There was the slightest trembling to her lower lip, and then her jaw tightened. Her lashes lowered, and she walked by him.

He felt a smile tugging at his lips, but he suppressed it.

"Well, I never!" Clara Jennings stated indignantly once Christa had gone. She flounced around in her chair, staring at Jeremy. "Colonel, I demand that you say something to your wife about this matter!"

He bowed deeply to her, doffing his hat. "Indeed, Mrs. Jennings, I do intend to speak with my wife!"

"Hmmph!" Mrs. Jennings said, somewhat mollified.

"I intend to tell her that I found her speech most touching and admirable. Nathaniel, you see, is my friend too. He grew up in the North, but I want to reassure him now that most northerners do not share your sentiments—and that we are heartily glad that we fought and won a war for the Union and emancipation."

He bowed again and turned to leave the gathering. As he walked away, he could hear Clara Jennings again.

"Well, I never! Never, never! Paul, I—"

"Shut up, Clara," her husband warned her.

Jeremy followed the trail that led down to the river, certain that Nathaniel would come to his "thinking log," a place he sought when his emotions were in an uproar. When he reached the break in the trees before the river, he paused.

Nathaniel was indeed there, as was Christa. They faced one another across the log. Christa was speaking.

"I hope you won't let her words hurt you, Nathaniel. She's a dreadful woman."

"Yes, ma'am, Mrs. McCauley. She is that."

"She's too stupid to know what she's saying—"

"It's the way a lot of folks feel, Mrs. McCauley."

"Not good folks, Nathaniel."

"I thank you for what you did, Mrs. McCauley," he told her, standing very straight and tall. "I heard what you said when I left, and I appreciate it. But there's no cause for you to go getting in trouble with those other army wives, ma'am. I've been called 'dirty nigger' half my life. It's not something you have to suffer over."

"It's not something that's right, either," Christa said. "Just because it's something that has happened."

Nathaniel grinned broadly. "Maybe southern folk aren't so bad."

Jeremy watched as Christa lowered her head, then raised her eyes back to Nathaniel. She sighed. "Nathaniel, I don't know how to judge this world anymore. Far more than half the southern boys who went to war never owned a slave in all their lives. Some who owned them were very decent to them." She hesitated. "There were cruel men and women too. Men who overworked their people. Who shackled them. Who beat them. I can't—I can't defend slavery."

Nathaniel walked toward her. He reached for her hand. It was very small and pale against the ebony coloring of his own. "You do know, Mrs. McCauley, that the black doesn't come off like dirt. That means a lot to me."

She smiled at him. "However it came about, Nathaniel, slavery is over. We just have to convince some people that we're all human."

Nathaniel's handsome jaw twisted. "It's a nice thought, Mrs. McCauley. But a hundred years from now, we'll still be trying to convince some people of that fact. You shouldn't worry about those people who call us dirty niggers, Mrs. McCauley. We have our ways of getting back."

"Oh?"

"We just call them 'white trash.' And that's what they are. That's what they are. I—" He broke off. Jeremy realized that Nathaniel had seen him standing on the trail watching them.

Nathaniel frowned, about to tell Christa that Jeremy was there.

Jeremy shook his head, warning Nathaniel that he didn't want Christa to know that he had been there. Nathaniel nodded, and Jeremy turned and walked away.

Sixteen

Jeremy couldn't return to the tea-time gathering on the lawn. Their guests would just have to get along without his or Christa's being present.

He had decided to double the guard—he was certain that Robert Black Paw would not return with any good reports about the smoke seen on the trail.

If Major Jennings was right, Buffalo Run was in a rage again, and though Jeremy's troops hadn't been guilty of any crimes against the Indians, it wouldn't matter. Just like some whites felt about Indians, Indians felt the same way about whites.

Jeremy could never guarantee that there wouldn't be a raid or attack against them. Not when they were in Comanche territory. He felt confident that his troops were capable of fighting the enemy, but he didn't want any surprises. Especially not now. There were far too many women present.

If Clara Jennings felt squeamish about a black man cutting her bread, just what would she feel about a red man whisking her away?

Actually, it might be total justice, Jeremy thought, a grin teasing his lips. He could just imagine the red-faced, corpulent Mrs. Jennings reduced to being a slave for some demanding Comanche squaw. The situation did have its humorous side.

But only in the imagination, Jeremy reminded himself somberly. The Comanche tortured their captives sometimes too. He knew that a number of officers in the West kept ammunition set aside to kill their own wives and children before letting them fall captive to the Indians.

A shudder ripped through him.

What of Christa?

No. He could never put a bullet through her heart. Christa was young and strong and beautiful. If the Indians took her, they might well make a slave of her, but the hope for freedom would always be there. She was a fighter. He would not take the chance for life away from her.

Besides, Christa's sentiments were just about the opposite from Clara Jennings's. To Christa's way of seeing things, she'd already bedded a Yankee. What worse could happen to her?

He paused in the trees for a moment, straightening his shoulders, stiffening his spine. God Almighty, what had he done to them both? Why in hell had he ever dragged her away from her precious Cameron Hall, her hallowed Virginia? How in hell had he ever made the stupid, stupid move of falling so deeply in love with her?

"Colonel!"

He gazed down the roadway as he emerged from the trail. Robert Black Paw was making his way toward him on his paint pony.

He saluted in return. "Robert. Did you look into the smoke that Jennings saw?"

Robert nodded gravely, throwing his leg over the horn of his saddle and slipping lithely to the ground. "It was a Comanche raid on a single wagon. Ranchers, I think, from near the Pembroke homestead. There were two men on the ground, both dead. The wagon was lit—that was the source of the smoke and the fire."

"Any sign of the Comanche?"

Robert shook his head. "I think it was a quick hit-and-run raid. In retaliation for the village that Captain Miller struck last week."

"Damn Miller!" Jeremy muttered.

"Yes, sir. Damn Miller. That kind of thing will start up some heavy wars with Buffalo Run. You know him, sir."

"Yes, I know him."

"The funny thing is, Colonel, I think that half-breed Comanche actually likes you. I think he believes you want to leave him and his people in peace. But if men like Miller keep on killing old men, women, and children, there isn't going to be anything that anyone will be able to do."

Jeremy clenched his fingers into fists at his sides. Robert was right. What the hell could he expect out of the Comanche when white men brutalized their people daily? Not that they weren't a warlike tribe—they were. But Buffalo Run seemed to know a hell of a lot more about making a treaty—and keeping his word—than the United States government.

"Damn Miller!" he repeated furiously.

Robert remained silent—there was nothing either of them could say on the matter. "All right," Jeremy said. "We'll have to take greater care. No small hunting parties heading out. I'll speak to the men, all of them. I think I'll ride out to the site myself." He started to walk away, then paused. "Keep a careful eye on my wife until I return."

The Cherokee nodded, placing a hand over his chest. "I'll guard her with my life."

Robert was his man, Jeremy knew. Fiercely loyal.

But he seemed to be falling under Christa's spell too. Don't love her too deeply, he wanted to warn the man. Don't let her hold your heart because she is clad in some prickly armor, and the knives she carries will cut and hurt you and you'll be bleeding before you even know that you were struck.

"Thank you," he told Robert. He strode away, calling for Staff Sergeant Hallie to bring around his horse. He called up Company B and ordered the men to prepare quickly. They were going to ride.

Nathaniel had gone about his duties, leaving Christa alone by the river, sitting wearily on an old decaying log, when she first heard the bugle calls.

At least one of the companies was leaving the camp. She jumped up and started for the trail.

Jeremy wasn't necessarily leaving, she assured herself.

It might be a very good thing if he was leaving. If he did she wouldn't have to face him for quite some time, and that would surely be a relief.

But she didn't really want him to go. If something were wrong, Jeremy would be looking into the matter himself. And he would take all manner of risks because he was the senior officer.

She bit into her knuckle, wishing suddenly that she could run to him, warn him that he must take care. But, of course, if she hurried to him he might not want to see her. He was probably ready to throttle her over the things she had said to Clara Jennings. He had warned her not to make trouble.

She started along the path anyway, determined that she would at least discover what was going on. But even as she hurried along the trail she suddenly stopped, aware that someone else had stepped onto the trail.

It was Robert Black Paw, the Cherokee. Tall and usually quiet, he was an interesting figure. Today he wore his long ink-black hair in twin braids, and his regulation cavalry trousers along with a white shirt and a heavily decorated doeskin shirt. His features were not handsome, but they were chiseled like hard rock, giving him an exceptionally striking appearance. She didn't know his age; he seemed as old as time. Wherever Jeremy was going, Robert Black Paw would know.

"Robert, my husband—"

"He will return before dawn," Robert said. She stared at him, then started to hurry past him. "Mrs. McCauley," he said, stopping her. She looked back to him.

"He is already gone."

"What is it? What's going on?" she asked him tensely.

"There is nothing for you to be afraid of."

She kept hearing that. All along this trail. But there were things to be afraid of, and she knew it.

There were Comanche.

"Has he ridden out against a war party?"

Robert shook his head gravely. "He will be back before dawn. You are safe. He is safe."

She realized suddenly that Jeremy could have found her if he had wanted to. He could have given her this message himself.

He hadn't wanted to see her. Maybe he hadn't trusted himself with her. Maybe he didn't want his officers and their wives to know that he was itching to throttle his wife.

This was all for the best. She could pretend to be sleeping whenever he returned. With any luck, she wouldn't really have to talk to him until he'd had a chance to cool down a bit.

I'm not afraid of him and I was right, she cried inwardly.

But something felt hollow and empty inside her. She was worried, worried that something could happen to him. Her heart beat too strongly. She pressed her palm against it. She couldn't bear to lose him.

How had she become so entangled? She could not love him! But perhaps she did.

Robert Black Paw watched her with that seemingly ageless wisdom in his dark eyes. "Thank you, Robert," she told him, and walked by. She skirted around the camp. She had no desire to return to the scene of their picnic. Bertha would lovingly tend to the beautiful silver and china that she had brought along with her from what had once been her hope chest.

She skirted around the campsite with its endless array of A-frame tents to come to their own much larger canvas structure. She entered the flap and closed her eyes, then opened them again. Home away from home. She had made their camp bed that morning, but she had done so quickly. Someone else had been in to clean behind her. Jeremy's desk was next to one of the center support poles, his papers neatly stacked. The smaller secretary with her own writing instruments and her books was across from it.

Just as if it were all laid out for a loving couple. One that could spend an evening together, silent but bonded by the emotions between them, each set upon his or her own task.

For a home in the wilderness, it was so very domestic! Her trunk lay open with one of her cool cotton skirts stretched across it. A clean cavalry jacket lay folded over Jeremy's. The beautiful quilt that Callie had made them was folded over the foot of the bed. The washstand, pitcher, bowl, and mirror were set to one side of the tent, while a small squat folding table that held the bottles of brandy, wine, and whiskey lay invitingly near the desks. Christa bit her lip, staring at it. Ah, the downfall of the wine.

Ah, the downfall of her own heart!

What would his feelings be when he saw her again? He had been so furious with her after their evening with Sherman! Would he return angry enough to half-kill, and would it turn into a tempest again?

Or perhaps it might be as he had said when she had warned him not to touch her. Perhaps she wasn't so special. Perhaps she would bring him to a point where he wouldn't care at all any longer.

She paced the tent, wishing that he hadn't ridden away. They should have had it out by now.

"Christa!"

Someone called her softly from outside the tent. She lifted the flap. Celia Preston stood there, tiny, delicate, so pretty in her silver-gray day dress.

Beyond her, Christa saw Robert Black Paw was standing watch over the tent. She lifted a hand to him in salute. He nodded gravely.

Celia slipped into the tent, swirled around observing it, then plumped herself lightly down upon the foot of the bed. She smiled. "What space you have here! Of course, our tent is larger than most since Jimmy is a lieutenant, but this"—she broke off laughing, her velvet brown eyes wide —"this is sheer elegance in the wilderness." Her smile faded. "Oh, Christa! I'm so nervous. Jimmy rode out with Colonel McCauley and Company B. What's going on? What's happened?"

Christa shook her head. "I don't know. But everything is all right, Celia. The men are just very careful, you know that."

Celia nodded. "I hope you'll forgive me for intruding. I was just so nervous . . ." Her voice trailed away, and then she smiled again. "Oh, Christa! Did you give that virago what for this afternoon! You were wonderful. She's still so indignant she's about to pop! She and Mrs. Brooks haven't stopped buzzing about you! May I have a glass of wine? Will you join me?"

"Yes, of course, I'm sorry, I should have offered you some already," Christa said.

"Join me?"

"Er, I think not," Christa murmured. She poured Celia a glass of the burgundy, handed it to her, and sat down beside her.

"How do you endure this awful waiting?" Celia said.

"I haven't had to endure it often," Christa murmured. Celia was staring at her again. She realized she had the young woman's total—and perhaps awed—admiration.

"You're so strong, so wonderfully strong!" Celia said. "And you manage with everything, no matter what happens! Jimmy tells me how wonderful you are all the time!"

"Maybe I will have a glass of wine," Christa murmured. She felt so guilty. She didn't deserve any admiration. She did everything that she did just so that her husband would never see her falter in any way, just so that she wouldn't betray the slightest weakness. That was hardly noble.

"I wish I could be like you," Celia said.

"Jimmy adores you."

She smiled. "Oh, I hope so. But you see, you manage to be beautiful and the perfect wife."

Christa swallowed down a long draft of wine, fiercely reminding herself that she needed to go slow, that she mustn't drink too much.

She had, after all, become an excellent wife at last because of it.

"Celia, trust me. Jimmy finds *you* to be a wonderful wife." She hesitated just a second. "And believe me, my husband does not often find me so perfect as you claim."

Celia stood, her pretty mouth curving into a small smile. "How can you say that!"

"Easily. I assure you that he wasn't very pleased with anything I had to say to General Sherman. Nor can he be very happy about today."

Celia giggled. "I think that the 'Dixie' was the finishing touch with General Sherman! But, Christa! You're very wrong! It's a pity you didn't stay this afternoon. I can't remember his words, but he assured Clara Jennings that he had far more to say to her than he might to his wife! Christa, the colonel applauded your words to her! Why, surely, all of the men and ladies present—other than that shrew herself!—were in sympathy with you!"

Christa felt as if her heart skipped a beat. Jeremy had defended her? Against Clara Jennings? Was it true, or was Celia trying to make her feel better about the disaster of a social?

Celia leapt up suddenly, setting her wineglass down upon the little table. She gave Christa a quick and startling hug. "Oh, if I just had the courage to speak as you did! You were wonderful. I try every day to be more like you!"

Christa shook her head. "Celia, don't say such things. Your husband loves you just the way that you are. You don't want to be hardened, believe me. I'm just the way that I am because I was . . ." She broke off. She didn't know how to explain the war, or the things that had happened after the war.

"A Rebel!" Celia supplied for her. Her brown gaze was still filled with affection and admiration. "Christa, I'm so sorry for you. For all the things that happened. I was so very far away. The war was just something I read about in the paper. Until I married Jimmy, of course, and he was assigned to Washington. Then the war was over before I ever found out that he had been with the troops sent in at the last. I can't even imagine what it must have been like to live in Virginia, with the battles going on constantly, with kinfolk involved, with the enemy swarming everywhere. I would have never survived it."

Christa smiled wryly. "We survived, Celia, just because it's natural to do so. And—" She paused again. "It is all over now, isn't it?"

Celia nodded happily. "I'm so grateful, because I just don't know how I'd endure this without you!" She sighed, then hurried toward the flap. She stopped and looked back. "Thank you, Christa."

Christa shook her head. "No, thank you, Celia."

Celia beamed. "I want to be there, waiting, when Jimmy comes back. Good night."

"Good night."

Christa watched her go. She sat for a while, wondering if it could be true, if Jeremy had really defended her.

A while later, Robert Black Paw called to her. He had brought her some of the buffalo stew left over from the ill-fated picnic.

She thanked him, but she wasn't hungry. She left it to sit upon her writing desk. He asked her if she wanted anything else and she hesitated, then asked him if he thought some of the soldiers would mind heating her some water and bringing in the ladies' camp tub. Robert assured her the men would be glad to serve her, and it seemed that they were. In less than thirty minutes she had her bath.

She used a few precious drops of her rose-scented bath oil and soaked and scrubbed until she felt wonderfully, squeaky clean. In the middle of her bath, she realized that she was doing it all for her husband. Tonight she felt that she owed him a certain debt.

Camerons always paid their debts. She had told him that once.

He could still return furious with her. He might have defended her just to save face.

Still, tonight she would wait up for him.

She dressed in one of her flannel nightgowns and sat down in the chair behind her desk. She brushed her hair a hundred strokes, then curled her toes beneath her and sat, waiting. Through the white canvas of the tent she could see the fire Robert Black Paw had built burning brightly. He was out there, warming his own meal, brewing dark rich coffee.

She watched the play of the flames.

The night drew on. She watched as the fire burned lower and lower.

Her eyes grew heavy. She slid more deeply into the chair, then rested her head on the desk and closed her eyes. She wasn't going to fall asleep. She was far too nervous to do so.

But she closed her eyes.

And she slept.

When she woke the tent was dark. She was stretched out and comfortable. There was a remarkable warmth at her backside.

Disoriented in the darkness, she slowly became aware that she was no longer in the chair.

And she was no longer alone.

Jeremy had come home.

She stiffened. He had picked her up and brought her here, to lie beside him. But he wasn't touching her. He was drawn to his own side of the bed.

"What's wrong?" She heard his voice, deep and low.

He wasn't sleeping. He had sensed her slightest movement.

She didn't answer him. Her heart was suddenly thudding and she was afraid. She wanted to feign sleep.

He wasn't going to allow her to do so. "What's wrong?" he repeated.

"I—"

"Jesu, when the hell did you become afraid to speak your mind?" he demanded impatiently.

He still wasn't touching her.

He had said that morning that she was half-dead herself.

She bit her lip. It was really difficult to thank him for anything.

"I didn't mean to offend anyone this afternoon. It was just that when that woman started on Nathaniel—"

"You didn't offend anyone."

"I didn't mean to make you angry."

"Well, that's new," he murmured wryly.

Her back was still to him. She was glad. She was glad for the darkness too. He certainly had no intention of making anything easy for her.

She inhaled quickly and spoke in a rush. "I understand that you—that you defended my position. Perhaps you thought that you had to. I just wanted you to know that I really didn't mean to antagonize you, that I simply couldn't stand what she was saying about Nathaniel. I didn't want you to be angry—"

"I wasn't angry, Christa."

"I—"

"I know, Christa. My God, what kind of a wretch do you think me? Nathaniel has covered my back for years. He's one of my best friends. Did you think me so low that I wouldn't defend him myself?"

"But it wasn't just for Nathaniel. It was for him and for Tyne and Janey and for so many other people. I've never heard anything so incredible as her attitude! She's a northerner—"

Hell, yes, Jeremy thought, Clara Jennings was a northerner. Christa didn't understand that many of the men and women in the North had never seen Negroes, just as many men and women in the North didn't understand that more than half of the southern boys in the Confederacy had never owned a slave in their lives.

"The war has been won," he said quietly, staring at the dark canvas above them, "but real peace and freedom will probably take decades."

"Jeremy—"

She broke off.

Jeremy rose up on an elbow. She was trying to apologize, and to thank him. It was a unique experience.

And if he reached for her, she might even respond. Out of gratitude.

But tonight he was weary. Riding out to the scene of the Comanche raid had sickened his spirit, and he was tired.

And he wanted more than gratitude from his wife. He didn't want her paying off any imagined debts. He wanted magic again. The kind he had touched last night.

"Go to sleep, Christa," he told her.

He sensed the stiffening within her once again. He turned his back to her, closing his eyes tightly.

She smelled like roses, sweet and delicious. Her hair fell in a cascade of ebony silk, enough to entangle him straight to hell and back. When he had come in, she had been so incredibly beautiful, curled upon the chair, innocent in her sleep, all her defenses down. She had appeared so vulnerable. He had wanted to take her into his arms. Cradle her. Love her.

The scent of roses still teased his nose.

He clenched his eyes more tightly shut. Not tonight. There would be no battles fought, no peace discovered. He did not have to have her. He had warned her that she was not irresistible.

Then why did her scent haunt him so? Why did he long to turn to her? Bury his face against her neck and the sweet-smelling silk of her hair and forget the frontier and the death that stalked it.

He grit down hard on his teeth.

Who am I taunting? Her? Myself?

The answer was easy. He was the one in torment.

But then, he was the one who had so foolishly fallen in love, lost his heart.

And still he lay there, angered by his torment, his back to her.

Pride. What a foolish vice. She lay beside him. She had waited for his touch. And just last night, it seemed, they had evoked the angels when they had made love.

Damn his pride. He would hold her again.

At last he turned, yet when he did, it seemed that she slept again. He felt her breathing, slow, deep, and easy. It was very dark. He smoothed some of the hair from her face and felt her cheeks.

They were damp.

Christa crying? She didn't cry. Camerons didn't cry. The men or the women. She had told him so. She had cried wretchedly and alone before leaving Cameron Hall, but not a tear had appeared in her eyes since. She was fierce, she was strong.

"What in hell is this we have made for one another?" he whispered softly aloud. He slipped his arms around her and pulled her close against him, holding her as she slept. His hand fell beneath her breast. Her back lay against his chest, his hips curved around her derriere.

The ache of his desire was not eased.

But something within his heart was. She slipped beside him so easily. Curved against him naturally.

It was good just to hold her.

Last night she had felt their child moving. There would be a new life created. He shuddered, remembering Jenny.

Jenny had died. With all his strength, he had to protect Christa. He had brought her to Indian territory. He should send her home.

But he could not send her away. He could only keep her safe. By his life, he silently vowed to do so.

He pulled her more tightly against him. He smoothed back her hair.
The night passed on.
Somewhere, a wolf howled.
In time, he slept.

Seventeen

Long, seemingly endless hours of rain and very hard travel kept Christa from seeing much of Jeremy over the next several days. Despite the rain they held a steady pace, and although he seemed not to choose to share any of his important decisions with her, James Preston was polite enough to always keep her abreast of what was going on. Captain Clark had moved on, being one of the messengers of the West, so he was no longer around to entertain them. But many of the other men were very kind, and despite her words with Sherman, they didn't seem to hold anything against her. Sergeant Jaffe had pointed a few men out to her, and to her surprise she learned that they had been wearing gray uniforms until just a short time ago. "Oh, we've an interesting army out here now, ma'am, that we do. A tough one! Half of these fellows have just spent four years shooting at other white men. They aren't going to bat an eye when they raise their guns to shoot at red men."

Christa didn't find that much of an encouraging thought. From the little that she did know about her husband, she knew that Jeremy was often appalled by the way his own army dealt with Indians. She knew that the reason he was so determined to move on was that he wanted to reach, occupy, fortify, and hold Fort Jacobson before harsh weather fell upon them.

For three nights they found high ground by the river when it was very late. The tents were not set up, and Christa spent the nights with Celia—and a parcel of the pointer puppies—in their wagon. By the fourth day the rain had abated. They passed a reservation of Indians, and Jaffe told her that they were Caddo Indians. They were "half-civilized" according to the sergeant, and Christa dismounted from her horse, intrigued and determined to buy whatever they were selling. One of the women was wearing a long cotton dressing gown in very pretty cotton. One of the men was adorned with a brightly colored kerchief about his head. A little child—very little, Christa thought, perhaps just a bit more than a year old —came running out and crashed into her legs. She laughed, a pain touching her heart as she thought of how he reminded her of her nephews and her niece. She scooped up the little boy and swung him around as she had once done so often with John Daniel and the others. The child, like any child—white, black, or red—let out a peal of laughter. The Caddo woman smiled slowly. Christa returned the child, and with Jaffe's help pointed out what she wanted to buy. They would soon be into an area where the majority of the nearby Indians would be Comanche and Kiowa, and neither tribe was an agricultural one. They followed the buffalo and made war upon their enemies, and supplemented their diets with berries and forage off the land. From the Caddo she bought numerous vegetables.

A number of the men were there, too, buying what they could. Thanks to Jaffe and some of the other cooks, Jeremy's men ate well, but army rations themselves were still rather sparse. A private in the army was paid thirteen dollars a month, Jaffe had told Christa. He was also allotted a weekly issue of salt pork, dry beans, green coffee beans, brown sugar, soap, and wheat flour. They were supposed to receive fresh meat twice a week, but since they had been hunting quite successfully—and since the buffalo kill—they had done much better than that. As far as fresh fruit and vegetables went, they were on their own. Even a number of the men who were known to gamble their pay before they received it were carefully buying up corn and greens from the Caddo.

They had started up on the march again long before Christa heard from Celia that Mrs. Brooks and Mrs. Jennings were back in Mrs. Brooks's ambulance praying for Christa's soul. "They're very upset about the way you played with the Indian child," Celia told her.

"You'd think they'd complain about the snakes and tarantulas instead of me for a while!" Christa muttered.

"Oh, they complain about those too!" Celia assured her, and laughed. Christa was glad of Celia's amusement. She had taken to the hardships of the last days very well. She was becoming a very well-adjusted cavalry wife.

They traveled well over twenty miles that day and camped on the Washita River. Nathaniel and Robert Black Paw had set up her portable home, and she was brewing coffee just outside the tent when she paused. It was dusk, but she could see that a cavalry officer had come into the encampment leading a group of three Indians.

There was something different about them, and it gave her pause. She rose slowly from the campfire, staring at the newcomers.

The night was cool yet they wore no shirts. They were dressed in high skin boots and breechclouts. There were paintings upon their horses in red, and their faces were also streaked with the color. The lead rider was wearing a headdress created from the head and horns of a buffalo. There was nothing civilized or tame about them. The very way that they rode seemed to speak of their freedom on the plains and of their fierce determination to cling to that freedom.

"Robert—" She turned quickly to her husband's Indian scout.

"Comanche," he said softly. He had been watching the newcomers too.

Her heart seemed to slam against her chest. "Why are they here? Were they captured? That can't be, the way that they are riding. How do they dare ride into the camp like that?"

Robert shrugged. "They've come to see the colonel. For now, they've come in peace. You do not need to be afraid."

She nodded. The Indians dismounted from their horses in front of the headquarters tent and disappeared within it.

Christa tried to settle into the tent but she couldn't do so. There was little for her to do. Robert had caught a prairie hare for their supper and quietly told her that he would tend to the meal himself. The bedding was arranged, the tent was comfortable. Celia was alone at last with her beloved James, and she certainly wasn't going to go pay a visit to Mrs. Brooks or Mrs. Jennings. Some of the other wives were very nice, but she only felt really close to Celia.

Nathaniel and Robert, ever concerned about her comfort, saw to it that after the long days of rain and mud the hip tub was brought in. She did relish her bath; she had felt almost as caked with mud as the earth itself.

She almost wished that Jeremy would come in while she was in it, since finding her in a bath tended to give him an urge toward action rather than conversation.

She was sure that she wanted to be held. To give in once again. To touch that shining pinnacle of paradise that came even here, in the wilderness.

She was so nervous about the night to come, because she had barely spoken with Jeremy since he had returned from his ride out on the plain. He hadn't touched her that night, and with the hardships of their ride, he had been a stranger since. It seemed that all she could remember was that he had called her "half-dead," but she had surely given him all that she had to give.

She left the bath, dressed, paced the tent, then sat at the edge of the bed. Jeremy still hadn't come. She leapt up suddenly. He was usually angry with her anyway—it didn't matter much if he wanted her with him or not now that the Comanche party had come. She was longing to see the Indians who kept even the most seasoned soldiers on edge.

She threw a shawl around her shoulders and left her own tent behind, heading straight for the headquarters tent. Private Darcy was on duty outside of it.

"Ma'am—" he began, ready to stop her.

She waved a hand his way. "It's all right, Mr. Darcy. I'm sure my husband won't mind."

Her husband would mind, but short of holding her back physically, there was nothing Darcy could do since she was on her way into the tent. She paused just inside the flaps, surveying the scene.

Captain Clark was the white man who had ridden in with the Indians. He was standing to the right of and just behind Jeremy. Two of the braves stood to the side of the desk. One of the Indians was speaking with her husband, and in an excellent English.

"It was just months ago when we gathered, thousands of us, Comanche, Apache, Kiowa, Pawnee, and more, on the banks of the Washita, hearing about the things that would be offered to us by the Great White Father of the Confederacy."

Christa's eyes widened as she realized that the man was talking about Jeff Davis.

Jeremy, seated behind the broad traveling desk that could be so easily transported to a wagon, nodded sagely to the man before him.

"The emissary from the Confederacy spoke to you in all good faith. But even as he was speaking, the government of the Confederacy was folding. Buffalo Run knows—"

"Buffalo Run knows that things happen—like the massacre at Sand Creek. He was glad when he learned that you were coming, for he remembers you well and he feels that you are, perhaps, the only honest white man he has met."

Jeremy leaned forward. "Eagle Who Flies High, I am pleased that Buffalo Run feels that we can negotiate. I have been very distressed. It was not long ago that I rode out here with a company from my regiment to discover that a stranded company of men from another regiment had been annihilated. And just days ago, I came across dead men on the plain. Is this Buffalo Run's message of good faith to me?"

"Just as you do not control all white men, Buffalo Run does not control all Comanche braves."

"Ah, but Buffalo Run can exert influence," Jeremy said.

The Indian before him—a man of medium height but with a solid, muscular build—inclined his head. "So he will speak with you. And his brothers Setting Sun and Walks Tall will await here in equal good faith."

"I am agreed," Jeremy said simply. He stood. The meeting had evidently been completed.

The Indian turned. He had been about to walk from the tent but he stopped, standing dead still as he saw Christa. Jeremy, who had been involved with his exchange with the man he had called Eagle Who Flies High, saw her too. His eyes narrowed, his jaw tightened. Christa felt a flush suffuse her as the Comanche studied her thoroughly from head to toe.

"My wife, Eagle Who Flies High," Jeremy said. The Comanche didn't really acknowledge Christa, he nodded to Jeremy.

"She is a fine wife." He studied Christa again in silence, turned back to Jeremy and bowed, then proceeded out of the tent, nearly brushing by Christa as he left. The other two braves followed him in silence, their dark eyes studying her with the same blunt appraisal.

When they were gone, Jeremy's wrath exploded. "What in God's name are you doing here?" he demanded, his tone low but shaking with the effort to keep it so.

"I just—"

"Colonel, sir," Emory Clark said, "surely it can't be Mrs. McCauley's fault to have stumbled upon us in the midst of—"

"Emory, I'll thank you to mind your own business!" Jeremy snapped, rising. He started toward Christa. "And you! You need to learn to stay out of business that does not concern you!"

"But it does concern me!" Christa retorted, wishing that she had never come, and miserable for both herself and for poor Emory. "The Comanche—"

"The Comanche are very fond of taking female captives!"

Emory cleared his throat. "He's concerned for your welfare, Christa—"

"Emory! I'll speak to my wife myself, thank you!"

"Yes, sir." Emory saluted. He didn't look pleased. He strode out of the tent.

"You didn't need to be so rude!" Christa cried.

"And you don't need to behave so stupidly!"

She stiffened, swung around, and strode out of the tent almost blindly. She nearly tripped over Private Darcy.

"Christa!"

She heard him, but she looked right at Private Darcy and pretended that she didn't. Furious, she strode on through the field of tents until she reached her own.

He was right behind, catching her by her shoulder, spinning her around. "Christa, don't walk out on me like that again!"

"Then don't yell at me like that again!"

"I'm just concerned—"

"Then you shouldn't have yelled at Captain Clark."

He threw up his hands. "Right. I wouldn't want to yell at the poor dear fellow who so resembles Liam McCloskey!"

"Oh!" she cried, and threw up her hands in aggravation. "You're right! He is poor Captain Clark. He will forever have to pay because of that!" Angrily, she pulled the pillow from the bed and threw it at him, hard. He caught it and tossed it to the bed, advancing on her. She backed away quickly, but found there was nowhere to go. He was nearly upon her when she began talking. "My God, I didn't mean to cause you difficulty!" she hissed out. "I didn't know if you were staying out all night or coming in. I merely wished to see—"

"You wished to see the Comanche!" he said.

She turned away quickly, trying to keep her fingers from shaking as she poured him a brandy, handing it to him quickly. To her surprise, he took it from her fingers. His eyes were still hard, silver and gun-metal gray. She quickly tried to ply her advantage.

"I've seen many of the Indians," she said.

"Not the Comanche."

"Yes, but they're important to you. There's so much that I don't understand. What was he talking about? What was the Sand Creek Massacre?"

"The Sand Creek Massacre," he repeated. He walked around his desk, pulled back the chair, and sat in it, his eyes remaining on her sharply. "You never heard of it?"

She shook her head. "There—there was a war going on."

"Yes," he murmured, looking away. "All right, you want to know. War came, and half the men out here resigned to go with the Confederacy. More men were pulled back to fight on the front. Once there was a fairly decent man named Wynkoop at a place northwest of here called Fort Lyon. Under terms, some Arapaho and Cheyenne Indians had put themselves under his protection. Wynkoop was too decent a man. Somebody decided to get rid of him and a Major Anthony came out to take charge. Governor Evans of Colorado and a militia colonel named Chivington wanted a war. Anthony managed to get the Indians to move away from the protection of the fort—he could attack them then. And he did. Chivington had given his men orders to attack all the Indians, to kill and scalp the big ones and the little ones because nits made lice. And so the men went in and killed, raped, maimed, and destroyed. A Captain Silas, a regular from Anthony's army, refused to follow the order. He was murdered in Denver soon after. Anthony and Chivington tried to make it sound like a noble battle, and still the truth got out to whites and red men alike. Buffalo Run is not a fool. He has seen the past, and by that, he sees the future. He doesn't trust many men."

Christa didn't think that she could blame Buffalo Run, not after the story Jeremy had told her. He didn't describe the slaughter in detail, but in his tone she could almost imagine what had happened and it had surely been horrible.

"It seems that Buffalo Run trusts you."

Jeremy shrugged. "He tolerates me—more than he is willing to tolerate most white men." He leaned forward suddenly, wagging a finger at her. "His men should have never seen you."

"But—"

"They are a polygamous society. Buffalo Run has several wives and probably wouldn't mind having another one."

"But—"

"The Comanche can move like the wind. They like to travel down to Mexico and trade with the Spanish. They trade women just like they trade buffalo meat and hides. They like to rape their female prisoners first so that they give the Spaniards a woman who is soiled. It's a way of being superior."

A chill was slipping over her. "But Jeremy, I came to the headquarters tent! I didn't wander out into open territory."

"But you've done so before," he reminded her tautly.

She felt a chill seeping into her. "I won't do so again," she said uneasily.

He was up suddenly, hands folded at his back, pacing the space between them. "See that you do stay close in!" he commanded. He stopped in front of her, his voice sharper than she had ever heard it to one of his soldiers. "Over the next few days, until my return, you must stay with Robert Black Paw. Always, always have him in sight."

"Until your return?" Christa said, startled.

"I am going with Eagle Who Flies High tomorrow to visit the place where Buffalo Run is keeping camp."

Christa gasped. "You're going—right into a Comanche camp? But you can't!"

"I've been in his camp before."

Christa shook her head. "But—how can you trust him? He kills people, he has his own set of rules, you just told me that!"

"I have to go, Christa. And I trust him more than I do most men, no matter what his color."

"If you trust him so much, why are you so angry with me?"

"Damnation!" he seemed to roar. "I've been trying and trying to make you understand!"

"Stop swearing at me like that!" she countered, her teeth gritting. "Mrs. Brooks will be in to get you!"

To her amazement, he paused. He sat down at the foot of the bed, staring at her incredulously, then smiling slowly.

"I have to go, Christa."

"But—"

"Will you miss me?"

Color touched her cheeks. "Jeremy, really—"

"Come now! Surely, you'll miss me just a little. I'm another body to fight off whatever threats may come!"

"You're a fool, marching into a hostile Indian camp!"

"Come here," he said suddenly.

"I—"

"Come here. I've got tonight. Then I've got to ride. I will not spend tonight arguing."

"You won't argue. No, you'll just yell and then expect me to jump at your beck and call."

"Fine!" He stood, strode the distance to her, lifted her high, and set her down upon the foot of the bed. "I'm not being a fool, Christa. Buffalo Run has sent two of his own brothers to be hostages here until I return safely. He and I are blood brothers. The Comanche are a very free people. There are many bands, usually created of family connections. Any Comanche is free to come and go from his band and a brave is certainly free to think for himself, but they all respect certain matters of honor among one another. Two minutes after I return here hostilities might break out. But while I'm under his promise of protection, I will be completely safe."

"Fine!" she said, repeating his words.

"You!" he said, pointing a finger at her. "I will never feel safe about you."

"But—"

"But! Will you miss me?"

She moistened her lips. "Perhaps."

His laughter was throaty.

"It will pain me every second that I am away."

"You are a liar!" she accused him.

"It's God's truth."

"Well, it's hard to tell. You do manage to keep your distance when you choose."

"And then I am furious with myself. There will be no distance tonight, Christa. When the night has passed, you will surely miss me. Whether you do with pain or pleasure, I can't be certain, but you will surely be aware of my presence tonight, and that it is gone tomorrow!"

A heat rose within her. She lowered her eyes quickly, avoiding his.

"What, no protests? No fury?"

The lamplight was very low and very soft. She stared down at her hands, studying them. No matter how she fought it, she felt a wave of crimson coloring rush to her cheeks and her words were soft and breathless. "You're mocking me. I truly don't know what you want! I surrendered everything the other night, everything. And you seemed pleased enough at the time, yet uninterested when you returned from your ride."

"I have never been uninterested!" he said, and he came down upon one knee, taking her hand from her lap to slide between his own. "Never."

"You said that I was half-dead."

"Because I wanted to shake you into the realm of the living."

She inhaled, feeling the fire of the silver in his eyes as they sought to impale her own. She refused to meet his gaze, shaking her head. "I did give in!" she murmured. "I swear, I ceased the fight! I—"

"You told me it was the wine," he reminded her. "I was palatable—because of the wine."

She lowered her head, wishing that he were not so close, so very demanding. "Perhaps it was. Perhaps it wasn't. I still don't understand what it is that—that you still want of me."

"More, Christa. I will always want more. But mainly, I want you to come to me. Not because I might defend you. Not because Camerons always pay their debts. But because you want me. Would that be so very difficult?"

She shook her head, swallowing hard. Her eyes met his at last. She tried to speak, moistening her lips with the tip of her tongue, seeking words, unable to find them. Perhaps he understood her dilemma, perhaps he knew exactly when to push her, and when to come to her rescue. He released her hands, his arms slipping around her. He rose, bringing her to her feet along with him. His mouth descended ardently down upon hers, seizing her lips in a fierce, hungry kiss. But one that gave so much more. One that teased, one that coerced. One that was hot and fervent, one that elicited fires to burn deep in secret places she had so recently discovered within herself.

Those fires seemed so quickly fanned! In the fierce sweetness of his kiss she swiftly understood more of what he sought from her, and with the honeyed excitement sweeping through her she dared to do those things she had dreamed before. Her arms slipped around his neck. Her lips parted more willingly to the pressure of his kiss, and tentatively at first, but more boldly with each passing second, she teased and taunted and elicited in return, her tongue playing with his, thrusting into his mouth, rimming it. Her fingers stroked the hair at his nape, caressed his cheek, curled into the muscles of his shoulders and arms. She felt the rampant beating of his heart, a hardness, a quickening within him. He lifted his head from hers at last, silver glistening in his eyes as they touched hers. "Jesu!" he whispered, and she smiled, unaware of how dazzling and beautiful the lights in her eyes could be. But he did not meet them long. He spun her around, his fingers impatient on the hooks of her gown. When the material fell from her shoulders, he spun her again, his lips touching down on her flesh, searing and wet, causing her breath to catch, and the flame within her to sizzle and soar. He eased her dress downward, and it fell in a pool at her feet. His fingers caught at the tie of her pantalets, and when they fell, she stepped from them. The lamplight seemed so gentle that night.

He sat, pulling off a boot. She knelt before him, taking off the other boot. She paused for a moment, aware that he was quickly shedding his shirt. Her eyes met his again and the searing spark of desire within them sent a flutter cascading from her heart to the center of her womb. She rose slightly, curling her arms around him. Her lips just brushed atop his, then pressed to his throat, to his collarbone, and trailed slowly across his shoulder. She teased his flesh with the tip of her tongue, tasting the salt there. Her fingers moved over the bronzed length of his arm, testing the ripple and feel of muscle. She sat back, watching with fascination as she brought her hands down over his chest, her fingertips dancing lightly over the crisp whorls of dark red hair upon it. She came close again, kissing his chest, testing with the hot tip of her tongue, finding a rich, rising excitement in the intrigue of his body.

"Christa!" He whispered her name huskily, rising suddenly, bringing her with him. Crushed against him, she grazed her knuckles over the length of his back, savoring the ripple and pull of his muscles. The soft sensations aroused him further. She stood on tiptoe. Her lips caught his, left them. Again she stroked his back. Lower. The evocative brush of her knuckles covering his buttocks. A husky groan escaped him, startling her. She found herself swept up and laid back upon the bed, dizzy with the sweet feel of her own commitment, so alive and vital, anticipating the wonder of what was to come. Yet when she saw that his cavalry pants were off him, she did not wait. He had said that he wanted her to want him. And she did. Her flesh burned. Ached for his touch on the outside. And on the inside . . .

The fire of her flesh was now searing inside of her, and the longing was deep and rich. Even as he walked toward her, she rose again. With a little cry, she raced toward him. She found herself swept up again. Her legs locked around his back as he spun with her, kissing her. He held still. She slid down the length of him. Fingers and lips covered his chest. Stroked his naked buttocks. Her eyes found his, questing, blue. "This . . . ?" she whispered.

A deep, guttural groan gave her sweet reply. "This!" he said. "This, this . . ."

Against the softness of her flesh she could feel the hard arousal of his sex. Her heart hammered. She didn't dare—she couldn't. She closed her eyes, leaning her forehead against his chest. She teased him first, inadvertently, with the brush of her knuckles. She felt his breath catch, his heart thud. She closed her fingers around him. An exclamation exploded from him. She grew bolder, stroking the hardness, exploring beyond, her hands touching the softness of his sac, coming against the sheer hardness of desire. Whispers fell from his lips that she scarce understood, yet she did not need to hear the words, for the desire and approval were so rich in his tone. She was lifted suddenly again and found herself breathless as she lay flat. She cried out softly, for he was within her and the feeling was delicious.

Her legs locked around him, holding him close. He brought her soaring to the very crest of a pinnacle, then withdrew. She felt his lips upon hers, upon her shoulders, upon her breasts. So sweetly upon her breasts, teasing, bathing, suckling, first one and then the other. She was whispering frantically herself, demanding that he cease the torture and come to her. But he did not. He stroked, caressed, and bathed the length of her with his kiss, with his demand. When he was done, he lifted her over him, drawing her slowly down, his eyes impaling hers even as his body did the same. He taught her to move, his eyes fully upon the lush fall of her hair, the sway of her breasts. His hands curved strongly around her buttocks, and he guided her until the natural force of her desire brought her hungrily against him, sweeping them both into a maelstrom that exploded into an ecstasy beyond all that she had ever imagined, sweet, volatile, and violent, and bringing her crashing down against him at last, entangling him in the wild fall of her hair even as it seemed that the world burst into brilliant sunlight, fell to darkness, and burst into a beautiful array of stars once again.

She slipped to his side, still amazed. His arm came around her and he held her tight against him. The feel of his flesh was still hot and slick and wonderful against her own. She lay still, grateful for the warmth that surrounded them.

She heard his whisper, deep, husky. Mocking perhaps, but yearning, too.

"Will you miss me?"

"Jeremy—"

"Will you miss me?"

God, yes! she might have cried out. I'll miss you like the sun, like air. More than I've ever missed anyone in all my life, more than I missed my brothers in the awful years of the war. I loved them but I love you. Oh, my God, yes, I love you.

"Jesu! If it takes that long, you're not convinced!"

A gasp escaped her. She was suddenly, fiercely, in his arms again.

He made love to her, slowly, fervently, thoroughly. He erased all thoughts from her mind, other than the hungers and the beauties of human sexuality. When she lay panting at his side once again, he repeated the question.

"Will you miss me? If not—"

"Yes!" she gasped.

And the sound of his laughter was warm, as were his arms when he pulled her gently within them.

"My love, I'll miss you too!" he vowed softly. "Dear God, but I will miss you too!"

Eighteen

The days that Jeremy traveled to Buffalo Run's camp—accompanied by James Preston along with a few other men—moved slowly. Although Major Jennings and Major Brooks had more western combat experience, Jeremy had left the regimental physician, Major Weland, in command. Christa knew that both Mrs. Jennings and Mrs. Brooks had their noses cleanly out of joint, and she couldn't help but feel a little smug about it. She also saw the wisdom in Jeremy's choice. Weland held a comparative rank, and though he was their physician he was also a curious man with an open mind, fascinated by people, far quicker to think than he was to take up arms.

She had promised Jeremy that she would miss him and she did, desperately. She was amazed to discover that she lay awake night after night, aching for him physically and within her heart and soul. She wondered if there would ever be a time when she could tell him the truth of her feelings. Still, she lay awake sometimes in agony, wondering at all the secrets he kept locked within his own soul, wondering about Jenny, wondering about the child she had lost.

Though Jeremy and his men traveled slowly, they moved ever westward.

On the third day after Jeremy's departure, Weland invited her to the command tent to sup with him, and she was delighted to discover that he had a letter for her from home. A messenger had found their encampment that afternoon and come through with a great deal of mail. The letter was for her and Jeremy, and there were bits and pieces in it from everyone in the family—including a scrawl from the oldest of the next generation, Jesse and Kiernan's son, John Daniel Cameron. Callie, Kiernan, and Jesse wrote little bits of cheerful news about everyday life. Daniel, who had always been the best correspondent in the family, wrote more. She bit her lip, reading that he and Callie had taken a trip to Fort Monroe, where Jeff Davis was being held. Varina had been so good to them when times had been different in her life, they had been determined to see what they could do in return. There was little. The Union didn't know what it wanted to do with Jeff Davis yet. There had been rumors that he should be hanged, but even Daniel was certain that such a thing would never come to pass.

I think they will incarcerate him for a while, and then let him go. Perhaps they are afraid that the South shall rise again. It cannot do so. We are the lucky ones among our countrymen, for our land is in good repair, our house stands tall, and we have weathered it well. Still, to travel the nearby countryside! Building takes place daily, but wherever one goes it seems there are still the remnants of once great manors to be seen. Fields lie fallow or are overgrown, and at times it seems—in truth—that locusts have descended. I am not yet pardoned, but we have been encouraging Jesse to seek public office. Someday, this madness will end. The government of the southern states will be returned to the states. It seems that some of our most fervent Confederates are now dedicated to the task of sewing up the rip in the country. Perhaps we can start that here. It is sad and bitter to imagine that it will take years and years for all of the land to return to its bounty, for homes to rise again free from bullet holes and cannonballs, but it cannot begin at all unless we set our backs to the task.

She let the letter fall into her lap, imagining what home would look like now. The autumn foliage would be upon them. The landscape would be alive in crimsons and yellows and oranges.

"Homesick?" Weland asked her.

"A little bit."

"But it's not so bad as it was at first?"

She shrugged, then smiled slowly. "I admit, the travel is fascinating."

"The wild, wild West!" Weland murmured. "It will become more fascinating still."

"But at home they're rebuilding the South," Christa said softly.

Weland stood, coming around behind her, and gave her a paternal squeeze upon the shoulders. "There are great things happening!" he told her. "So many men and women have seen the downfall of the Confederacy as the end. Christa, we are entering upon a new age. We have battled ourselves at last. Now we can look to the future. The West will explode.

The South will rebuild. It is an exciting time to be alive. It makes the choices all the more difficult."

"What choices?"

He came back around the dinner table, smiling at her. "Whether to explore the new world, or rebuild the old. Will your home be in Virginia, or in the West?"

She shook her head. "I don't think that I have any choices," she said ruefully. "Jeremy is a cavalry officer. I will go where he—" She paused. She had almost said "commands." "I will go where he goes."

Weland smiled. "Home has always been where the heart is. That is what you must discover. In time you will." He shook his head. "It is the poor Indian I pity!" he said.

Christa's eyes widened. She heard enough descriptions of what the Indians could do to wonder how Weland could speak so broadly.

"They are the true losers!" he told her. He spread out a hand. "Day after day, more wagon trains come now. The war kept us from this expansion. But now Americans, from the North and the South, will head here in droves. They'll settle and they'll force the government to break more and more treaties." He leaned forward. "Why do you think the Comanche hate the Texans so much?"

"I didn't know—"

"They hate the Texans! Why, they don't even think of the Texans as Americans. Other settlers are other settlers. But the Texans—the Comanche feel the Texans already stole all their land."

"Did they?"

"Sure did." Weland lit his pipe and winked at her. "That's progress for you!"

She smiled. She liked Dr. Weland. He always made her feel comfortable and as if she belonged. As if she was wanted, loved, cherished.

"Well, now. Will you have more coffee?" he asked her. She shook her head and thanked him. "I'm going to go and write back to my family," she told him. She wished him good night and returned to her tent.

As she walked back, she could hear some of the men singing soft songs to get them through the long hours of camp life. She didn't hear footsteps following her, but she sensed them. When she reached her tent, she paused. "Good night, Robert Black Paw!" she called out softly.

There was silence. Then she heard, "Good night, Mrs. McCauley."

Feeling curiously happy, she slipped into her tent, wrote a long letter home, and went to sleep. She only stayed awake awhile, staring at the canvas of the tent.

Jeremy had said with conviction that he would be safe. He would return.

The troops moved onward while awaiting his return. The country they came upon grew more and more intriguing. They were upon the Canadian River, Nathaniel told her, at a place near the line dividing Indian territory and the upper part of Texas.

The river was fascinating, being full and broad sometimes, then seeming to disappear. Nathaniel showed her how the water ran beneath the surface.

In the afternoon they came upon the "Antelope Buttes." They amazed Christa, being high tables of rock with the tops apparently perfectly flat. The sides of the buttes sloped precariously steep. The way that they dotted the landscape seemed so unique to her that she spent long hours staring at them once they had camped for the night.

It was because of this that when the sun ceased to sparkle so brightly against her eyes, she saw the pole sticking out of one of the buttes.

Curious, she rode Tilly to the headquarters tent. Weland was deep in conversation with Jennings and Brooks, charting their course for the next day, and no one noticed her at first.

"We are dragging our feet enough as it is!" Major Brooks said gruffly. "Colonel McCauley was the first to want to make haste. If he doesn't return tomorrow, we must push on harder!"

"Gentlemen, I have followed his orders precisely, and see no reason to change my course of action," Weland argued in return.

"Except that you can't trust that Comanche half-breed, Buffalo Run!" Jennings insisted wearily. "Major Weland, if the colonel doesn't return tomorrow, I'd say it's very likely that he and the other men might well be dead!"

Christa didn't realize that she had cried out until all three men stared at her. Weland was instantly on his feet. "Major!" he declared. "What a way to speak!" He rushed to Christa's side. "And the colonel's lady with child here in the wilderness. You should be ashamed of yourself, sir!" He forced Christa to sit. She saw him wink and shrugged.

"Oh, I do feel faint!" she moaned.

Jennings was quickly up, the poor henpecked man. "I'm sorry. So sorry, Mrs. McCauley! It's just that we have the whole of the regiment to worry about."

"Jeremy said that he'll come back. He will," she insisted.

"Yes, Mrs. McCauley," Jennings said. He cleared his throat and twirled his mustache. "Well then, I'll be on my way! Brooks?"

"Yes, yes, I'll be joining you."

The two majors left hastily. Christa burst into laughter watching them go. She smiled at Weland. "You were wonderful."

"No, you were wonderful—getting them out of my hair like that!" His smile faded. "You are feeling all right? I promised Jesse a healthy nephew or niece, you know. And of course, if I let any ill come to you, Jeremy would simply hang me."

"Oh, he would not!" Christa protested.

He stared at her, then smiled. "But he would! Well, never mind that now. Did you come to me because you were feeling sick or social—or both?"

She shook her head. "There's something up on one of the buttes."

He frowned. "What?"

"I don't know, but I'll show you."

He accompanied her out, calling to a private for his horse. He rode with Christa to the last tent, from where they could see the pole that seemed to extend from one of the buttes."

"I'll have Robert Black Paw see to it," Weland said. "I'll ride back and have him sent for."

Christa smiled. "Oh, there's no need to do that!" She raised her voice, whirling Tilly around. "Robert! Robert, where are you?"

Weland glanced to her, his brows arched, as Robert sheepishly rode out from behind one of the tents. He pointed to the pole. "Do you think you can reach the top of the butte?" Weland asked him.

Robert Black Paw nodded, but he looked to Christa. "I'll climb the butte. But—" He paused.

"I promise that I won't leave Major Weland's side until you return," Christa told him.

That satisfied him. With a few other men, Robert started out for the butte. Weland and Christa paid a visit to Celia, trying to cheer her up. Then they returned to the headquarters tent and waited, engaging in a game of chess.

Weland took so long to move at one point that Christa sat back, staring at him.

"Robert knew what was on the pole," he said.

Startled, Christa raised a brow. "Do you know?"

"I'm afraid I might."

She didn't have a chance to ask him what he knew. He was staring over her shoulder. She looked back to see that Robert had returned. He carried nothing with him, but stared at Weland.

"Whatever it is, say it, please!" Christa demanded.

"Christa, I don't know if you should—"

"Oh, please! You both know that I will not pass out or go into fits of hysteria!"

"A scalp?" Weland asked.

"Yes, a scalp. A white scalp."

She didn't get hysterical, she didn't pass out, and she didn't shriek.

But she did panic. Cold, black fear filled her. She felt the first taste of bile and terror rise to her throat. "A white scalp. Oh, my God, Jeremy—"

"No, no! Christa," Robert Black Paw said quickly, forgetting his customary manner and using her Christian name. He knelt down beside her. "It is a woman's scalp. The hair is long and light."

"Oh!" She locked her fingers together in her lap, holding them tightly.

"And how was it found?" Weland asked.

"Stretched out on a hoop, secured to the pole by sinew ties."

"You think it's a warning?"

"Perhaps."

"Do you think that Jeremy is safe?" Christa whispered.

"Buffalo Run gave his word of honor. Jeremy will be safe," Robert said flatly. Weland didn't say anything at all.

Christa leapt up. She felt so nervous. She had to be alone. "I—I think I'll go to bed then. We'll probably rise early. I'm—I'm very tired."

"Christa!" Weland said.

She paused, looking back at him.

"Jeremy will be all right."

She nodded. Fear had begun to live within her. She could not control it.

In her own tent she paced up and down.

She felt the baby moving and bit her lip, wondering if Jeremy might have been able to feel the strength of the movement if he had been with her. She sat on the bed, remembering how he had withdrawn from her the night she had said the baby was moving.

He hadn't told her then, but of course he had been remembering. Remembering Jenny and the child who should have lived.

She pressed her fingers to her cheeks. She was in love with a man whose thoughts were with someone else.

No. He had said she was the perfect cavalry wife. Her cheeks colored when she responded to him. She didn't think she could do anything but respond now.

She stood up, poured herself just a touch of brandy, and sipped it. It warmed her.

She dressed for bed in warm flannel, then curled up on her pillow. She

could see the campfires burning beyond the canvas. She had to sleep.
She turned down the lamp.

The fires burned low. She had to sleep, for the baby. For their son or
their daughter. A child who would grow in the new world. In Weland's
age of discovery. Sympathetic to the misfortunes of the South, sympathetic with the ideals of the North.

She closed her eyes and dozed.

Something was moving. She tried to awaken. All that she could see in
the mist between wakefulness and sleep was the rise of the butte. And
the pole upon that butte.

She could hear drums, she thought. War drums. She could see warriors, Comanche warriors, dancing to the rhythm of those drums.

Jeremy was there, staked out upon the dry earth. One of the Comanche braves, his face painted red, was bearing down on him with a razor-
sharp knife aimed at his skull.

She awoke, gasping for air, leaping from her bed. There was someone
within the tent. A scream rose in her throat. The Indians had come!

Arms encircled her in the near darkness. "Christa!"

It was Jeremy. She gasped, trembling. She forgot that he had ever been
her enemy. "Jeremy! Oh, Jeremy! You're back! You've returned."

He was startled by the vehemence of her greeting. He smoothed back
her hair, determined to enjoy her welcoming of him rather than analyze
it.

"I told you that I'd come back."

"Yes, but they found a scalp!"

He didn't tell her that many, many a scalp could be found in the West
—and many, many of those Indian scalps taken by white men.

"I heard. I've seen Weland," he told her. Still holding her, he tossed his
hat from his head. She didn't seem anxious for him to let her go. In the
dim light he tried to study her eyes, but they were shielded by the darkness. Still, darkness couldn't shield everything. Every time he left her and
returned to her, he was struck anew by her beauty. Her skin was flaw-
less, her face so delicately, classically, beautifully molded. And the softness of her! Her breasts were very large with her pregnancy, her belly just
beginning to round with it. She was sweetly warm in his arms. He could
hear the ferocity of her heartbeat, feel the unsteady rhythm of her breath.

"So you missed me?" he said lightly.

"I—" She paused, remembering the way that they had parted. "Of
course I missed you," she murmured. "You left me here alone with those
horrible Brooks and Jennings people!"

He laughed, familiar with the slightly tart twist of her voice. She may have claimed to have surrendered. But she had never done so. He might be battling all his life.

His smile faded. He didn't mind that. He didn't mind the skirmishes, nor did he ever mind trying to win.

If only he could rid them of their ghosts!

If only she could love him in return. But he didn't place his heart on a platter before her.

Camerons, among other things, could be ruthless.

"Well, I'm back now," he told her softly.

Her smile eased. She slowly withdrew her arms from about his neck. "Well, how did things go with the Comanche, with this Buffalo Run person?"

"I don't want to talk about Buffalo Run or the Comanche at this moment."

"Oh. Then, I . . . would you like wine? Brandy? A whiskey."

"No, thank you." He unbuckled his scabbard, casting it aside.

"I could make you some coffee—"

"There is only one thing I want," he said flatly.

Even in the darkness, he could see the color that rushed to her cheeks. "Oh."

"Well?"

"Well?" she whispered.

"Am I being offered that for which I truly hunger?"

Her lashes fell. "You know that you can always take what you want!"

"That's not what I asked you."

Her lashes rose. There was a flush of fury in her eyes. "Why do you do this to me?"

"I wasn't aware that I was doing anything to you. Yet!" he added with a smile. He touched her chin, lifting it. His eyes searched hers again. "You were all that I thought about the hours I was gone. I should have been concentrating on the importance of words spoken between Buffalo Run and me, but my mind kept wandering. I would close my eyes and see you here, naked, the fall of your hair about you, a sheen upon your flesh, the slightest curl of a smile to your lips. What have you done, Christa, bewitched me? Are Camerons so talented?"

She gazed at him, her eyes widening. She didn't reply, and he pressed his point. "I'm hungry, Christa. Starving for the touch and taste of you. Tell me, do you offer yourself up as freely as you would pass out whiskey or wine?"

"I can't play these word games!" she whispered.

He caught her arms, pulling her against him. "No games, Christa. Tell me! Will you come to me?"

"Yes!" she gasped. She truly couldn't say anything more. But tonight, the darkness and her own hungers were her shield. She slipped her arms around his neck. She rose on her toes and kissed him. The long hours of worry and waiting added to the savoring hunger of her kiss, and he marveled at the feel of her in his arms.

He lifted her up, thanking God in heaven, and brought her to their bed. She said nothing more and he forced nothing more from her.

He had no desire to break the fragile magic.

It lasted through the night.

He felt her get out of bed. Still drowsy himself, he watched her with half-closed eyes. She was so graceful and supple, sliding from the covers in the pale dawn, tall and naked and elegant, no matter that slight rounding of her stomach. He enjoyed watching her when she thought that he slept, dousing her face in wash water from the pitcher on the trunk, shivering fiercely, then dressing as silently as she could, determined not to wake him.

He tried not to smile, certain that she would go out and start the morning coffee, then come back to him. At the moment, he didn't care what time the regiment started moving. He'd earned his rest.

He watched her slip out of the tent and luxuriated in the comfort of his camp bed after the nights spent sleeping on the ground with his saddle as a pillow. She would return soon enough, bringing him coffee. The morning would be sweet.

He rolled over, glad to keep his eyes closed for a few minutes longer as he mulled over his days with Buffalo Run.

There were numerous bands of Comanche. They were all still friendly with the Wind River Shoshone, the tribe from which they had sprung and with whom they shared a common language. They had formed alliances with the Kiowa to create bigger raiding parties, but they fought the Utes —with whom they also shared their language. They acknowledged no central tribal chief or government, but each band recognized its own chief who might also hold some sway with the chiefs of other bands.

Buffalo Run was such a chief.

He was an intelligent man, a half-breed, a renegade. Many people thought that the Comanche were responsible for a majority of the white deaths in the West, but Jeremy didn't feel that Buffalo Run enjoyed the spectacle of death.

He had simply watched what happened with white men and learned from the misfortunes of others. When Jeremy had sat with him in the four-poled conical dome of his tepee, he had listened to Buffalo Run and admitted that he was listening to a history that placed a dark cloud upon his own people.

"Think on this, McCauley!" Buffalo Run had said, waving a hand in the air to create a picture. "It was just eighteen forty-six when your General Kearny took Santa Fe, until then the capital of Spanish and Mexican New Mexico. Navaho raiders stole some of his beef and went on to raid the settlements. Yes, white settlers were killed. Yes, the Navaho stole thousands of sheep, cattle, and horses. But General Kearny began a campaign against the Navaho that ended with over eight thousand of their number becoming prisoners at one of your white forts. Since eighteen sixty-four they still reside there."

"Perhaps it was Kearny's way of warning other tribes that they mustn't raid and steal."

"Perhaps it is his way to trick other tribes into submission. I tell you McCauley, I have seen the white man's ways. Your people will not be happy until they have annihilated mine."

"Your mother was white," Jeremy reminded him.

Buffalo Run smiled. He was a striking Indian. Despite his white blood, his eyes were an obsidian black, his features strong, bronzed, and clean-cut.

"I have never minded a white woman or child who lives with the *Numinu,*" he said, using the Comanche's own term for the tribe. It meant "the people." "They learn our ways and they become one with us."

Jeremy had sat back then, still wondering why Buffalo Run had determined to have him come to his camp. He had been greeted as a friend. Buffalo Run's three wives, two of them sisters and the third a cousin to the other women, had seen to it that he had been brought the best of their buffalo meat, clean water, and a bottle of good Irish whiskey—one that had been traded for or stolen, he didn't want to know which. He was an honored guest, but he was certain that Buffalo Run wanted something.

He did. "I've not brought you here to make promises that you cannot keep, nor can I give you promises when the Comanche are a free people."

"Why am I here?"

"White men in gray uniforms have taken my youngest wife's sister. I have promised to take her in as one of my own. I am a powerful man, able to care for many women."

Jeremy nodded. A Comanche might take as many wives as he desired —and could handle.

Personally, Jeremy was certain that dealing with one vixen was enough.

"I hear that you have acquired a wife," Buffalo Run said.

"Yes." He didn't know why he felt so uncomfortable.

"Eagle Who Flies High tells me that she is a very beautiful woman."

He nodded again. "Yes." He hesitated. "We are expecting our first child."

"May you have a son."

Jeremy refrained from telling Buffalo Run that he did not care if his child were a son or a daughter—he cared only that his child be born alive and that Christa endure the labor with her life and health intact. "Thank you," he told the Comanche chief. "I still don't understand—"

"I want my wife's sister returned to me. I want you to go after the men in gray, and I believe that you will do so."

"Men in gray must be Confederate soldiers. Turned outlaw perhaps," Jeremy said. "I don't know what I—"

"They stole Morning Star," Buffalo Run interrupted, "and I would kill them, but they are armed with the Colt revolvers the Texas Rangers are so fond of using against us. I would lose many men. My braves are not afraid—to die in battle is the honorable way to die and a way to join one's ancestors."

Jeremy understood that. The Comanche believed in an afterlife—but that afterlife was denied men and women who died in the dark, who were strangled, drowned—or scalped. Burial ceremonies were important and sacred among the Comanche, and to die in battle was always the way for a warrior to fall.

"Then—"

"These men also held up the trading post just this side of Indian territory. They killed Joseph Greenley who was your friend, I understand. Eagle Who Flies High followed them. They also attacked a Union pay wagon, and slit the throats of the men who threw down their weapons."

"I would like to find them."

Buffalo Run nodded. "There is more. The men carried off Comanche arrows when they took Morning Star. They have made their acts look like the work of Comanche. They have left these arrows with their victims, and they have scalped the men and cut their tongues from their mouths."

Jeremy nodded again. Buffalo Run had asked him to come to his camp as a gesture of true friendship. He was being given the honor of bringing these men in.

Back in his own tent, he punched his pillow and laid his head back down on it. He could smell the coffee Christa was making. In a matter of minutes she would bring him a cup and he would take it gladly. Maybe they would share it. Then he would have to find a way to convince her to take off her clothing even though it was early morning.

She was coming in. Carrying a tin cup of coffee, just as he had known she would.

She walked to the foot of the bed. He anticipated the light tones of her voice, the rich taste of the coffee, the softness of her flesh.

"You—bastard!" she hissed.

He jumped up just in time to avoid the heat of the coffee spraying over tender parts of his anatomy. The cup nearly hit him on the head.

Her hands were on her hips, her hair was wild, her eyes were a blue glistening fire. She didn't seem to care in the least that she had nearly endangered the prospect of a sister or brother for their unborn child.

"You, you—bastard!" she spat again, furious.

The end of magic, he thought.

Christa had seen the Confederate prisoners.

"Madam, may I suggest you cease," he warned her harshly, "unless you would share their fate?"

"Gladly! Imprison me with them, tie me up, do your worst! How dare you! They are lost, they are beaten, and you would cage them like animals! How dare you! How—"

He jumped to his feet. His hand clamped over her mouth. "Shut up! You test me too far, Christa! All of the camp can hear you when you rage like that, and I won't—not even for you—become the laughingstock of an entire regiment! I have my reasons for what I've done, and I'll be damned if I'm going to endure this outburst before you know what my reasons are. Now, shut up!"

Slowly, warily, he eased his hand from her mouth.

"Yankee bastard!" she hissed out.

He suddenly felt exhausted, worn down by forces he couldn't fight.

"That's right, Christa, Yankee bastard. Then, now, and always. Christa, I am sorry!"

Her eyes were glittering. Were there tears within them? He wanted to put an arm around her, he wanted to hold her close, to explain.

She would never let him touch her now.

She tried to jerk free from him. He held her firmly, clenching his teeth.

Then he freed her.

She turned from him and ran.

Nineteen

Christa hadn't been sure at all how a morning that had begun so gloriously could have darkened so quickly.

She had awakened so relieved to have him back! To have him at her side, his sun-bronzed hand so dark where it lay over the ivory flesh of her hip, his hair-roughened leg casually tossed upon hers. It had felt so good, so sweet, so secure, just to lie with him.

But when she had risen and dressed to start the coffee, she had seen the Confederates.

Someone had rigged together a ramshackle stockade in which to hold the men. There were four of them, worn, thin, tired, and weary looking, still wearing their uniforms. Stunned at the sight of them, she had found herself hurrying toward them.

Private Ethan Darcy had been guarding the group. She knew he was an excellent sharpshooter and could bring down a man or a beast at a tremendous distance. Her heart quickened, and despite herself she felt her temper rising.

Why were they being so cruelly held? There was little over their heads to shield them from the elements. They'd been provided with nothing to sleep on, and they were huddled before a waning fire.

"Mrs. McCauley, you need to be leaving these prisoner fellows alone now," Darcy warned her.

She shook her head at Darcy, studying the men. One wore a captain's insignia, one a sergeant's, and the other two appeared to be privates. She had never seen a sadder-looking group of men, so lean, so hungry-looking. They were the losers of the war, she thought, and they looked it. Emaciated, tattered, pathetic.

"My God!" she whispered. "Why are they being kept here like this? Who ordered this?"

"Mrs. McCauley, maybe you'd better speak with your husband," Darcy told her.

"He's taken the word of an Indian over a southern white boy," the man with the captain's insignia on his shoulders told her. "We're suffering for it, ma'am. Your colonel doesn't seem to know that the war is over."

She moved closer to the man. His beard was unkempt, his hazel eyes were watery. She didn't think that she'd ever felt quite so sorry for a human being, and she suddenly felt ill.

She gasped suddenly. There was the caked blood on the arm of the man's uniform.

"You're injured!" she cried.

He shrugged. "It's just a scratch, ma'am. But I admit, I would take kindly to any small mercy."

Last night, Jeremy had come back. She had been so glad to see him. He hadn't wanted to talk. She had been so glad to hold him. She had lain with him in warmth and ecstasy while he had been doing this to these men. She had been so deceived.

"I'll get the doctor out here," she said. She stared hard at Darcy. "They need better shelter! A warmer fire. What are you doing treating men like this?"

"Mrs. McCauley, we're just keeping a watch on them. We'll be moving into Fort Jacobson sometime very soon, and they'll be taken care of from there."

"I'm going to see to it that these men are treated better now," Christa said firmly.

She turned around to start back to her tent. Darcy called to her softly. "Ma'am, your husband is the one who brought these fellows in. And he was right firm when he did so. I don't think you understand—"

"I don't think that you understand! Jeremy has to treat these men better! The war is over."

"That's not it, ma'am. Mrs. McCauley, he's not going to bend on this matter—"

"Then I'll see to it that certain things are done!" she said firmly.

This time, she left Darcy behind, shaking his head. She clenched her eyes tightly together as agony ripped through her. She had fallen in love with him. She had greeted him with such heat and fever, and all the while these men had stood out here starving and wounded. He had told her that he didn't want to talk.

"Oh, God!"

She stopped in front of her tent, then looked down at the coffeepot and at the fire before it. With shaking hands, she poured coffee into Jeremy's tin mug and stepped back into the tent.

He was so damned comfortable, sprawled out with his long limbs, his skin so bronzed and healthy, his muscles corded and powerful. He was the picture of health.

"You bastard!" she swore and threw the tin. She didn't really intend to scald him; she hadn't really thought about what she was doing at all. Once she had seen the prisoners, she had felt only that somehow he had used her and betrayed her. He had said that the war was over. It was not.

He was up, of course, being too alert and agile a man to lie still while she hurled missiles of coffee at him. Then, of course, he started railing at her like the supreme commander, cold, distant, harsh. Warning her that she had best stop before she share the prisoners' fates.

She wasn't sure exactly what she said. She only knew that she was furious and very hurt. Yes, she would share their fate! She was a Rebel, just like those men. But she had spent the night comfortably, lying with a Yankee.

He shook her and held her in his merciless grip. She felt her teeth chattering in her head. He wouldn't take this rage from her. She could feel the searing anger and strength that radiated so freely from his naked body to hers, and she hated herself again.

How could she care so much? How could she have fallen so completely? How had she ever let him make such a fool of her? How had she loved him?

She couldn't break his hold. He released her at last, and she ran. Ran from his touch, from the strength of his hold. From the heat of him. From wanting him.

When she was free of that touch, she could think again.

She snatched up the coffeepot and a tin mug from her own fire and marched back to the makeshift stockade with it. "Darcy, let me in!" she commanded.

"Ma'am, I don't know—"

"Darcy, I have just come from my husband. Let me in. I've brought coffee. These men need to be warmed. Has it become our policy to sit judge and jury on those who have lost a country? Let me in to tend to these men!"

Darcy, very displeased, did so.

The captain took the coffee cup from her with shaking fingers. He paused to smell the brew before sipping from it, then offered it to the other men. "Thank you, ma'am. Thank you, right kindly. Do I take it you were a southern sympathizer, ma'am, or merely an angel straight from heaven?"

"I'm a Virginian," she murmured, looking to the rest of his band. One of the privates was a boy, no more than eighteen or nineteen.

That hadn't been so young in the last stages of the war, she reminded herself. Drummer boys and buglers far younger had perished. "Where are my manners, ma'am?" the captain said. "I'm Jeffrey Thayer. Sergeant Tim Kidder there, and my privates, Tom Ross, Harry Silvers."

Christa nodded to each of them in turn.

"Why—why are you here?" she asked.

"Some fool Indian told the Union colonel we were guilty of his own outrages!" Thayer said indignantly.

"Don't that beat all?" Sergeant Kidder asked. He'd drained the coffee.

"There's more," Christa said hastily. "I'll get you some food too. And Darcy can stoke up the fire. My God, and your arm, Captain! I'll get the doctor here."

"You are an angel!" Jeffrey Thayer said.

She shook her head. "I don't understand—"

"There's lots of ex-Confederate boys heading south from Texas," Jeffrey told her. "We were on our way to be among them."

"South?" Christa said, confused.

"Right on down to South America. We're going to start a new colony down there, ma'am. A rebel colony. You're right welcome to come now, if you wish. It'll be a place where Yanks don't come and burn down every food source in sight! Where the old ways can live again." He grit his teeth suddenly, clutching his arm. "My, my, but this does hurt."

"Good thing the colonel couldn't aim," the young boy, Tom, said.

She heard a sniff from Darcy. "Don't fool yourself, kid!" Darcy called. "Colonel McCauley hit the captain right where he aimed. If he'd have been aiming differently, the captain'd be pushing up daisies right now."

"Private Darcy!" Christa admonished. She looked up to the sky. It was barely dawn. John Weland would probably still be sleeping. She didn't care. She was going to wake him up. "Captain, I'm going to see about someone to help with your arm."

She started to turn, but he clutched her hand. His eyes were damp, his fingers trembling with emotion. He spoke in a whisper. "Ma'am, we've survived so much fighting. If there's anything you can do to get us out of here, I'd be beholden for life! They're going to hang us for what heathen Indians did. They're going to hang us just because they hate us still. They didn't kill us during the war, so they're going to do it now. Lady, please . . . !"

Shaking, Christa disentangled her hand from his grasp. She couldn't. She didn't have the power to help them escape. And if she did she wouldn't dare.

She closed her eyes, swallowing hard as she remembered the scalp they had found on the butte. The Comanche were savage and brutal. Jeremy couldn't really believe anything they might tell him about someone else! Jeremy had gone to see Buffalo Run. Buffalo Run had surely given Jeremy some lie to make up for an atrocity he had committed himself.

And Jeremy was willing to believe him! Because these men were in gray uniforms!

"I'll get the doctor," she said. She whirled around. As she made her way through the tents, she saw that only a few of the men were beginning to rise.

Jeremy didn't need to worry about men having heard her tirade against him.

They all seemed to have slept through it, she thought wryly. The few who were awake greeted her politely and courteously, making way for her. She reached Weland's tent and hesitated. "John?" she called softly.

"Christa?"

"May I come in?"

He wasn't really dressed, but he had on his long johns and his trousers and suspenders. He lifted the tent flap and let her in.

"Jeremy brought back prisoners—" she began.

"So I heard."

"What?" she said, amazed. "Then, John, why didn't you tend to the wounded man?"

"It was a scratch, or so I heard. He said he just nicked the man to get him to stop."

"He's in pain. Major Weland, please. For me, would you come look at this man's arm?"

A light suddenly seemed to shine in his eyes. Christa thought that he was a lot like Jesse. When it came time to heal the sick, Weland was ready to go.

"Let me get my shirt."

He did so and picked up his surgical bag and followed her out. They walked through the encampment until they came to the stockade at the far edge.

Private Darcy was still standing guard. Christa looked at the landscape beyond them and understood why their precautions against escape could be so lenient.

There was nowhere for the prisoners to go. Not on foot, and not in Comanche territory. With horses, yes, they could escape.

"Go on in, John, please," Christa encouraged him. "I'm going to go to see what I can find for them to eat."

"Sergeant Jaffe will be bringing them something—" Private Darcy offered.

"I want them fed now," Christa said firmly.

She found Jaffe, and to her relief he was already preparing food to be brought to the prisoners. She returned behind him and leaned upon a fencepost, pressing her cheeks against the cool wood as the men ate.

They had been near starving. They ate like animals. Even Doc Weland had stopped his treatment of the captain's arm to allow them to eat. When Jeffrey Thayer had finished, Weland set to bandaging his arm again. When he was done, the doctor stood with Christa while Thayer spoke. "I don't mind dying. Me and my boys, we stood in battlefields so long that death is like a long-lost cousin. But it just beats all that your colonel is going to see to it that we hang for some awful business done by a pack of savage Comanche."

Christa glanced uneasily at Weland. His face looked a little pale too.

"Did you—did you try to explain the truth to my hus—to the colonel?" Christa asked.

With a pained expression, Thayer nodded. "God's my witness, ma'am. I tried. But it seems that savage Buffalo Run has some kind of crazy influence over the man. And we're—"

"What?" Christa pursued.

He shook his head. "Same old story, angel. We're Rebels. A Yankee just can't believe a Rebel."

Christa turned away and walked some distance from the stockade. A second later, she felt a gentle touch on her shoulder. She spun around. It was Weland.

"Are you thinking of helping them escape, Christa?" he asked her.

She started to shake her head. "I—I—"

"Well, I am," he said bluntly.

She gasped.

"Shush!" he warned her quickly. "Come on. Let's get to the med tent. We don't want to be heard."

She stared at him in amazement, at the misery in his eyes, then nodded quickly. He was like Jesse. He couldn't stand the suffering.

And for Weland, the war was over.

She followed him hastily to his tent, nodding good morning to the men they passed, barely daring to breathe. When they reached the medical tent, she burst through the flap and spun around. Weland quickly came in behind her, pouring her a sherry from his stock on his camp desk.

"It's too early in the morning!" she whispered.

"You need it. And keep your voice down!" He began to pace. Christa decided that he was right and she swallowed the sherry down. He stopped pacing and stared at her. She knew that they were both thinking of the scalp on the pole on the butte. How could Jeremy have believed the Comanche over the emaciated men in his stockade?

"What are we going to do?" she whispered.

He sank into a chair. "I could be court-martialed for even thinking this way," he said with a groan.

"Then you can't do anything. I've got to do it."

He looked up at her, studying her. "Christa, you are the only one who can do anything."

Her fingers started to shake. Her knees went weak and she sank down to the foot of his bed. "How, what?"

Weland ran his fingers through his hair. "Well, we should have ridden into Fort Jacobson today but I think Jeremy planned to camp over, tie up some loose ends with the men, write some dispatches. He should be busy in the headquarters tent all day. Not that they could possibly escape during daylight . . ."

"The dawn?" Christa said.

Weland nodded. "And they'd have a day's rest. Jeff Thayer's arm could heal a bit. They'd have some food in their bellies. What a pathetic lot! How could Jeremy . . ." His voice trailed away and then he looked at Christa guiltily. "I'm sure he had his reasons, of course."

Yes. The men were Rebs.

"I can see to it that some of the horses are tethered near the stockade for the night," Weland continued. "If you could just slip out very early, before dawn, and do something about Darcy."

She nodded. "Distract him?"

Weland nodded. He stood. "It wouldn't be so difficult. Because, you see, it would be impossible for them to escape from here without help, so no one will be worried very much. And when they do escape . . ."

"I won't ever let anyone know that you were involved, I swear it!" Christa promised him fervently.

He shook his head. "You have to play innocent too, Christa."

"I doubt if Jeremy will believe I'm innocent," she murmured.

He slammed his fist against his hand. "But is it the right thing to do?" he demanded suddenly. He answered himself. "It has to be. I can still see that scalp, stretched out, dried . . ."

"Stop, please!"

He swung around. "You must be careful. Very careful. Jeremy will see that you're very upset."

"Oh, he knows that I'm upset," Christa murmured. "I'll just stay away from him during the day. I don't think it will be difficult."

Weland stretched out a hand to her. "Oh, God, Christa! I can't believe that we're conspirators—against Jeremy!"

"I never meant to be!" she whispered.

"Nor I. You mustn't let him suspect, Christa. And you have to keep him in his tent through the night, so that I can casually see that the horses are moved around."

"Yes," she said flatly, staring at him. Keep Jeremy in the tent? They weren't even speaking!

"They will die if we don't help them," he said. "They'll hang."

Christa nodded, her fingers digging into her palm.

She turned and fled Weland's tent, grateful that he was first and always a humanitarian.

It wasn't difficult to keep her distance from Jeremy during the day because it seemed that he had no desire to see her.

She knew that he would be in the headquarters tent all day and that he was busy with correspondence. She tried to spend time with Celia so that she wouldn't stay too near the prisoners, but she couldn't even be near Celia without betraying her emotions.

Jeremy didn't come to their tent for supper. Robert Black Paw informed her that Jeremy was dining with Majors Brooks and Jennings and sent his apologies.

Ah, yes, he was sorry!

The hour grew later and later. She couldn't eat, and she certainly didn't dare sleep.

Keep him in his tent . . .

She couldn't even get him here, she thought.

But as the hour grew very late, she heard him coming back at last. He paused to speak with Robert Black Paw outside their tent, and she went into a sudden swirl of motion. She stripped to the flesh and lowered the lamp to a shadowy, soft glow. Before he entered the tent, she plowed beneath the covers and pulled them to her chin.

She felt his eyes on her when he came in and listened to the movements that had become so familiar. He removed his scabbard and sword, and she heard the clink of metal against his desk. She felt his weight on the bed and heard the soft fall of his boots beside it. Then the sounds were just whispers in the night as he shed the rest of his clothing and crawled into bed beside her. She opened her eyes just a slit, certain that she would find him lying there awake, his fingers laced behind his head, his eyes on the canvas above them.

His eyes were hard on her. He had known she wasn't sleeping.

"Christa, stay away from the prisoners," he warned her.

"I don't want to talk," she told him coldly.

"Christa—"

"I don't want to talk!"

"Well, maybe I do."

"You didn't want to talk last night, I don't want to talk tonight."

Aggravated, he started to toss the covers back and sit up.

But with the covers drawn back he noted her state of nudity and inhaled softly, his eyes riveted to hers. Silver, glittering, they spoke a silent demand.

"I—I said that I didn't want to talk," she whispered. She didn't really know how to play this game.

Yes, she did, she realized. She didn't want to talk. She was furious with him. She was heartsick over what he had done.

But, she realized with the pounding of her heart, that didn't change certain things. She wanted him. Perhaps she was even afraid that it might be the last time she would ever have him. Maybe after tonight, they would never be able to forgive one another.

She had to keep him in his tent.

It was not going to be so hard a task.

"Christa—!" His voice was harsh, rough-edged. She came up quickly, leaning over him, draping the length of her hair about his shoulders and chest. She pressed her lips to his shoulders, sliding the length of her body against him, her breasts brushing the dark hair and muscle of his chest, her body warm against his. She let her kisses fall where they would, her tongue teasing his flesh. She rose against him, her tongue sliding over the small hard peaks of his nipples, sweeping over the muscled structure of his chest. She moved against him again, the softness of her hair brushing where her kiss had just been. She pressed her face against the ripples of his belly, bathing him again with the warmth of her tongue.

She moved lower against him. Nipping at his hip, always allowing the soft flow of her hair to sweep around him. She felt the pulse of him. The powerful trembling of his fingers as they moved into her hair. She heard his tense whisper. She felt the hard, searing shaft of his desire beneath her, and allowed her touch to fall all around it. Then she took him into her hands, into her caress, and bathed him with the slow, luxurious slide of her tongue.

Impassioned words exploded from him. The force of his desire sent longing and excitement sweeping into her. She gasped at the violence with which he clutched her, lifting her, bringing her atop him, impaling her there.

She could not meet his eyes, could not meet the bold hunger in them. She closed her own and felt him. His fingers curled around her buttocks, guiding her. She gasped, her head falling back as he thrust more deeply into her. The night seemed to take flight, the rhythm exploded, and she became aware of nothing but sensation, the force of her own desire to touch the peak, to reach out and feel the stars cascading, to feel the ecstasy and the splendor he could create.

She rose and rose, soared so high. Yet when she would have cried out, she suddenly found herself beneath him. She was devastated, for he had withdrawn. Then she gasped, feeling the rise of a greater fever as he touched and caressed her. Teased and tormented her flesh, touched her with the searing liquid fire of his kiss, stroked her with the evocative draw and thrust of his fingers and caress. She thought that she would die if the sweet anguish went on any longer, yet just when she reached that point, he was with her again, moving in the darkness, in the night.

And then it came, that honey-sweet explosion of the stars, of the world, of the velvet of the night. Shattering, violent, delicious, leaving her to cling to him while she trembled.

He fell beside her, his arm flung back, his breathing still harsh, his body hot and wet despite the coolness of the night. She closed her eyes tightly, thinking of the depths of her betrayal.

"Christa—" he began anew. The sound of his voice still seemed harsh. She didn't want to hear it! He would chastise her again about the prisoners. She reminded herself that she had to hate him for what he had done, taking sides with Comanche just because the men had been in the Rebel army!

"I don't want to talk!" she said fiercely.

"Damn you—"

"I don't want to talk!"

She heard his teeth grating in the darkness. "Fine. Have it your way, my love. Don't talk!"

And so he said nothing more, but minutes later she felt his hands in the darkness again.

It seemed hours later before he slept. The dawn was finally coming.

Christa bit her lip, threw back the covers, and rose. He stirred, but she turned her back to him, dressing. He knew that she was up.

But he never suspected her of this treachery, she was certain. She washed and dressed and headed out of the tent, looking back.

Her heart seemed to plummet. He lay at rest, his hair a rich dark red against the snow white of the covers, his face so handsomely defined. She stared at the hard, sinewed length of him, and a trembling seized her. How could she lie with him as passionately as she had, and do this?

How could she love him as she did, and do this?

Because he didn't understand. Even Dr. Weland realized Jeremy didn't understand. He had fought men in gray uniforms for so long that he couldn't let it go. He was being deceived by a Comanche. She wasn't doing this to hurt him. She was doing it to save her countrymen.

Christa slipped from the tent.

The rest of the camp lay sleeping. Mist was all around them. She hurried through it to the makeshift stockade where Ethan Darcy was once again on duty in the early-morning hours.

"Good morning, Private Darcy!" she called to him softly, walking over to him. "Don't tell me that they keep you here all day and all night!"

"No ma'am, Mrs. McCauley," he said, watching her warily. "Lennox and Fairfield were on duty before me. We stand guard in shifts."

He turned around, following her. Christa nearly allowed her eyes to widen and betray her as she saw Weland coming up silently behind Darcy. He brought the butt of a gun down hard on Darcy's temple.

Darcy never knew what hit him. He crumpled to the ground.

Christa stared from the fallen soldier to Weland. "Will he be all right?"

"Of course," Weland said softly. "Hurry now. I've the horses around here. Let's free the men."

He hurried around and slipped the slide bolt from the stockade. Jeffrey Thayer stepped out immediately. The others didn't follow.

"Come on!" Thayer commanded.

"I—I ain't going back out into Comanche territory," Tom Ross said.

"It's an order!" Thayer told him.

But Tom Ross was stepping back.

"Leave him!" Weland commanded.

"I—I ain't going either," Sergeant Tim Kidder said.

"Harry!" Thayer barked to the last of his men. "Are you coming or have you turned on me too, boy?"

"I ain't going to turn you in, but I ain't going with you," Harry said.

"I don't understand—" Christa began.

"It doesn't matter, let's just get this going!" Weland said. He caught hold of Christa's arm and led her along with Thayer to the horses. "Ride out with him a ways—if the sentries see you, they won't stop him!" Weland commanded her.

She shook her head. "John, I can't do that—"

She broke off in sheer amazement. He was aiming his gun at her. The same gun he had used to knock Darcy senseless.

"Get up on that horse, Christa," he commanded her.

"John—"

Someone suddenly interrupted them. She heard a low, dangerous voice. "What are you doing?"

She spun around. It was Robert Black Paw. She was never far from his sight, she remembered.

But that wasn't going to help her now. She cried out as Major Dr. John Weland took careful aim and shot the Cherokee scout.

No sound escaped her because Jeffrey Thayer had a bony but powerful hand wrapped tightly over her mouth. "Get her out of here—fast!" Weland ordered. "And see that she doesn't come back. Trade her to the Indians. Strangle her! Just see that she doesn't come back. It's your price for freedom."

Christa bit the hand covering her mouth. Thayer swore savagely, jerking her back against him. "When I get you alone, angel, are you going to pay!" he drawled.

She inhaled for a long, high-pitched scream. It never left her mouth because Weland had aimed his gun at Darcy. "One word, Christa, and I shoot Darcy too!"

Furious, she demanded, "Why? What did I do to you? What did Jeremy do to you?"

Dr. John Weland, her friend through so much, smiled. He tried to stroke her cheek, and she wrenched her head away. "It isn't you, Christa. I really like you."

"Then Jeremy—"

"And it isn't that proud husband of yours, Christa. Pity you wouldn't listen to him. You played right into my hands. I had myself assigned to this division purposely. I've spent months—no, years—planning this revenge. I had a better method of torment devised, but you ruined that."

"I don't know what you're talking about!" she whispered. If she could just stall for time, help might come. She was always being watched.

By Robert. And Robert was bleeding on the ground.

God! What had caused this?

"You married McCauley," Weland said quietly. "I could have had the house. I made a lot of money, putting in with those fool southern blockade runners! Not the noble boys. Fellows like Thayer here who knew how to make a dollar out of a war."

She gasped. "But—why?"

"Jesse Cameron," he said simply.

She was feeling faint. She couldn't begin to comprehend what was happening. The house! That seemed so long ago now. Yet, even when she had been about to lose it, she had been convinced that the enemy must have been Daniel's enemy.

"Jesse?" she repeated, stunned.

"Jesse Cameron," Weland repeated. "The one, the only, the majestic, the wonderful. The great healer, second only to Christ!" He spat on the ground suddenly. "The man given every promotion I should have had."

"You'd kill—because of that?"

His eyes had been distant. Now they were riveted on her. "He was the great healer. Until it came time for him to operate on my little brother. Then your goddamned sainted brother couldn't do a thing. Gerald died screaming on the operating table. They said that he'd been a coward. That he'd been running away from the battle when he was hit. It was a lie. But your brother killed him anyway. He opened him up and he killed him."

"You're wrong!" Christa said. "Jesse would never let anyone die if he could stop it, never, for any reason." She spoke very quickly. "I thought that you were like him! I thought you were a doctor just like Jesse, so concerned with healing! You believed in men's right to live, whether they were red or white or black. You—"

"I thought that seeing Cameron Hall burned to the ground would wound him forever. But this is better," Weland said. "He'll never know what happened to his precious sister. Whether the Comanche have you and rape and mutilate you daily, or whether some renegade, murdering Reb kidnapped you down to South America to serve his comrades. He'll never know and it will hurt him all his life. It will cut like a knife. I hope he lives a long, long time."

"You're sick—"

"And I'm going to hang with those other fools if I don't get the hell out of here!" Jeffrey Thayer said.

"This is a sick man!" Christa tried to tell him.

"I don't care if he's a raving lunatic! He's set me free. And you're my way out. Let's go!"

"Go with him. Or I'll shoot Darcy right in the head. As a matter of fact, let me get Darcy up on a horse. Then Thayer can shoot him the minute you give him a word of trouble!"

Thayer jerked her around while Weland threw Darcy's prone body over one of the four horses brought for the Rebels' escape.

"Get up!" he commanded her.

She stared at him. "You are a murderer, aren't you?" she asked. "My husband believed the Comanche because the Comanche was telling the truth."

"Get on the horse. I've killed before. But there's a lot I'd rather do to you than kill you, angel. So keep quiet and—"

"I'll see you hang!" Christa promised.

Thayer smiled, the kind of smile that showed her, too late, what kind of man he was.

No matter what the color of his uniform.

"You want that private dead on your account?" Thayer asked, indicating Darcy.

She swallowed hard, then walked to one of the horses and mounted it. She stared at Weland. "They'll hang you too!" she promised.

He lifted a brow complacently. "I won't give a damn."

"Ride, angel," Thayer commanded her.

Just then they heard music. Someone was singing a hymn. "Onward Christian soldiers . . ."

"Christ Almighty!" Weland groaned. "It's that holier-than-thou Brooks woman!"

Mrs. Brooks had come upon them with her Bible, ready to read a sermon to the erring Rebel prisoners, Christa was certain.

Now the plump and proper old harridan stared at them all, open-mouthed.

Weland turned, aiming his gun at her. "Mount up, Mrs. Brooks. You're going for a ride."

"Her!" Thayer protested. "Shoot her! Just shoot her!"

"Jesus, no!" Christa cried.

"What in the Lord's name—" Mrs. Brooks began.

"Just mount up! Mount up!" Christa urged her.

"I will not!" Mrs. Brooks said indignantly. "I will not be a part of this treachery—"

"He'll shoot you, Mrs. Brooks!" Christa cried. She leapt down from her own animal, prodding Mrs. Brooks toward one of the mounts. "He'll shoot you!" she hissed, trying to show the woman how serious the look was in Weland's eyes—and Robert Black Paw on the ground, blood oozing from his chest.

"Oh! Oh, Lord Almighty! I'm going to faint—" Mrs. Brooks began.

"Get on a horse!" Christa ordered her. Mrs. Brooks was heavy. With a strength she didn't know she had, Christa boosted her onto one of the horses.

If they could just ride, they could escape Thayer. He'd be on his own without Weland behind them.

When Mrs. Brooks was mounted at last, white-faced and wavering, Christa leapt up on one of the horses again.

"Good-bye, angel," Weland said. He stared at Jeffrey Thayer. "If she survives and comes back, you're a dead man."

Thayer started to laugh. "She'll be with me—until death!" he swore.

He slammed his heels against his horse.

And all four mounts—his, Christa's, and the beasts carrying the unconscious Darcy and the blubbering Mrs. Brooks—began to race across the plain.

The first pink streaks of dawn were just beginning to show on the eastern horizon.

Twenty

It was still dark when he opened his eyes. He didn't stretch his arms out over the covers—he knew that she was gone.

How strange, he thought, to have had a night so sweet and spectacular, and to awaken now, feeling so pained and miserable! She still wouldn't let him speak. She didn't want to hear the truth. She wouldn't believe anything ill of a man dressed in a Confederate uniform.

He punched his pillow bitterly, wishing he could gain just a few more minutes' sleep. But thoughts of her plagued him, and he couldn't close his eyes. He jerked up suddenly. He had heard something. Not Christa. He didn't smell coffee brewing. In fact, he hadn't heard her since she had so silently risen and left the tent.

"Jesus!" he gasped out leaping off the bed, for a bloodied hand was reaching up, dragging the covers off him.

Robert Black Paw, huddled, broken, bleeding, had come to him. Crawled upon his belly to reach him.

Jeremy cried out again, shouting for help. He lifted the Indian scout who had been his friend and companion for so long, trying to find the wound. It was in his chest. Blood was pouring from it. He ripped up the sheets, packing the wound to stop the flow.

"Jeremy—" Robert was trying to speak.

"What the hell happened? My God! Someone get in here—"

Nathaniel rushed in. His eyes opened wide at the sight of Robert, and he exhaled quickly. "I'll get Doc Weland—"

"No!"

Robert found the strength to rise. Shaking his head vehemently, he fell back.

"Clamp down on the wound!" Jeremy ordered Nathaniel, reaching for his clothing. He slipped into his trousers, speaking to Robert at the same time. "Robert, don't die. Damn you now, don't die! I'm going for the doctor—"

"No!" The Cherokee thundered out the word again despite his wound. He beckoned to Jeremy to come close to his lips and he whispered quickly, knowing that his strength was failing him. "Weland—in on it. Something to do with your wife's—brother. Thayer loose. With Christa."

There was blood everywhere. Jeremy felt as if it drained from his body. "Christa?" he whispered.

Robert's bloodied hand reached for him. "She thought—him innocent. Didn't know. Weland—hurt her." He tried to speak again. He fell silent.

"Robert! Robert, damn you, don't you die!" Jeremy cried.

Nathaniel looked at him. "He's still breathing. If I can just stop the blood—it seems the bullet made a clean hole through him."

"Nathaniel, if you can, save his life!" Jeremy commanded swiftly, reaching for his sword and scabbard and guns. He tore from the tent. Christa!

Damn him, what a fool he had been! Why hadn't he seen it? Yes, she had been furious. She hadn't forgiven him a thing, she hadn't missed him. She'd seduced him to go and set the Confederates free.

But Weland had something to do with it. Why would Weland want to hurt Christa, or Robert? It didn't make any sense.

He passed by one of the young buglers just staggering from his tent. "Call the men to arms!" he commanded quickly. "Get help down to the stockade!"

He rushed on and burst onto a scene he hadn't begun to imagine.

The gate they had so hastily rigged when they'd brought in the prisoners was down. But three of the men remained.

Dead.

Three of the soldiers were strewn about the ground, bright red bloodstains oozing out over the tattered gray of their uniforms.

John Weland stood in front of the stockade, staring at them, shaking his head.

"Jeremy, thank God!" Weland said. "It was the damnedest thing! Christa—I'm sorry, Jeremy, really sorry, but you, well, you know your own wife. She was determined to free these fellows. She got Thayer a gun somehow. Robert came after Christa, and Thayer killed Robert. Then he turned his gun on his own men!"

Jeremy stared at Weland. Everything was going mad here.

And Christa was gone. All that mattered was that Christa was gone. She was heading across the plains with a merciless cutthroat who had killed heedlessly already.

He watched the doctor cautiously. The man he thought he had known. He strode into the fenced yard where the dead Confederates lay. The first was definitely gone. There was a bullet through his head. He moved onward. The second was dead too. Jeremy didn't think he'd ever seen so much blood. The bullet must have pierced him right through the heart. He moved on. He thought he saw the slightest movement. He knelt down.

It was the sergeant, the man named Kidder. His lips were moving. His eyes opened.

Jeremy could just see Weland through the fence. Weland didn't seem worried.

Because he was innocent?

Because he was certain that the dead could tell no tales?

He leaned closer to the sergeant. The man was whispering. "Your Yank's a traitor, Colonel. The bastard killed me."

A cold shiver ripped through Jeremy. More horrible than anything he had known through all the years of warfare. Weland. He had coldly shot Robert Black Paw and these men.

Why?

He stood, looking at Weland. "I'm sorry, Jeremy, there's nothing I can do for any of them. Or Robert."

"Robert isn't dead," Jeremy told him.

John Weland's eyes flickered. "Not dead? He's right over there on the ground! I found him first. I—" He turned. He saw that the Indian wasn't there. He stared back at Jeremy.

He was caught. They both knew it.

"Well, it really doesn't matter. There's nothing you can do. Thayer will see that she lives and dies miserably."

"Why?" Jeremy cried out incredulously. Weland just stared at him. Jeremy swore suddenly, fists clenched, teeth grating. It didn't matter. It couldn't matter now. What mattered was Christa. He had to find her.

He knelt quickly down to the Reb still breathing. "I'll get help, son."

The boy's eyes opened. He was trying to talk again. "I didn't never want to kill no one, sir, honest. I didn't take the Indian girl and I didn't shoot any cavalrymen at that pay wagon." He moistened his lips. "Thayer is going to head for Texas, so he can get to South America. I couldn't go. Hell, I'd rather be hanged than have the Comanche get me any day." He started to cough. A fleck of blood appeared on his lips.

"I'll get help," Jeremy said.

The boy clutched his hand. "Be careful. Thayer has the man who was guarding us, Darcy." Something almost like a smile touched his bloody lips. "And some battle-ax of a lady who sings psalms."

"Mrs. Brooks?" Jeremy said incredulously.

"That's how Thayer's going to keep your wife in line. She—she didn't know, sir. She just thought that we were ex-Rebs, unfairly treated."

Jeremy nodded. "Don't talk anymore. The men will see to you." He started to rise.

"Watch it, Colonel!" the young sergeant cried.

He swung around. Weland was at his back, his gun aimed. Jeremy instinctively reached for the Colt at his side. Even as he fired, he felt the flesh tear at his arm.

John Weland had missed his target.

Jeremy didn't.

He walked across the stockade yard. Weland was on the ground, dead, his eyes wide open and staring. Jeremy still didn't understand.

He looked up. Men were filing out. He saw Lieutenant Preston. "Saddle up, Company D! Five minutes, men," Jeremy commanded. "James— get Morning Star to ride with us. And somebody, dear God, get some help for this poor Reb!"

He strode past them, anxious to reach his horse.

Dear God, Christa was out there somewhere, in Thayer's hands.

They rode desperately hard until Thayer realized he would kill the horses if he pushed them any further. By then, Darcy was just beginning to come around, and Mrs. Brooks was finding her voice once again.

Jeffrey Thayer gave them all fair warning. "I need the whole set of you right now. If the cavalry starts closing in again, I can drop you back one by one and buy myself a little time. Except for you, angel," he told Christa, smiling. "You come with me. All the way."

"You're out of your mind," she told him.

He aimed his Colt, another gift from Weland, straight at her heart. "What? Have you lost your devotion to your cause? Angel, you were willing enough before!"

"I was willing to see you freed instead of hanged when I thought you were an innocent man," she told him.

"Honey, we had some fun with one little Indian maid. And I killed a few Yanks. Hell, I killed them by the dozens during the war. What difference does a few months make?"

"A world of difference," Christa told him. "You are nothing but a murdering bastard."

He grinned. "You'll get to like me. I like you. And I'm going to like you a whole lot more."

"Take her! Just take her!" Mrs. Brooks cried out. "We're far from camp now. Just leave me here alone, and I'll tell her husband that she wanted to go with you, she's always been a Rebel, she'll always be a Rebel, so take her, and the devil can have the two of you—"

"Mrs. Brooks!" Darcy cried feebly. Christa ignored both Mrs. Brooks and Jeff Thayer and turned her attention to Darcy. They had stopped by a creek to get water for themselves and for their horses. She ripped up her petticoat and soaked it and came over to bathe Darcy's face. "Jesu, Ethan, I'm sorry!" she whispered.

He caught her hand. "Weland hit me?"

She nodded.

"Why?"

"It's a long story."

"Come on, you're taking too long!" Thayer warned them. "I want to get started again. You, Miss Christa-belle, one false move and I put a hole the size of Richmond through the Bible bitch or your Billy Yank, understand? And you—" he warned Darcy. "No heroics. Or the noble little Reb gets to ride and bleed at the same time."

They all mounted up. Darcy looked woefully at Christa. "He has to sleep sometime!" he whispered hopefully to her.

She nodded. Would they get to that?

They started out, riding hard once again. They reached an outcrop of rock. To Christa's surprise, Jeff Thayer suddenly seemed uneasy.

She began to feel it herself. The sensation of being watched.

She turned around. Her heart flew to her throat.

They *were* being watched.

Atop the ridge behind them, silent as statues, Indians had appeared. Six of them. Painted in red, some bare-chested, with designs upon their flesh. All armed with rifles or bows and arrows and incredibly long lances, decorated with feathers and . . . scalps.

"That son of a bitch! Buffalo Run! He had McCauley followed, wanting to make certain the Yank executed me!"

"What are you talking about?" Christa demanded, staring at him.

"If you've got an extra gun," Darcy said, "for the love of God, give us all a chance—"

"You're on your own!" Thayer shouted. He spurred his horse cruelly. The animal leapt into the air, then started to race. The other horses, without cue from their riders, did the same.

Terrified, Christa leaned low against her horse's neck, praying as the dirt of the plain flew up at her.

To no avail. She sensed the colors of the horse and men at her side long before she heard the first wild war whoop. Her horse was forced to the side, slowly made to come to a halt as the Comanche rode a circle around her.

Darcy and Mrs. Brooks were being held in the same circle, she realized.

Jeffrey Thayer was not within it.

She stared in front of her, awed and horrified.

The ex-Reb had been forced from his mount. He tried to shoot the Indian bearing down on him.

Thayer screamed. The Indian's lance went thrusting through his middle, followed by a rain of arrows.

Each Comanche had shot at the man. The arrows pierced him. His legs, his arms. His eyes. Yet sounds were still coming from him.

An Indian knelt down beside him. Thayer was still barely alive. The Indian began to cut away the man's scalp.

Mrs. Brooks began choking and gagging. Behind Christa, she was sick. Even Darcy let loose with a little sound of terror.

Christa was too horrified herself to make a sound or to move.

The last of the Indians mounted up again. She instinctively slapped her reins over her horse's shoulder. The horse bucked and bolted and started to race once again.

But before many minutes had passed, a Comanche was riding at her side, their horses brushing sides.

He leaned over and was almost off the horse he was riding. He reached out for her, grabbing her while his animal eased into a canter. Christa cried out, grasping for something to hang on to.

Comanche could bring about a terrible death, she knew. She had just witnessed one, and death could be worse out here. But instinct assured her that she would not be trampled to death beneath the horse's hooves.

She needn't have feared. Her Comanche captor did not intend to release her. He was a strong man and rode his horse effortlessly, keeping her atop it as he did so. The animal raced across the plains easily, and it seemed to Christa, forever. She was not alone, though. Other Comanche had seized Mrs. Brooks and Darcy.

She thought about the way Jeffrey Thayer had died. Then she thought about Weland. She still couldn't grasp how the man, after failing in his effort to take Cameron Hall and burn it, had managed to get himself assigned to Jeremy's regiment.

Jeremy! She had betrayed him. She might lead Jeremy to death, and she definitely might kill their child.

She had already been hungry and weakened from her sleepless night of lovemaking. The constant slap of her body against the animal and the roughness of the endless ride quickly sapped what little strength she had left. During the long harsh ride, she must have blacked out.

Such a merciful condition! It ended too soon. She came to as she was dragged from the haunches of the horse, warm brown hands powerful and insistent upon her. She struggled to free herself from the hated touch of the warrior, staggering as she tried to swirl away. A choked cry escaped her as he reached for her, dragging her back, tying her hands together with rope. Another of the braves came up to the warrior she faced, saying something to him in his own language.

Furious and terrified, Christa lashed out. "You wait! You just wait until the cavalry comes. They'll slice you into little pieces! They'll fill you with bullet holes. They won't leave enough for the buzzards to eat!"

To her amazement, the Indian smiled. He spoke to her in perfect, unaccented English. "Will the cavalry come for you, do you think? Why would they think to rescue you—when you were so determined to free a murderer?"

She gasped, blinking. He knew that she had freed Jeff Thayer.

"My—my husband will come," she responded quickly. Maybe she was wrong, but she was determined to defy this Comanche. "You have taken another man's wife as well—"

She broke off. The other Comanche was saying something in his own language again. The one she faced started to laugh.

"What?" she cried out, wanting it to be a demand but feeling her knees shake.

"My friend has suggested that this other woman's husband might pay us a ransom not to return her."

Mrs. Brooks was still carrying on, screaming, crying, screaming again. Christa couldn't blame her. She felt much like doing the same herself.

When their captives made too much noise, Comanche sometimes cut out their tongues.

"Let her go, then!" Christa suggested suddenly. "Let her go back to camp. Maybe they won't come after you then. Maybe—"

"Your husband will come," the Indian said flatly. "I know him, and he will come. And then we shall see."

"You know my husband," she murmured. Of course. It all made sense, the fact that this Comanche spoke English so well. "You're Buffalo Run."

"I am."

She remembered Jeffrey Thayer's curious words just before he had been killed.

"This party—did you ride out to see that Thayer was—killed by the whites?"

He indicated one of the other warriors. "It was Eagle Who Flies High's war party. He advised and I listened, and he was right. Your husband has never betrayed me. But it seems you have betrayed him."

He turned and the rope he held jerked her along. She nearly tripped but was determined not to cry out. This was different from what she had expected. This man understood her. She felt that he was still the worst savage she had ever come across, but he did speak her language. There was hope that he might reason.

Yet what did she have to reason with? He knew the truth that was so horrible to face herself.

He jerked upon the rope, then caught her when she nearly tripped a second time. "You're carrying his child?" he said.

"Yes!" she said swiftly. "Yes!" Would that buy her some mercy from this man?

He grunted and turned again. He walked her to a brook of fresh running water and released her leash long enough to allow her to drink. She was desperately thirsty, yet even as she drank she tried to think of some manner of escape.

He didn't intend to allow it. He caught hold of the rope again and, dragging her along with him, tethered her to a tree near the water. Then he left her, conferring with the other warriors. She waited miserably, her back to the tree, her wrists chafing before her. They had ridden most of the day. Now there was minimal light, for beneath the moon they had lit only one fire. She determined that they had decided to camp there that night under the stars.

What was to be her fate, she wondered.

Dear God, she didn't want to think about it.

Some instinctive numbness in her mind kept her from it. Oddly, she had nearly dozed again when Buffalo Run approached her, offering her a dried strip of meat. She was starving and she took it from him, not caring in the least that she should, perhaps, have clung to her pride and refused anything from the Indian. He watched her eat. As he did so, she suddenly heard a screaming again.

Mrs. Brooks.

The dried meat stuck in her throat. She looked at the Indian. "Don't kill her. Dear God, please don't kill her!"

"Because she is your cherished friend?" he inquired politely. She knew that the Comanche was mocking her.

"Because it will be my fault if you do kill her," she said honestly.

"They are not killing her," he said.

He did not tell her what they were doing to her—that was left to Christa to wonder, and she did so wretchedly.

He rose and watched her again beneath the moonlight. He was very tall, far taller than the other Comanche warriors. His eyes were dark, his hair long and smooth and almost ink black. His face seemed a little bit narrower than some of the other braves' and Christa remembered that Buffalo Run was a half-breed.

Not in his heart, she realized. In his heart, this man was all Comanche.

"Are you going to kill me?" she asked him.

"Not tonight," he told her, and turned and walked away.

Mrs. Brooks's screams slowly faded. The Indians talked around their fire for a long while. Christa wondered what Jeremy was thinking, what he was feeling. She leaned her head back with misery. He had to hate her for what she had done. She had been so self-righteous about the poor wounded cavaliers of the Confederacy that she hadn't had the sense to realize that there were rotten apples in the ranks of Rebels.

And she hadn't given Jeremy the least opportunity to explain anything about his captives. Now she knew, and knew too late. Jeremy had taken the men instead of allowing the Comanche to take them. Jeff Thayer had played upon her sympathies and made a fool of her.

She couldn't hate Jeff Thayer for what he had done. She couldn't hate anyone who had died the way that he had. She could only despise herself for her stupidity.

Jeff Thayer had paid the ultimate price.

Oh, God! There had been Robert Black Paw! Ever there for her and for Jeremy. Teaching her and caring for her.

Dying for her.

"Oh, please God!" she whispered. She could well die herself.

She couldn't die. Not with the baby. But she didn't feel any movement, and she thought of all that had happened in the last twenty-four hours. She prayed that she hadn't killed her child.

Jeremy's child.

If only she had managed to tell him that she loved him! If only she hadn't been so proud, so stubborn.

She might have listened to him. She might have seen the truth.

She lowered her head, fighting the great wash of tears that threatened to cascade from her eyes. She had fallen in love with him, but she had been too proud to forget her past, and too proud to give either of them a real chance. Now she might never see him again.

And she had, perhaps, cost him another child.

He will come for you, Buffalo Run had told her. Was that the truth? Did the hostile savage know her husband better than she did herself?

Perhaps Buffalo Run couldn't begin to understand that her husband had never courted her, that she had forced him to marry her for a house, for bricks and stone and wood, for something that meant nothing out here. She hadn't even been willing to meet him halfway, not until something had turned somewhere within her heart, not until she had discovered that she could do nothing other than admire him, respect him, and love him.

Perhaps he would come. Perhaps his honor would dictate that he must. Perhaps he would come for their unborn child.

And perhaps, her heart seemed to whisper, perhaps he would even come for her!

But if he came, would he be risking his own life? What was he thinking at this moment? Was he hating her for what she had done? Thinking that she had brought this upon herself and that she deserved whatever happened to her? Was he missing her?

"Dear God, Jeremy! I'm sorry, so sorry!" she whispered out loud. "I love you, loved you. I—"

It didn't matter. It was too late.

Twenty-one

Jeremy dismounted from his horse and knelt down by the bloodied and battered body on the ground. It didn't take more than a few seconds, despite the condition of the corpse, to recognize the Confederate Jeffrey Thayer. His gray coat was blood spattered and stuck with a half-dozen arrows. The man's face had been slashed, his scalp expertly taken.

Jeremy felt his muscles tensing, the whole of his body quickening with anguish.

He no longer had to fear what the ex-Reb planned to do with Christa. Jeffrey Thayer wouldn't be doing anything with anyone ever again.

"Comanche?"

Jeremy turned. Jimmy Preston was watching him unhappily.

Jeremy nodded. "Search—" he began. He had to pause. In his heart he had to believe that the Indians wouldn't harm Christa. "Search the area for other bodies," he said. James stared at him, swallowed hard, then turned around and called out the order.

Company D dismounted from their horses. Jeremy walked across the dry plain and stared across it. Buffalo Run, he thought. He'd come to see if the whites were going to handle the matter of the murdering Reb.

Buffalo Run had taken down Thayer himself.

"You fool!" he hissed to the body of the dead man. He wanted to feel compassion for any man so brutally killed. But Thayer had murdered unsuspecting, innocent men. Red men, white men. He had, perhaps, come to his just reward.

"And you used my wife, you goddamned son of a bitch!" he swore savagely, fighting the temptation to kick the corpse.

"There's no sign of anyone else," James reported to him.

"Not Darcy, or Mrs. Brooks?"

"Or Christa," James said quietly.

Jeremy stared off across the plain. "It was Buffalo Run, then," he said.

"There are many bands of Comanche," James warned him.

"But only Buffalo Run would kill Thayer this way and take the others." He was quiet a moment, then said, "I'm going to have to go to him alone."

"My God, you can't go alone! You could run into other hostiles and get killed before you reach him."

"You'll accompany me with Company D until we reach the outskirts of his camp," Jeremy said.

"Even then—"

"James, if I were to take the whole regiment against him, it would be an even match. The death toll would be terrible. And the Comanche might kill the captives immediately on principle. If I go alone, I've got a chance. I won't be entirely alone," he said. "I'll have Morning Star."

"Colonel, sir!" one of the men called.

Jeremy looked back at the twenty-three enlisted men of Company D. Private Jenkins was staring at him awkwardly. "Do we bury him, sir?"

Jeremy's throat seemed to constrict. He'd tricked Christa, and Jeremy had been too damned angry and proud to try to explain things. God knew just how far Thayer intended to go with her.

Let the buzzards eat the man! Jesu, he was in anguish! He knew the Comanche well. And he knew Christa well. Don't fight Buffalo Run, Christa, don't fight him.

And please God, don't let him hurt her.

"Sir, do we bury him?"

"Dammit, yes, go ahead. Hurry, we've got to ride!"

There was so much at stake. They had to make haste. He was responsible for Darcy and Mrs. Brooks. He had to reach the Comanche before they could kill any of their captives.

He could die going for Christa. But if he couldn't bring her back, he didn't know if life would be worth living. He had been in love before, but he had never known the passion of emotions he felt for Christa. Perhaps they were like the pieces of the country, torn and bruised, suffering bitterly for all that they had done to one another. Yet nothing but broken fragments without one another. He had married her under duress, but nothing in the world could have forced him to do so if he hadn't been willing somewhere in his heart. He had been determined to bring her with him, to demand that their marriage be whole. He had forced her to live it. In his way, he had tried to give her life. And she had given it to him in return.

Night was coming in all around them.

He looked to the darkening sky. Against the night were curious, winged shapes. Buzzards were circling over him. They'd been seeking a meal of Thayer. He prayed that he would not see them circling in the sky again.

He leapt up on his horse and shouted to James. "Let's ride!"

They would have to stop soon enough. The Comanche before them would have to stop in the ebony darkness too.

In the morning, Buffalo Run untied her and directed her down through a scruff of trees and foliage to a narrow creek below them. For a moment she felt the incredible wonder of her freedom, then realized that her hands were still tied together before her and that he had given her freedom only to perform the most necessary of human tasks. Yet as she came along the trail, she caught her breath, trying not to make a sound. She had come upon Private Darcy.

Like her, he had been bound to a tree. She wondered why they hadn't killed him yet, then she feared that he was dead, and she wondered why they hadn't taken his scalp. His eyes opened, slowly, miserably. He saw her. It looked as if he was going to cry out, but Christa shook her head, turning around to look at the camp.

The Indian braves were gathered around the fire. It seemed that they were exchanging stories about their exploits.

For the moment, she and Darcy were not noticed.

Christa quickly moved into the shadow of the tree and knelt down by Darcy. Trickles of blood had hardened along his neck. She bit her lip. "Are you injured so that you can't rise, walk, or ride?"

His eyes, filled with pain and weariness, found hers. He shook his head. "They nicked at my ears and scratched my throat. They know how to keep a captive alive and in pain and terror a very long time," he told her.

Christa, with her hands bound together, struggled with the knots that held him to the tree.

The Comanche also knew how to tie very good knots, she realized. Her fingers began shredding before the rope did. Darcy started talking swiftly. "Pull up my pant leg. There's a small sheath at my ankle and I think my knife is still in it."

It was awkward, the way that she was tied, but Christa found the knife and managed to pull it out. A fine sheen of perspiration broke out on her forehead despite the coolness of the morning. She managed to balance the knife between her hands, and in a matter of minutes she had Darcy freed.

He leapt to his feet, quickly cutting her bonds. "We might have just signed your death warrant," he said.

"And yours."

"I was already a dead man," he assured her. "We've got to get horses."

"And Mrs. Brooks!" Christa said.

He stared at her as if she had lost her mind. "And Mrs. Brooks," he said.

She looked back up the trail. The horses were to the left of the fire and small encampment. Mrs. Brooks was somewhere to the far rear.

"You go for the horses," Christa told Darcy. "I'll go for Mrs. Brooks."

"If she opens her mouth just once," Darcy warned her. "Leave the old witch!"

Christa nodded. She slipped around the trail. Apparently, the Comanche seemed assured that their captives weren't going anywhere. The six braves remained around the fire, and though Christa couldn't understand a word that they were saying, she found them surprisingly similar to their white counterparts, probably telling tall tales around a campfire.

Mrs. Brooks had been very quiet during the morning, and Christa felt a surge of fear rise to her throat. The Comanche had cut out her tongue.

But when she found the woman, her eyes were closed. And she had been silenced with a gag made out of her petticoat. Christa, with Darcy's little knife, began sawing at the ropes that bound her to her tree. The woman awakened, her eyes flying open in terror. Christa pressed a finger to her lips.

For once in her life, Mrs. Brooks had the very good sense to keep silent.

Christa reached down for the woman. It seemed for several minutes that Mrs. Brooks wasn't going to find the strength to stand, she wavered so. "Please!" Christa whispered to her. Mrs. Brooks seemed to realize that they were dealing with life or death. She had no remonstrations for Christa; she looked at her with eyes as appealing as a child's.

"Come on. Quietly. Carefully."

She led the woman the long way around the braves once again, feeling as if she died a little with every step. They reached Darcy, who had untethered three of the horses. Between them, she and Darcy lifted Mrs. Brooks onto one of the horses before leaping atop mounts themselves. Darcy loosed the others from their tethers so that the horses would be gone when the Indians came after them.

Darcy swallowed hard and nodded to her. They broke away from the group slowly and carefully.

Then Darcy cried, "Ride!"

As if the flames of hell themselves were in pursuit, the three slammed their heels against their Indian mounts. Darcy knew his way, and Mrs. Brooks and Christa followed. She didn't know just how long they had ridden before she heard a cry behind them.

The Comanche were alerted at last.

Darcy leaned low over his horse and looked at Christa. The expression on his face warned her that they were all dead.

She looked back. Only three of the Indians were following them. Only three had managed to recapture their horses after Darcy had loosed them.

"Split!" she cried to Darcy.

"Jesu, Christa, no!" he warned her frantically.

But there was no choice. They could all die. Or she could lead the Comanche away. They might follow her.

They would kill Darcy now. Maybe they wouldn't kill her.

She reined in slightly and quickly before she could lose her courage. Darcy and Mrs. Brooks went racing by her. She turned toward a more northerly course and slammed her heels against her horse.

She raced the beast cruelly. Her heart beat with the same awful rhythm as that of the horse. Dirt and dust spewed up around her, yet despite the terrible pounding of her horse's hooves, she felt the tremor of the ground when another mount came in pursuit.

She turned slightly.

The Indians were in pursuit of her. One of them was nearly upon her. She could ride, and ride well, but the man coming after her was surely one of the most talented horsemen on the plains.

Buffalo Run.

She cried out as he bore down upon her. When he reached for her, she was certain that she was dead, for he would send her spilling down to the earth at their frantic pace.

But he did not. He pulled her from the horse and across his own, slowing his gait. In moments they walked. He made a curious sound with his tongue against his palate, and in a few minutes the other racing horse returned to him.

Miserable, beaten, Christa lay across his horse tasting dirt, animal hair, and sweat.

Buffalo Run's horse began a jolting trot. In another few minutes they were back with the other Indians. Buffalo Run shoved her from his horse and she fell into the dirt. She scrambled quickly to her feet, looking around. She was surrounded by Indians.

There was no sign of Darcy or Mrs. Brooks. The two had escaped.

Because Buffalo Run had come for her. She had gambled, and she had been right. She was the greater prize.

She backed away uneasily because the Indian was coming for her. He struck her hard on the cheek and she fell to the dust once again, reeling from the blow. He reached down a hand for her. She tried to shimmy away from him in the dirt, but he caught hold of her firmly, jerking her to her feet. He called out an order to the other men, then lifted her over his horse. They still had plenty of mounts, their own six Indian horses, hers, and Jeffrey Thayer's mount. But they weren't trusting her to ride alone anymore.

They started out slowly, allowing the horses a chance to breathe.

Buffalo Run rode behind her, a creature composed of flesh and steel, she thought dully.

"Are you going to kill me now?" she asked him.

"Not yet."

"Jesu!" she breathed out. "Then let me go!"

"It's never that simple. Not with the Comanche. Has no one warned you?"

Yes, she had been warned!

"Why don't—"

"You not only cost me two horses and two captives, you nearly killed the animal you rode so hard and those we rode to catch you!"

"Then—"

"I may still kill you!" he warned her. "And I may cut you up in bits and pieces to feed to the buzzards first."

"Yes, I cost you two captives!" she informed him, thinking herself a fool. "And two horses. And nearly four more! So do what you will—"

"The horses truly grieve me," he said roughly. "And if you wish to keep your tongue in your head, keep it still!"

"My husband will come for you. He will cut you into little bits and pieces!"

"Shut up."

"The cavalry will—"

"I will slice your tongue out myself if you do not take care!"

He meant it, she knew. A trembling seized hold of her.

Jeremy! She would never be able to tell him that she loved him.

"Please!" she began.

"One more word and it will be your last!" he said.

So warned, Christa fell silent.

* * *

The whole of Company D was still riding with Jeremy when he looked across the rolling plain to see the two riders.

He saw them from quite a distance at first, and he had to blink to assure himself that they were appearing before him. Because his vision was very sharp or perhaps because of instinct, he knew right away that the riders were connected with him, and he called out a warning to James. He then spurred his horse and went racing over the plain. There were only two. Mrs. Brooks and Darcy.

His disappointment when he neared the two—who had broken into a gallop at the sight of him—was difficult to conceal, and he swallowed it down with bitterness. He didn't have much chance to speak as he dismounted from his horse, for Mrs. Brooks threw herself into his arms, screaming and talking gibberish all at once and sounding something like a Comanche herself.

Darcy was far clearer.

"It's Buffalo Run, sir, I'm certain—"

"Christa!" he said hoarsely. "Darcy, where's my wife?"

"I know she felt responsible, sir. And I don't think that the Indian knew quite what he had on his hands. He loosed her to go to the stream. She managed to free me and go back around for Mrs. Brooks. Then we all started to race out of there but the savages were on our heels. Mrs. McCauley suddenly cried out that she was going to split up and I couldn't stop her, sir. She knew that they'd let us go and follow her. Sir, you don't know the half of it! Colonel, Doc Weland went mad on us! If he's still back there, he's dangerous, sir. He—"

"He's dead," Jeremy said flatly.

His heart sank. Christa was still with the Comanche. She had caused trouble and Buffalo Run had caught up with her again. She might still be fighting him.

No, Christa, no. They'll hurt you! I've warned you about the Comanche. I don't know if he'll remember that he's my blood brother or not, or if he'll see only that I was responsible for Thayer and that he was riding free. Christa, don't fight him.

Move, fool, he warned himself. He was still at the very least a day's ride from the encampment. Time might well be of the essence.

He turned to James, thrusting the wailing Mrs. Brooks upon his lieutenant. "I'm going on alone from here. I can ride faster."

"It's dangerous territory—"

"It's Buffalo Run's territory. If he sees me coming in with a company, he might decide to slaughter us all, and that will do Christa no good."

"We can go back for reinforcements," James said.

Jeremy shook his head. "If they were to see us coming, they might kill Christa and any other captives on the spot. We might annihilate half of them, but they'd do a damned good job on us too. I've no right to risk the entire regiment, although I'd do so if I thought it would save her life. But it won't. I have to go in alone. I have to bargain with Buffalo Run."

"Colonel, sir, I'll come with you—" Darcy began.

"Darcy, I guarantee it—you'd be a dead man. You and Mrs. Brooks hurry straight back to the encampment."

"Yes, sir, but I'd be willing to come with you, just the same. She was the bravest woman I ever saw, Colonel."

"She's a Reb," Jeremy said softly. "She learned how to fight with some of the best." He mounted his horse once again. "James, you're in command here. Bring them all back. Jennings is in command at the encampment. He knows to move the men into the fort."

James swallowed hard. "If you find her, sir—"

"If I find her, I'm going to do my best to convince her that the fighting is over," he said. He tipped his hat to the company.

He turned away from them and rode on alone, only the Comanche girl, Morning Star, following behind him.

Twenty-two

They came to Buffalo Run's encampment late that afternoon. It was a curiously peaceful sight. Perhaps two dozen tepees were set up along a slowly moving stream. Children were at play in the water and dogs roamed the camp. Women dressed in cotton shirts, skirts, and buckskin clothing were busy with their tasks, some sewing skins with large bone needles, some at work with what looked like mortars and pestles, and others working on skins that were strung across long frames by the sides of the tepees.

As they moved into the encampment, an old Indian with a broad, brown, and heavily leathered face came toward them, a wool blanket about his shoulders, his still pitch-black hair hanging in braids down his back.

Buffalo Run spoke to the old Indian with deference. The old man nodded, observed Christa where she sat before Buffalo Run, and nodded again. He raised his hands and spoke. The women, who had come running in when they had seen the braves returning, now milled around.

"Now you are with the Comanche!" Buffalo Run told her. He lifted her and set her down in the midst of the women.

They began shouting and poking at her. Some of them carried sticks. She tried to back away but she was encircled by them. She swirled, trying to see her tormentors, shouting at them in return.

There was a white girl among them, a long scar down the side of her left cheek. The lobes of her ears were missing. But whatever torture she had met at the hands of the Comanche, she was one with them now, shouting at Christa. She shoved at Christa so hard that she fell.

Christa rose and turned around. A very tall Comanche woman had joined in with the tormenting. Her eyes were obsidian dark, her words a singsong with a curious roll to the R's that was almost melodic.

Christa nearly fell again, her knees shaking horribly, when she saw the newly arrived, tall Comanche woman.

She, too, had been mutilated. The tip of her nose had been clipped off. It seemed to have made a very vicious woman of her. While the others chanted and laughed and poked at Christa, the clip-nosed squaw struck her again and again with her pointed stick. Christa cried out, trying her best to fight off the woman.

There was a sudden, sharp roar of command. The women backed off. Christa found herself facing Buffalo Run again as he walked into the melee surrounding her. He called out orders and the women melted away, murmuring. Buffalo Run took her by the arm, shoving her into a tepee. She stumbled into it, then gained her balance, swirling back around, ready to face him. She was dizzy, and so terrified. All of the things that had been told to her about the Comanche came bubbling to the front of her mind.

She backed against the rear of the tepee, watching Buffalo Run warily. It was horrible to be so terrified, to be living with such terrible images of death in her mind, and to know that she had to keep some sense of dignity about her or lose all hope for a future.

"All right, we're here now!" she said. She wanted her words to be so commanding! They were barely a whisper. After all, she had seen Jeff Thayer die. "What are you going to do with me?" she demanded.

He smiled, arms crossed over his chest. "You think that we are an exceptionally savage people, do you?"

"Yes," she admitted flatly. "There is a Comanche woman out there with most of her nose cut off. She is one of your own. What should I think?"

"Basket Woman knew the consequences. It is the Comanche way."

"The way for what?"

"She lay with another warrior."

Adultery. It carried a heavy fine, Christa thought.

"You are savage to your captives!" she whispered.

"The white man has been savage to us," he replied. "But perhaps we're not the worst of the tribes," he said, walking around the low-burning fire in the center of his tepee. "The Pawnee have an interesting ceremony—carried out with a captive man or maiden. It is a religious ceremony, a sacrifice to the god Tirawa. The Pawnee may take many captives and welcome all but one into their tribe. That one captive is given the finest food; if it is a man, women are sent to dine with him. He is treated with the most respect and deference. But then he is taken naked and tied to cross poles. The Pawnee who captured him shoots an arrow through him, in his one side, out his other side, while a fire is lit

beneath him. Every male in the tribe then shoots an arrow into him, and
the fire builds until he is burned to cinders. The tribe prays to Tirawa,
especially the warrior who took the captive, so that he knows that a
human life was taken. When this is done, the tribe has good fortune with
its crops and does well in its wars. The captive can be a woman. The
Pawnee hate to sacrifice their own. Perhaps I could trade you for many
horses!"

"You're not going to give me to the Pawnee," she said. "And if you are
going to kill me, why don't you get it over with?" Christa asked. She
wasn't going to be able to stand much longer.

"We are masters of torture," he told her.

She heard a soft voice speak suddenly, the R's rolling, the whisper very
gentle. She spun around and saw that a young Indian woman was curled
down on a bearskin bed against the edge of the tepee. She hadn't been
sleeping, she had been waiting, sewing a shirt, and she watched now.

Buffalo Run answered her angrily at first, then seemed to soften. He
looked back to Christa. "My youngest wife, Little Flower," he said. "You
will serve her and do as she says. It was her younger sister, Morning Star,
who was taken by the outlaw soldier."

"What?" Christa asked quickly.

"The white man we killed kidnapped and raped Morning Star, Little
Flower's sister, whom I meant to take for my fourth wife. They also killed
the cavalry soldiers guarding a pay wagon and a white trader called
Greenley. He deserved to die."

He turned and started to leave the tepee.

"Wait!" Christa cried out, and she was startled by the plea in her voice,
and then more startled that he seemed to hear it and take pity upon her.
He paused and turned back slowly.

"I—I didn't know. I didn't know until it was too late what kind of a
man Thayer was. I'm sorry that he hurt Morning Star."

Buffalo Run grunted.

"Please—what is going to happen to me?" she asked.

"That we will see."

"But I—"

He seemed to relent, just barely. "You are my captive," he told her.
"Because you are my blood brother's woman, I have already granted you
mercy. The women will leave you be. You will serve Little Flower. And if
you do not anger me, then you will live—until your fate is decided."

"And that—"

"That will depend!" he said angrily.

"On—?"

He walked toward her. She forced herself not to shrink back. "It will depend on McCauley, and it will depend on you. If McCauley dies, perhaps I will take another wife, if Little Flower and the others find you acceptable. Then, perhaps we will sell you to the Apache or the Spaniards—when we are done with you. It is not decided."

He turned and left the tepee.

Christa, aware of the Indian girl but heedless of her, gasped in a breath of air. She could stand no longer. She sank to the ground.

To her amazement, she felt a very gentle hand touch her hair. "You needn't fear," the girl said. Christa looked up. Her eyes were huge and dark and expressive. Her English was far more hesitant than Buffalo Run's, but it was very good. "Buffalo Run does not like to hurt captives. He is against some of our ways."

Christa looked at the girl and swallowed hard. "I just saw women out there who—"

"The white girl was not his captive. And Basket Woman was not his wife."

She needed to take comfort in that, Christa thought. She needed to take comfort from anything that she could—it was the only way she would maintain her sanity.

Little Flower, she thought, studying the Indian. The name was fitting, for she seemed as gentle and tender as the petals of a rose, as soft, as beautiful. Christa was amazed to realize that she was still discovering all that had really happened.

"I am really so sorry that your sister was hurt. Is she—is she all right now?"

"I don't know. She had strayed from her work by the stream. We found the basket of clothing she had been washing. We found some of her things, torn from her. But Morning Star was missing. Perhaps McCauley found her. We don't know."

"He will think I deserve to be hurt!" Christa murmured.

"He will be patient. He will not let others hurt you," Little Flower said.

Christa hugged her knees and shivered, grateful at last to be able to show some of her fear. "But he may! It's my fault he lost two other captives and two horses."

Little Flower was silent for a moment. "Perhaps he feels that he was at fault himself for carelessness? But that doesn't matter."

"What does?"

"Your husband."

Christa buried her face in her hands, fighting the savage wave of pain that streaked through her. Jeremy. Even when he wasn't with her, he was protecting her. Just by being the man that he was, the man she hadn't wanted to see for so very long because of the color of the uniform he wore.

"I don't know if he will come," Christa said dully. But she gripped the girl's arm fiercely. "Little Flower, your English is so good—"

"Buffalo Run taught me," she said proudly. "If I am to best whites, I must understand them, while they cannot understand me!"

Christa nodded. Buffalo Run could be an extremely intelligent man. "Little Flower, I'm going to have a baby—"

"Yes. McCauley told Buffalo Run."

Jeremy had discussed her with Buffalo Run?

She inhaled and exhaled, praying suddenly that at least the baby was still all right.

"Little Flower, I know that my baby isn't due for months, but if you have any influence with him and they should decide that something is going to happen to me, would you try to see that the baby is born first, that—that it is given to my husband?" she whispered.

Little Flower arched a dark brow. "That is what you wish?"

"It's what I wish."

"Then I will try. And I will try to help you while you are with us too. If you learn to work, you will be tolerated."

"I can work," Christa said simply. And she could. She had learned to work well on the plantation, and long hours and back-bending labor meant little to her now.

In the few days that followed, with help from Little Flower, Christa quickly learned about the Comanche way of life and tepee etiquette.

When the flap was open, a guest might enter directly. When the flap was closed, a guest announced his presence before being invited in. Guests invited to dine brought their own bowls and spoons—it was extremely rude not to eat everything offered. Guests did not pass between the fire and those seated around it, but around those seated who leaned in to afford room for movement.

Women did not sit cross-legged as did the men—they sat on their heels or with their legs to one side. Christa hated bowing down to Buffalo Run on any principle whatever, but she was too grateful to be alive and unharmed to fight with him—or even let him notice her—over such a small detail. All of society followed certain rules. Tall Feather was the peace chief, and in matters that did not concern warfare he was highly respected. He called his warriors to council and he looked to Buffalo Run for much of his advice, but all of the warriors had a say in things, and any one of them could initiate a raid or a battle. Young men did not speak unless they were invited to speak by an elder. Although some Indian societies were matriarchal, the Comanche society was dominated by the males.

She was expected to work with the women, and as long as she stayed with Little Flower she was glad of the tasks that lasted throughout the day. She quickly learned that the Comanche did not eat fish, nor did they, as did some of the Indians, eat dogs or coyotes, for one of their gods was a dog-god. They cooked fresh buffalo meat right over an open fire, suspended from a tripod, and they made stew from buffalo meat by making a cooking pouch from the lining of the animal's stomach and dropping hot stones into it. They were never wasteful, drying strips of the meat into jerky and making sausages from it flavored with wild onions and sage. They made pemmican from the jerky, pulverizing the jerky into powder with a stone maul, then mixing it with dried berries and fat. The pemmican was stowed away in parfleches, or rawhide cases, where it could preserve food for the winter months when hunting might be scarce.

The night was another exercise in misery, for she was kept in Buffalo Run's tepee. Besides Little Flower, Buffalo Run had two other wives and a growing family of children. His other two wives were sisters, Dancing Maid and Running Doe. Running Doe had a babe that was just a few weeks old, and Dancing Maid had a child Christa estimated to be about six months.

Throughout the night, the babies cried or gurgled off and on, or made suckling noises as they nursed. At night she could also hear Buffalo Run with Little Flower. She lay with her teeth clenched, her face flushed. She was horribly embarrassed—and cast into a realm of memory, thinking of her own husband. Thinking of him, tall and naked and sleek, coming for her, sweeping her into his arms.

But the cries in the night were not hers.

When he finished with Little Flower, Buffalo Run prepared to sleep. His eyes caught Christa's, open in the dim firelight. He looked her way and smiled slowly, then laughed out loud.

She knew that he was aware that she was afraid he might decide she would do for an evening's copulation, and he enjoyed tormenting her.

Christa couldn't understand the lack of jealousy among wives, but Little Flower seemed very adapted to the lifestyle. In the morning she tried to explain it to Christa. "We each had our time alone with him when we were wed," she said. "Dancing Maid and Running Doe are now busy with their infants. My time will come, and I will tend to my child while they tend to Buffalo Run. And if he takes you on as a wife, you will have your time."

"Oh, God!" Christa whispered. They had come to the stream to bathe. Little Flower, she had discovered, loved water. She didn't mind that it was very cool. Christa had been terrified to part with her clothing, but Little Flower convinced her that the Comanche respected one another's privacy.

She so longed to bathe. She had ridden so long, through so much dust and mud. And though none of the violence had actually touched her, she had felt as if she were covered in blood. Robert Black Paw's blood. Anguish filled her. His death would lie forever on her conscience.

If she was with Little Flower, she tried to assure herself that she was safe. She had to change her clothing, for Little Flower told her that her dress had offended Dancing Maid, and as she was the first of Buffalo Run's wives, she had the right to want their slave dressed as she pleased.

Dancing Maid wanted the dress, Christa was certain.

But Christa didn't mind if Dancing Maid took her clothing. Not so long as Christa got to keep her nose, earlobes, and health intact. She meant to keep her peace with Dancing Maid. She had also discovered the doeskin she had been provided with to be very soft, and she knew it would be very warm against the coldness of the night.

Oddly enough, she also discovered that none of Buffalo Run's wives really seemed to wish her any harm. She was careful to work as hard as the women did, no matter how exhausted she became. And it was easy to care for the babies. They didn't know that they were Comanche, or that she was white, and Christa had long ago discovered that an infant was an infant, black, white, or red, and ready to love and trust anyone who offered it love and tenderness. Because she was so good with their children, Dancing Maid and Running Doe were more tolerant of her. She knew that if Buffalo Run decided to take her on as a wife, his wives would not protest. There was a great deal of work for a Comanche woman to do—less if she shared it. And since warriors died in battle so frequently, the Comanche would have found it foolish for a young woman of childbearing age not to have a husband. Christa would have been the only one to feel abject horror if Buffalo Run decided that he would have her.

Little Flower frowned at her. "Buffalo Run is a fine war chief, and an excellent hunter," she told Christa. "He is half white himself. He was taken into one of the forts for several years when he was small. That is where he learned to speak English so very well."

The water seemed to have grown very cold. She hugged her arms around her chest. "He is a fine warrior. It is just that—" She paused, feeling the anguish sweep over her. "It's just that I love the husband I already have."

Little Flower nodded. "He is very handsome and noble, especially for a white man."

Christa turned away from her, hugging herself against the chill as she climbed up the embankment to find her clothing. Before she could reach the doeskin dress and boots, she paused, feeling the hair rise at her nape. Chills danced down the entire length of her spine.

An Indian brave blocked her way. He was the next tallest of the warriors to Buffalo Run. His breeches were made of animal skin, his shirt was cotton, covered by a fringed vest with beadwork. His long black hair was in braids, and a kerchief interlaced with rawhide was tied around his forehead.

Eagle Who Flies High, she thought quickly. She remembered the night when Jeremy had been so angry because she had made an appearance in the tent when he was there.

He'd been angry because the Indian had seen her. Eagle Who Flies High had initiated the war party to come after her and Jeff Thayer.

Now he was staring at her, blocking her path. She didn't move, but felt her nudity more keenly with each passing second.

"Little Flower . . . ?" she whispered.

The Comanche girl came from the water, her soft voice full of reproach, her language swift and intriguing with its rolling R's.

But it did no good. Eagle Who Flies High answered her curtly and angrily. Little Flower argued back, but the warrior seemed to grow angrier by the minute.

"What is he saying?" Christa asked nervously. Surely, he couldn't hurt her. Only Buffalo Run could hurt her, if he chose. Unless Buffalo Run were to be killed.

Then she might be sold, or traded, or given away.

"Little Flower!"

"He says that he saw you first. That by right, you are his captive. He says that Buffalo Run really has no right to you, that he has pampered you, that he has scorned the Comanche ways. He says that you should be his slave, and that he intends to take you."

"Jesu, no!" Christa cried. Eagle Who Flies High took a step toward her, and she didn't care if there were nothing but desert and dust and death if she ran from the encampment, she would not stand still and wait for this man to attack her. She spun around, naked still, and shrieked with terror. She raced across the water and started to run through the scruffy foliage on the other side of it. Brambles and branches tore at her flesh. Rocks bruised her feet.

He was slowed by the water between them. Christa continued to shriek and scream as she ran, but she wondered if she could be heard, and if she were heard, would anyone help her?

The calf-high boots that had slowed Eagle Who Flies High as he made his way through the water became his advantage when they were both on solid ground. She couldn't run over the rocky terrain the way he could. Pain seared into her foot and she cried out, holding it, as a jagged rock tore the bottom.

And even as that cry left her mouth, another formed inside her, for the Comanche had caught up with her. She went spinning around and fell flat to the ground. With deadly serious eyes he started to lower himself upon her.

Christa struck out, kicking him with all the vengeance and desperation inside her. She must have struck thoroughly and well, for the warrior who never betrayed emotion showed signs of the pain she had inflicted. His bronzed features tightened, his teeth grated loudly. He fell away from her, rolling to his side. Words of fury escaped his lips, directed toward her. She leapt to her feet, certain that were he to set his hands upon her now, she would be brutally raped, mutilated, and perhaps, if she were lucky, killed.

She started to run again. She screamed as fingers wound into her hair.

But before she could be dragged back to the ground, a bullet exploded, splintering a rock near her feet. She shrieked and spun about, just as Eagle Who Flies High did.

Buffalo Run had come. Christa was certain that Little Flower had gone for him. The shot he had fired from a U.S. Army issue Colt—surely taken in some raid—had been meant as a warning one.

Angrily, Buffalo Run began speaking. Eagle Who Flies High responded in kind. Christa didn't wait for the argument to finish. She shot back toward Buffalo Run, hiding behind him. Little Flower was there, awaiting her with a blanket. She wrapped Christa in it.

Others from the tribe had come around by now, but they all remained quiet, listening to Buffalo Run and Eagle Who Flies High. Tall Feather, the peace chief of the band, had come. He began speaking and the others listened.

"What are they saying?" she asked Little Flower.

But this time, there was no chance for Little Flower to answer her. Buffalo Run turned around angrily and caught her by the arm. He brought her back to the camp, dragging her along.

"I didn't do anything!" she cried out. "Please, tell me what is going on!"

But Buffalo Run wasn't going to explain anything to her. She felt a new rise of fear as he dragged her past his own tepee. He stopped before one that had been erected near his own. It had belonged to a warrior named Eagle Claw who had been killed in a recent raid. His young wife, childless, had returned to her father's home. She was being imprisoned in a neutral territory, she realized.

He threw her into the tepee. "You!" he charged her. "You are nothing but trouble!"

"But I didn't do anything this time! He just came after me—"

"This time! You freed the other captives, you cost us good horses. You were captured yourself to free the gray soldier." He spat on the ground. "The gray murderer! For McCauley, I have kept you from punishment. Your nose should have been clipped! You wouldn't have created such a lust in Eagle Who Flies High!"

"But I—"

"Stay here! I will come for you soon enough. You are a dangerous prize—someone will pay the price for you. And tonight—you will pay yourself!"

Furious, shaking, he turned and left the tepee. Terrified, she tried to come after him.

Basket Woman waited outside, grinning cruelly. She held a knife, and quickly raised it to Christa's throat.

The woman would gladly kill her, Christa knew.

She moved back into the tepee and sat. A few minutes later, she heard a soft whisper. Little Flower had brought her clothes. She came in and hastily started a fire, speaking as quickly as she could. "I cannot stay. There is tremendous trouble now, over you."

"What will happen?"

A blaze started up in the center fire. "You will be warm at least."

"Little Flower, please—?"

"I don't know! We have never had such an argument before. I don't know how it will be solved. Eagle Who Flies High says that he will use you as a captive should be used if Buffalo Run will not do so, as you should be his captive by right. Buffalo Run told him that Morning Star was to have been his wife, so you are his captive in exchange. He also says that he snatched you from your horse. There is great trouble, so something must happen. But now, in the midst of this there is more. I don't know quite what happened myself, but Tall Feather and Buffalo Run and Eagle Who Flies High have all gathered with—"

A sharp command came from outside. Basket Woman was warning Little Flower to come out.

"I don't dare stay longer! Their tempers are so high! Someone, I think, must die—"

Another roaring command came from the outside. Little Flower jumped up, stared at Christa, then hurried from the tepee.

Christa dressed and sank down upon a pile of furs, trying not to shake. Jesu, she should just die and end this agony!

But then, just as the thought came to her, she felt movement.

The baby was moving again! After everything. The baby was alive inside of her. She had to live. No matter what happened to her, no matter what was done to her, she had to live. If nothing else, she meant to see to it that she delivered her baby. If Buffalo Run had any sense of honor, and he did, he would see to it that Jeremy received their child.

She lowered her cheeks to her knees and fought the tears that threatened her. What would come now? Maiming, torture at the hands of Eagle Who Flies High?

Or would Buffalo Run return. He had said she should have had her nose clipped. Perhaps he would only rape her.

It was then that she heard the drums. A slow, steady beat. Continuous. Threatening. They seemed to go on for hours and hours. Hours in which she thought that she would lose her mind. Thump. Thump. Thump. They beat on. Warning of dire things to come.

What things?

Jeremy would know.

Tears, unbidden, slid from her eyes. She wiped them away.

It was then that she looked up, and terror struck her heart once again.

Someone was there. Tall, indomitable. Filling the entrance to the tepee.

A scream, silent and terrible, welled in her throat as she watched him come into the tepee.

Twenty-three

He hadn't traveled much beyond the point where he had parted from Company D when he began to feel the sensation of being watched.

He was, indeed, in Buffalo Run's territory.

There was something so unnerving about the feeling, that he was upon occasion tempted to turn his horse about and race as hard and fast as he could in the opposite direction. He could never do that. Even if the desperate, all-consuming need to find Christa should suddenly and inexplicably fade, he could not turn and run.

He was being watched. He was close to the encampment and Comanche warriors were watching his progress.

He wasn't alone. Morning Star was with him.

Thankfully, when he had come upon the ex-Reb outlaws, they had been so busy with old Joseph Greenley's money and trading goods that they hadn't had time to give much attention to Morning Star. She was just a girl, younger than her sister Little Flower, but by Indian standards she was certainly old enough to wed, and it would not be at all unusual for Buffalo Run to take her into his household, where he would then have two sets of sisters, and those sisters cousins with one another. Morning Star was quiet, with a curious wisdom far beyond her years. He'd tried to talk with her, but there was very little she would tell him. She was grateful to be with him. She had known him from Buffalo Run's encampment, and she had come to him when he had seized the outlaws with an implicit trust that had been both frightening and endearing. "McCauley bring Morning Star home," she had told him, and of course she had been right. No matter what happened, he would see to it that she was returned to Buffalo Run and the Comanche encampment.

But he didn't imagine that he would be riding into the territory in the company of one small Indian girl. Nor had he ever imagined that she would be part of his bargaining power when he asked for the return of his own wife.

Moments later, he saw a warrior on the wave of ridge he approached. As he moved closer, a second warrior appeared, and then a third.

Within a few minutes, the Indians had slowly encircled him. No violence was offered. They kept their distance as an escort, bringing him the rest of the way into the camp.

He hadn't quite reached the first pathway through the tepees when he saw an old Indian step out, barring his way. For a moment he felt his muscles tensing, then he relaxed.

It was Tall Feather, the peace chief. The Indian lifted a hand in greeting to him.

"McCauley," he said.

Jeremy dismounted from his horse, walking the few feet that remained between them. "I've brought back the girl, Morning Star," he said. "And I've come for my wife."

"You wish to trade women?" Tall Feather said.

He shook his head. "I would have brought Morning Star home no matter what. If my brother Buffalo Run seized my wife, I wish to think that he would bring her home to me—no matter what."

Tall Feather lifted his arm, indicating his own tepee. "There is some trouble over your wife," he commented.

Jeremy felt his heart careen against his chest. He tried to still the panic rising in his breast and followed Tall Feather into his tepee. A good guest, he entered carefully to the left and sat with his legs crossed.

Tall Feather spoke to one of his wives in his Comanche tongue. Jeremy couldn't follow all of the words, but he knew that he sent the woman for Buffalo Run—and for Eagle Who Flies High.

Tall Feather produced one of his pipes. It was an exceptionally fine pipe, made with a stone bowl polished with buffalo grease. The stem was decorated with beads and horsehair, and Jeremy knew it was the old chief's best pipe, which was an encouraging sign. The Comanche respected him and wanted to remain his friend. Also, no serious business could possibly be done without the smoking of a pipe between men.

Jeremy tried to conceal his fear and impatience, inhaling deeply on the pipe before returning it to Tall Feather. "What is this trouble with my wife?" he asked, his heart pounding. All manner of horrors raced through his mind. They had punished her for freeing the other captives. They had slashed her legs or her face. They had clipped her nose or ears. "As Buffalo Run is my brother—"

"Buffalo Run does not refuse you your wife. He has been waiting for you to come."

"Then—"

"Buffalo Run said that we must leave the problem of the outlaws to you. They were white men trying to commit crimes as Comanche. He knew that you would believe us. But Eagle Who Flies High gathered the force to ride to your encampment to see that the white men had been taken. They found that the white man was escaping, and they passed their own judgment."

"I know that," Jeremy said. "I found the man."

Tall Feather nodded sagely. "We hear many things, so we know that your wife was with the army of the men in the gray coats." He leveled his finger at Jeremy. "A man should have control of his own home."

At that particular moment, Jeremy's fingers itched to slide around Christa's neck. "I bow to your wisdom, Tall Feather," he said to the Indian.

The tepee flap moved. Buffalo Run and Eagle Who Flies High entered, came around the left, and accepted the pipe so that they could be involved in the business at hand. Buffalo Run stared levelly at Jeremy. Eagle Who Flies High seemed to be staring above him. Jeremy realized that the man who had come to him before as Buffalo Run's emissary was gaining an equal footing with Buffalo Run as a war chief.

"She is well," Buffalo Run assured him, and Jeremy wondered just what of his fear he had given away. "For my part, my brother, I give up my rights to her, as you have returned Morning Star to me."

"Then I may take my wife and leave—" Jeremy began.

"No," Eagle Who Flies High said.

"There is the matter of which man here has the right to the captive," Tall Feather told Jeremy. "Eagle Who Flies High was the warrior to lead the raid. Before we knew of your coming today, they had disagreed about her. Eagle Who Flies High challenged Buffalo Run, and they agreed to meet with knives to settle the dispute."

"I will not give her up," Eagle Who Flies High said flatly. His eyes met Jeremy's at last. "It was not my woman you returned. I owe you nothing."

"I will not leave without my wife!" Jeremy insisted softly.

"Then Buffalo Run must be taken from this dispute," Tall Feather said. "And you, McCauley, must be ready to meet Eagle Who Flies High in his stead. Is your wife worth this?"

She is worth everything, he might have said.

But he had to take care. "She is mine. And I will leave with her."

"Or die in the trying," Eagle Who Flies High said with quiet menace.

It was more than just keeping Christa from this brave, Jeremy realized. It was a power struggle within the tribe.

"Or die in the trying," Jeremy said.

"It is settled," Tall Feather said. "You will meet in the morning with knives. The fight will be fair, between two warriors, in our fashion. The tribe will be witness."

"If I win," Jeremy said, "it is agreed, on your honor, that I leave here in peace with my wife?"

"It is agreed. You leave with our gratitude, for Morning Star is returned."

Tall Feather started to knock the burned tobacco from his pipe—a clear sign that the meeting was ended. It was time for them all to rise and leave the tepee. Jeremy, though he knew the etiquette, sat still.

"I will fight in the morning. I want to be with her tonight," he said.

"That I will not agree to—" Eagle Who Flies High began.

But Buffalo Run protested before Jeremy could. "The woman is Mc-Cauley's wife. And has been. And carries his child. He may well die. There are matters to solve between them. I say that he should have the night." He looked to Tall Feather.

Tall Feather nodded. "This is only just. We have kept our two good war chiefs from meeting one another and injuring one another when all braves are needed, when we can trust so few of the white soldiers and settlers. Neither will Buffalo Run and McCauley, who are brothers with mingled blood, meet one another. The fight will be good and fair, the outcome just. Buffalo Run, you will see that your white brother reaches the woman. And you will tend to his needs for the fight to come in the morning. Eagle Who Flies High—you will wait until then."

They all rose. Jeremy could feel the heat and fury emitting from Eagle Who Flies High. He knew the Indian longed to slit his throat then and there, but his tribesmen had spoken against him, and to retain face he must wait for the fight.

And win it.

That gave Jeremy the night. The night, if nothing more.

They walked through the camp. Here and there, Jeremy was greeted with a call by those who knew him. But mostly the Indians paused and stared at him. They all knew that Christa was in the camp.

They knew about the trouble over her, and now knew that he had come.

A white man walking alone amongst them.

Buffalo Run came to a halt in front of a tepee not far from his own.

"You must leave her at dawn," he said. "You will come to my home. I'll see you are dressed properly, and Dancing Maid will cover you in bear grease, so that your opponent will not have an advantage."

"Thank you."

"You are a rare white man, McCauley. You have always kept your word with me. I hope that you live to do so again."

Jeremy smiled. "So do I!" he said. Buffalo Run nodded and left him.

The battle-ax of a woman keeping guard in front of the tepee moved aside for him. He unpinned the flap, leaving it open, and stood there for a moment trying to see in the darkness. His heart started to pound suddenly, his loins to quicken. Christa. Buffalo Run had said that she was unharmed.

A fire was burning low in the center of the tepee. He could just make out a shape beyond it. He strode into the tepee anxious, fury and fear suddenly mingling within him along with the simple desperation to hold her. She wasn't moving, he realized. She was frozen as still as ice. He heard her shifting her position, inhaling sharply.

"You!" she cried.

He heard her startled gasp and realized that she hadn't known until that moment that it was he who had come upon her.

She was against the hide wall of the tepee, curled as close as she could come to the skin. The fire played over her, and he saw that she was dressed in soft skins, that her hair was free and long, flowing down her back. Her eyes were huge in the firelight, her face pale. She was terrified, he thought, and trying very hard not to show it. He was suddenly afraid himself. Not afraid of meeting Eagle Who Flies High in combat; he had fought too many times in hand-to-hand combat against white men in the midst of screaming cavalry horses to feel himself incapable of fighting Eagle Who Flies High.

He was only afraid that he had found her at last, only to lose her still to death—his own.

Christa, damn you, he thought. Why couldn't you believe in me? Weland was a traitor to us all, but you let him use you to thwart me!

He felt his hands shaking. He was so glad to see her safe and unharmed. Suddenly, if he was going to die, he wanted to do so with the memory of the sweetness of her kiss on his lips, not with the bitter taste of betrayal in his heart.

He reached down his hands to her, catching her wrists when she continued to stare incredulously at him.

He wrenched her to her feet and brought her crashing hard against him.

"Tomorrow, madam, I may die for you," he told her. He didn't mean to sound so harsh, but the depths of his emotion and hunger combined to give his words a rough-edged quality. His fingers were tense upon her, making his hold a rough one. He brought her closer against him. He wanted to touch her, all of her. From the soft planes of her face to her fingers and toes. To see that she was really unharmed.

He stroked and cupped her chin, tilting her face, forcing her eyes to his. His fingers threaded into the wild tangle of her hair. His eyes traveled the length of her. He held her head steady as his lips lowered until they hovered just above hers. His grip was forceful. The length of him seemed to shake with electric energy, be it passion or fury. And hovered there, continuing to whisper, the warmth of his breath bathing her lips, her face.

"Tomorrow I may die. Tonight . . ." He paused briefly, seeking out the shimmering blue beauty of her eyes. Yes, her arms were around him. Yes, dear God, she was glad of him tonight. The last time he had seen her she had seduced him to trick him. Sometimes she had been his because she had felt her debts deeply, and sometimes because he had learned to fire her passions. Yet, he realized, none of that mattered. Tonight, she would love him because the drums were beating, because he would live or die for the glory of her touch.

Tension seemed to burn in his body, hotter than the bluest streaks of flame within the fire. "Tonight," he told her. "Tonight, my love, you will make it worth my while!"

His lips descended down upon hers, hard, questing, demanding.

And bringing up all that fire within her.

"Jesu!" she whispered when the bruising force of his lips left her mouth at last. Again her gaze met his. Bluer than the sky, than the sea, deeper than the earth. The fire within him had touched her. The sound of the drums had entered her blood.

She threw her arms around him and clung to him. His fingers moved over her hair, reveling in the length of it. He drew her away from him, the fury, the passion, still alive within him.

"Life—and death. Make them both worthwhile," he told her harshly.

She stared at him. He swept her up into his arms and bore her down to the furs upon the ground.

"Love me!" he commanded her fiercely.

She was silent as he stripped, her eyes on his, waiting. Then he was down beside her, his hands upon her, stripping her of the fine doeskin tunic the Comanche had given her to wear.

She lay against his burning, naked flesh. He could feel the length of her, and he began to shake, certain at last in his heart that she was all right. They had not touched her, had not maimed her. He had come in time.

She would keep nothing from him, he decided. She wouldn't fight the sensations, she would do nothing but surrender. He whispered harshly to her. "Give in to me! Everything, Christa, everything."

He straddled her. Her flesh was beautiful, ivory and gold in the fire-light. Her breasts were so large now, full, evocative, the nipples nearly crimson, hardened. He could just feel the slight rise of their child in her abdomen, and he prayed suddenly, fiercely, that they all might live. Beneath him she began to tremble, and he didn't know if it was with fear or with desire, or if the endless incantation of the drums had entered them both.

She reached out her arms to him, eyes wide, luminous. She moistened her lips to speak, and her words were soft, quavering, yet filled with a passion that touched his heart, soul, loins.

"I will give you everything!" she vowed, and added in a vehement whisper, "And make the night well—well worth your while!"

Tonight was different from all others. Tonight the words, the accusations, the anguish, the whispers, all hovered within his body, locked within his soul. He loved her. He didn't know how long he had loved her so fiercely, maybe it had been forever. For all else paled beside this. No love he had known could be so deep, no hunger could be so shattering.

He found her lips. They trembled beneath his and parted. Heat rippled and burst between them, spreading rampantly. His hands moved swiftly, circling the heavy fullness of her breasts, rounding over the rise of her belly, touching her.

The softness of her body seemed to meld to his. She twisted and turned, accepting his touch, wanting his touch. Soft sounds escaped her, sounds that sent desire rocketing more deeply into his mind and body.

"Death holds no threat, my love. Indeed, you have made it all worth my while!" he promised her.

He felt the urgency of her touch, pressing against him. Holding his breath, he let her have her way. Upon her knees she kissed his shoulders, her fingers biting into the flesh and muscle. She kissed his lips, his chest. Swept into a newer, even sweeter fire, he caught her hand and guided it to the fullness of his sex.

A ragged cry escaped him. He swept her up into his arms, then laid her flat against the hides and fur of the bedding again. He caught her ankles, spreading her legs. He hovered over her, lips ravaging hers again, eyes seeking her own.

His body screamed that he must have her then.

But something within him knew that he could not for he had to touch her more, had to feel her, see her, kiss her, touch her, taste her.

Again, his lips covered hers. They covered her breasts. They bathed her belly, and even as she cried out, his kiss, his lips, his tongue stroked and teased her inner thighs, the throbbing sweet cleft between them. A cry escaped her, then whispers and gasps. She urged him to her, near sobbing as she brought him into her arms.

"Jesu!" he cried out.

He felt so alive, so volatile. So damned, desperately hungry. He scooped her into his arms. Sensations sheathed and sheltered him as he thrust himself into her. Her limbs wrapped around him tightly, the liquid fire of her body accepted and encompassed him. He moved and let the thunder of the drumbeats call his rhythm, for he was far beyond reason, feeling the incredible rise of his climax. He fought the explosion, savoring the feel of his wife beneath him, the sleekness of her flesh, the undulation of her body, rising against his and meeting him. He felt the ragged rise and fall of her breath, the pure thunder of her heart.

But the splendor that night seemed as savage as the beat of the drums. Desire soared within him, then burst in a violent climax. He felt her shuddering beneath him, felt the explosion within her. "My love . . . ."

The words escaped him. He didn't know if she heard him or not. It didn't matter. He grit his teeth, feeling the final thrust of his body, the last of the little explosions that shook him.

For a long while he held still. Felt the satiation fill his body. He lay down beside her, sweeping her damp, cooling body into his arms.

She started to speak.

"Shh!" he said softly. "We have the night."

She curled against him. She touched his cheek, but her eyes would not rise to his. "I can't!" she whispered. "I don't think it's possible to forget this fear long enough to . . . make love."

He smiled. "Give me a chance!" he said softly, and they both remembered another night he had made such a request.

She rose up, trying to see him in the flickering gold light. "Jeremy, I know that I betrayed you. I have no right to ask you to understand, but you can't know the whole of it. Dr. Weland—"

"Is dead," he told her flatly.

She inhaled sharply. There was a glaze of tears in her eyes. "Then you know? He killed Robert Black Paw."

Jeremy hesitated. "Robert may still be alive. It's possible."

"Oh, God!" she whispered. "Oh, God! I pray that he is!"

Her words were fervent, and he knew that they were honest. He prayed himself that the man who had been his good and loyal friend through so many things might still be alive.

But Robert seemed distant now. The cavalry encampment might have been a million miles away. The real world was here, in this tepee, with the sound of the drums all around them, the flickering fire bathing them in its gold light, and the promise of the violence that would come with the daylight.

"Jeremy—"

He reached up to her, threading his fingers through her hair, amazed himself that he could want her again, so desperately, so quickly.

It might be all that he would have.

"Come here," he whispered, pulling her head down to his. His lips just a breath from hers, he told her, "We haven't that long." He rose, pressing her back down to the furs. But she moaned deep in her throat, protesting, tossing her head. He released her captive lips, and she looked up at him, her eyes wide and incredibly blue, her hair wild and entangling them both.

"Jeremy, you said that you might die. I don't understand—"

"I am to meet Eagle Who Flies High in the morning. We will fight for you. With knives."

She gasped, and a tremble shot through her. "You—you can't meet him. He could so easily kill you—"

"Thank you for the vote of confidence!"

She shook her head raggedly. "Oh, my God, Jeremy, it's just that he's an Indian, a savage—"

"He is a savage? Jesu! You should have seen the way your friend Jeff Thayer killed poor Joe Greenley and the Union soldiers on the pay wagon!"

She swallowed hard, her lashes falling over her eyes. "I didn't know, Jeremy—"

"It doesn't matter!" he said roughly. "Not tonight."

He tried to capture her lips again, but she was speaking quickly. "Don't you see, it does matter?" she whispered. "Damn you, Jeremy, I don't want you to die for me! I don't want you to die for honor, not for my sake. I forced you into marriage, I—"

"Christa! You're carrying my child!" he reminded her.

She fell silent, inhaling, her lashes once again covering her eyes. She stared at him. "Before you came, I asked Little Flower to make sure that the baby was brought to you in the event of anything happening to me.

She would have helped me. She—will help me get the baby back to you if choose to leave now—"

"Christa, if I wished to, I couldn't leave now. My honor is at stake here, my credibility. I cannot go."

"But—"

"Christa! The night is short, the hours wane. Dawn will come soon enough."

"Dawn?" she whispered miserably.

"I have to prepare."

"Then you have to sleep!" she cried out fervently.

"I will sleep," he said. He threaded his fingers forcefully through her hair. "I will sleep soon enough."

"I—"

"Shush, Christa!"

She had no chance to disobey for his lips seized hers firmly, and the kiss was deep and demanding, stealing the breath from her.

When he finally dozed, she stared down at his face, biting her lip, feeling tears form and fall. She jerked back, lest her tears hit his flesh.

If something happened to him tomorrow, she wouldn't want to live. Once she had loved Liam, but never like this.

"Don't die!" she whispered. "Please, don't die! I cannot live without you!"

At long last, she lay down beside him, certain that she would never sleep.

Yet she did.

Jeremy awoke with the first light of the new day. He stared down at the woman entangled with him. Her flesh was so ivory and soft against the brown fur, her hair so black and richly cascading, her face so beautiful. Her abdomen seemed more rounded this morning; in the midst of this chaos, their child grew.

He leaned low against her and reached out and touched her cheek. It was damp. Tears lay upon it.

Tears she had been shedding for him.

He kissed her forehead, then silently drank in the beauty of her curled before him once again. He placed his hand upon her belly and wondered in sudden awe if he had actually felt movement. Life. If he were to die, he prayed God that Christa and his child might live. Gently, tenderly, he pressed his lips against the flesh of her abdomen, and then he rose. He hastily gathered his clothing, then left the tepee, moving on to Buffalo Run's home so as to prepare.

* * *

When Christa awoke, she heard the chanting and the cheers. She lay staring into space for a moment, and then she remembered.

She leapt up and found her doeskin dress and shimmied into it. She was afraid that Basket Woman would be waiting just beyond the tepee to stop her, but she was too desperate to care. She burst out of the tepee and found that she was not going to be stopped at all.

It seemed that all of the Comanche, Basket Woman included, were attending the fight.

She raced through the line of tepees until she came to a spot before the river where a circle had been drawn in the earth. The men were both there, surrounded by the tribe.

She hardly recognized her husband at first. He was dressed in a simple breechclout and nothing more. His flesh had been so rubbed with bear grease that it seemed nearly as dark as Eagle Who Flies High. When Christa reached the gathering, they were parted by a medicine man who danced between them, chanting and sprinkling herbs upon the ground. He carried a bear paw. He called something out and Eagle Who Flies High stepped forward, presenting his back to the man. The shaman brought the bear claw tearing down the Comanche's back. Bright streams of blood appeared. Eagle Who Flies High stepped back. He hadn't made a sound, nor had he flinched. He appeared smug and well pleased with himself.

Jeremy stepped forward, turning his back to the shaman.

Christa cried out.

A hand clamped upon her arm. Dancing Maid was beside her, shaking her head. Christa opened her mouth to speak and then fell silent. She closed her eyes, feeling a numbing terror steal over her. She heard the Comanche give out a roar of approval and she opened her eyes. Blood was streaming down Jeremy's back. Her knees grew weak.

"Oh, God!" she whispered. "Please don't let him die, please don't let him die . . ."

A drumbeat sounded. The shaman left the circle.

Knives in hand, Eagle Who Flies High and Jeremy slowly began to circle one another.

Twenty-four

The two men lunged at one another simultaneously. There was a curious sound as their greased bodies smacked together. For a moment, they hovered in the air, then they were down on the ground, rolling. A streak of blood appeared on one arm, and for a moment Christa couldn't figure out to which fighter the arm belonged. She cried out again. The blood was dripping from Jeremy.

"You mustn't cry out so!" a voice suddenly warned in her ear. Little Flower was at her side. "Please, Christa, you will distract him."

She bit her lip. She wanted to go back to the tepee, she wanted to look away. She couldn't bear to do so, but neither could she bear to look.

The two men tore away from one another. Once again, they were up on their feet. Circling. Stalking.

Jeremy was a cavalry officer, she thought. Trained to fight from the saddle. He was excellent with a Colt and with a saber. But the Yanks and Rebs hadn't fought their battles with greased bodies and razor-sharp knives.

Jeremy and Eagle Who Flies High appeared to be evenly matched. Both men were superbly muscled, agile, and alert to the slightest movement from the other. Jeremy was slightly the taller of the two, Eagle Who Flies High was stockier. Christa bit her lip, praying that the Comanche's added weight would not make the difference in the end.

Eagle Who Flies High made another flying lunge at Jeremy. The two men went down.

The Indians gathered tightly around the circle. Christa couldn't see anything. She tried to burst through the crowd. "Dear God, dear God, please! I'll do anything, I'll tend the sick, I'll work for the poor—I'll be nice to Yankees everywhere. Oh, God, please, I'll never ask another thing of you, just let him live, please, please, let him live . . ."

She weaved her way through bodies, but was blocked again. She tried to twist through, and fell to the ground, plowing through the dust to land at the edge of the circle where the men were fighting.

A gasp escaped her. Tears welled into her eyes. Jeremy was down. A red gash had been cut across his chest; another sliced his shoulder. His eyes were closed; he lay on his side, prone, in front of her.

"Dear God, no!" she cried in pain and anguish. "Jeremy . . ."

From some distant fog, he heard her call his name. He fought the pain that seared through him. Fought the exhaustion. So much blood was draining from him now, it was making him weak. He had made a few strikes too. Eagle Who Flies High had to be hurting. Jeremy had cut him soundly about the hip and struck deeply into one leg.

But still, he hadn't been able to fight the dizziness. Death had not seemed so horrible until he had heard her voice.

He could see her, yes! Christa thought. He was not dead!

His lip curled suddenly. "I won't fail you, Reb!" he whispered.

He pulled up to his knees. Christa suddenly felt herself wrenched to her feet. She was being held back by one of the braves. She wasn't going to be allowed to come close anymore.

"Please!" she cried. But the brave did not intend to release her. She could see the men moving again. Circling, coming closer and closer to one another.

A war whoop shook the air. Someone had lunged once again. She could see the bodies entangled upon the earth. Flailing, fighting, one man gaining an advantage, then losing it.

Damn! The bear grease made fighting nearly impossible. Every time Jeremy thought he had a good hold on Eagle Who Flies High, the man slipped between his fingers.

But then, the grease worked to his advantage just as well. He saw the warrior's dark eyes on him, sizing him up as they both paused.

Jeremy grit his teeth. They were both losing blood. The blood dripping into his eyes from the wound on his forehead was blinding him. He had to win. He could see many things in Eagle Who Flies High's eyes. The Indian hated him. Hated that he had come to him in peace so many times. He could be a war chief now. As powerful as Buffalo Run. This fight was over many things, with Christa the main prize. And the Comanche coveted the woman.

Eagle Who Flies High had chosen the weapons. He had known his own expertise with the knife. Just as he knew that most cavalrymen were adept with their swords and guns. He had known he had the weight advantage. He had known he was a proud, fierce, good warrior, a strong fighter.

But he hadn't realized that weapons wouldn't matter, that fear wouldn't matter, that nothing would except Christa.

Love could be the strongest weapon of all.

He would not die.

"McCauley!" the Comanche taunted. "Come, McCauley, taste my steel. Taste it deep in your throat!"

He shook his head. "No, Eagle Who Flies High. You have chosen. You must taste my steel."

For the last time, the two of them lunged for one another, knowing that it must now be to the death.

There was a jarring, sickening crunch as steel met flesh and blood and bone.

One wearied fighter fell.

The other, severely wounded, staggered back.

Christa couldn't see them anymore. She heard an explosion of sound from the crowd of Comanche, and hands rose and struck the air, lances were raised, and loud cries sounded fiercely all around.

One of the combatants was down.

Down and dead, or dying.

She could not see which man.

"Please!" she shrieked, trying to tear away from the warrior who held her. He didn't release her, but the squaw in front of her moved.

She saw the bronzed back of a man. He lay with his face in the dirt. He was covered with blood and grease. The hilt of a knife protruded from the side of his rib cage.

"No!" she whispered. She started to fall. It was Jeremy and he was dead and she really didn't care what happened to her anymore. Her knees were too weak to allow her to stand, and she would have fallen if the Comanche warrior hadn't held her upon her feet.

"Tall Feather! Buffalo Run!" She heard the words, and she gasped. It was not Jeremy who had fallen. He was alive, and he was speaking, and the Comanche who held her so rigidly was at last moving forward.

He was alive but just barely. He was covered in as much blood as he was covered in grease. Standing seemed difficult for him, but he was determined to do so. He was addressing the chiefs, Tall Feather and Buffalo Run, his friend and his brother.

"I am sorry that it came to this. I am sorry for the life of a fine opponent. I ask that it be the end. We have all been betrayed by men we thought to be our friends. And in this, Tall Feather, and my brother,

Buffalo Run, we have all learned that there can be honor among our enemies. I have met Eagle Who Flies High in fair battle, man to man. The gray-coat, Jeffrey Thayer, is dead. Even the man who betrayed me, who sought to bring down my wife's family, is now dead. I want to take my wife and bring her home. We can't stop the great tide of violence that goes on between our peoples. We can remember the honor in one another. Let me take my wife and go."

Christa felt the warrior's hold upon her tighten as he awaited word from the head men of the band. Buffalo Run and Tall Feather exchanged glances. Tall Feather looked at Jeremy a long while, and then nodded. He lifted a hand.

The brave released Christa. Suddenly, she was free.

With a soft cry, she raced the distance to her husband. The impetus of her weight against him almost caused him to keel over. She straightened quickly, made painfully aware of how he had been cut and injured. She tried to support his weight upon her shoulders, yet he would not lean upon her.

"McCauley," Buffalo Run said. "You are right. There can be honor among enemies. Take your woman and go home."

Christa inhaled a ragged breath, looking to Jeremy. He smiled and took a step forward.

But they weren't going home. Not quite yet. Jeremy took a step and fell flat into the dirt. Christa cried out, falling to her knees beside him.

Little Flower was quickly at her side. "Bring him!" she told the men gathering around. "Bring him quickly. We must stop the flow of blood."

When Jeremy opened his eyes again, Christa knelt by his side. He heard the tinkle of water and realized that she was bathing his wounds and his forehead again and again.

He blinked, trying to see her. Her face was very white and drawn. He tried to smile, but the effort seemed too much. He tried to rise. There was powder on his chest. He frowned, trying to dust it off. She caught his hand. "Leave it!" she said softly. Her gaze wandered elsewhere in the tepee, then returned to his. "It's all right. I really do know quite a bit. Before the war, I helped Jesse a lot, and he told me that a lot of Indian medicinal herbs were really very good. This is just a salve of yarrow, fine for cuts and bruises."

He nodded. He wanted to talk to her. The effort seemed too much. He closed his eyes.

When he awoke again, he felt much stronger. There was warmth at his side. He half rose. Christa slept there.

But they were not alone. He heard a soft whisper, and saw that Little Flower had come to him. She brought a bowl of a thin-looking gruel. She smiled, offering it up to him. "It will give you strength," she promised him. He sipped the substance. It was something made from buffalo meat, he was certain. He downed it all, determined that he would get his strength back.

She took the bowl from him. "Thank you, McCauley."

"For what?"

"For Morning Star."

He nodded.

"It was only fair that you should have your wife in return. That is why the gods smiled on you."

"Is it?"

"You should leave with your wife in the morning, McCauley. You mustn't stay too long."

"I'm not welcome here any longer?"

"You're always welcome here. But our worlds are not the same, and there is more bloodshed to come. And you need to take her home and have a healthy child."

"Yes, I will take her home."

Little Flower smiled. "She has waited for you. She loves you very much."

She disappeared. Jeremy lay back down, wishing he were still unconscious. They had survived. He closed his eyes. She was so warm beside him. He reached out, putting his arm around her, pulling her closer.

He slept again. When he awoke, it was morning. Christa was awake and watching him again, setting cool cloths on his head.

He sat up. "We have to go."

Alarm touched her eyes. "You shouldn't ride yet. You were seriously wounded."

He touched his forehead and his arm and chest. He was well bandaged with strips of cotton from Christa's old plain petticoat.

"We have to go," he insisted. He staggered to his feet. She followed along with him, supporting him. He stepped outside of the tent. Buffalo Run stood just outside with Tall Feather.

"Thank you for your hospitality, my brother," Jeremy told him. "We are ready to leave if we can take just the horses I came with."

Buffalo Run nodded gravely. Dancing Maid brought up the two horses. She said something in her own language and Buffalo Run nodded. "There is jerky in the saddlebags and a canteen of water. It will take you some time to ride home. Your men will be at your Fort Jacobson now, won't they?"

Jeremy nodded. "Yes. We will be there for the length of the winter."

Buffalo Run nodded. "Perhaps it will be a peaceful season." He reached out a hand to Jeremy. Jeremy grasped it.

Buffalo Run set Christa up on the army horse which Jeremy had brought Morning Star back on to the Comanche camp. He assisted Jeremy onto his own horse. Then Buffalo Run grinned and saluted. Jeremy saluted in return.

Following Jeremy, Christa slowly rode from the camp. She looked back. Little Flower was watching her.

"Thank you!" Christa called.

The Indian girl smiled. Christa turned again to continue following Jeremy. She didn't look back.

They rode for several hours, not racing, but plodding along. Christa, worried, hurried up alongside Jeremy.

"You need to rest!"

"I need some distance between us and the camp."

"But we've been freed—"

"I want more distance," he said stubbornly.

A while later she tried to talk to him again. "Thank you, Jeremy."

He didn't reply.

"Thank you for coming. Thank you for risking your life for me."

"Christa, dammit, you're my wife. You're carrying my child."

"I'm grateful—"

"I don't want you to be grateful!"

She fell silent and allowed her horse to fall back.

He was a very stubborn man and a very determined one. They rode until it was twilight. He dismounted from his horse, wincing at the movement. But before she could leap down from her own mount, he was beside her, reaching up to her.

She allowed him to ease her to the ground, but then she quickly broke away from his touch. Tears stung her eyes. How could they have come from the searing, intimate passion of just two nights ago to this?

They had stopped by a beautiful, bubbling little stream that was shaded by tall trees. Christa unrolled a saddle blanket and spoke to Jeremy behind her. "Sit, please. I'll get some water and the jerky."

He stood for a moment, but then he obeyed her. She brought him water in the cup from his saddlebag, then returned for more, drinking what felt like half the brook herself before coming back to him. She produced the jerky and he ate it hungrily, wincing when his back moved against the bark of the tree.

She stood and walked away from him.

Jeremy watched her. He realized that the pain from his wounds wasn't half as great as that which now seared his heart. She was standing so proudly. Trying to talk. But what was there for her to say?

She was a Cameron. Camerons always paid their debts. But he didn't want her owing him anything.

He wanted more.

"Jeremy, I don't know if you can forgive me or not, or even believe me, but I'm sorry."

"It doesn't matter."

"It does matter!" she cried suddenly, passionately. She fell silent, then spit out, "All right! If it doesn't matter, I'm going home. Home to Virginia just as quickly as I can, and I will not let you stop me!"

Agony seemed to sear into him. His head was pounding; his flesh hurt. His heart was tearing in two.

"You're not going home."

"I'm going home because of all that has happened—" she began, but he cut her off furiously.

"Dammit, Christa, it doesn't matter!" he said fiercely. The scratches on his back were driving him crazy. He wanted to sleep, to ease the pain. The last thing he wanted now was another fight. His hands were trembling. What in God's name was this over now?

He thought that he knew. The Comanche had really frightened her. She wanted no more part of Indian country, and maybe she was right. Maybe he should send her home just as quickly as was humanly possible.

"All right!" he snapped out harshly. "I understand. The Comanche frightened you. And if the hatred in your heart is too much—"

"Hatred!" she exclaimed. She had been standing by the stream, her back to him, a very noble pride to her stance, her hair free and falling down the length of her back, as if she were an Indian maid herself.

But now she spun around, staring at him. He knew he was having some difficulty with his vision, but he must also be losing his mind, for he was certain there were tears in her eyes. "You stupid, stupid Yankee!"

"Christa, I am in no mood for Rebel abuse at this moment—"

"Abuse! I don't want to go because I hate you! I want to go because *I love you.* And I don't want you being honorable anymore, or having to suffer for the things that I do—"

"What!" he exclaimed. Painstakingly, he got to his feet. He must have thundered out the word because she looked frightened for a moment, as if she would back away from him.

"Little Flower said it," he told her. "Little Flower said that you had been waiting for me, that you loved me. But I didn't dare believe. Tell me!"

"I—" she began, and faltered.

He took a step toward her, fighting for strength. His fingers suddenly curled around her arms, exerting a power he hadn't known he possessed. "Tell me!" he exclaimed raggedly.

"You shouldn't have had to come for me. You shouldn't be bleeding and injured now. You shouldn't—"

"Not that!" he thundered, shaking her, pulling her closer into his arms. "The other!"

Her eyes widened. She moistened her lips nervously with just the tip of her tongue. "I might well have ruined your career with Sherman—"

"Damn Sherman. Go on!"

"I—"

"Say it, Christa! Dammit, was I imagining things, or did you say that you loved me?"

"I—" She paused. "I said it!" she whispered.

"And you meant it?"

She lowered her gaze and then her head. "I meant it." Then her gaze rose to his again, blazing blue. "It's not that I mean to take anything from you, Jeremy. I just don't want to stand in your way, or cause more horrible grief. I know that you would never have really wished me dead rather than someone else, but I've lain there some nights and wondered if you didn't wish that I were your Jenny—"

"Oh, Christa! Christa!" He closed his eyes tightly, wrapping her tenderly in his arms. "Christa, she was fine and sweet and gentle, and yes, I loved her, and dear God, yes, I'm sorry the war killed her, just as I'm sorry the war killed so many! But Christa, I have never wished that you were anyone but you, and I have prayed only that our child might survive. If you haven't read my heart, Christa, then you are a stupid, stupid Reb as well!"

She jerked away from him, her gaze crystal and doubting.

He smiled. "You stubborn, wayward little fool!" he charged her, glad to see the sizzle of anger touching her eyes. It was the Christa he knew—and loved. "From the moment I was legally able to get my hands on you, I was obsessed. I wanted you so badly, Christa, that it didn't even matter if you wanted to close your eyes and pretend that I was Liam at first."

"I never—"

"I never wanted to let you, but it wouldn't have mattered. More than anything in the world, I wanted you to respond to me."

"I was afraid to!" she whispered. "Because I knew that once I did, I would have to admit to myself that I did love you. Oh, Jeremy! It is horrible in a way. I never, never wanted to love a Yankee!" She smiled ruefully. "It was one thing to have one for a brother, but to fall in love with one . . ." Her voice trailed away. She looked down to the ground once again. "Jeremy, I'm so sorry. I didn't even think when I was so determined to release the Rebel prisoners. How can you forgive me?"

He lifted her chin. "Christa, I forgave you long before I came for you. I was furious with myself for not having understood how you would feel. I should have talked to you. If I had talked with you all along, you would never have doubted me. I never wanted you to know that I was afraid, but I was worried about you and about our child. Sometimes I was furious with myself for what I had done, forcing you out on the trail. And then I knew that I couldn't let you go. That I couldn't live without you anymore. Christa, we've been such fools, going in such ridiculous circles. I felt that I was competing with a ghost. And so much more. The past. The present. The war, and even peace!"

"Oh, Jeremy!" she murmured suddenly, searching out his eyes. "I could never understand it, all those years, watching Callie and Daniel and Kiernan and Jesse. It was so tragic for them. To love the enemy—"

"I'm not your enemy, Christa!"

"But, oh, God, Jeremy, you were for years! I used to fear the sight of blue uniforms horribly. Every time I saw a soldier in blue I prayed fiercely that it was Jesse. Jeremy, you have to understand. The Union soldiers came onto the peninsula to burn and destroy."

"They had to reach Richmond!" he said softly. His strength was suddenly failing him. He'd been so swept up by her words, so torn, so anguished.

And then so awed. Watching her speak now, watching her eyes, still so wet with tears, he knew that everything she was saying was the truth. She loved him. He didn't know if it was the blood that he had lost or the simple miracle of those words, but he could stand no longer. He started to fall.

"Jeremy!"

Supporting him, she lowered them both to the ground. He leaned against the tree, his eyes closed. He opened them. Tears were damp against her cheeks. He touched them tenderly.

"Camerons don't cry."

"Oh, my God, Jeremy!" she whispered. "Don't you die on me, please, don't you die on me!"

He smiled very slowly. "I wouldn't die now for all the promises of heaven!" he said.

She caught his hand and kissed it. "You need to rest."

He nodded, then shook his head sadly. "My God, Christa! What a miracle. You've just said that you love me. We're all alone in some of God's most beautiful country, sweet green trees, a bubbling brook, and I can't even stand!"

She exhaled on a shaky sigh, her fingers curling more tightly around his hand. "You are going to live, I think!" she whispered. She sat beside him, leaning her head against his. He was silent for a minute.

"Christa, it's still going to be hard. There is so much bitterness. Most southerners do hate northerners. There's equal hatred in the North. The hatred will live for years. For generations. The difference, of course, is that—"

"The difference is that you won!" Christa interrupted.

"Right. The difference is that we won." He shifted, tilting up her chin. "Can you live with that?" he asked her very softly.

She smiled, lowering her lashes, resting her head against his shoulders. "Yes."

"You're certain?"

"I can live with anything, if I'm living with you."

"But I'll still be surrounded by a lot of Yankees."

"It doesn't matter," she said.

"You don't hate Yankees anymore?"

She turned, smiling ruefully. "I still hate lots of Yankees," she admitted. "It's just that—it's just that I love you far more than I hate them."

"You hate them so passionately!" he stated.

Her smile deepened. "Right. So just imagine how very, very deeply I love you."

He leaned back. His fingers moved in her hair. Branches stirred and rustled over them. The brook bubbled by. "Christa!" he murmured.

"Yes?"

"You are, in every way, the perfect cavalry wife." He mustered all of his strength together and turned, taking her into his arms. He planted a very tender kiss upon her lips. "And I adore you!" he whispered.

Then, his strength spent, he leaned back against the tree and slept.

She stood in the stream, stripped of her doeskin, doing her best to scrub her flesh as the Indians did, with the clean rocky sand from the shallow water. A sudden noise alerted her and she looked up quickly. She had imagined that they were so deeply in Indian territory that they wouldn't be disturbed by any casual passersby.

It was no casual passerby. Jeremy was up. He had shed the uniform he had so carefully donned over his wounded flesh. Ripped and bruised, he was beautiful still, she thought.

No. More beautiful than ever. The long red gashes had been gained in his quest for her. Some of them would scar. Maybe it was good. She would remember for all time just what he had sacrificed for her.

"You shouldn't be up!" she whispered to him.

He stopped before her in the water. The sunlight was playing upon it, mirroring both of their images. They were both, she thought, rather beautiful at the moment. Naked and glistening in the sunlight, as natural as Adam and Eve.

If the Comanche were near, she thought, they would never disturb them now.

It was the wild, wild West.

It was almost Eden.

He walked toward her. No, maybe not Eden. They were not so perfect as Adam and Eve. Despite his rippling bronze muscles, he was torn and wounded. And she was beginning to round more daily now.

But maybe that was why now they were so especially beautiful to one another.

He came before her and took her into his arms, kissing her with a slow burning fever and passion. "You're injured," she reminded him.

"Oh, no, I'm feeling much, much better now. And I don't care if every gash in my body breaks open, I can't wait to make love in a new way."

"A new way?" she asked huskily.

"With you whispering against my kiss that you love me, and with me crying out those same words every step of the way."

"Oh!" she said simply. He began to kiss her. Her lips. Her throat. Her shoulder.

"Jeremy."

"Yes?"

"I love you . . ."

Winter seemed very slow and domestic after all that autumn had brought.

On October fifth, a treaty was signed with the Comanche, among other Indians. Christa had thought that Jeremy would have been pleased, but he didn't seem to have much faith in it.

"I don't think that our side really intends to keep with it," he told her frankly. But winter and cold came to Fort Jacobson, where they had finally settled with Jeremy's regiment, and there were no disturbances over the long months.

There were miracles.

Robert Black Paw survived. Once she returned with Jeremy—and was greeted like a heroine by all the men and women, including Mrs. Brooks —she tended to her husband first, then to Robert, seeing to their wounds with the doctor they found stationed at the fort, Remy Montfort.

Dr. Montfort was a civilian. He had been in the Indian territory for the duration of the war, and he claimed he had never taken sides. Christa didn't know if that was true, but he was a lively old codger with twinkling blue eyes, and she liked him very much.

When Jeremy and Robert were fully on their way to healing, she let him know her own fears about the baby. "Life is miraculous," he assured her. "And wee ones are far stronger than we imagine. You wait and see. Things will come along just fine."

They did. On the morning of Saint Patrick's Day, she awoke with startling pains in her back. She didn't say anything at first, because Jeremy was expecting a company from a fort along the Canadian and she didn't want to disturb him if it was a false alarm. She went over to Celia's cabin where a number of the women had gathered to knit booties—Celia was expecting her own baby in the early summer. An hour later, she felt a pain so strong that she jumped.

"Christa McCauley! You've been in labor some time, haven't you, young woman?" Mrs. Brooks demanded.

"I—I don't know, Mary," Christa said. Now they all knew that Mrs. Brooks's Christian name was Mary. Jeremy had seen to it that the fort had been supplied with a likable young reverend, and Mrs. Brooks had been so pleased that she had actually learned to smile. Maybe the Comanche had changed her.

"I've never done this before!" she said. The pain came again, almost on top of the other one.

Clara Jennings jumped to her feet.

Things weren't perfect. Clara was still awfully hard to swallow upon occasion. But even she had changed. She had taken it upon herself to teach Nathaniel French.

Nathaniel didn't particularly want to learn French, but in the interest of interracial relations, he had determined to do so. "There's a great difference between a man like Nathaniel and a field hand!" Clara had announced.

"The difference is in the learning," Nathaniel had told her.

That had seemed to go over her head. But it didn't matter, not to Nathaniel. He was a wise, peaceful man who knew that changes could take a lifetime. Maybe several lifetimes, he had told Christa.

"I'll go for the colonel!" Clara said.

"No, no, please! I do know that this will take lots of time," Christa said.

"Now, Christa, how—"

"My brother is a doctor," she reminded them. She bit her lower lip for a moment. "He was probably the finest doctor in all the Union army!" she said. But then she gasped because the pain had come again, very quickly.

"Oh, dear!" Celia was on her feet, too, but it didn't matter, because Mary Brooks hadn't waited. She had taken the initiative and gone for Dr. Montfort. "Well, well, so this is it, eh, Christa McCauley? Let's get you back to your own bed in your own quarters, young lady. When did you first feel the pains?"

"Early this morning. Before six. But still—"

"This young one could come at any time, Christa! You've been as active as a worker bee all this time, and that often speeds things along."

"What can I do?" Celia asked quickly.

"Why, boil water, of course!" Dr. Montfort said, his eyes twinkling. "And maybe somebody had best go for the colonel!"

Dr. Montfort said that the baby did come incredibly quickly. Christa supposed that it did, knowing how long it sometimes took other women.

But in the time that it took the baby to come, she was assuredly wretched enough!

She grit her teeth against the awful pains and she tried hard not to cry out. But after Montfort told her that the babe was almost there, she felt one pain so tearing that she could not keep quiet, and she cried out.

She was surprised to hear a soothing voice. Fingers curled around her own. She opened her eyes. Jeremy had come. They had told him to wait outside, in their parlor in the fort. He hadn't done so.

"This is it, Christa. Bear down now, push!"

She pushed, and she fell back exhausted. She pushed again. She was certain that she nearly broke Jeremy's fingers. Montfort chuckled, very pleased. "The baby's head is here, Christa, now just one more . . ."

And the baby was born. Her baby. Jeremy's. "It's a boy!" Jeremy cried out. He stood beside her and kissed her, and she smiled, exhausted as she was, and reached for the little bundle.

He was beautiful. No, he was red and wrinkled and screaming furiously, his little fists batting away.

Jeremy kissed her forehead, marveling at their new creation along with her. "I think that noise he's making is a Rebel yell," he teased.

"Nonsense," Dr. Montfort told them. "He's simply too young to announce politely that it's a very frightening new world and that he'd like some warmth and sustenance, please!" He arched his brow at Celia and Mary, who were still in the room. The three of them quietly left the new parents alone. Just a bit awkwardly, Christa loosed the nightgown she was wearing to feed the tiny bit of new life in her arms. She gasped, startled, at the first fierce tug, then laughed. "Oh, Jeremy, I was so frightened so often for him! Yet he seems so strong!"

Jeremy drew a finger down the baby's downy cheek. "Oh, of course, my love. He's outstanding. Look at his parents. And that was a Rebel yell. My God, look at that hair. Pitch black. And his eyes are blue—"

"I think most all babies start out with blue eyes," Christa told him.

"Well, we'll see," Jeremy murmured. "He needs a name."

"Josiah!" she said quickly. She leaned her face against the baby's soft, damp hair. "Josiah, for your brother."

"Christa, it isn't necessary—"

"He was your brother, and Callie's brother, and you two loved him very much. Both of my brothers came home."

"He was a Yankee."

"I know." She nuzzled the baby's head. "But his father is a Yankee, too, and I love him very much. Josiah first, for your brother. James for a half-dozen Camerons."

"Josiah James McCauley," Jeremy said softly. He kissed Christa's forehead. "Thank you. And thank you for my son. He is exquisite! Like his mother."

There was a tap at the door. Dr. Montfort stood there, clearing his throat.

"Let's take the little one, shall we, Colonel? Your wife really needs some sleep."

Jeremy nodded.

"She came through it fabulously, Colonel!" Montfort added proudly.

Jeremy smiled. He smoothed back Christa's hair and spoke softly to her. "I knew you would do fabulously. After all, my love, you are a Cameron."

Her hand slipped into his, seemingly so fragile and so feminine. He remembered what Darcy had told him. "She was the bravest woman I ever saw." The bravest, the finest. Despite her delicate beauty, she was incredibly strong. She had survived so very much to come to this day.

Her fingers squeezed his. She was exhausted, but her eyes were brilliantly blue and very beautiful, and her smile was soft and enticing.

"I was born a Cameron," she told him. "But I am a McCauley now."

His smile in turn was miraculously tender. He leaned low and kissed her lips. "Mrs. McCauley, my dearest Reb, I do love you! This Yank has surrendered most willingly to the South."

Epilogue

June 1866
Cameron Hall
Tidewater Region
Virginia

Christa sat upon the window seat, draped in the long sleeves of Jeremy's white cotton shirt, her knees up, her elbows resting upon them, and her chin resting upon her hands. They were in the summer cottage, staring back out over the cemetery and onward to the lawn and porch and gardens beyond.

She looked something like a waif in the oversized shirt, but even as a waif, Jeremy decided, she was elegant. Christa, with her fine, beautifully sculpted features, sky-blue eyes, and jet-black hair. Even the way she curled the trim length of her body was elegant. She reminded him of a cat, sleek, glorious, and at the moment, purring.

He sat behind her, lifted the full rich sweep of her dark hair, and brushed his lips against her shoulder. She moved back against him, her arms falling upon his as they encircled her.

"You're happy to be home, aren't you?" he asked her.

He felt her smile and he felt her hesitate, careful with her answer. "Of course I'm happy to be home. It's nearly summer, and everything is growing so beautifully. The grass is so green, the air still just cool enough, the sun radiant. Virginia is beautiful in summer."

"And in spring," Jeremy agreed.

"And in fall, too, of course," she murmured. She twisted and her eyes danced with a blue fire as she continued, "Then, of course, I'm glad to be home because it's wonderful to see Callie and Kiernan doting over

Josiah. I confess, I adore my son, but I'm grateful for the time we've managed alone here."

Jeremy felt his eyes drawn back to the furs upon the floor before the fire. He was feeling quite grateful himself. There were two half-full wineglasses awaiting them. And he had to agree, it was very nice to be alone. He'd found the invitation to the summer cottage beneath his breakfast plate this morning and he'd been delighted to find his wife there before him, without the child he too adored. The long miles home had been worth it for just those moments.

But, of course, the journey was worth it for so many more reasons. The sense of belonging here was wonderful. Daniel and Callie and their little ones had been at Cameron Hall almost constantly since they had arrived. Christa had been watching her brothers and their wives and the Cameron toddlers—and their own little bundle in his cradle—out on the lawn from the window for the last several minutes. The Camerons were all here. But the homecoming was even richer than that. Joshua McCauley and his young wife, Janis, had been invited down as a surprise for Jeremy just as soon as Callie had known when they were arriving. Since the southern household had been filling with Yankees, Jesse had suggested that Kiernan's father, John McCay, come spend time with them too. The Joshua McCauleys were home now, and John, too, had returned to his own house. But for a while the household had been tumultuous with children everywhere and the discussions both serious and laughable.

Daniel and Callie and their brood were still at Cameron Hall, and it was those two Christa watched now, along with Jesse and Kiernan and the children. They were wonderful to watch. Kiernan and Callie were stunning in their gowns, sipping cold drinks on a swing and rocking the baby while Jesse was down on the ground and Daniel was directing the children, one after the other, to climb atop his back. Then Jesse was standing, insisting that it was Daniel's turn to play cavalry horse. Then Callie stood up, always the peacemaker, but before she could chastise them she shrieked as Daniel brought her down—elegant day dress and all—onto the lawn. The children couldn't let Kiernan be the only dignified one among the adults, so they dragged her onto the lawn too.

Jeremy and Christa couldn't really hear the words from where they were, they could only hear the laughter that occasionally floated to them, making them both smile.

"Think they know where we are?" Jeremy asked Christa.

She nodded, smiling. "Well, they know I'm here, so I'm sure they know you're here! But it's always been a private place. When we were children and we were in trouble, we used to come here to bind our little wounded souls! We all knew to stay clear until that someone reappeared. Then . . ."

"Then?"

Her lashes fell and she smiled. "Then . . . well, I'm quite certain that Kiernan met Jesse here before the war, before they were married. I carried messages for them now and then, and one of them was about fur . . . and well, you've seen how it's furnished!"

He laughed. "Minx! Spying on your brother!" he chastised her.

"I certainly never did such a thing!" she protested, but she leaned against him still smiling. "Oh, Jeremy! Look out there. It's almost like it was before the war!" Christa said softly.

"Because the war is over. Really over," Jeremy said, and he threaded his fingers through hers, lacing them together.

She sighed, leaning her weight against him. "But there's still so much that isn't healed!" she said. "Carpetbaggers and riffraff are still half of the ruling force. Daniel's had to ask another pardon—and it doesn't sit well with him, I assure you! The schism had remained."

"Yes, in a way," Jeremy agreed. He smoothed back her hair. "Christa, you can't take something as agonizing and devastating as the War of Rebellion—"

"The Civil War," she corrected.

"We Yanks do call it a War of Rebellion," he continued patiently, "and think that it can be over because the firing has ended. Christa, it may take years, it may take decades. Our country is just a pup when you compare it with others. The war has come and gone, and we've made it as a union! Maybe you can't see it yet. But it's time for growth again. Men and women are looking to the West, they're looking to the cities, they're searching for opportunities—searching for ways to live, and in living we'll heal the breach. In little ways, first. Like we've healed the breach here!" he said very softly. "We've found our peace. Others will find theirs. And a hundred years from now, maybe the Camerons living here will know that the war had to be fought, and had to be lost, for the whole country to be strong."

She looked up at him, smiling, her blue eyes radiant. She stroked his cheek. "I love you, Jeremy."

He caught her fingers and kissed them. He cleared his throat. "I love you, too, Christa. More than I could ever say. And I've lain awake nights lately, thinking about it."

She arched a brow. "I thought that love made you sleep well. When Josey isn't busy waking us up, that is."

He smiled. "Yes, but I've been thinking."

"Oh, dear! Yanks are so dangerous when they think!" she teased.

He ran a finger down her nose. "I'm going to tell you what I've been thinking despite that comment, Mrs. McCauley!" He paused just a second, then continued. "Jesse wrote me while we were still at Fort Jacobson—"

"Jesse wrote you?"

"Yes, your brother wrote me privately!" he teased, then sobered. "He wanted me to know that your father had left him instructions about a certain parcel of land. It was to be yours if you ever wanted it, once you were married and settled. I imagine Jesse was afraid it might cause a dispute if you had wanted to come home, and I had wanted to stay in the West."

"The two of us? Have a dispute?" she said, wide-eyed.

He grinned. Since the day he had taken her from Buffalo Run's encampment, neither of them had ever denied the depths of their love or would ever do so again. But they had learned that not even love curbed hot tempers completely, and that the making up from their inevitable disagreements was a wonderful thing.

"Well, my love, Jesse did grow up with you. He knows, of course, all about your temper."

"My temper!"

"Errant Rebs seem to come with them," he teased. She smiled, but then her smile faded. "Oh, Jeremy! I was so grateful for the way that you handled things last night!"

She had made him promise that they would never tell Jesse that John Weland had been seeking revenge against him. The danger was all over, but Jesse, being Jesse, would hound himself about it endlessly.

At dinner they had been talking about traveling, and Jesse had cleared his throat and commented that he was still afraid of being away from home too long—since someone had nearly succeeded in burning down the place just a year ago.

Jeremy had apologized profusely for not having told Jesse earlier that he had come in contact with a man who told him that he knew who had been after the Cameron estate, and that it had been a deranged major who had, since that time, passed away.

Jesse would never know the truth.

And they would all breathe more easily feeling that Cameron Hall was safe.

"You were wonderful!" Christa told him. She kissed his lips, then lay back in his arms, studying him. "You were always wonderful. Even when I was being incredibly rotten, you were considerate of my family."

He brushed a kiss onto her brow.

"You were quite good to my sister when she came here, too, you know," he reminded her.

"I loved her right away. Even for a Yankee, she was a sweetheart."

"Well, I admit, I was partial to your brothers from the start."

"Even the Reb?"

"Especially the Reb."

She smiled, leaning against him again, luxuriating in the quiet time and the rare solitude they were enjoying.

"Well?" he said softly.

She opened her eyes wide. "Well?"

"Christa—" he said, then he paused, swallowing. "Christa, when I married you, I dragged you away from here. I took you from everything that you loved, from your family, from your home. I forced you out west, to hardship, to danger. I had no right—"

"You had every right!" she corrected him. "I forced you to marry me, remember?"

"If I hadn't been willing, no one could have forced me," he said softly.

"And no one could have forced me west!" she replied.

He disentangled himself from her for a moment, pacing before the fire. Christa, watching him, hugged her knees more tightly and felt a rush of warmth sweep through her. He was naked, and very comfortable and natural that way.

And excessively handsome and alluring, too, so tall, so tautly muscled and sleek, so bronze, touched by the fire that took the chill from the air.

She swallowed and watched his eyes, reminding herself primly that he was trying to talk to her.

He came back to her, a foot upon the window seat, and he stared down at her. "Christa—"

"Out there," she interrupted him, "in the graveyard, are many of my Cameron ancestors."

"I know, Christa. That's the point—"

"The first Camerons to come here were Jassy and Jamie. He was a lord. She married him—"

"I've heard this story from Jesse," Jeremy warned her. "Jassy was a bit of a tart who married Jamie for his house and holdings in England. But he brought her here—"

"Precisely!" Christa whispered softly. "She was a bit of a tart! But she was strong-willed and determined, and she built this home with Jamie and stayed with him here. Because she fell in love with him, you see. And do you know what else?"

"What else?"

"He had to rescue her from Indians too. They were the Pamunkeys, I believe. And they roamed all this land. They're mostly all gone now." She flashed him a rueful smile. "Except, upon occasion, you meet a tall blue-eyed, very blond man or woman who happens to be a descendant of Pocahontas and John Smith! Is that what will happen out west, do you think?" she asked him.

He shook his head. "I don't know. But we do seem to be a gluttonous people. The railroads will go farther soon. We'll continue to call them savages while we kill their food supplies and steal their land. Maybe one day there will be a peace. I'm afraid that there will be tremendous loss with it. But there's so much only time will tell."

She smiled, watching him, feeling a warmth sweep around her. She loved him so much, yet it seemed that she loved him more daily.

She touched his russet hair, marveling at the color and the thick rich feel of it. "The point of this story," she told him, "is that Jassy gave up what she thought she wanted so much—"

"It was my understanding that he told her she was coming or he would see to it that she did so by force."

Christa waved a hand in the air. "The point is that she discovered that she loved him with her whole heart. And they came to love this land together, and they built their home here."

He took both of her hands. "So we will build a home here," he said.

She shook her head. "You're not paying attention to me. It doesn't matter where, Jeremy," she said.

"There's still tremendous danger in the West," he told her. "The Indian problems will not be solved for years!"

"There's danger, yes, but tremendous excitement and beauty too!"

"There's beauty here."

"There's so much to explore and build in the West," she argued.

"And there's so incredibly much to rebuild here, in Virginia," he said. "I—I brought you from your home. But then discovered how much I loved you. Christa, you and Josiah are my life. And love is far stronger than any need for honor or glory in the West! You hold my heart in your hands. Carry it tenderly, my love. But carry it with you wherever you would go. The future is yours to decide."

Her eyes widened upon his as she realized just how serious he was. "But you're up for promotion again—"

"Christa, there's a great deal I could do here too."

She started to tremble. She threaded her fingers through his hair. "Oh, my God, Jeremy!" she whispered. "I love you!"

He caught her hand and kissed her palm tenderly. "Christa—"

"Oh, Jeremy! How strange, and how very sad and curious! That's one thing that John Weland told me once."

"Weland!"

She nodded. "He told me that home was where the heart was. And it's very true. Don't you see, it doesn't matter. It doesn't matter where we are at all. In your arms, I'm home."

He rose, and lifted her into his arms. She stared at the glittering silver in his eyes.

"So?" she whispered.

"So . . ." he said. He whirled around with her and lowered them both before the fire and onto the fur. He came upon his knees and drew her up likewise against him, entwining their fingers together.

"So?"

"So . . ." He paused and kissed her. Kissed her long and leisurely, savoring the taste and touch and feel of her lips, the brush of their bodies just barely touching one another.

"So?" she repeated one last time.

He smiled, his mouth just a breath away from hers. "So we will worry about it later. As wonderful as Josiah's aunts are, he will want his supper, and soon. And for now—though I would deprive my son of nothing—I'm afraid I want his mother too. And so I must take my time now."

"And the future?"

"It will come tomorrow. It always does."

She smiled. And then her smile was captured in the heat of his next kiss.

The fire raged high and golden around them. The summer cottage enveloped them, a haven for their love, providing them sweet secrecy and enchantment.

Somewhere nearby, the river drifted ever onward. The breeze stirred over the James. Timelessly.

Life went on.

The war was over, Christa reflected. Wherever she was, the war had ended.

They might ride westwardly once again. There was so much to be done in the years to come, the expansion would be tremendous. The frontier was opening as it never had before. There were so many ready for war with the Indians in the West, ready to decimate them. Men like Jeremy—men of peace and strength—would be needed.

They might build here. There was so much needed in the South too. A lot had been done. The land itself was beginning to cover over some of the scars of war. But so much more would be necessary. And yes, it would take years. Decades, maybe. But like a phoenix rising from the ashes, a new South would form. Different. They would be entering an age of progress, of learning, of growth. The South needed good men and women too.

Which would it be for them?

She didn't know. They needed time. To think, to dream, to talk.

And, she thought, meeting the silver of his gaze and smiling slowly in the comfort of his arms, it didn't matter.

Just as she held Jeremy's heart in her hands, he held hers within the tender grasp of his own.

He stirred, holding her close, kissing her forehead.

She smiled within his embrace. It had been a long, long road. A long time since she had stood by the gates of the family cemetery, feeling that she was being torn from her roots, from all that she loved. From all that Jassy and Jamie had built.

But she knew now that Jassy and Jamie would most certainly understand.

Truly, it didn't matter where she was.

She had finally come home.